ALICE'S ISLAND

ALICE'S ISLAND

a novel

DANIEL SÁNCHEZ ARÉVALO

ATRIA BOOKS

New York   London   Toronto   Sydney   New Delhi

ATRIA
BOOKS

An Imprint of Simon & Schuster, Inc.
1230 Avenue of the Americas
New York, NY 10020

First Atria Books hardcover edition April 2019

ATRIA B O O K S and colophon are trademarks of Simon & Schuster, Inc.

For information about special discounts for bulk purchases, please contact Simon & Schuster Special Sales at 1-866-506-1949 or business@simonandschuster.com.

The Simon & Schuster Speakers Bureau can bring authors to your live event. For more information or to book an event, contact the Simon & Schuster Speakers Bureau at 1-866-248-3049 or visit our website at www.simonspeakers.com.

Interior design by Kyoko Watanabe

Manufactured in the United States of America

10 9 8 7 6 5 4 3 2 1

Library of Congress Cataloging-in-Publication Data

Names: Sánchez Arévalo, Daniel, 1970– author, translator.
Title: Alice's island: a novel / Daniel Sanchez Arevalo.
Other titles: Isla de Alice. English
Description: First Atria Books hardcover edition. | New York: Atria Books, 2019.
Identifiers: LCCN 2018016388 (print) | LCCN 2018019557 (ebook) | ISBN 9781501171970 (eBook) | ISBN 9781501171956 (hardcover)
Classification: LCC PQ6719.A53245 (ebook) | LCC PQ6719.A53245 I7413 2019 (print) | DDC 863/.7—dc23
LC record available at https://lccn.loc.gov/2018016388

ISBN 978-1-5011-7195-6
ISBN 978-1-5011-7197-0 (ebook)

To my mother, my sister
and all the women who have taught me
how to write life.

PART ONE

MOBY DICK

It is not down in any map; true places never are.

Truth hath no confines.

There are certain queer times and occasions in this strange mixed affair we call life when a man takes this whole universe for a vast practical joke, though the wit thereof he but dimly discerns, and more than suspects that the joke is at nobody's expense but his own.

—Herman Melville, *Moby-Dick* (1851)

PERHAPS DAY 0 doesn't exist on the calendar, but in life, it does. My Day 0 was the day Chris died, though I've also considered it might have been the day I moved to the island. But in the end, death struck me as more decisive than a move.

When the phone rang, I knew it was him. I was taking a bubble bath that had two spoonfuls of olive oil and a big glass of whole milk in it—home remedies to stave off stretch marks on my enormous belly—while I ate Belgian chocolate ice cream, an homage to my ancestors. I didn't make any attempt to step out of the bathtub and pick up the phone. I just hoped it wouldn't wake up Olivia; it had been hard for me to get my six-year-old daughter to sleep, and my moment of relaxation and self-indulgence had finally come. Chris would understand.

The bath was over when I'd polished off the pint. I dried off; rubbed almond lotion on my chest, belly, and butt; and listened to the message he'd left on my voicemail:

Hey, honey. I just wrapped up. I wanted to make it home for dinner, but there was no way. My client insisted we have something here in New Haven, at one of the off-campus bars. I'm headed home now. I should be there around twelve. You don't need to wait up for me. Kisses, my love.

I didn't call back, I just sent a text:

I was in the bath gorging myself on ice cream when you called. Don't call me tubby, I'm sensitive! Have a good trip home. The three of us are here waiting for you. ILY.

My cell phone rang again two hours later. It didn't really ring; it vibrated and the screen blinked. I'd fallen asleep watching TV in bed. I

3

wasn't alarmed when I saw it was Chris. When he traveled at night, he sometimes called me on his hands-free to keep from dozing off. I loved that he relied on me to keep him awake. I wasn't being a submissive wife; it's just that I had an incredible capacity to close my eyes and fall asleep anytime and anywhere. So not only did those brief interruptions not bother me, I actually enjoyed them. They reminded me of when we were teenagers, and I'd take the cordless house phone into bed, and he would do the same, and we would spend the whole night talking, and in a way, we'd fall asleep together.

"Hey, honey, where are you?" I asked, still drowsy.

"Good evening," a woman's voice answered. Then I got scared. I looked at the cell phone screen again. Chris. There was a lot of noise from cars in the background. "Is this Alice Williams?"

"Uh . . . Yeah, that's me." Immediately my hands started to shake.

"Your husband has been in a traffic accident. We're taking him to Saint Luke's Hospital in New Bedford."

"What do you mean, New Bedford?"

"Your husband is Christopher Williams, resident of 668 Hope Street, Providence?"

"Yes . . ."

"He ran off the road on Route 6, close to Marion."

"Marion? Where's that?"

"Marion, Massachusetts. Next to the Weweantic River," the person added, as if that would help me orient myself.

"I'm sorry, but I don't know what you're talking about," I said, stunned, fighting not to wake up. As long as I was asleep, all this would be nothing more than a nightmare.

"I repeat, ma'am. Your husband has been in a traffic accident twenty-two miles east of New Bedford. We're taking him to the hospital . . ."

"No, there must be some mistake," I cut her off, relieved, finally getting my thoughts in order. "That's impossible. My husband is—was—at Yale."

We lived in Providence, Rhode Island. Yale is in New Haven, a hundred or so miles to the west. New Bedford is to the east, the opposite direction. I didn't know exactly how far then, but less than an hour by car.

"Ma'am, I've just looked through his documents," she said patiently, understanding how difficult taking in such information can be. "He's Christopher Williams."

"Can I talk to him, please?" I asked in anguish.

"He's unconscious. His condition is very serious, Mrs. Williams. It's important for you to come as soon as possible. Saint Luke's Hospital, New Bedford."

When I hung up, I looked instinctively at the time on the digital clock on my nightstand. I watched it go from 12:01 to 12:02 on May 13, 2015. From the time I was a little girl, my favorite number had been thirteen. It was the number I always picked when I played a sport, the number displayed on my jersey. And since no one ever chose thirteen, all its luck was for me. But that was over now.

And that day, May 13, 2015, became Day 0 for me.

———

After driving for five minutes, which seemed like endless hours, a shiver coursed through me when I realized I'd left Olivia alone, as if I'd just gone out to the mailbox to pick up the paper.

I immediately called my parents in the car on the hands-free, hoping my father would pick up.

"What is it, honey?" It was my mother, alarmed by the late hour.

"Mom, Chris has been in a car accident. They're taking him to the hospital."

"Oh my God. Is it bad?"

"I don't know. I'll call you later. I just ran out and Olivia is alone at home. I don't want her to wake up without anyone there. Please go over there right away."

"Sure, honey, we're on our way. Oh Lord, George, wake up, Chris has had an accident. Where was he, honey?"

I didn't want to have to go on giving explanations.

"Close to Yale, where he was working."

———

I hate hospitals. As soon as I went in, I got queasy, even more than usual given my distress. My legs were about to give out. I don't know how

I managed to drive there. A porous veil started clouding my vision. I suffer from asthenophobia, an irrational fear of fainting in public. It almost always strikes me in stressful situations, when I feel trapped, when I'm surrounded by strangers or when I'm the center of attention. Any combination of those factors can lead to tachycardia, chills, difficulty breathing, and a feeling of panic.

A nurse accompanied me to a waiting room next to the ICU.

"Stay here, please. The doctor will come out as soon as he can. They're still operating on your husband."

I saw a soda machine and realized I needed sugar and caffeine. I didn't even have time to reach into my pocket to fish out the coins. I faded to white at more or less the same time that would later appear on Chris's death certificate.

———

I woke up in an examination area in the emergency room. The doctor and the head nurse looked at me so gently, with such empathy, that I knew Chris was dead. Not long after they confirmed it, I wondered whether I would have to honor his wishes and call our baby daughter Ruby or whether I could choose whatever name I wanted. Tricks the mind plays to survive. Those little unimportant details you grab onto when life stops moving on solid ground.

They'd put an IV in my arm to give me saline and injected me with a tranquilizer. Vital anesthesia for facing the nightmare of death. Was it appropriate given my pregnancy? Probably better than taking the risk that I would give birth then and there, wracked with heartache.

"The circumstances of your husband's death are still far from clear," the doctor told me. "We think it was cranioencephalic trauma caused by the impact when the car crashed. But the police have informed us there were no skid marks on the asphalt, so it's likely he fell asleep at the wheel or lost consciousness before going off the road or . . ." He stopped, thinking it inappropriate to continue speculating on the subject. "A coroner will perform an autopsy to clear things up and determine the exact cause."

It was then that I realized he was insinuating that Chris might have committed suicide.

"How long does that take? When can they send the body to Providence?"

"There's a special area in the hospital set up where you can stay and receive family and friends." Seeing that I didn't react, he added, "A psychologist will come now to assist you and your family. I'm very sorry, Mrs. Williams. If you want, we can help you get in touch with them . . ."

"No, I want to take my husband home as soon as possible, please," I said, or thought. At that moment, I couldn't really distinguish between the two. All I was certain of was that, yes, of course I would call our daughter Ruby.

———

The sun was coming up outside and the effects of the tranquilizer were wearing off. It was time to call my parents. I would break down, cry, tell them what had happened, and say that I couldn't stop thinking that if only I'd picked up the phone when he called, he might still be alive. That I didn't know what Chris was doing there, that he'd lied to me and I was so sad, that I felt like none of this was happening, that it was all a nightmare. That they'd asked me to identify his body, and when I saw it, I'd thought, *No, it isn't him.* Because it couldn't be him, because Chris never lied to me, and when he did—usually about something insignificant—I always knew it and he'd laugh like a naughty child, and I adored him for it. So the body I had identified in the morgue wasn't Chris; it was a false Chris. It wasn't my Chris. None of this was real. *Right, Dad? Right, Mom? Tell me none of this is happening.* I called my father's cell phone. My mother picked up.

"Yeah, Mom, it's very bad . . . I don't know, on a road close to Yale. He was on his way home . . . Mom, I don't know anything else. I'll call you when I have some news . . . No, I don't want you to come . . . No, not Dad either . . . I don't want Olivia to suspect anything and then get scared . . . I'd rather you both stay there and take care of her . . . I'll keep you informed . . ."

I didn't know I could lie so easily, because it was something I'd almost never had to do. Why hadn't I been able to tell the truth? I couldn't even say that Chris was dead. It was as if I needed more time. For what? I had no idea. I only knew I needed two hours or so. At that moment, it was hard to foretell that the time I'd need wasn't a matter of hours or weeks or months, but of years.

MY HUSBAND JUST died two days ago, and I didn't even know him, I thought. The first time I had smiled at him wasn't because he was handsome, funny, popular and smart, but because I felt like I'd known him my whole brief life. And from that first fleeting smile we shared in a hallway in high school, I felt like he was part of me, and I part of him. Who was my husband? And, since I had spent eighteen years in love with his smile and with the smile he evoked from me, who was I? *Hi, my name is Alice Williams, I'm thirty-three years old, and I'm sitting in the hallway of the Monahan Drabble Sherman Funeral Home listening to Dire Straits on the PA.*

A PA? Seriously? In a funeral home? *Brothers in Arms* by Dire Straits, the first CD Chris ever bought, at a yard sale, when he was a kid. His favorite. How did they know? "So Far Away" was playing. How appropriate, how macabre. How ridiculous. But who had told the funeral home? Suddenly I realized it had been me. *Is there any particular music you'd like to have played during the viewing? You can personalize the selection,* the kindly woman in charge of making our loss more bearable had said. I don't remember how I'd answered, but it was obvious that if this was playing, it was because I had requested it. Though it could easily have been Tricia, Chris's sister. I was having problems with my memory. And when I say problems, I mean I was forgetting everything except what I really wanted to forget: that I was a widow.

Everyone was there. My parents, my grandmother, my aunts and uncles, my cousins, Chris's parents, his sister and other family members, acquaintances, the friends we had in common and the ones we kept to ourselves. My entire little universe, controlled and orderly, until now. My bubble. A bubble that exploded with that call in the middle of the night, waking me to a hostile world I didn't recognize, didn't want to live in. And so, in just two days, I had built a new temporary bubble,

9

where I kept myself relatively alive, in a state similar to hibernation, being there without being there. Even when people were in front of me, I didn't see or hear them. I didn't want them to talk to me or touch me. I couldn't comprehend why I took no comfort in their words of consolation and their gentle, sincere embraces.

I didn't tell anyone about Chris, about how he hadn't been where he was supposed to be. I was ashamed to.

Olivia came over when "Walk of Life" started playing. She was the only one with a key to get in and out of my emergency bubble. Her and Dire Straits.

"Mommy."

"What, honey?"

"Where's my present?"

"What present?"

"The one from Daddy that he always brings when he goes on a trip."

"I don't know, love."

"Did you look to see if it was in the car?"

"No, babe, I didn't look."

"Do you think it was my fault that he died?"

"Why do you say that, sweetie?" Sweetie, babe, love, honey. I didn't know what to call her to soften the blow.

"Maybe he was going to buy my present and he died. On the way."

"No, Oli, I'm sure he had bought it and I'm sure it's in the car. I'll look tomorrow and I'll get it for you."

"If it's not my fault, whose fault is it?"

"No one's. It's no one's fault."

"So it's not a bad thing, then?"

I looked at her without understanding. "Daddy says if something bad happens, it's always someone's fault."

After reassuring her that it also wasn't any of her grandparents' fault, or her great-grandparents'—one at a time, the living and the dead—or Tricia's, or mine, or anyone she knew or didn't know, she said to me:

"So if it wasn't anyone's fault, was it Daddy's fault?"

"No, honey, it wasn't Daddy's fault either."

"Why is Daddy's box closed? I want to see him."

The coffin was closed. It had been my decision in order to protect Olivia, to keep alive the image she had of her father.

"No, Oli, like this it's better."

"When I close my eyes, I see him. I see Daddy."

"That's good, so you remember him."

"I see him dead in the car. Pieces of his face are gone. An eye and a bunch of teeth and other stuff. And he's bleeding a lot. It makes me really scared to close my eyes, Mommy."

I didn't think my soul could break any further. Olivia was six and had never expressed obsessive thoughts, at least not such palpable ones, just little hang-ups, nothing important. I stroked her hair. That was something that calmed her down a lot. Her and me both. I liked to run my fingers through her fine blond hair, which was just like Chris's. Along with her father's hair, she had inherited his mouth and smile, and my green eyes, nose and freckled cheeks.

"When we get home, I'll print you the photos from when the three of us were on the cruise to Alaska last summer, OK?"

"It won't work, Mommy. I need to see him. In the box."

I looked at her and thought: *How smart my daughter is. Maybe she's gifted. I should buy her a piano or give her a chess set. But today, so when she becomes the first female world champion of chess or she's playing at Carnegie Hall, she'll say in the interviews: "The day we buried my father, my mother bought me a piano—or a chess set. That was my salvation. I want to dedicate this concert—or this world championship match—to my late father and to my mother, for turning my pain into art and passion.* My daughter had some hidden talent, and my purpose in life was to discover it. The thought cheered me up a bit.

"It's not called a box; it's called a coffin, honey."

That was all I managed to say. Then I took her hand and, despite my original plan, led her into the room where Chris's coffin was.

It was cold, very cold. But that was normal. That's how you have to store meat.

The first person who realized we were going in there was my mother. She was talking and crying with my aunt Sally. Mom walked over and rapped her knuckles on the glass door that separated us. I couldn't hear her, but I could see her lips moving: *What are you doing? You shouldn't be in there.* I walked up to the door. I looked at my mother for two or three seconds. She looked back at me, waiting for me to say something, but I just pulled the curtain on the door shut to get a little privacy for Olivia and me.

I took a metal wastebasket—what do the dead need a wastebasket for?—turned it upside down and stood Olivia on top of it, so she could peep inside the coffin.

"Are you sure, Oli?"

"Yeah, Mom, come on . . ."

I opened the lid. Olivia smiled immediately. It was a smile so full of life that I thought she was going to resuscitate Chris, that he would rise up and say: *It's freezing in here, let's go home.*

The autopsy had determined that Chris hadn't died from the impact of the crash, as the police and the forensic investigator had suspected. He'd suffered a brain aneurysm that made him pass out at the wheel, and that caused the accident. He had an arteriovenous malformation. A time bomb nestled in his brain that had suddenly burst. Painful and clinical as the explanation was, it relieved me to hear it, because it ruled out the possibility that Chris had committed suicide. The absence of skid marks on the asphalt had raised the suspicions of the police and the investigator the insurance company had hired. I wasn't worried about the claim not paying out; I was worried because even though I'd told the police in no uncertain terms that Chris was a cheerful person who always overcame anything in his way, in my heart I doubted; for the first time in my life, I doubted him. When they confirmed the cause of death, I couldn't help but show my incredulity because Chris had lead a very healthy lifestyle. The coroner told me it had nothing to do with that; it was a congenital disorder. In many cases, hereditary. No one in his family, which I knew very well, had died under similar circumstances or had anything like that. And then I doubted a second time.

"Daddy's so handsome."

"Yes. Very."

"And he smells good. He smells like Daddy."

Betty, Chris's mother, had come to our house beforehand to take a suit, tie, shirt and his favorite shoes from the closet, as well as his usual aftershave and deodorant.

"It's like he's sleeping."

Olivia stroked Chris's pink cheek. The undertaker had gone a little too far with the makeup, perhaps to conceal some cut or bruise.

"He's really cold. Why is it so cold in here, Mommy?"

"So the body doesn't go bad."

"Like hamburgers in the refrigerator?"

"Yeah, more or less."

"Is someone going to eat Daddy?"

"No, honey, of course not . . ."

"I always loved you more than Daddy. If you died, I would have been much sadder. Much more . . ." she said, caressing her father the whole time.

"Come on, sweetie, let's go now . . ."

I tried to close the coffin lid, but Olivia stopped me.

"Wait . . ."

Olivia shut her eyes to be sure the image of her father she had in her head had changed. After a few moments, she opened them again. She seemed relieved.

"OK, we can go now."

A piano, I thought, *I'm going to give her a piano. An enormous grand piano, the best in the world.* It would rise up in the air and fly whenever she played it, transporting the three of us right out of there.

I KEPT MY phone on each night, as if a part of me were hoping he would call, that the ringtone associated with his number would start to play. "As Long as You Love Me" by the Backstreet Boys. Back in 1998, he was finishing his last year of high school, I was in tenth grade, we liked each other, we'd say hi to each other in the hallways and eye each other in the cafeteria while talking in our respective groups. He sent his friend Troy to tell my friend Suz that he liked me; I sent my friend Suz back to his friend Troy to say I was crazy about him. I went to see his tennis matches; he came to watch me play lacrosse; and one day, at a party at his friend Melvin's house while his parents were away blowing their money at Foxwoods Resort Casino, we finally talked. After three hours and six beers for him and three for me, right when that song started to play, he finally dared to give me my first kiss while we danced, intoxicated in every sense of the word, and we were sentenced to adore that corny song for life.

The morning after the funeral, I woke up in Olivia's tiny bed. I couldn't remember when I'd gone in there.

"You were kicking me," she said, more amused than irritated.

"It wasn't me; it was the baby."

Olivia laughed. So far it seemed like she was all right, no trauma or lingering damage.

An hour later, while I was cleaning up after breakfast, she came into the kitchen in her fluorescent pink down jacket.

"What are you doing with the feathers on? It's really hot, Oli."

"No, it's really cold there."

"Where's there?"

"In the refrigerator . . . Can we go see Daddy in the refrigerator?"

OK, so maybe she wasn't completely *all right*.

———

I was named Teacher of the Year at the Seekonk River School, where I taught art—the same elementary school I had attended as a girl. It was a family affair. The award was something I'd always hoped to achieve. It was an open process, democratic and clean. The children voted, and I have to confess that the month before the voting, we teachers were always a little more attentive and agreeable. We were struck with a healthy and barely concealed competitiveness, and that was welcome, because it was to the children's benefit. But the rivalry wasn't so much about winning as about not coming in last. Not that the final results of the voting were made public. No, they only announced the winner. But of course, the rest of the teachers all knew their places in the ranking. And naturally, who wanted to come in last? In my eight years there, I had always made it to the top three, but I'd never won, and that was the fault of the marvelous Mr. Buck, the science teacher, who was a cross between Indiana Jones and MacGyver. He organized elaborate scavenger hunts to help the kids learn while having fun investigating and discovering the small, unfathomable wonders of nature, facing great *dangers* all over the schoolyard, then turned all this into a documentary worthy of *National Geographic*. His motto was: *Don't look at life, try it!* So receiving the honor should have made me feel pleased and proud. But no, I knew why they had given it to me. Even though the relevant voting had taken place, I was sure that no one realized that the teachers, with the reigning champion Mr. Buck at their head, had decided unanimously to award me the distinction.

And there it was, the longed-for honor, in my living room. A framed certificate shaped like a scroll with a red apple on top of a textbook, an unimpeachable symbol of the teacher's art and an homage to Isaac Newton. Behind it, a blackboard with my photo with a big smile on my face. *Mrs. Williams, Teacher of the Year.* My own students had painted the frame with bright colors that emphasized my freckly nose, green eyes and long red hair. I didn't hang it up, but my father did, on my mother's express orders. I found it when I came back from the funeral reception at Chris's parents' house. I thought seriously about giving it back: going back to the school, entering the teachers' lounge, and smashing it onto the table. *Take your damned charity and shove it . . .* But no, I didn't.

———

The principal was startled to see me in the teachers' lounge. Nick Preston liked to get there an hour before the rest of the staff to enjoy the peace and quiet of the school before the arrival of the hordes of adorable little devils—as he called them. *And when I say adorable little devils, I don't just mean the students,* he would say, laughing.

"Hey, Alice. What are you doing here? You shouldn't have come," he said with an affected tone of worry, as though he wished to make clear how upset he was for me and how much he regretted all that had happened. "You didn't get my email?"

He had written me to offer his condolences once more—in addition to attending the funeral, of course, and sending one floral wreath to the funeral home on behalf of Seekonk River School and another to my home on behalf of the Preston family—and told me to forget about my obligations at the school, that what was important was my recovery and gathering strength for the next semester. In other words, I didn't need to come back. There was a little more than a month of classes left.

"Yeah, I got it, and thank you, Nick, but . . . I came here to drop Olivia off, and . . . I'd rather get started again."

"Alice, don't worry. Mr. Wolf has taken over your classes. You're seven months pregnant. By law you have a right to take time off."

"We agreed that if I felt well, I would hold out till the semester was over."

"Sure, Alice, of course . . . But do you feel well? Do you really feel well?"

I fell silent and promised myself I wouldn't cry. He wasn't worried about me, but of daily having to face a woman who had lost her husband. A very pregnant widow was too morose an image for the jovial atmosphere of the school. Having me there, they couldn't have a good time openly—he and the teachers—laughing between classes over coffee in the teachers' lounge or during lunch in the cafeteria while they chatted about the various home teams' scores. No, everyone would have to be worried about poor Alice. *She's just so fragile.* The principal must have said something like that to Mr. Wolf when he asked him to take over my classes. I wanted to vent all this to him, but I didn't dare.

Maybe because I really was fragile and confrontation was just too hard for me then. Or maybe just because my mind was playing a nasty trick on me and I was getting paranoid. Why did I doubt Nick Preston's intentions? Why didn't I believe he was genuinely concerned for my well-being, when he'd always been so kind to me before?

With all that's going on, Alice, do you really want to be here? I asked myself. The principal was right. At that moment, the elementary school wasn't where I needed to be. But I also didn't want to be at home where the walls came crashing down on me, especially when Olivia wasn't there. So where then? I tried to think of a place, somewhere that would make me feel better, an activity that would help me, a friend I could talk to, cry to, even laugh with, but nothing and no one came to mind.

I DIDN'T KNOW where to put the bouquet of flowers. On the guard-rail? I had forgotten to bring duct tape. The flowers wouldn't last long on the ground. But what was I doing there? *Honey, you have to go leave flowers at the scene of the accident*, my mother had said. *We'll go together*, she insisted. It was hard for me to convince her not to come, that it was an intimate act, something I wanted to do alone. I didn't want to turn it into a circus or a pilgrimage site for the family. Luckily, Chris's parents agreed with me. *And besides, Mom, you see, Chris died in a place far from where he was supposed to be. He lied to me. I know it shouldn't matter to me, because he's dead and no one can do anything about that, but what was he doing there, on that road along the coast? Where was he going? No, not where was he going. Where was he coming from?* Obviously, I didn't say this to my mother. I contented myself with saying to her, *Mom, I'm going alone; that's all there is to it. I need you to stay with Olivia, because you certainly aren't suggesting we should take Olivia to see the place where her father ran off the road.* I left the house before she could say something like: *It's not the place where he ran off the road; it's the place where his soul rose up to heaven.* My mother is fervently religious. I'm not, though at that moment, I would have liked to be. Everything would have been much easier, I thought.

The guardrail was still broken, and there was some weary-looking police tape that had outlived its purpose. I tore it off with one hand, because it seemed disrespectful to me, as though they had treated Chris like a criminal. Was he one? The tape skittered off down the road, borne by the wind. I peeked over the shoulder of the road. A thirteen-foot fall. In front of me, the Weweantic River, flanked by lovely houses with their own private docks. A lovely spot to take photos, watch a sunset, med-itate. Anything but die. I confirmed that there weren't any skid marks, which implied he had lost consciousness before going off the road. At least it was a gentle death. I didn't say that, the doctor did. Had he said gentle? No, he hadn't said gentle. He said something else. I should start to take notes about things.

I didn't leave the bouquet on the road or on the guardrail. Instead, I walked two hundred yards along the road and made my way down the embankment along the river's edge. I left the bouquet where the car had overturned, right on the bank, where there were still leftover blotches of motor oil, broken glass, and a small crater from the violent impact.

I thought about praying but decided against it. Then I thought of swimming in the river. But I was afraid of the water's siren song, that I would let the current take me and get lost at sea. I took a piss among the wild rushes, after looking around first. I felt ashamed and ridiculous. A woman, seven months pregnant, peeing in the place where her husband had suffered a fatal accident. Not a particularly charming image. But I had to go really badly. The pregnancy had made me somewhat incontinent. It was then that I noticed a tiny gas station, Sam's Gas, on the other side of the road. *Alice, there are security cameras there; do you want to end up on YouTube? Category: pregnant pissing redhead.* While I was going, I repeated over and over in my head: security camera, security camera . . .

———

Being seven months pregnant has its benefits. It wasn't something I liked to take advantage of, and I didn't like to let people wait on me or give me preferential treatment. As a pregnant woman, I felt strong, powerful. At least until Day 0. But now it was going to work in my favor, because it's very easy to empathize with a pregnant woman, especially if her husband died in a traffic accident right in front of your gas station. And if the woman starts to cry unconsolably, forget about it. It was the first time I had cried openly in public. And it was for self-interest, to satisfy a clear objective: getting hold of the security camera footage from the night of the accident. Why? I still didn't know. But I wanted it. Maybe because I had listened to the message Chris had left on my voicemail a thousand times, looking for something in the tone of his voice, an air of hesitancy, of guilt, or at least some background noise. A clue. Whatever it might be. We had spent most of our lives together.

I could decipher his most casual remarks as well as his silences. And because I found nothing suspicious, everything was suspicious. Our relationship had seemed like the autumn sun, sweet and peaceful. Now I asked myself if that had made it unexciting, uninteresting. Did Chris need more? Did I need more, without realizing it? But right now I was looking for Chris's more.

"The police took the footage to investigate the accident," the owner of the gas station told me.

OK, better, just let it go. Good try. Get back home now.

"And you don't have a copy?" I asked.

"Maybe," he said, becoming intrigued. "But tell me something, miss. What do you want the footage for?"

I couldn't come up with anything that might sound remotely convincing. I was going to throw in the towel and hope that no one would post the video of me peeing on YouTube. But then Ruby spoke for me: she gave me a powerful kick. Or was it a succession of them? I doubled over for a few seconds, and then realized it might seem as if I were going into labor. Maybe I prolonged this gesture longer than necessary and uttered a few (rather overacted) muffled cries because . . . that would likely unnerve the calm gas station owner on this little-used secondary road. Get her out of here, the sooner the better.

Five minutes later, I was on my way back home with a CD containing a video file with the camera footage. Thanks, Ruby.

———

The SUV was utterly destroyed. It had been a lark of Chris's. A Cadillac Escalade, top of the line, with all the extras imaginable, so ridiculously large that I used to joke with him that if we got in a fight, he could always go live in it. Ironically, he had died in it.

I identified with the state of the SUV; maybe that's why, when the mechanic at the garage they had towed it to told me it needed to be hauled to the junkyard, I looked at him very sternly and said, "No."

I examined the Escalade from top to bottom. I opened the glove compartment and found the registration and insurance papers, all in order. A few chocolate wrappers (mine). Nothing else, not even a measly ticket. Chris was a very responsible driver.

The GPS screen was shattered, but it still functioned. I turned it on and looked to see if it had any preprogrammed routes. Nothing. He never used it because he boasted he had a singular sense of direction and needed no help finding his way. *Are you sure you weren't lost, Chris?*

Last of all, I opened the trunk. There was his black leather laptop bag, the one I gave him, and a stuffed bear. A Big Smelly Bear. With a pink ribbon and a pompom around its spongy waist. The bear that Olivia had spent weeks begging for. Where had he bought it? Why wasn't it in a toy store bag? Why wasn't the receipt anywhere to be found? I took the bear and sniffed it instinctively. It didn't smell like anything. *So, why's he called the Big Smelly Bear, then?* I asked myself.

———

When I gave it to Olivia, her face lit up. She hugged it and kissed it as if it were her best friend in the world. "Is it from Daddy?"

"Of course, honey. See? He didn't forget your present."

"But is it from this trip, or the one before?"

"What's this trip, Oli? What do you mean?" I asked as softly as possible.

"Grandma said Daddy's still going somewhere."

Brilliant, Mom. Thanks. What do I say now?

"One question, Oli: Why's he called the Big Smelly Bear?"

She squeezed the creature's behind. A farting sound came out.

"Dirty pig!" Olivia said, cracking up laughing. "You're supposed to fart in the bathtub!"

I knew I wouldn't find anything else of interest in his bag. Chris and I didn't have secrets. I knew the passwords to his Facebook, his email, his cell phone. Well, it's not that I knew them per se, but Chris was a bit of a wreck as far as remembering those things, so he had them all written down on a Post-it stuck to the computer monitor on his desk. In plain sight. But it had never occurred to me to go in there and snoop around. I trusted him. And he trusted me.

When I used them after his death, it was impossible not to feel like I was betraying our trust. I looked through his email, his Facebook, his LinkedIn, his Twitter, his Instagram, his (our) bank accounts, credit card statements, drawers, cabinets. I didn't discover anything I didn't already know, except that he was following Taylor Swift on Instagram. Along with 103 million other followers.

I compared his cell phone contacts with mine, to make sure they coincided, that he didn't have some compromising number camouflaged under a colleague or family member's name. Nothing. And I called the rest of the contacts that didn't coincide with mine from a prepaid mobile I bought. I listened to their voices, and if they seemed to match their profile in his contacts, I hung up. I didn't find anything suspicious there either.

Our life had been a puzzle we made together, piece by piece. We knew we loved each other. We had an image of our perfect life and the pieces we needed to put it together. We lived in a New England colonial house on Hope Street. Sufficiently close and sufficiently far from the homes of his parents and mine, equidistant from both, so there was no bias and everyone got along fine. We were faithful to the city of our birth; the city where we grew up, where we fell in love (the high school was just minutes from our house, a coincidence that pleased us both), where we separated to study our respective majors at our respective universities (Chris chose business administration at the University of Virginia, and I studied art at Brown, the prestigious Ivy League university just a few minutes from our house); the city that took us back in when Chris returned, with a love more solid and mature, resistant to the seductions of university and the dangers distance brought with it; the city that paid us back with a daughter, Olivia. Ruby was the final piece. We always wanted to have two, a little pair. We both loved her already, despite our arguments over her name. We both sought her out and made her with great pleasure. Those were the pieces to our puzzle. And it was finished. The landscape of our life defined, precious and ideal, ready to be put in a frame and hung up on the wall to admire. But now it was as if I had just opened the box to a five-thousand-piece puzzle and didn't know what the final image would be.

—————

The roadway was abandoned. A few scarce cars passed before the Cadillac veered off, tumbling down the embankment and disappearing from the frame. It was traveling at a moderate speed. I hit Pause on the player. The recording said 23:15. I hit Play again. I sped the image up. A car with two passengers pulled over to help. The driver peeked over the embankment and then brought his hands up to his head. In the meantime, the other person seemed to be calling 911. The ambulance took twelve minutes to arrive. Not long afterward, a Plymouth County police car and a fire truck from Marion, the next town over, pulled up. The paramedics couldn't get Chris out of the SUV. After the firemen intervened, cutting the driver's side door with a circular saw, they finally managed to load him onto a stretcher. He wasn't moving. After they put him in the ambulance, the police and the firemen stayed behind at the scene of the accident. *Why are you watching this, Alice?* I asked myself as I cried in silence.

I DREW AN X over the scene of the accident on a map. US Route 6, beside the Weweantic River. I drew another X over our house in Providence. And with another X, I marked where he was supposed to have been, at Yale in New Haven. As if it were necessary to corroborate the lie visually.

Hey, honey. I just wrapped up. I wanted to make it home for dinner, but there was no way. My client insisted we have something here in New Haven, at one of the off-campus bars. I'm headed home now. I should be there around twelve. You don't need to wait up for me. Kisses, my love.

I had listened to the message dozens of times. He didn't say the name of the client, didn't say the name of the bar . . . There was no recognizable noise. If anything, there was too much silence. Strange. *Off-campus in New Haven. Kisses, my love.* He almost never called me *my love*, because he said it was too important a word to wear out, to turn into a routine crutch. That's why it had made me happy to hear it in that message. But now when I heard it, I kept thinking of those fake cakes placed in the windows of bakeries to attract your attention. A truth that turned into a lie when you touched it. That's what I was trying to do, touch Chris's truth to uncover his lie.

If he hadn't had the accident, he would have arrived home right at the time he'd said. At twelve. Wherever he called me from, he'd made sure to be the same distance from Providence as Yale: a hundred miles away. I turned back to the map. The scene of the accident was 40 miles away. So he'd been driving for 60 miles or so. Taking that distance for a reference, I traced a line from the Weweantic River away from our home to the east, to figure out what the farthest point he could have driven from would be. Seeing the results of my calculations, my emergency bubble cracked like the windshield of a speeding car struck by a stone, and before I could patch it up, it shattered and soaked my entire body in a cold sweat. One hundred miles to the east. That encompassed practically every corner of eastern Massachusetts, including Boston, as well as virtually all of Cape Cod.

On the refrigerator, among the magnets and Olivia's drawings, was a sheet of paper that read: *Daddy's Trips*. Back in high school Chris had been on his way to being a tennis star. He won the Rhode Island State Championship in his junior and senior years, and that earned him a full scholarship to the University of Virginia, which had one of the best tennis teams in the country. His career there was brilliant: he made it to second place in the US Open Junior Tennis Championships, where he lost to Andy Roddick. Although he graduated with honors from the business administration program, he still wanted to be a professional tennis player. In just one year he made it to the 143rd slot in the ATP world rankings. When he tore his Achilles tendon, his newly minted career was cut short. But he didn't let it get him down. *Nowadays in professional tennis (and in almost anything in life), what you haven't achieved by age twenty-five, you won't ever achieve. So, if by the time I'm twenty-seven, to give myself a few years of wiggle room, I haven't gotten my face on a cereal box, then I'm giving it up*, he said, half as a joke and half seriously. When the day came, I made him a special edition of his favorite cereal, Fruity Pebbles, with his photo on the box, smiling with a headband on and holding his racquet. It wasn't a way to remind him of his failure, but to make him see that there are lots of ways to get onto a cereal box, that even if it wasn't the way he'd dreamt of, that didn't necessarily mean it would be worse, just different. And he seemed to take it that way, because he got very excited over it, so much so that he placed it in his trophy case, next to his second place in the US Open Juniors, the high point of his career and his most treasured defeat, as he called it. That same day, in front of the entire family, he announced he was quitting tennis, without the least hint of rancor or frustration. Now I couldn't help but wonder whether that decision to give up on professional tennis, which he seemed to take so naturally and so calmly, might not have plunged him into some kind of depression or grief that could have provoked a fatal wound to his self-esteem, to his dreams of grandeur—which he'd cultivated from a very young age. An emptiness impossible to share—because he couldn't stand anyone feeling sorry for him—that might have fed into whatever it was he was doing behind my back.

Not long afterward, he started a business installing tennis courts, which allowed him to pursue a career while remaining close to his passion. He developed and patented an artificial surface, using recycled materials, that not only dried in record time, but also absorbed the impact of players' footsteps, helping to prevent injuries of the kind he had suffered. He already controlled the better part of the tennis court market in Rhode Island and was starting to expand into Connecticut and Massachusetts. It was just the beginning, according to him. On his last trip, he was finally (supposedly) closing a contract with Yale University to renovate all the tennis courts on campus. If it turned out well, his business would take off. *Most universities follow Yale's lead. If Yale picks me, they'll all pick me*, he affirmed.

He tried to bunch his trips together so he could spend the minimum amount of time away. He was a real homebody, devoted to his routines, devoted to me. That was why all this had to have some kind of explanation.

Newport, Charlestown, Worcester, Manchester, Boylston, Hartford, East Greenwich, Block Island, and Yale. Those were the trips he had made so far that year. And once again, not a trace of hotel expenses, local restaurant bills paid for on the credit card, nothing at all. Hadn't that surprised me before? Not really. His father always said you had to actually pay your bills, with cash, with greenbacks, not with plastic. Because if not, it feels like you're not earning anything, and you spend more, naturally. You have to be conscious of what you spend because if not, someday, without realizing it, you'll be left without anything, he used to say. Yeah, the Williamses were a little tight-fisted—though Chris thought of himself more like the thrifty ant in the fable. So even if it had drawn my attention, he would have reminded me of his father's words and shown me the stack of bills he always kept in his pocket, in a silver clip he'd inherited from his grandfather, and I wouldn't have had the least doubt he was telling the truth.

In my painting studio in the basement of the house—it had been in the attic until Olivia was born—there was a table in the center crowded with all my junk: paint jars (oil and acrylic), brushes, pencils, plastic picnic plates where I mixed my colors, rags, canvas, frames, sketches, a light table, lots of books, and my laptop, accented with paint drips and splatters from my brushes. A controlled chaos. I liked it that way. Though it wasn't idyllic, being humid and lacking natural light, it was my corner, my world, where no one but me ever went. I liked how it filled up with life and experience. But now I didn't hesitate to clear off the entire table. I needed space and privacy.

I opened a road atlas my father had given us years ago and tore out the pages for Connecticut, Rhode Island and Massachusetts, laying out the sheets to create an enormous, detailed map of the Northeast. Then I traced all of Chris's *business trips* in different colors, following the most logical routes. None of these supposed trips would have taken him anywhere near US 6.

———

His side of the bed still smelled like him, revealing to me the abyss of his absence. A dark, endless precipice, a black hole of sorrow. And yet I refused to change the sheets. Before I went to bed—luckily, I hadn't lost sleep, for the less I was aware, the better—I thought: *I have the surveillance recording of Chris coming back. But naturally, if he passed through that spot on his return trip, he probably did the same on his way out, to wherever it was. Would that date coincide with the day he supposedly went to Yale? What was the owner of the gas station's name? It doesn't matter, Alice, his name's on the gas station. Now get some sleep.*

And I did sleep, but first I wrote everything down in a notebook. I had started to always keep one on me to prevent myself from forgetting the few lucid thoughts I had.

I don't know at what point I got up, went to Olivia's room, and got into the bed. I was sleeping; I'm sure of it. But I knew what I was doing and that it wasn't a dream. It was a strange conscious somnambulism. It would have been lovely to stay in that state the whole day long.

"Mommy, why can you come to my bed when you want and I can't go to yours?" Olivia asked drowsily, not expecting a response, curling up in the fetal position next to my belly, in the exact same position as Ruby, as though pretending she was inside me.

———

Sam, the owner of the gas station, was overwhelmed as he examined the long list I had just handed him with the dates of the security camera footage I wanted. The dates of Chris's trips.

January 17–22 and 28–31. February 6–11 and 24–28. March 4–7 and 17–23. April 15–19 and April 28–May 3. And finally, May 9–13.

"Are you going to go into labor again if I ask you why you want this footage?"

"Probably," I said, rubbing my belly.

"Just one question: Is all this about the person from the accident?"

I decided not to answer and just see what happened. It seemed to work.

"I have good news and bad news," he said. "Which do you want first?"

"Are we really going to play this game?" I asked, but Sam just imitated my silence. "OK," I said. "Give me the bad news first."

"I'm going to give you the footage."

"That's the bad news?" I asked.

Sam grabbed a grimy calculator with plastic over the keys to keep them from getting dirtier than they already were.

"Ma'am, you're asking me for forty-eight days' worth of recordings." He typed. "Forty-eight times twenty-four is 1,152 hours of recordings. That's a little crazy, ain't it? What are you looking for? I know, an SUV. You want to know if that Escalade passed by here other times. I read lots of mystery novels." He went back to his calculator without waiting for me to respond. "So, if you watched the complete tapes, sped up to two times normal speed, still slow enough to see any cars that might pass by, for an average of eight hours a day, like a regular old job . . ." He typed again. "Divide 1,152 by two . . . that's 576 hours . . . by eight . . . you'd need seventy-two days to see all of it," he said triumphantly, as though he'd just beat me at poker.

"Then what's the good news, Sam?" I asked, woozy at the cavalcade of numbers. The truth is I hadn't thought about all that.

"Well, the majority of closed-circuit systems erase the images they've stored little by little. It's not a legal thing. Here in this state, you can keep them for the rest of your life if you want. But it's a practical matter, a question of economics. The recordings are stored for twenty-eight days. Why twenty-eight and not a whole month? I don't know . . ." Sam looked back at the list I had given him. "So I can give you the recordings from April 15 through April 19 and the ones from April 28 through May 3 in addition to the one you've already got." He looked up and smiled at me, now more mocking than triumphant. "That's the good news. That you'll just have to watch . . ."

He started computing again. I wanted to slam that greasy calculator right over his head. But I didn't.

AT THE BEGINNING, every car that passed before my eyes made my heart shudder. *That's the one!* I kept thinking. And I would stop and rewind, and it would turn out to be a little pistachio-colored Chevrolet Spark, for example. I was looking for a rather large black Cadillac Escalade. But soon enough my eyes became adapted to the darkness of the vital moment, and in the end, I could even pass through the images at 4X speed.

Of the six journeys, both back and forth, I managed to find the SUV in five—two trips out and three back, including the moment of the accident. They didn't always coincide with the days Chris left or came home. So it occurred to me that on his trips, Chris would take care of his obligations, but that he could wrap them up in a day or two before running off to who knows where for who knows what reason. Following that highway, US 6, to come and go somewhere. Was it always the same place? Did it matter? He had already shown that he'd lied to me, and that lie apparently always led him to the same place. *Fine. Enough. Your dead husband was doing something bad. Did it have to be bad, necessarily? He had his big little secret he didn't want to share with you. Can't you live with that, Alice? Is it really so impossible to bear? Didn't he treat you well? Love you? Didn't he show it? Didn't he respect you? Want you? Make love to you? No, yes, yes, yes, yes, yes, yes, yes and yes.*

Someone knocked at the door to my studio—it was locked from the inside, something I had never done before. It was my mother.

"Honey, what are you doing in there?"

"The same as you when you're in the garden, Mom."

"You have rosebushes in there?"

"No, I have my things, the things I like to do by myself, for myself, without anyone bothering me."

"It doesn't bother me if you look at me or keep me company while I care for my roses."

"Well, it bothers me."

"But you don't even have rosebushes . . ."

Silence, I sucked in and held my breath.

"Oh, you mean whatever it is you're doing in there. Well, you could have told me, dear; you know I'm very respectful . . ."

I continued holding my breath.

"So why don't you plant some rosebushes? It would do you good to get some fresh air now and then instead of being shut up in there all day."

After she left, I held my breath for another fifteen seconds.

————

I traveled along US 6 from the scene of the accident toward the beginning or endpoint, depending on how you looked at it. To trace out the route Chris had followed. I had reserved the red marker for him. What should I call that route? I had to give it a name. The route of death? The route of the secret? Of the lie? And why was he on a secondary road, instead of I-195, which would have taken him much less time?

I passed in front of the gas station. I was about to stop and say hi to Sam and give him a gift by way of thanks. *Here, Sam, it's a new calculator, so you can go on calculating your pointless life . . . Poor guy, don't take it out on him, he even helped you out.* But maybe that was the thing that bothered me. If he had told me no, he wasn't going to give me the recordings, what would I have done? Would I have let it all go? Would I have given up my quest, unconsciously thankful to him for stopping me in time?

When I got to Wareham, I stopped at the main intersection. I'd already been driving a long time, hypnotized, going up US 6 slowly, like a zombie, afraid to look to either side, totally overwhelmed, ignoring all the houses that lined the road. The infinity of possibilities, of alleys, of turnoffs, of origins and of destinations. I was about to give up. *Go home, Alice. Forget all this.* Until a bird landed on the branch of a cherry tree at the same height as my red Jeep Cherokee. It was a cuckoo. It leaned its head to one side and looked at me. Chris always leaned his head to look at me when he noticed I was irritated and wouldn't say what it was that had made me angry. It was a little gesture to say, *Come on, A. You're angry, you know that I know, don't make me ask you why a thousand times, and don't say a thousand times that you're not, because in the end you'll tell me, and by then we'll both be angry after playing this goddamn game.* And what would I do? The same thing I was doing just then. I would stay there quiet, avoiding any eye contact with him. Finally, Chris would get tired of waiting, get up and go. What if the spirit of Chris had taken up residence in that cuckoo. *Aren't those the birds that lay their eggs in others' nests? Is that some kind of subliminal message? Is he trying to tell me something?*

The cuckoo took flight just as this thought flitted through my head. It was Chris, no doubt about it. Where was he going? I followed him with my gaze. He left in the very direction I'd come from. *Aha, you're going home, coward. You want to lead me away from the scene of the crime.* I went pale. The scene of the crime? I hadn't thought about it. What if now . . .

A horn honked loudly behind me, startling me. When I said I had stopped at the intersection, I mean I was literally in the middle of the road blocking the flow of traffic. An impatient driver was making a fuss, as if to say, *Woman driver!* I moved forward a few feet and parked on the shoulder of the road. *Pay attention to the cuckoo; go home . . . Left or right . . . ? He was warning you. Don't go poking around in other people's nests . . . Left or right? Where do I go . . . ? Backward, back home. You still have time to make it to your water aerobics class for pregnant women . . . Look, the guy who honked at you stopped in front of a bank . . . A bank, so what? What do I need with a bank right now? Alice, banks have security cameras.* I'd had these kinds of internal dialogues all my life. They weren't the result of some trauma. I'm an only child; I had no choice but to get along with myself.

––––––

It was called Pilgrims' Bank and it was almost a toy. There were security cameras installed outside. And who was behind the counter? Yes, the man who had honked at me impatiently at the intersection. He had greasy hair slicked down on one side, probably covering up an incipient bald spot. He was fat and had a stain on his tie. It was either going to be very easy or very difficult to get him on my side. *How far would you be willing to go to get what you want, Alice? Would you pay for it, for instance? Would you jerk him off in the bathroom?*

"I beg your pardon."

He looked at me without understanding.

He doesn't recognize you, Alice. Don't say anything. Change the subject. "I was blocking the intersection before."

Great, Alice.

"Oh, don't worry. No problem." He smiled affably. "I apologize for honking. It's just that right before then some coffee spilled on my tie. I'm a disaster with things like that, eating in the car, you know, and I always end up spilling something on myself. But I can't help it. Anyway, so I made you pay for it, honking my horn like a jerk." He extended his hand. "My name's Karl. Yours?"

"Angela."

"Nice name. How can I help you, Angela?"

Suddenly, the fat horn honker with the stain on his tie and an urge to get jerked off by a pregnant woman in the bathroom became Karl, an employee at a humble bank who liked his job and really wanted his clients to get the most out of their savings.

"Look, Karl, the thing is, I'm a little desperate. I need your help."

"No problem, take out your pistol, I'll give you what's in the safe, it's not much, things being what they are, and that's that." He raised his hands and laughed, a little high-pitched, considering his corpulent body.

I told him my brother had died not long ago in a traffic accident. They had done an autopsy on him, and he had tested positive for meth (I'm a big *Breaking Bad* fan). They found traces of the drug in his car. He had just gotten high. The meth had been cut with something bad, and he had a stroke, which made him run off the road. The police had closed the case because for them, my brother was just another drug addict who deserved what he had gotten, but I needed to know where it had come from. I was certain I'd just seen his dealer, and I needed to find the person responsible for my brother's death. What I'd just told him was the plot from a dreadful TV movie I'd seen one afternoon a few months back, one of those you start watching and can't take your eyes off of till the end, no matter how bad it is. It was called *Avenging Angela*. Who would have thought it would end up being useful?

There were tears in Karl's eyes as I told the story; they started just after I said I was going to name my baby Derek, after my brother. And that was how I discovered prior footage of Chris heading east on US 6. I realize it probably wasn't necessary to lie about all that. I guess I was training myself for all the lies to come. Chris's and mine. Mainly mine.

THE NEXT DAY, I had a lawyer's appointment and couldn't go on mapping out Chris's route and tracing it with the red marker.

My mother called at my studio door.

"Are you all right?"

"Yes, Mom, I'm fine. You don't have to ask me if I'm all right every half hour."

"Well, I put my ear up to the door, and I didn't even hear you breathing . . . Remember you've got an appointment with the insurance lawyer today?"

"Yes, I remember."

"Are you sure you don't want me to go with you?"

"No, thanks . . ."

"Or Dad? You know they might try and scam you. I don't trust lawyers."

I opened the door, wedging my body so that my mother couldn't peek inside.

"Don't worry, Mom. It's nothing . . . I'd rather go by myself. I'll work it out."

"OK, fine . . . But seriously, honey, why do you spend so much time shut up in there?"

"This is my painting studio, Mom. I'm a painter. I like to paint. It relaxes me. It makes me forget everything for a while."

"It doesn't smell like paint, honey," she said to me without a trace of hostility. The opposite, in fact: she wanted me to know she was there for me. Suddenly, I realized I had turned my mother into a threat instead of a possible accomplice. I was about to break down and confess everything. Everything.

"I'm drawing, Mom. Pencils don't have a scent."

I closed the door. And locked it.

———

The lawyer looked like he'd come straight out of central casting and was seated in a typical lawyer's office in a typical law firm.

"Your husband had a life insurance contract that covered accidental death. After looking over the autopsy report, which determined that he wasn't under the influence of controlled substances or driving recklessly, and since the accident was the result of natural causes, the board has approved payment of the policy in full. Would you like to know how much it is?"

"A million and a half dollars . . ." I said inexpressively. We used to joke a lot about how well a fatal accident would work out.

When the lawyer began to advise me about various investments I could make to derive maximum benefit from the money, I stopped him gently. I didn't want to speculate with the money. I didn't want to use it. It was dirty money, and it wasn't going to bring Chris back. *But it might help you find him.* It was a fleeting thought that passed rapidly through the corners of my mind, but I caught it and never let it go.

———

When I returned home, the piano had just arrived. No, I hadn't forgotten about the gift for my presumptive child prodigy. I'd bought it that same day after returning from the funeral home. I'd shut myself up in the bathroom because I needed to cry alone. Then I opened the browser on my cell phone and typed into the search bar *Piano stores buy online.* I clicked the first link in the results. The grand pianos looked too ostentatious and pricey for me. *A genius can make any piano sound good,* I thought. So I bought an upright digital piano, a glossy white Roland (which sounded like a good brand). It cost $1,999 and took me less than four minutes to order.

Now that pretty piano, because it was very pretty, was in the living room against the wall where we had all the family photos.

"What's that for?" Olivia asked, holding on to her Big Smelly Bear. She hadn't let it go since I gave it to her.

"What do you mean, what's it for? It's a piano, Oli. For playing music."

"Yeah, but why's it here?"

"It's here for you. It's a present Daddy ordered for you."

She looked under the lid and lifted the mat that covered the keys.

"Don't you want to learn to play the piano?"

Olivia looked closer. I turned it on and she touched a key. A few times, but only that one key.

"You can touch more," I said. "They all sound different."

I played a complete scale. Do, re, mi, fa, sol, la, ti, do . . . Olivia watched me with obviously disdainful curiosity.

"This isn't a gift from Daddy."

"Yes, it is."

"No, Daddy doesn't give me presents like this."

"What do you mean?"

"Daddy gives me better presents. Fun ones. If you had died, Daddy would have given me a pony to make me feel better, not a piano."

At this point it was clear she wasn't a genius, but she was certainly clever. She was about to leave the living room when I snatched the stuffed animal from her hands.

"Leave Big Smelly Bear alone! Give him to me! Mom!"

I used a voice at once reedy and garbled, as if I was the Big Smelly Bear.

"Olivia, if you don't want the piano, I'll take it. I love pianos."

"Don't use that voice. I don't like it!"

I ignored her.

"And you know why I like pianos? Because then I can fart while I'm playing and nobody will hear it."

I sat Big Smelly Bear in my lap and banged wildly on the piano's keys with the animal's front paws.

"You like it? It's an original composition. It's called 'Poop Melody in Fart Minor.' Dance for me, Olivia! Dance for me!"

Olivia had stopped trying to force the bear out of my hands and was laughing and dancing and turning around in a circle. Two weeks after Chris's death, I had finally managed to make Olivia laugh. Not that she hadn't laughed the entire time, but it had never been laughter I had provoked. Just for that, buying the piano had been worth it. Anyway, I had forty-five days to return it.

———

With the assistance of Karl, the banker with a heart and stains on his tie, I managed to figure out that Chris crossed the Wareham River on US 6. I traced his path until I made it to a minigolf course on Cranberry Highway called Sand & Surf, where I saw there was a security camera. A security camera on a minigolf course? The place was completely empty.

The manager, Charlie—I read it on his nametag—was walking indolently over the worn-out Astroturf surrounding the holes, a putter resting on his shoulder like a rifle. He had a shaved head with a scar down the center, ending right between his eyebrows.

The story of my brother lost to drugs moved him so deeply it made him cry, without tears, because according to him, when they opened up his head, in addition to losing 11 percent of his brain matter, his tear ducts dried up. He had to use drops throughout the day to keep his eyes from drying up. It turned out he'd split his head open when he was coked out of his gourd on a trip to Miami with a friend he met who was a gun nut like himself. "Nothing weird, no gay stuff, get it?" he added. He got the idea to do some balconing, which he explained to me, without my asking, was when you jumped from the balcony of your hotel into the pool. Clearly, he didn't make it. Charlie had always wanted to be a marine, but they turned him down because he had a slight limp.

Afterward he applied for practically every branch of the US armed forces, then the state and county police, forest rangers, highway patrol . . . Zilch. So he'd ended up there, with a putter his lone weapon to fend off the local drunks and pranksters. They installed the security camera, he explained to me, when one father accused another of kicking the wooden beam at the boundary of the hole to make his son's ball go in so that he would win the championship. In the subsequent fight, the accused father wound up stabbing the other man in the stomach with the flag marking the hole.

Charlie not only offered to give me the footage I needed, but also wanted to join me in my investigation. If I was going to delve into the underworld, I'd need protection, someone to cover my back, and he wasn't afraid to take a bullet in the chest for me and "the little creature I was carrying inside me."

I gently declined his offer and left with the recordings safely in my possession.

Not all the characters who helped me trace out what I silently referred to as "the route of the red marker" toward Chris's point of departure or destination were so peculiar. Several refused to collaborate and didn't feel moved in the least by my story or my personal circumstances. Others even threatened to turn me in for trying to bribe them. Some only had the security cameras for show and others erased footage daily. Occasionally, I was forced to make decisions blindly, assuming I was following Chris's route, only to discover he hadn't passed through there, and I'd retrace my footsteps and try another one. But luckily for me—or unfortunately—we lived in a society that was obsessed with defending its territory.

Eventually, I found that Chris had crossed Buzzards Bay, passing by the Bay Motor Inn—information courtesy of the manager, Hugo—until he reached a huge traffic circle close to Bourne Bridge, where a number of main roads meet. There was a gun shop there with an on-site shooting range.

It turned out that the owner of the place, a coarse-looking woman of about fifty, had all of her security footage from more than five years back. Her father, the former owner, was in a nursing home with senile dementia. She went to visit him every Monday morning—the only day the range closed—and took him the tapes for the week, because they were the only thing he liked to watch, the only thing that roused him from his slow and agonizing decline.

"So, tell me, Angela," she eventually said, "how many pistols are you willing to buy to get me to give you what you want?"

———

Chris had taken the exit onto US 28 East and crossed Bourne Bridge, one of only two bridges leading onto or off of Cape Cod. Cape Cod? Chris didn't like the cape one bit. At least, that's what he said. I had spent a few summer vacations with my parents in Chatham when I was a little girl and then a teenager, and had lovely memories of it, but I'd never gone back since, in part because of Chris, because places with too many crowds made him nervous, especially during vacation season. He'd say, *You go on vacation to feel calm, not stressed out all day sitting in traffic or going nuts trying to find a parking place. I can't take the idea of everyone going to the same place like sheep, as if there weren't other magnificent places, calmer and cheaper, all up and down the East Coast.* I vaguely remembered that on one of his business trips, at least two years ago, he had been in a country club in some part of Cape Cod. But the deal hadn't panned out, as I could corroborate when I looked through all his contracts without finding any pertaining to the cape.

Could he have been lying to me? I suddenly asked myself if the motivation for that visceral rejection of Cape Cod might have been to keep me away from there, from whatever it was he was hiding. No, it couldn't be. Chris couldn't stand crowds. He didn't like big cities. *And besides, a place you can only get to by bridge makes me claustrophobic,* he had said to me once. Yet there he was now, on my computer screen, turning onto the exit leading directly onto Cape Cod.

I PROGRESSED—OR, better said, I rewound—at an average of a mile or two a day. Slowly. Without telling anyone. I took Olivia to school. Six hours. That was the time I had to find out what I could, tracing the route in red marker. Then I'd go back, pick up Olivia, play with her awhile, bathe her, make her dinner, put her to bed, read a story to her and Big Smelly Bear, and then go back over all the material I'd gathered. That routine kept my head busy and helped me play hide-and-seek with the despair that flooded everything and the crippling longing for Chris to come back. I felt guilty, like someone looking through her husband's cell phone or email or pants pockets while he's in the shower—things I had never done. But at the same time, it connected me to Chris, as though I was keeping him alive, because in a sense I was seeing him in those recordings, I was following him. Every night before going to bed, I opened Chris's email, his Facebook, his LinkedIn and his other social media accounts. As if I were his secretary taking care of business in his absence. In case a new notification suddenly popped up, a clue. But nothing, it was almost all spam or work stuff.

I kept his phone on. The screen had been shattered in the accident, but it still worked. I carried it in my bag, waiting for some call to come through. Maybe a person with some connection to his secret. If it rang, I never picked up—whether it was someone known or unknown; I always waited for them to leave a message. I didn't want to chase away or tip off whoever was calling. I had to activate his voicemail, because he always had it off. It was a business tactic of his that I never understood very well, though apparently it worked. *Lots of people call you at weird times, when they know you're not going to pick up, to leave you a voicemail. People don't like to say no to your face.*

In the three weeks since his death, he had gotten nine calls: one from the deputy director of athletics at Yale to confirm that the renovation of the tennis courts had been approved. He had won the contract, and we were all happy and sad at the same time. There were two calls from T-Mobile, to offer him a good deal on business phones; three from various purveyors of material for his courts; and three from a hidden number that didn't leave a message. Could that have to do with Chris and his lie? At times I called it a lie, at times a mystery, at times a secret.

After Chris's death, his father, Christopher—they had the same name—and his sister, Tricia, had taken charge of the business, to tie up the loose ends, the unfinished jobs, invoices, outstanding payments. They had decided to dismantle the business, even though the accounts were up-to-date and it was solvent. They would push ahead with the contracts that were already signed and even with the deal with Yale— that would be a nice homage to Chris. But then, they would shut it down. It didn't make sense to keep it going without Chris. He had built it up alone and hadn't wanted to bring anyone in, taking care of everything on his own, keeping all the bases covered. The ubiquitous Chris. Everyone he contracted was on a per-job basis. He knew that at some point, he'd have to expand, but everything in due time. Step by step. Yale was going to be the turning point, what took him to the next level.

My mother was becoming increasingly concerned about me. *Honey, where do you go for so long? You're not in any condition to be running around like that, you're about to give birth.* And I'd invent activities: childbirth education classes, gynecologist appointments, yoga, music therapy, shopping for baby clothes.

———

I discovered that on Cape Cod, Chris had followed Route 28, exiting onto Route 151 East. He'd turned off on Falmouth Road around Mashpee.

That is how I reached the small Barnstable Municipal Airport, close to Hyannis, where a number of streets merge and the Airport Shopping Center is located. Among the businesses situated along US 28 (with their security cameras witnessing the flow of cars) was a garage and parts store called World Tech Auto Center, an aesthetician's called Salon

Centric, a rug and carpet store called Kent's Carpetland, and a spy store called Night Eyes.

By now I'd become experienced and knew it was pointless to try my luck at the franchises, because they generally had strict security and privacy policies, and any request like mine had to go through the higher-ups. So I went to places where the decisions depended on a single person I could negotiate with directly. My instincts had gotten sharper, or at least that's what I thought, until every business at the shopping center turned me down and all I had left was the spy shop.

Night Eyes turned out to be a small, rundown shop, despite its sign reading *Security and Electronics Superstore,* and the speaker outside was playing the theme from *The Pink Panther.*

The store was empty. Behind the counter was a middle-aged man eating an orange as he watched a small TV of a kind I thought no longer existed.

"Hey, Blondie, how can I help you?" he asked in a foreign accent I couldn't quite manage to place.

I thought maybe it would be harder to lie to this guy, since his job was selling gadgets that revealed people's lies. Was it better to tell him the story about my drug-addict brother or get straight to the point? Insecure after my recent defeats, I hesitated.

"You can say whatever problem open. All you say here confidential. Me priest, this confession. Amen."

"Well, see, my brother . . ."

"Had car accident, right?" he cut me off. "Died behind steering wheel, driving, drug overdose."

I looked at him, unable to believe it. Had I already gone in there in my madness? I wouldn't have forgotten his accent or his peculiarly kind way of talking.

"Eddie, from car shop, call me," he clarified. "He say, look, pregnant crazy trying get security camera footage. He tell all businesses in area. Don't give nothing. Not legal. Illegal. Don't give. Watch out pregnant bitch."

I wanted to run out of there. *Alice, it's over; you're going to end up in jail.*

"That brother story? Very bad," he stated. "Film was on TV recently. I watch much TV to improve English. Getting better, every time is better. At first when I arrive, I only know say *hello* and *fuck you*."

I turned and started heading for the door.

"Wait. No leave. I make fun of you. Eddie a jerkoff, no like him, he no give discount when I take car to get fixed. Probably he call me and everyone else so you go back to him and he get more money from you."

"I offered him a lot of money." Those were my first words since I had come in. "I have money." *How much money you want I pay you?* I almost said to him, so he would understand me, accept, and just give me the tapes.

"Why you no come here first? You want information. Confidential. Secret. This spy store. Birds of feather. Clear as water. You disappoint me a little. Why you no trust me? Plus, here no ask question. Here only find answers."

He reminded me of Yoda from *Star Wars*. But he wasn't from a galaxy far, far away, nor was he a Russian ex-KGB agent. It turned out he was Spanish. From Malaga. His name was Antonio, like Antonio Banderas, also from Malaga, as he made clear. The orange he was eating was from Valencia, because according to him the oranges from Florida and California were *piece of shit compared to Spanish*. The financial crisis in Spain had led him to emigrate in search of the promised land. That and, a week after he got laid off from the security firm he worked for, his wife hooked up with his boss. It took him a long time to figure it out, and he thought: *If only someone helped me then the way I helping people now*. That was where he got the idea for the spy shop.

I liked Antonio. Maybe it helped that I'd had a Spanish boyfriend. When I was studying at Brown, I studied abroad for six months in Madrid—the first time I left the country. That's where I met Diego. I was going through a crisis with Chris (yeah, we had crises then) due to the distance between our universities, but also because we'd been together *all our lives* and had never had other relationships, other experiences. He wanted to experience other things (hook up with other chicks), and I wanted to discover the world (fall in love with other guys). Diego was a sweet parenthesis in my life. A professor in the art department at the Complutense University in Madrid, he was a painter as well as a sculptor and photographer. He was sensitive, fun and a great dancer. I loved his hands and the way he touched me. During those six months I experienced things I never had before and never would again. With him I felt artistic, bohemian, as if I'd gone outside myself, outside my world, and was someone else. *Maybe you were that person you'd always wanted to be but never dared.* Diego had a sister I adored, whose name was Olivia. I never talked to Chris about Diego. We agreed that what had happened during that time had happened; we didn't want to give explanations to each other and didn't feel we owed them either.

Recently, when we had discussed what name we should give our baby—I was seven months pregnant at the time—he had said: *You chose for the first baby; you wanted something international that could be spelled the same in English, Spanish, Italian, and French. And I was fine with that: Olivia. I liked it. But now it's my turn. I want a name that sounds like a jewel, because that's what we're going to have, a precious jewel: Ruby,* he said.

And I said: *Sorry, no way. Find another one; Ruby sounds to me like a hooker from a soap opera.*

Looking offended, he said: *You just tarnished the memory of my great-grandmother Ruby, Alice.* He never called me by my full first name except when he was trying to unnerve me. Most of the time he called me Ali, or preferably A. I liked A.

"So, Blondie, what I help you with? Shoot."

Just then, Eddie from World Tech came in. He was very annoyed. He thought Antonio was negotiating with me to get more money for the recordings. *Son of a bitch, you come here and you take away our money and our jobs. Go back to Mexico where you belong!*

"I'll give you what you need for a thousand bucks," Eddie said.

Before I could say yes or no—I would have said yes—Antonio beat me to the punch.

"Seven hundred, Blondie, and all yours."

"Five hundred," Eddie offered.

"Three hundred," Antonio said, undercutting him.

"Don't be an asshole!" Eddie said. "She can give us a thousand, and we'll split it."

Antonio ignored him. He looked at me and winked.

"A hundred dollars, Blondie."

"I'll turn you both in to the cops! This is illegal!" Eddie threatened. But far from shrinking, Antonio counterattacked:

"Of course, Eddie. How you want? Police come. Then you explain them those cars that come in morning and no return from garage. Or return, but in pieces you sell illegally. Explain that to police, cocksucker."

Suddenly, his English had gotten better. Eddie went pale.

"You think I talk shit? Go put stolen exhaust tube up your asshole."

Eddie took off, spouting all sorts of threats that Antonio ignored while he slowly finished his orange.

"So, what your name, Blondie?" he asked me when we were alone.

"Grace." *Avenging Angela* had officially given up the ghost.

"Well, pleasure, Grace. Like Grace of Monaco. Also blond."

"I'm not blond; I'm a redhead."

He ignored the comment.

"You really going to pay Eddie so much money?"

"Yes. And if you want, I'll pay you more."

"More, no. Just what's right. Just thousand dollars, Blondie." He gave me his hand. "Oh, I'm color blind. You for me always blond."

I smiled and shook his hand. The aroma of the Valencian orange lingered. A scent that reminded me of Spain and of Diego. *You're a widow, now; you could find him*, I thought, and I felt very dirty.

Back in the car, with the recordings on a USB drive, I decided to stop fooling around and go back to offering money, plain and simple. Wasn't I a millionaire? Didn't I feel that money was dirty? Well, blow it and don't look back. To hell with it. That money reminded me all the time of what had happened, and the sooner it disappeared, the sooner I'd resolve Chris's lie/secret/mystery. In any case, back home, I stopped at my bank branch and opened an account for Olivia. I deposited $300,000, to be split with her sister when she was born. It was one thing to blow my small, dirty fortune and another to leave my daughters unable to go to college.

CHRIS HADN'T CROSSED Route 28 close to the Airport Shopping Center. I checked twice. That meant he'd entered Hyannis. I checked again. I vaguely remembered being there as a girl. Maybe it had been just one of our many outings during those summers in Chatham.

That night I called my father.

"Dad?"

"Yes, honey."

"When we spent the summer in Chatham, were we ever in Hyannis?"

"Yeah, once or twice. But just passing through."

"What do you mean, passing through?"

"Hyannis is where you can catch the ferry to Martha's Vineyard and Nantucket. Don't you remember when we went to Martha's Vineyard? It's the island where they filmed *Jaws*."

"That's right, now I remember . . ." I recollected with a smile. "And apart from remembering it being a pretty island, why does Nantucket seem so familiar to me?"

"Well, probably because I drove you up the wall telling you over and over how Nantucket was a whaling port, and it was there that Ishmael set off on the *Pequod* under the orders of Captain Ahab."

Moby-Dick is my father's favorite book.

"Ah, right. You used to read me bits of that book when I was a girl."

Nantucket. Whales. Moby Dick. Was Chris Moby Dick, and was I Captain Ahab? How did *Moby-Dick* end? Who won? Did he catch the whale? Did Captain Ahab end up half-mad after trying to chase down the impossible? I didn't remember, but my impression was it turned out badly, terribly badly. That was a sign. *Let it go, Alice. It's not legal to hunt whales anymore.*

"Hey, Dad. Do you have a copy of *Moby-Dick*?"

"Of course. A first edition, 1851."

"Can I borrow it?"

"What for?"

"To read it."

"Honey, it's worth thirty-five thousand dollars. I don't know if it's a good idea to handle a thirty-five-thousand-dollar book. I'm leaving it to you in my will. After I'm gone, you can do what you want with it."

The next day, my father came over with a hardcover copy of *Moby-Dick*. I was surprised, because he said he was going to buy me the e-book. But he wasn't much of a fan of digital.

"The feel of the paper will bring you closer to the characters. When you turn the pages, you'll feel the breeze of the sea as you navigate aboard the ship."

"Thanks, Dad." I opened the book and flipped through it. "What did you say it's about? I don't mean the plot, but the message."

"Well . . ." He reflected a few seconds; he didn't like to talk idly. "It's about the need to face evil. About creating demons and chasing them to the point of madness, or out of our own madness, basically to keep from examining the ones we have inside us."

"Got it . . ." I tried to keep him from detecting in my voice the fire-ball that was blazing in my mind. "But just one thing, Dad. The book ends badly, right?"

"No, honey, it ends the way it has to."

He gave me a kiss and left. My father never wants to be a bother or interrupt whatever someone is doing. Because he also doesn't want to be bothered or interrupted in his discreet passage through life. Beyond that, he never asks me how I am, because my mother already takes care of that a thousand times a day. My father reads me; he smells me from a distance. He looks at me and knows, without asking. His love is silent. He's like that old pilled blanket you bundle up in on the couch at night to watch television. Not because you're cold, but because it makes you feel cozy, protected, comfortable.

———

"Where are we going, Mommy?"

Olivia was sitting in her booster seat in the back of the Chero-kee, paging through the maps with the routes marked in red marker.

I suddenly realized it was a pigsty back there. Empty water bottles, Styrofoam containers from all the places I had stopped to get food—I always ate in the car, like Karl the banker—containers I hadn't thrown out, because I wanted to recycle them. Paper cups, markers, notebooks, CDs, and traffic tickets. I'd gotten more than one, and every time the cops stopped me, the first thing I thought was I was busted, they were going to arrest me, and I'd end up in jail, charged with a crime against Chris's privacy.

It was midafternoon. I could have left Olivia with my mother, but I wasn't ready to start up her questioning machine yet. So I did the only thing that occurred to me, I took her with me.

"What are we doing, Mommy? Where are we going?"

"Put that down, honey."

"It looks like a treasure map. Are we looking for treasure?"

"Yes, Oli," I said, taking the map out of her hands.

"What treasure?"

"I don't know; we won't know what it is until we find it."

"Whose treasure is it? Did Daddy leave it for us?"

"Yeah, more or less."

"Are we going to find pirates?"

"I hope not."

"Did a pirate kill Daddy?"

Maybe it would have been better to leave her with my mother.

———

The preceding days had been a blur. On June 5, I found out that Chris had entered (or left) Hyannis by way of Barnstable Road. (Courtesy of the Church of the First Born. Donation: one hundred dollars).

———

June 6 was a washout.

———

On June 7, Chris's mother, Betty, turned sixty-five. My mother had warned me: *We can't skip, honey; we have to maintain a good relationship with them. They love us very much. And we love them, too; of course, that goes without saying. I know it's going to be a sad day, but it's important we're all together, don't you think?*

Olivia got sick during the celebration, due to the heat—to top it off, she was wearing a princess costume—plus the games, food, excitement, ice cream and candy. She ended up vomiting. And naturally, there was a lot of sadness and yearning, because the scene was normal only on the surface. The absence of Chris consumed almost all the available oxygen.

———

June 8. Chris had crossed Main Street to continue up Ocean Street. (Courtesy of the owner of the Yankee Peddler Pawn Shop. Five hundred dollars and a children's illustrated edition of *Treasure Island* acted out by mice, which immediately became Olivia's favorite book).

———

June 9. Chris had proceeded down Ocean Street until he reached the port, where the various ferry companies disembarked. (Courtesy of the bartender at the Black Cat Tavern. Four hundred dollars.) And he had turned left on Ocean Street, entering what looked like a parking lot. (Courtesy of the manager of the Hyannis Harbor Hotel. One thousand dollars. I paid that ridiculous sum not because I had the feeling I was getting closer to the end—or to the beginning—and that the information was therefore more valuable, but because I was unusually nervous and incapable of haggling.)

———

And now it was June 10. I stopped the car right where Chris turned, where I'd lost sight of him. It was the entrance to the parking lot for the ferry terminal. Tachycardia. The pier for the Robin Island Ferry. Robin Island? I'd never heard of it. I had trouble breathing. From the Weweantic River along US 6 to the Robin Island ferry terminal: 37.5 miles. Would the red-marker route end there? My legs shook when I got out of the SUV. "Stay here a second, babe," I said to Olivia with a trembling voice. "You never let me get out, Mommy; this is stupid; I want to look for treasure, too," Olivia complained.

I approached a worker who was directing cars onto the ferry.

"Excuse me, does this ferry go to Robin Island?"

"Yes, ma'am, that's why it's called the Robin Island Ferry. We're original around here, as you can see," he answered, without any trace of malice.

"And it only goes to Robin Island?"

"Yes, ma'am."

"And can you go elsewhere from the island?"

"You can get to Nantucket and Martha's Vineyard, but only in the summer months. Anyway, it'd be silly to do that because the ferry terminals for Martha's Vineyard and Nantucket are right over there, they go direct, they're more modern, and they take a lot less time. There's even an express service. So if you want to go to Nantucket or Martha's Vineyard, it's not worth it to go to Robin Island."

He looked at my car and at Olivia, who had ended up disobeying me and getting out.

"One vehicle, two people?" he asked.

"Are we going to get on the pirate ship?"

"Olivia, get in the car."

"Round trip?"

"I want to get on the pirate ship."

"Forty-five dollars. I'll only charge you for one, the girl can ride free."

"We're going to Treasure Island!"

I was falling out. I was starting to faint. The euphoria I thought I felt at my discovery was just the beginning of an anxiety attack. The fastest way out, I thought, was to pay, and that's what I did, trying to hide the shaking of my hands.

"Go to lane one," he said, indicating the spot. Two vehicles were already waiting there.

I got into the car with Olivia and started it up, putting it in reverse. I nearly rammed the car behind me, and they honked. I didn't apologize and instead pulled away. In the rearview mirror I could see the worker waving his arms as if to say, *Hey, lady, where are you going?* while Olivia complained bitterly.

"But, Mommy, I want to go to Treasure Island!"

Despite the nausea, I managed to make it home. I didn't stop. The only reason I didn't faint and collapse right there was the animal instinct that took over to protect my daughter. My two daughters. I was enraged with myself. *Why did you have to do all this? What's the point? Do you want to ruin your life? But you can't turn back now, you're fucked.*

We entered the house. Olivia asked me to watch TV, something I didn't usually let her do. "OK," I said. I went up to the bedroom and vomited in the bathroom. When a person vomits, no matter how unpleasant it is, there's always a certain relief afterward. This time, I didn't feel it. My tangle of emotions had subsided somewhat but still remained. I had Moby Dick within me, fighting for his life, or trying to put an end to mine.

———

There was a security camera in the sales office of the ferry terminal. I saw it the first time I went in. By now, I'd developed a talent for sniffing them out. It watched over the parking lot and the ferry entrance. Why didn't I try to get the recordings? The worker had seemed nice, and he clearly liked me. Surely, he would have gone along, and if not, someone who worked in the terminal building would have.

What was going on with me? I had found Chris's hideout, and all of a sudden I had run away in terror. But besides the fright, there was something more. I was so close that a single false step could startle my prey. I had to proceed with caution. I couldn't bribe anyone to get the security camera footage because that would alert everyone on the island. I couldn't come in and pass undetected. Nor could I show the worker a photo of Chris and ask him if he knew him, if he'd ever seen him before. They could even be pals. If Chris took that ferry often, he probably gave the man a friendly greeting. Chris was like that, attentive and kind to everyone. Maybe I was just inventing excuses to keep from solving the mystery/secret/lie. I was terrified. But . . . *Fine, what if I show the photo to the worker, and he says,* Yeah, Chris went to the island all the time; I remember him perfectly; I never forget a face. *From that point on, I've shown my hand. It's not a matter of figuring out if he went to the island or not; it's about figuring out what he was doing there. The worker could notify the person he was supposed to notify, saying:* Hey, we got a pregnant woman asking questions about Chris, watch out. *No, I can't ask, or try to get the security camera footage . . .*

That said, maybe Chris didn't go to the island. Maybe he just left the Escalade parked in the lot. It was public, free, unsupervised, and open twenty-four hours a day.

June 11. The guy who runs the garage had called me several times complaining that he couldn't keep Chris's SUV there any longer, and no matter how often I told him he could charge me whatever he saw fit, he kept repeating it wasn't a matter of money, but of space.

So I went there to look the car over one more time before sending it to the junkyard. While I examined it, the mechanic went on with his litany of complaints.

"Mrs. Williams, you need to understand, the vehicle can't be repaired, it's totaled, and I understand your situation, I really do . . ."

At that point, I stopped listening, because I had lowered the driver's visor—I had already looked there the last time—and under a plastic flap—where I hadn't looked the last time—I found two keys on a bare ring. One was a car key with a button in the center to control the locks. *Ford*, it said. The other was small, Master was the brand, for a padlock or a locker. Two keys, one ring. A Ford? Did Chris have, had he ever had, a Ford? Was that key a talisman, a relic he had kept from his first car? He inherited his first car, an old Buick Skylark Gran Sport, where our first sexual encounters took place, from his grandfather. And the other key, the small one? Did he have something locked up at home? Was he a member of a gym, club or some other place that had lockers?

"Besides, with all due respect, Mrs. Williams, I don't think it's good for you . . ."

I cut him off.

"Get rid of it."

Before I went back home, I went by Chris's parents' place to pay them a visit. On the front porch, I edged over toward the garage and pushed the button on the key fob, hoping one of the cars would react. Nothing.

After having coffee with Christopher and Betty, and worrying—genuinely—about how they were, I went up to Chris's room, which had been left as it was since he was a teenager, with posters of his tennis idols (Agassi, Sampras, McEnroe and Chang), his musical idols (Guns N' Roses, AC/DC), and his movie idols (Bruce Willis in *Die Hard*). The shelves were packed with tennis trophies, and on the corkboard there were photos of him with his classmates from high school and with me at the prom. Now it had become a mausoleum in memoriam. When I shut myself up in there, his parents took it to mean I needed a little time alone with Chris. Maybe it was true. I couldn't help crying as I looked over his things, but I found no clue to the Ford or the other key.

When I got back home, I scoured every corner of the house trying to find a lock that fit the little key that I had already started calling the Master Key. Later, I went to bed exhausted and fell asleep with the two keys in my hand, trying to fit together the pieces of the puzzle. I woke up at six thirty the next morning with an overwhelming urge to piss and a new resolve to return to the ferry terminal.

———

June 12. When I arrived at the ferry terminal, there were seven vehicles in the lot, two of them Fords. A Taurus and a Ford Ranger pickup truck. First I tried the Taurus. It didn't open. I discreetly approached the truck, pretending to talk on my cell, convinced that my intuition had failed me. The truck was gray, a color Chris detested, and at least fifteen years old. It was also filthy. Chris was meticulous about his cars and how they were maintained. No, it couldn't be.

But it was. Again, I felt the urge to run off. I didn't get into the truck right away. I glanced around first to make sure no one saw me, even though I was in the rear part of the terminal, the most discreet and least trafficked area.

The truck was practically empty. A few rags, a bottle of water, an empty Dunkin' Donuts cup, and a kid's Ninja Turtles backpack, very old and worn out. Also empty. I had the feeling it had been Chris's; I even thought I might have seen it somewhere in the attic at home.

I got behind the wheel and put the key in the ignition. The engine hesitated, then started up. The tank was almost full. I opened the glove compartment. The registration and insurance were inside, in his name. He had bought it, and paid in cash, at MBM Auto Sales, a secondhand car dealership in Hyannis. Almost three years ago. Three years? My Lord . . .

I don't know how long I was there, still, with the motor running, absorbed in my thoughts, until I noticed three small rectangular stickers, different colored, stuck to the windshield. I got out to take a closer look. They were passes for the Robin Island Ferry, for the years 2013, 2014 and 2015.

I thought that if the key to the truck Chris took to the island for more than two years was on the same ring as the Master Key, then whatever it opened had to be there, on Robin Island.

THE FERRY TO Robin Island was small, with a capacity of roughly twelve cars on deck, arranged in three rows. It took forty-five minutes to reach the island. On that trip, there were only three cars, a roofer's truck, and a UPS van. None of their occupants got out to enjoy the scenery. Just one got out at all, to smoke a cigarette. They obviously were regulars, people for whom this was a mere journey from point A to point B, not a scenic voyage through Nantucket Sound where one enjoyed the sun, the breeze and the mild warmth of early summer.

When Olivia and I had arrived at the terminal, the man we had met three days earlier asked me why I had bolted. I told him I'd felt indisposed, pregnancy, you know. He refused to charge me and was very agreeable without a glimmer of suspicion. Even so, I was constantly expecting someone to ask me: *Why the hell are you going to the island?!* But the only person who would ask me anything in that tone is myself. *Besides, why should it be odd? It's an island. People go visit islands, to spend the day, to picnic on the beach. It's almost summer.* Even if Robin Island was small and had a population of barely 450 inhabitants, it was proud of having avoided mass tourism, unlike the neighboring islands of Nantucket or Martha's Vineyard.

I had taken Olivia with me because I thought that going with my daughter would make it easier not to arouse suspicion. And she was elated, obviously.

"Look, Mommy, a boat!"

"Yes, it's a sailboat."

"Look, another boat!"

"It's a barge."

"And another boat like ours!"

"Yes, a ferry going in the opposite direction."

Look, a bird. A seagull. A fish. I don't know what kind of fish. Look. Look. Look.

While I named everything Olivia pointed out, I thought about Chris's trips, the sheet of paper from the fridge that had been my road-map, with the dates of the trips he'd made so far this year. I had only traced his steps for those five months. But now it turned out he'd been going to Robin Island regularly for well over two years. I made some cal-culations. He was twenty-five when he tore his Achilles tendon. A year and a half of back and forth until he decided to give up tennis. Right when he turned twenty-seven. Then he worked two years for Williams Consulting, his father's company, which he'd been groomed for like a prince to inherit and run one day. He quit because it gave him claustro-phobia that turned into asthma attacks, which he had never had before or after. He hated having to follow his father's orders. *I listened to him for all these years without complaining or questioning anything. A father is a father, but it's my turn to be one now*, he told me. I don't know how he did it, but he worked it out so well that his father felt neither hurt nor rejection, and he passed the hot potato, the burden of succession, along to his sister, Tricia, who had just finished her degree. Chris was very good at avoiding conflict and confrontation, and even so, he man-aged to get his way. Then he started WTT, Williams Tennis Tech. By that time, he was thirty. It wasn't till a few years later that the business started to take off and he began to travel. When he was thirty-two. For three years, he'd been traveling regularly, at least twice a month. How was it possible I hadn't noticed anything? Never in my life had I focused on Chris's weaknesses or defects. He had them, of course, but I didn't waste time or energy on them; I just concentrated on his achievements and virtues. Had that been my big mistake?

"Welcome to Robin Island. Established in 1652. Population: 455" read a plaque at the ferry terminal. There was a bronze map with the island in relief situated it in the center of the triangle formed by Nan-tucket, Martha's Vineyard and Hyannis. Beside the map stood an im-pressive totem pole, some fifteen feet high, made of cedar and crowned with a sculpture of a robin with outspread wings. An inscription stated that the totem was the work of the Native American Wampanoag tribe. "Robin Island. Formerly known as Opechee Island, the island of the robin. For the Wampanoag, the robin symbolized the path of the wisdom of change."

The terminal was much smaller than the one in Hyannis and had no security cameras. Far from disappointed, I felt relieved. It pleased me to see the island hadn't given in to the country's generalized paranoia. I had decided to keep a low profile and ask nothing, so no one would ask me anything. The second thing I noticed was that people took off in electric golf carts. Later I found out it was due to a municipal ordinance requiring all residents to use electric vehicles on the island. Very ecological.

"Is this Treasure Island, Mommy?"

"Yes, I think it is."

"Let's go see the pirates!"

And we did. It didn't take us long to go the six miles from one end to another in the car. We didn't get out, again because I was afraid of looking nosy and suspicious. I had to make a great effort to keep from being seduced by the beauty of the landscape. I wanted information and needed to maximize that first visit. I couldn't fall in love with the island. I had to skin it and tear out its guts.

There was a small port, Hiese Harbor, with moored leisure boats, a few fishing vessels, an ambulance motorboat. A store, Burr's Marine, that sold and rented leisure boats, golf carts and electric bicycles. A main street, Grand Avenue, which had nothing grand about it, with a café, a bank, a post office, a church and several stores.

An oyster farm: Bishop Oysters.

Houses, of all kinds and colors, and a horse ranch, which I avoided passing by so Olivia wouldn't pester me again about the damned pony.

A mill that looked straight out of a Van Gogh painting.

A lighthouse on a tiny island accessible by a narrow wooden bridge.

A lookout atop a hill, crowned with an imposing oak, from which the island could be seen in all its small, grand splendor. There, on Kissing Tree Mountain, as the marker read, I decided we should stop and enjoy the view. *How beautifully everything is laid out*, I thought.

Where are you, Chris? What corner are you hiding in?

"Why did we come here? To forget Daddy?"

"No." *Quite the contrary*, I thought. "We're never going to forget Daddy."

"Why is that tree covered in letters?" Olivia asked.

The trunk bore hundreds of initials of couples framed by hearts, sealing their love. What if Chris's initials were there along with those of another woman? I didn't dare to look because I knew any *C* I saw would pierce my heart. I wasn't ready, and even less so with Olivia as an eyewitness. Anyway, it seemed a pointless exercise that could only bring shadows. *Right, because everything else you do is super-productive and fills you with light.*

"Mama, you peed on yourself . . ."

My water had broken.

In a matter of seconds, I realized that I'd seen no hospital on the island. I started to panic. *I can't breathe; I don't know how to breathe. Why didn't I go to childbirth classes? You've already got a daughter, Alice; you've already given birth; you've had all sorts of classes. Yeah, sure, six years ago, I've forgotten all of it. How long did it take us to get here? How long does it take to give birth after the water breaks? When's the next ferry back? Have I passed my due date? I don't even know; I've lost track of time. I'm irresponsible. No, I haven't passed my due date, because my mother would have reminded me a thousand times. Do something. Come on, get in the car and drive to the port. I don't know if I can drive. It hurts, a lot. When my water broke with Olivia, it took me less than an hour to give birth. There wasn't even time for the epidural to take effect. Olivia is scared. She's about to cry.*

"I'm fine, Oli. It's Ruby; she's already on her way. Let's go to the car, babe."

I couldn't walk. A powerful contraction made me buckle, and I fell to the ground.

"Why is Ruby hurting you, Mama?" Now Olivia was crying.

Then somebody was running toward us. But he was jogging, not coming to my aid. Well, just for the first few yards, then he saw what was happening.

"Relax, I'm a doctor. Well, actually a dentist, but pulling out a baby can't be much harder than pulling out a wisdom tooth, right . . . ? Sorry, bad joke. It's no time for joking . . ."

He helped me sit up. The scent of his body soothed me.

"My name's Mark."

"Alice. That's my daughter Olivia."

"Hello, Olivia. Are you looking forward to having a little brother?"

"Sister," she corrected him. "And not yet, I still have to draw a picture to welcome her." Mark's presence had calmed her down. I mean, it had calmed me down, and Olivia had noticed.

"I'm sure you'll have time before it happens. Come on, let's go to the car."

"Are there pirates on this island?" Olivia asked Mark while he helped me stand and get into the car. I should never have given her that damned book. She made me read it to her every night.

"It depends. Do you want there to be pirates on the island?" Mark asked.

"Yessssss!"

"You're not scared of pirates?"

"No, because they're just little mice."

"Oh, yeah?! Well, I'm Long John Silver! And I'm a rat!!" he said, swooping Olivia up and depositing her in the car so we could get out of there fast. Olivia cried out from pleasure, not afraid in the least.

Before we took off, Mark made a call.

"Ben, there's a woman here about to give birth. We need to get the emergency transport ready. We're heading to the port."

On the way, Mark explained to me that there was no medical service on the island. They just had one paramedic, Ben, an older guy who gave first aid to patients—running IVs, performing CPR, stabilizing vitals, etc.—while they were transported to Cape Cod Hospital in Hyannis.

"But don't worry, it's no more than ten or fifteen minutes on the ambulance boat," Mark said when he saw my terrified face as I tried to breathe past a contraction to keep from frightening Olivia. It had only been a couple of minutes since the first one.

I couldn't even make it to the dock. When I tried to step out of the car, my strength gave out and another contraction hit me.

"I don't think I can walk."

"Do you mind if I take a look downstairs to see how far you're dilated?" Mark asked.

Just then, Ben arrived. Calling him an older guy was a euphemism, he was well past eighty, and I'd swear he had the first signs of Parkinson's.

"Everything's ready. Let's go."

"Wait. She's dilated about ten centimeters. Minimum."

Ruby seemed to be coming out with the clear purpose of breaking her sister's record.

"Ten centimeters? Let me see." Ben put on his glasses and peeked inside.

At that moment, my embarrassment was overcome by my fear and pain. Moments later, the chief of police, Margaret, joined the party, having heard the bulletin over the radio. She was a small, wiry woman of around fifty, with an unpleasant-looking face. *Don't call me Maggie, my name's Margaret*, her gaze seemed to say. After confirming the degree of dilation, she offered her verdict: "I don't think this girl's going to make it to Hyannis."

They spoke as if I couldn't hear them, as if my opinion didn't even matter. But actually, I was thankful for it, because I was in no state to make decisions.

"Let's go to my office," Mark said. "Alice, you're going to honor the island's well-known nickname: Mom's Island."

He and Ben picked me up while Margaret took care of Olivia. On the way, to show me I was in good hands, Mark told me the *Boston Globe* had written an article about Ben called "A Lifesaver on the Island," because at eighty-six he was the oldest paramedic in the United States, handling around three hundred calls per year, always with the utmost professionalism.

When we went into the dental clinic, there was a patient in the waiting room.

"Barbara, your filling's going to have to wait, but you're going to be a big help. Can you assist us in pulling a wild colt into the world?" Mark said in a rush. "She's one of the vets from the horse ranch," he explained, as though that would calm me down.

Barbara didn't hesitate a second. She jumped into her role as if she'd been there waiting for us the whole time. She smiled at me with blue cat eyes and lovely dimples. Opening the door to Mark's office, she cleared a path for us.

"All right, up into the chair," Mark said. "On the count of three."

"No, don't put her up there," Margaret cut in. "She's better on the floor, on her side, her left side, so there's no pressure on the vena cava."

They laid me on the floor, on top of various waterproof sanitary gowns. At that point Gail, the chief of the volunteer fire department, and Mayor DeRoller joined the entourage. Months later, I observed that women had the most important jobs on the island. But right then, I could only concentrate on breathing, in short, painful gasps.

"That's it, breathe. In through the nose, out through the mouth, nose, mouth. Very good," Mark encouraged me. "Resist the impulse to push. Let her come out on her own. Terrific, you're doing a great job, Alice."

Despite the scene around me, I was surprised by how easy and natural it was. Everything turned out well except for Olivia out in the waiting room, who didn't have time to finish her drawing to welcome her sister, and for Barbara, the veterinarian, who against all expectations became a little faint during the birth. I said, "What did you expect, that a colt would come out of my womb?" The moment I held Ruby in my arms, I felt an enormous peace. Nothing was important anymore. I had come to the island looking for Chris. And I had found him. Chris was inside Ruby.

After I pushed out the placenta, and with Ruby happily clinging to my breast, they put me in the ambulance boat along with Olivia to take me to Cape Cod Hospital in Hyannis. Various onlookers had come over to snoop or to show their support and solidarity, who knows? I realized that news spread fast on that island, and no one went unnoticed. That was favorable for my purposes.

From that day on, I was known as "the redhead who set foot on the island and gave birth."

AFTER THE BIRTH, I did what I had to do: be a good mother and a good daughter. I cleared out all the junk I had accumulated in my studio to make the red-marker route. I put it all in boxes, sealed with duct tape, and labeled them: "Chris's Trips." Then I crossed out *trips* and wrote *trip*, because it was always the same one. Then I crossed out *Chris's* and finally I crossed out *trip*. It was hard for me to label all that, to put a name to it. It was better that way, as a blur, a crossed-out part of my life. But Ruby's birth had restored me back to life. I had been in limbo, halfway between the living and the dead. Ruby guided me to the positive side of life. The luminous side. She slept well, ate well, and soon began smiling. It seemed like a reward for the suffering I'd gone through. Before long I went out to run every morning, putting Ruby in a light, three-wheeled stroller that Tricia had given me. I started off doing two miles until eventually I made it to six, the exact diameter of Robin Island, curiously enough. Was I unconsciously preparing myself for something? At midday, we went to Mommy and Me Yoga classes, ideal for reconnecting with your body while you enjoy your baby. And in the evenings, I did hypopressive exercises to rehabilitate my perineum and pelvic floor. I got my figure back quickly.

Once in a while, I surprised myself by thinking that at some point, I should try to rebuild my sentimental life, which invariably provoked feelings of sorrow and defeat. But the fact was, I was thirty-three years old. I still was young, and people in my family lived a long time. If disaster didn't strike again, I had almost two-thirds of my life left. It seemed only logical that there would be other men. I missed loving and being loved. I liked living as a couple, sharing. Watching TV series in bed with someone beside me, after making love, if possible. But it turned my stomach to think of anyone but Chris in those circumstances. I concluded that I had already experienced everything that I ever would as far as the love of men was concerned. And that didn't even bother me.

Strangely, when I felt the worst was when people were around. The emergency bubble I had built had alienated me from reality. At first, that had been necessary, but now I couldn't get past it. I wanted to be more connected to my friends, colleagues and family. I wanted to laugh and share moments, dinners, anecdotes. And I did, of course. Every day there was someone at the house. People came, brought something to eat; we talked about the same old stuff, that is, everything and nothing; and the day ended. Yet I was still there without being there. Normally, in such situations, night is the most fragile time. Ghosts stalk you in the darkness, in every silent corner. But it was my favorite time. To sleep, to fall asleep and disappear. This was my refuge. Sleep hadn't abandoned me. On the contrary, it had accepted its responsibility, its inherent importance in this new phase of my life. Nobody took my eight hours from me. Four and four. I woke and breastfed Ruby, she went to sleep, and I went to sleep.

But despite the appearance of normalcy, while everyone thought I was doing well and getting over everything little by little, inside I felt a void that weighed heavily on me. It didn't get better with time. It got bigger. It's not that I wasn't well; it's that I wasn't there. *Postmortem depression? Should I go to the psychologist? Take antidepressants? Don't be hard on yourself, Alice; it's normal to feel a void. The void Chris has left inside you. It's part of the process. You'll fill it in, one bit at a time. Or if not, you'll get used to the void; it will become part of you, an additional room. And it won't necessarily be something dark or bad. You can decorate it, put flowers inside. No, plants, they don't wilt.*

One day, I looked for Diego on Facebook. More to provoke myself than anything else. I did it almost apathetically, while I was breastfeeding Ruby. I wanted to lash my emotions, to stir something up inside. Diego Sánchez Sanz. I found him. That's the good part about Spanish people having two last names. It makes them easier to find. Diego used to laugh at me because I was incapable of pronouncing the Castilian Zs in his name. I hardly reacted when I saw his Facebook page, even though he was living in New York. Less than four hours away by car. It seemed like things were going well for him. His photos—public—were of an exhibit of his at an art gallery in Chelsea in Manhattan. The exhibit was entitled *The Ones Who Looked at Me*. They were hyperrealistic portraits, enormous, six by six feet. Close-ups of people who had passed through his life, all of whom were looking straight at the camera. Might I be there? I didn't deserve to be, of course. I had left him promising we'd meet again. We cried, broken-hearted, in Madrid-Barajas Airport, unable to let each other go. Once back home, I planned on applying for a scholarship to study in Spain. I was going to do what I'd always wanted: Get to know other cultures. Be an artist. We had decided to spend the summer together, crossing Europe with a rail pass until we made it to Greece. There, on an island, we would paint and love one another. But I disappeared. Chris was waiting for me at T. F. Green Airport in Warwick, with a bouquet of red and yellow roses in honor of the Spanish flag. And all of a sudden, everything I had lived through in Madrid was in the past, far away, like those dreams you experience so intensely but forget upon waking. A week later, I wrote an email to Diego telling him I'd gotten back with Chris, that we wanted to give things a second chance, and that, even though what we'd had was very special and marvelous, well . . . goodbye, Diego Sánchez Sanz.

Suddenly, I wanted to go to his successful exhibit in New York because, of course, I must have left an indelible mark on his life. He must have been traumatized, and the picture of me must have been a cry in the desert, a desperate message in a bottle, hoping to recover a love as brief as it was intense. And then I saw myself. *The Two Alices*, the picture was called. I remembered the moment vividly. We were in his miniscule attic in the La Latina neighborhood in Madrid. It was hot. We had argued and then had made love. One after the other, the sex mingled with the still latent anger. Just after we reached orgasm, almost simultaneously, he grabbed his camera. He had me sit on the bed right then, to take advantage of that moment, because according to him, there was only a brief interval when the setting sun would filter in through the window. I got mad, but I obeyed him. *How unromantic! You could have held me for a moment after coming*, I said to him.

He ignored me. He moved me until I was situated right at the dividing line between light and shadow. The sun literally split me in two. *The two Alices. The bright side and the dark side*, he said, taking his camera and focusing.

I don't have a dark side, I replied impudently—though in fact I was pleased.

We all have a dark side. And he snapped the photo. I was holding on to my right leg, hiding my nudity, my chin resting on my still-sweaty knee, with tear streaks and mascara running down my face. A single shot. He put down the camera. He stretched out in the bed, hugged me, and we had sex again.

I didn't friend him on Facebook. I didn't *like* his photos. I wrote down the gallery's phone number, then called and asked about the piece. It hadn't sold. The price: $20,500. I was envious that he'd managed to fulfill his dreams and become a successful artist. *And you, Alice? Did you even try?* Diego looked good. Even better than before. Mature, with his beard—he didn't have one before—and his first gray hairs. *Get in touch with him. Go see him in New York. A coffee. A reunion. You'll tell him your story, all of it. He'll be your confidant. You'll cry, and he'll console you. It'll be nice, that's all. Nothing has to happen. He probably has a girlfriend. Normal. Better. A walk in the park. You'll hold hands and remember old times. A kiss at sundown. Maybe a fuck. A fuck without blame, without consequences. It won't be sex; it will be tenderness. And you'll go on with your life.* Life. That's what I saw in the photo. It was full of life. I was full of life. I bought it without thinking twice, while I burped Ruby and she threw up milk on my shoulder and stained my T-shirt. I didn't even make the excuse that it could be a good investment. I didn't want Diego to track me down, but since he didn't know my married name, there was no danger. They told me they couldn't send it to me until the exhibit was over, in a month and a half. That seemed fine. The picture would never arrive at my home in Providence.

————

My slow trajectory along the highway of normalcy took an abrupt turn the day I took the girls to the cemetery, and the poison entered me again. The poison of needing/wanting to know. Maybe it wasn't poison; maybe it was a lifesaving antidote. I wanted Chris to *meet* Ruby, who had just turned one month old and for the four of us to share a moment as a family. A picnic at his grave.

"Where are we going, Mommy?" Olivia asked me once we were in the car.

"You remember when we said goodbye to Daddy?"

"That place with the swans?"

"Right. That's where we're going."

"I like the swans."

We had to stop and go back home. Olivia wanted to take one of her drawings to her father. She ran into the house. She came out a minute later with a number of pictures, because she didn't know which one she wanted to give him, and wearing her fluorescent pink jacket.

"Honey, it's hot out. You're going to roast yourself."

It didn't matter. She associated her father with cold. At home, we couldn't use the air conditioner. And she refused to enter anywhere cold, which in the middle of summer basically eliminated any restaurant that lacked outdoor seating, as well as supermarkets, stores and movie theaters. Even *Frozen* was no longer her favorite movie. She had stopped watching it, though the Christmas before, she had had it on loop and dreamed of being Princess Elsa. What would happen to her—to us— after the autumn? Would she have gotten over it by then?

True to its name, Swan Point had a lovely lake filled with ducks and swans. Chris was buried in a plot his family had purchased, beside his grandfather Richard, in the grave that would naturally have gone to his father. His tombstone wasn't the typical sort, but a rough block of marble that had been hewn by his deceased grandfather, a stonemason. He had given it to Chris with a hammer and chisel so that he could carve it through the years, sculpting his dreams, polishing his ideas, getting out his frustrations, reflecting, making decisions, quashing his fears. It was a multipurpose stone, a stone that had helped Chris forge his character. Chris was very attached to it. He kept it in his parents' garden, and when we got married and moved to our present home, it was the first thing he brought with him. He turned to it to ward off the bad and celebrate the good. His rock was his totem, his oracle, his confessional, his pet, his faithful companion. Chris was a creature of habit, and every day he was home, he passed a little time with his rock. If only it could have spoken. Something tells me that rock knew things that I didn't. Moreover, I confess that after his death, I went over it meticulously to see if I might find some clue in one of its cracks or hollows.

I laid out a blanket at the foot of the grave. Sandwiches, juice, assorted sweets and the Big Smelly Bear. Still in her down jacket, sweating like a pig, Olivia did another drawing—she decided the ones she had brought with her weren't good enough. I breastfed Ruby discreetly. The few people who walked by smiled at us, with a bit of pity and perhaps skepticism. While we were there, I thought: *If I miss him, someone else must miss him too.* Click. Poison/antidote. Rage/curiosity. Torture/diversion. Void/fullness. The vicious cycle started up again. What was Chris doing on the island? That question hogged all the headlines in my mind. I imagined that someone else, who must have had to live through all of this in silence, alone, would want to go *see him*, to cry for him, to say goodbye. Why was I taking it for granted that there was *someone else*, that the secret/mystery/lie concealed a second life, a lover, a story with another woman? Maybe one of the girls he hooked up with during our six-month parenthesis in college?

Olivia finished her drawing. Her father on the back of a swan flying among the clouds, and the three of us greeting him—or saying goodbye—from the ground. But that wasn't what I saw; it's what she told me she'd drawn. I saw a giraffe suspended in the sky with a gnome on its humped back and three angry rats with sharp teeth on the ground looking up, as if waiting for gravity to bring their prey back to the ground so they could devour it. My hope of having a child prodigy for a daughter had completely dissolved. At that point, the keys of the piano in the living room were being eaten away by the termites of indifference.

We gave the rest of the sandwiches to the swans to eat, though feeding the animals was prohibited, and left.

A few days later, taking advantage of the fact that Chris's parents had taken Olivia with them to see a couple of second cousins her age who lived in Berlin, Vermont, I went back to the spy shop, Night Eyes.

Antonio recognized me as soon as I walked in. I had Ruby in a baby carrier, with her head leaning on my breast.

"Blondie! Nice see you! Already have baby! Much congratulations! How she called?" he asked, lowering his voice and motioning for me to be quiet, because Ruby was fast asleep.

"Hi, Antonio. Her name's Ruby." Should I have told him another name? *Come on, Alice, don't be paranoid.*

"As pretty as mother."

"Thanks."

"So what do you want? More security camera footage?"

"No, now I want to buy a camera."

"Ah. Very good . . . Your turn become spy. Take action."

"Yeah, more or less . . ."

"Not your husband? I hope not typical story of husband have kid and lose interest. Look at other women. I can't believe anyone cheat on beautiful woman like you. If I was husband, I would put video cameras because I no believe you would stay with me."

At that moment, I deeply regretted driving almost two hours to buy a simple camera I could have gotten on the internet in complete privacy. But I didn't want to leave a single trace of my steps and actions. Was what I was doing wrong? Illegal, maybe, but wrong? Maybe it was wrong, too. But that wasn't what was on my mind just then. Chris hadn't left a trace (almost). And I didn't want to either. If he had been so careful to erase every possible clue, it must have been for a reason. *Yeah, Alice, to keep you from finding out.*

"Sorry, I lose myself; I doesn't need explanations. Here no explanation never," Antonio corrected himself once he saw he was losing me. "Tell me what you want, and I tell you what you need."

"A security camera. A small one."

"There are hundreds of models of cameras: India, Kerala, pinhole, button, keychain, belt, webcam, wireless, night vision, motion sensor. Where you want to put it? And what use? Photo? Video? Both. I say again: you tell me what you want, and I tell you what you need."

I felt just as overwhelmed as when I'd looked on the net.

"I don't know, small, easy to hide, to take photos of people who pass by or go to a specific place. One I can leave there and not have to change the battery. You know, long-lasting. Oh, and for outside shots."

The winner was a camouflage Bushnell Trophy Cam that Antonio told me was used for big-game hunting. He saw that I was hunting something as well. It was the size of a small radio and cost $290. Completely waterproof, made to withstand the most adverse weather conditions, with eight megapixels, a motion sensor, and a 64 GB flash memory card, it was capable of holding twenty-two thousand photos in HD. With eight AA batteries that could easily last more than a year on standby. Antonio formatted the memory card and set the camera up to take photos—it took video as well—at three-second intervals whenever it detected movement, with the date and time marked. *That way no animal with horns cheat and get away*, he said. I thought if anyone had cheated, it had been Chris, but I just smiled and paid, in cash, obviously.

In the car, I told myself: *Great, you've got your toy, now go home, think about it a little, and . . .* My internal dialogue stopped there, because I had decided to go straight to the cemetery and set it up. Every day counted. Maybe *someone else* was already there crying for him.

In front of Chris's grave was a thick perennial shrub with solid branches. A guard passed by and waved at me cordially. I waved back. When he was gone, I approached the shrub. The camera had a clip to help mount it. I placed Ruby's stroller—she was sleeping inside—in front of the tombstone to have a reference point that would help me set the frame. But I wasn't convinced. *The stroller's short, it doesn't work, an adult is much taller.* I looked around and saw a rake several graves away. I grabbed it and placed it against the stroller, taking pains not to wake Ruby. I stood beside it. *All right, more or less the same height. Would he have looked for a woman the same size as me? Why do you keep insisting it's another woman? Too obvious.* I returned to the shrub and aimed, then shook the branch to make sure the camera was secure. Perfect, it didn't come undone. I turned it on. And thus was immortalized the first of thousands of images to come.

———

I don't know exactly when I decided to move to the island. Maybe it was just after setting up the camera in the cemetery. That rush of adrenaline that surged through my entire body when I pressed the button and took the first test shot. That feeling of being awake, interested in something,

alive—really, it felt more like an antidote than a poison. Or maybe it
was a few weeks later, after going to the cemetery every day—changing
the course of my daily walk to pass by there—and clicking compulsively
through the photos on the camera without finding anything remotely
interesting, till I got frustrated and realized I couldn't wait for the person to come. I would have to go find whoever it was on the island. So
I organized in my mind, in chronological order, all the steps, little and
big, that I would take toward my new destiny.

In any case, I had made my decision, following one of Chris's golden
rules. A Zen rule that said something like that you had to treat matters
of vital importance with ease and easy matters as vitally important.

One day I searched on the internet for *Robin Island Real Estate
Agency* and the first hit that came up was McCarthy Realty.

Then, another day, I called on Miriam McCarthy, the owner of the
only agency on the island. When she saw me with Ruby in the baby
backpack, she put two and two together, and said, "You're the redhead
that set foot on the island and gave birth, right?" I nodded and she
added, "You're already famous on Robin Island. It only makes sense
you'd want to come live here." I smiled, shook her hand and told her
my name was Alice Dupont and that all I wanted for now was to take a
look around, that no matter what, even if I found something, I'd only
be renting for a year. Miriam explained to me that there were no rental
properties there, that the island was like a co-op and the neighbors had
made the unanimous decision to prohibit any kind of renting or sub-
leasing to keep tourism at bay—there was only a single six-room inn.
Despite my reticence, she insisted on showing me a few of the houses,
trying all the while to convince me that renting was throwing money
down the drain and that I should take the opportunity to buy. The area
had suffered damage when Hurricane Sandy swept through, and since
there were more homes for sale than ever now, prices had plummeted.
But the market was already heating up again.

Then, another day, I went to the courthouse and changed my name
back to Dupont, my maiden name, which made me feel absolutely
terrible, but I thought it was necessary for me to pass unnoticed on the
island. I also changed the name on my bank account.

Then, another day, I looked for a nearby school where I could register Olivia and found out there was a very good one in Nantucket, the Nantucket Lighthouse School, and that a little seaplane came every morning to pick the children up and take them there, just like a school bus.

Then, another day, I asked Olivia if she'd like to live on that pretty island we went to visit one day, and she said, "Which? The one with Kissing Tree Mountain?" And I said yes, that one. And she responded, very excitedly, "Yes, I love it there, and I didn't have the time to put my initials on the tree."

Then, another day, I told my father about my plans to move, before my mother, because I knew he would understand me and because my head was burning up and I was afraid.

Then, another day, I started to choke, as if I'd forgotten to breathe, and I wound up in the emergency room and they told me I'd had an anxiety attack and I decided the fault lay with all that madness and I let it drop and I tried to forget the whole idea.

Then, another day, I choked again, and I ended up back in the emergency room.

When it happened a third time, I didn't go to the emergency room because they had given me an anxiolytic—Xanax—for my anxiety attacks.

Then, another day, it happened again, and my father told me that most likely what provoked the anxiety attacks wasn't the idea of leaving, but the idea of staying. *Honey, you're no Captain Ahab, and you're no Moby Dick either. You're young Ishmael. It's your story. You're the one who survives,* he said, addressing a doubt I'd never examined. I cried on his shoulder and told him I loved him very much.

Then, another day, I returned to Robin Island, and Miriam, the woman from the agency, once again showed me the three houses I had liked most and that were best suited to my needs—after an obsessive examination of all the details—and I fell in love, definitively, with a Victorian-style home, two stories plus an attic, three bedrooms, two bathrooms, a garden, and a porch with views of the beach. Miriam thought it was wonderful because it was next door to her house and she loved the idea of having me for a neighbor.

Then, another day, they called me from the art gallery in Chelsea, in Manhattan, to tell me the exhibit was over and they were going to mail me Diego's picture.

Then, another day, Miriam called to tell me she'd gotten an offer on the house I'd liked so much, and I thought she was bluffing, but I took a Xanax because I was afraid of losing it.

Then, another day, I put down a deposit to buy myself a bit of time.

Then, that same night, I said to myself: *Alice, why do you want to buy more time? That's wasting time; buy the house and go; that's what you want to do. Every day counts, remember? Each day that passes makes it harder to resolve the mystery/secret/lie.*

Then, the next day, I walked into the bank to let them know I would be making a sizable withdrawal.

Then, two days later—the time the bank needed to complete my request—I bought the house on Robin Island, with a $785,000 bank check, and I didn't have an anxiety attack partly because I held on for dear life to a phrase Miriam said as she winked at me: *In a year, I can assure you it will be worth between nine hundred thousand and a million, at the least. That's a hell of an investment, neighbor.*

Then, that same day, I called the art gallery and gave them the Robin Island address—48 Shelter Road—so they could send the painting to me there. And I thought: *What a pretty name for the street where I will live my new life.*

Then, another day, I told my mother, and she almost died from disapproval, and she got very angry with me and even more with my father for encouraging me and especially because I didn't tell her earlier. *Because I'm sure you told your father before; I'm sure of it!*

Then, another day, I thought about having a going-away party, but I decided that no, I didn't want too many people to know I was going, or where.

Then, another day, I thought about dyeing my hair since a redhead always attracts more attention—and I was looking to do the opposite—but in the end, I decided not to, because I was already known on the island as "the redhead who set foot on the island and gave birth" and a change of color would have been suspicious. I did cut it, a lot, shorter than I ever had in my life, much to the displeasure—once again—of my mother.

Then, another day, I spoke with Nick Preston, the principal, and told him I was leaving my position at the Seekonk River School, and he understood I needed a change of scenery, and he got excited and then sad and told me my job was for life and I could have it back whenever I wanted, and he took leave of me with a soft kiss that grazed the corner of my lips and told me how good the new haircut looked on me.

Then, another day, my mother insisted on coming to live with us even if it was just for a few months to help me get set up, and I thanked her and told her it wasn't necessary.

Then, practically every day, I thought that I was running away, until the very morning of the move, when I decided, who knows if just from a pure instinct for survival, that no, running away was staying there, running away was doing nothing.

A YEAR, I promised my mother to placate her sorrow. *A school year, then we'll come back.*

A year, I promised myself to calm my vertigo. *What I can't find in a year, I won't ever find. But a year from Chris's death or a year from today? No, a year from Chris's death. From the time you started to investigate. Don't set yourself any more traps.*

And so, with those promises behind me and a string of doubts playing over and over in my mind, we moved to Robin Island. Olivia, Ruby, my new haircut and I. Oh, and the white piano. I forgot to return it, or didn't want to. Maybe Ruby would be the one to heed the call to virtuosity.

Now ensconced in our house at 48 Shelter Road, I still awaited two things: the picture by Diego Sánchez Sanz and the resolution of the mystery/secret/lie.

Chris's story was to continue here, and mine was to begin. Or perhaps mine would continue, and Chris's story would end. I couldn't yet tell.

———

I didn't finish *Moby-Dick,* and I didn't take the novel to the island either. It wasn't absentmindedness; I did it on purpose. I preferred to write the ending myself. And yes, the beginning as well.

"Call me Ishmael (*Alice*). Some years ago—never mind how long precisely—having little or no money (*over $700,000*) in my purse and nothing particular to interest me on shore (*besides my daughters*) I thought I would sail about a little and see the watery part of the world . . ."

PART TWO

TREASURE ISLAND

We'll have favorable winds, a quick passage, and not the least difficulty in finding the spot, and money to eat—to roll in—to play duck and drake with ever after.

I'll be as silent as the grave.

—Robert Louis Stevenson, *Treasure Island* (1883)

THE BEACH IS deserted. The reeds are dancing to the sound of the northwesterly wind. The sand makes little whirls on the dunes. It's cold, even though it's early September. A man is standing on the shore, hypnotized by the sea. I can't see his face. I don't need to see his face. His hair is disheveled and frizzy from the salt breeze. He's barefoot, with khaki pants rolled up a few times. The waves break with a wild beauty. The receding surf traces furrows around the soles of his feet. I come over slowly, as if I want to surprise him or am worried I'll a frighten him. I'm naked, except for a baggy turtleneck sweater that hangs almost to my knees. I think I just made love to the man, and the sweater is his. The neighing of wild horses. A seagull suspended in the air. Peace is what I feel. Love for the man. That's why I don't want to scare him away. I reach him and embrace him from behind. His shirt is unbuttoned. I wrap my arms around his waist and play with the hair on his stomach. I know he likes it. He grabs my hands. Softly. Entwines his fingers with mine. And he squeezes tighter and tighter. What seems like a gesture of love, of togetherness, becomes unsettling pain, anguish. He turns. *You're hurting me, Chris; let me go,* I think, but I don't say anything, because his face, as he looks at me, terrifies me. His face is bloody after the accident. *What are you doing here?* he shouts at me. *What are you doing HERE?!*

When I awoke, I thought at first I'd had the dream at the same time as I got the call from the woman from emergency services telling me about Chris's accident, 12:01. But no, it was 3:24 in the morning. After Chris's death, I dreaded the thought of waking up at exactly the same time as that call. I normally went to sleep earlier, but if, for whatever reason, I was still awake at that time, I paused whatever I was doing. It wasn't a tribute to Chris. It was pure superstition. Irrational fear that some other tragedy would occur. And once the clock struck 12:02 and that fateful minute was over, I would simply go back to my activity as though nothing had happened.

I felt paralyzed the first few days, defeated, penitent, surrounded by packed boxes, barely able to go outside—the atrocious fear of being *discovered* was still very present in my mind. I had only unpacked Ruby's things and a few boxes for Olivia with her toys and paintings. The rest of the boxes stayed literally right where the movers had left them.

When the doorbell rang, I was still disoriented from my nightmare. I didn't react, in part because I had never heard it before, and I thought: *There it is; they've caught me.* Only when the chiming was followed by a few friendly taps did I go over to open up. It was Miriam, the owner of the real estate agency that had sold me the house. She had a lovely basket of purple New England asters.

"I picked them myself, the island is full of them at the end of the summer."

"They're beautiful," I said, accepting the bouquet. "Thanks so much."

"This isn't a gift from me as your real estate agent. I already got the money out of you; I don't have to suck up anymore. This is a gift from me as a neighbor. I mean, really we're all neighbors here, but I count the most." She lived on the same street, a few hundred feet away. "I was going to come by earlier to give you the official welcome, but I said to myself: Miriam, let a few days go by, let the girl get settled, give her time to breathe after the move. You know how the psychologists say it's one of the most stressful things, along with a divorce, getting fired, and losing a loved one." She stopped when she realized she had slipped up. I had told her my husband had died, but a few months before it actually happened, and in a flying accident, in a prop plane, something almost impossible to track down and corroborate. There were around five air accidents a day and more than five hundred deaths a year in America. I had looked. "Oh, I'm sorry . . ."

"Don't worry," I said cheerfully, so she wouldn't feel bad. It hadn't bothered me. In fact, I was happy to see her, with her wavy blond hair, her enormous smile, and her purple asters. I knew we were going to be friends. *You have to be good friends, Alice; you need allies, information; you need to dig into everyone's life.* "You can see that as far as arranging things, really arranging them, I haven't made it too far." I realized I hadn't invited her in. "Sorry, come in if you like."

"No, that's fine, I already know the house well enough. And I'm not a typical snooping neighbor. I suppose you're planning to go to the Labor Day picnic on the beach. You know there's a picnic, right?"

"Yeah, I saw a couple of posters for it. But I don't know; I've got so much going on . . ."

"You feel awkward, right?"

No, I feel scared, terrified.

"A little, yeah."

"Like, I don't know anyone, what will they think of me, widowed mother with two kids, and all that stuff."

That they're going to catch me. That they're going to catch me.

"I'm going to be honest with you, Alice."

I can't let myself go, no matter how much I like you right off the bat.

"I just got separated."

Why did they separate? Could it have something to do with Chris?

"And I have a baby, Chloe, who's about to turn one," she added, showing me her baby monitor.

Chris has a cousin named Chloe. Or was it an aunt?

"I still haven't told anyone, but here on the island, everyone knows everything."

Everything? We'll see about that.

"And I don't want to go because I can't bear how gossipy these people are, and especially, because I don't want to talk about things that are painful for me. But if I don't go, it'll be even worse. Because I'm sure my asshole ex will already be there downing beer after beer and telling his side of the story to his friends and badmouthing me. So I've got a proposition for you: let's go together, with our daughters, that way you won't feel out of the loop or overwhelmed. We'll stay a little on the out-skirts. I'll introduce you to people, because everyone's going to be there; and I'll catch you up on who's who; and since I'll be with you, no one will ask me things I don't feel like talking about. A win-win situation for both of us. What do you think? By the way, I love your new haircut," she added, in case that would sway me.

But there was no need. She already had me hooked. My second day on the island, I was going to meet all the inhabitants, and even better, I'd hear something about their lives. Two months' work in a single day.

After she left, I made sure my phone was fully charged and opened a few boxes to look for a macramé bag I had made myself, a perfect place to put my cell phone and record conversations. I even tested it out in the house to be sure the sound made it clearly through the holes in the bag.

I felt like I was back at my first day of school. Agitated, nervous, excited, afraid. Each year as a teacher I would still smile in sympathy when I saw the frightened faces of the new students. But now I was the newcomer, the one who had to make friends, get good grades and be popular. And like a little girl, I felt small and inadequate sitting next to Miriam on our towels under a beach umbrella with my sunglasses, a Boston Red Sox cap, SPF 50 sunscreen, Olivia beside me, and Ruby in my arms. All to shield myself from everything and everyone. The slightest noise startled me. The barking dogs running in the sand, the seagulls searching for scraps of food, the waves breaking softly on the shore, the shouting children scampering and the laughing adults conversing. The Frisbees, kites and beach balls seemed like weapons. As if, instead of at a pleasant beach, as its name indicated, surrounded by people having a good time, I was at the epicenter of a dire battle, surrounded by enemies.

"The two people stationed by the barbecue are Karen and her husband, John. Karen is the owner of the only inn on the island: Karen's Petite Maison. She opened it because she felt lonely. John's an engineer with the navy and spends several months a year away from home in a submarine. Almost all of us are thankful for it, but her especially . . . and their son, Rick."

"Rick, what did I tell you?!" John yelled at his son, who was playing an improvised game of football with other boys more or less his age.

"Let him be; it's just one day," Karen rebuked her husband.

"One day is all it takes to get hurt. Stop playing those stupid games and come help us with the burgers."

Miriam explained to me that Rick was the captain of the high school's sailing team in Nantucket and that his father was determined to make him an Olympic medalist. It was his senior year, and he was hoping to receive juicy scholarship offers from top universities, but to do so, he had to have a good season, with no injuries and lots of trophies. Rick obeyed his father with his head lowered, somewhat humiliated at being treated like a child in front of his friends, who didn't try to disguise their mockery of him. It reminded me of the kind of pressure Chris's father made him suffer with tennis. I suddenly had the urge to cry.

"Sooner rather than later, Karen will invite you to dinner at the inn," Miriam went on, "to introduce you to her brother, Keith, who lives by himself in a castle, on a private island next to Martha's Vineyard. He's loaded and single; his sister doesn't get why and is always trying to remedy the situation."

A spectacularly pretty and lively girl in a loose-fitting tank top and short shorts that showed off her ass cheeks walked over to the grill to grab a couple of hot dogs.

"That's Summer Monfilletto. Just turned eighteen. She's the island's official babysitter. All the boys are wild about her. Not to mention their fathers. She was expelled from school in God knows what state in the Midwest, and her mother shipped her off to her aunt's house on the island for a while so she could get her act together and make a little money taking care of kids in the process. It looks like she'll end up staying. Rumor is, she's pregnant. We'll know soon enough."

After provoking the badly concealed stares of almost all the men she came across, Summer went over to a woman in her forties sitting in a nylon chair beneath a multicolored umbrella with a serene expression, as if she were the possessor of a secret no one else knew, which put her above everyone else, though she didn't want to boast of it.

"That's her aunt, Jennifer. She almost never goes out in public. Her husband, Stephen, has been confined to the house in a vegetative coma for the last three years. The chance he'll come out of it is basically nil, but she refuses to unplug him. She takes care of him at home, all by herself. Lots of people ask—I mean, I do too—how a woman that pretty, still relatively young—she's just forty-nine—can live in a prison like that."

I hardly followed anything Miriam was telling me. The conversations, the introductions, the greetings, real life, were all nebulous, as if I was seeing everything through a pane of glass, disconnected and lethargic. I had my cell phone with its microphone on in my bag, but I didn't think it could pick up what Miriam was saying. The test I had done at home hadn't had any background noise, whereas on the beach the wind was roaring—at least, it struck me that way. But none of my anxiety must have been obvious, because Miriam spoke without stopping, not as a boor, not trying to be the center of attention, but cordially, kindly, instructively, like an audio guide in a museum. She spoke because I'd asked her to, and she was trying to please me and make my admission into the island's society easier.

One woman must have realized that I'd been observing her for some time and looked back at me. I thought I knew her from somewhere. Far from looking bothered, she waved at me kindly from the distance. I returned the gesture, dying from embarrassment, and glanced away.

"I just waved at someone I must know, but I have no idea from where," I told Miriam under my breath.

"Which one?"

"To the left, about sixty feet away. Ten o' clock sharp," I said without looking or pointing. "Brown-haired girl, with an older guy."

Miriam looked in that direction before I could tell her not to.

"Thirtyish, very dark skin, with a long pony tail, eating a plate of pasta?"

"Yeah, I think so."

"That's Barbara." The name meant nothing to me. "And that's her father, Frank Rush, next to her. He's a veterinarian. He has a clinic and pet store on Grand Avenue. He owns the horse ranch, Horse Rush Farm, but since his wife, Rose, died a few years back, his daughter Barbara takes care of the ranch. She's a vet too; she specializes in horses."

"Oh, the girl with the horses," I said, with a certain feeling of relief. I even dared to look at her discreetly. "She was there when I gave birth; she had a dentist appointment."

A guy her age approached her. He had just been out swimming. He took his things, gave her a peck on the cheek, said goodbye to her father and rushed away.

"That's her boyfriend, Jeffrey Sorenson. He's a pilot. He has an air taxi service. He must have just gotten a call."

I looked at Olivia. Well, really I looked for her, alarmed, thinking I had lost her, as if hours had passed and not a minute since the last time I had seen her. She was twenty feet away, playing on the seashore, making sand castles with other children her age. I couldn't believe the ease with which she made friends—she had clearly inherited that natural gift for getting along with people right away from her father. She was with a dark-haired boy with green eyes.

Olivia: *What's your name?*

The boy: *Oliver.*

Olivia: *Oliver? I'm Olivia. Almost the same as yours.* It was clear she liked the coincidence as well as the boy. *Oliver, did you know my mom promised to buy me a pony so I would be happy because my father died?*

"How easy everything is when you're a kid, right?" Miriam realized I had disconnected from her monologue and was looking at Olivia.

I nodded. "You go over and say hi, you start playing, and then you're friends."

"Or boyfriend and girlfriend, you know they start earlier and earlier. That's Oliver, Mark and Julia's son. Mark you know, of course . . ."

Mark? What Mark? I thought for a few seconds, unable to recollect a single name from all the ones she'd told me in the hour and a half she'd been talking and introducing me to people. Then Miriam pointed discreetly with one finger to where he was. Mark, of course, what an idiot I am. Mark the dentist, the one who took charge of my emergency delivery, the guy who even smelled good when he sweated. He had his back turned to a woman, or maybe she had her back turned to him, and to everyone and everything else, because her gaze was focused out on the sea, completely estranged from the celebration. She didn't even make the occasional gesture of checking up on her child, an involuntary action that all parents have embedded in our autonomic nervous system, like breathing. Mark ate in silence, without gusto; she hadn't even touched her plate. The tension between them was obvious. Both sat under an umbrella in the same posture, with their backs turned, as though reflected in a mirror, two symmetrical realities, joined and separated by a single edge. They looked like they were posing for a magazine article on marital crises.

"I don't know if you know, but Mark was a big-time dentist in New York, the kind who takes care of billionaires and celebrities. But they decided to escape the rat race and came to live on the island. It was her decision, especially. Julia's a writer. Have you read *The Funeral Dress*?"

"Julia Ponsky?" I asked admiringly. Miriam nodded. "Wow . . ."

Of course I had read *The Funeral Dress*. Who hadn't? It was her first novel, and it spent weeks on the bestseller list.

"Well, for weeks she's been depressed, and she can't get out of it."

"Writer's block?"

Miriam shrugged. No one knew. *She's pretty, right, Alice? She could easily be Chris's type. Is she depressed because Chris is dead? Ask Miriam how long she's been down. Go ahead, do it. It's an innocent question. Mere curiosity, worry for one of your favorite writers. It won't seem weird or suspicious.* Yeah, it would have been easy, but I couldn't do it. I glanced mechanically at my phone, like a person looking for a new message, even though the ringtone hadn't sounded. Did it have some time limit? Of course it had a time limit. Or maybe I had forgotten to touch the button?

"You see all the alpha males gathered over there?" Miriam asked, pointing out a group of men drinking beer. I nodded. "Well, in December, when the temperature's below zero, they keep walking around in Bermuda shorts to show everyone how tough and macho they are. They just swap their sneakers for Timberlands and put on a down vest over their T-shirts. The blond one with his hat backward, the only good-looking one, is my ex, Mike."

Though there was no way they could hear us, when Miriam said the word *ex*, Mike turned and glanced at us with a slightly disdainful air. He looked like a dangerous wounded boar, I thought of saying, but decided to keep my mouth shut. I had often seen friends or acquaintances badmouth their boyfriends or husbands, but watch out if someone in the conversation agreed or added a criticism—the friend or acquaintance in question would get pissed off and immediately go on the offensive.

"He's on the rebound; his ego's bruised; he's waiting for me to fuck something up so he can take custody from me, just to get at me. Because he doesn't pay a bit of attention to the girl. He has a waste management business. But as far as I'm concerned, he's the real piece of trash."

"So, I finally get to meet the redhead who set foot on the island and gave birth . . ."

Karen had come over to us with a bottle of white wine and plastic cups. Miriam introduced us.

"Karen, this is Alice. Alice, this is Karen."

Karen, Karen . . . What did she do?

"Hi, Karen, pleasure to meet you."

We shook hands. Firmly, both of us, which I liked.

"Likewise. Welcome to Robin Island. The best-kept secret in all of Cape Cod." Karen touched Ruby's nose with her index finger. "And this little creature?"

"She's Ruby." At least I could remember my daughter's name.

"Well, we're going to toast to your arrival. A little cold wine?" Karen winked at me and showed me the bottle.

I thought how nice a glass of wine would be, but I didn't want to look like a bad mother since you're not supposed to drink while you're breastfeeding.

"None for me, thanks. I'm still nursing Ruby."

Miriam and Karen looked at each other and laughed.

"Come on now! Don't be old-fashioned! Oh, sorry, modern!" Karen said, pulling out the cork, which had been jammed halfway into the bottle. "Who runs things here, the mother or the baby? We've had enough nonsense. My mother knocked back plenty of shots of bourbon before, during and after she had me and my siblings. And look at us. Fit as fiddles."

"I'm in," Miriam said.

I didn't know what to do. *You have to be popular, Alice. You can't be the wet blanket in the group. You have to fit in.*

"Well, if it's good for the mother, it must be good for the baby too, right?" I finally conceded.

"That's what I like to hear!" Karen passed me a cup, which I held out so she could serve me. "You're going to be happy on the island. You'll see. And by the way, pardon the indiscretion, but I don't see any men around here, so you came alone with the kids, huh? Does that mean there's not a man in your life?"

"Karen, don't pry; she'll think we're just a bunch of gossips here and get the wrong impression, besides Alice is a widow." Miriam interceded ironically.

"I am sorry about your husband. I wasn't prying. Standard hospitality and courtesy. It's getting to know a new person, and . . . OK, fine, I am a gossip." She cackled. She was pretty lit. I could see her husband looking at us from a distance, smug and disapproving. "It's just that you're really pretty, Alice. You know my brother has a weakness for redheads? You need to meet him. One of these days I'll organize a dinner at the inn. You'll love it." *Ah, she's the one from the inn! The one with the rich brother.* "His name's Keith and he has an island, Napoleon Island. With a castle and a one-hundred-and-twenty-foot yacht. All for him and the woman of his dreams, whoever she may be."

Miriam and I exchanged glances.

"Whenever you want," I told her. "I'd love to meet your brother."

"Great." Karen looked at Miriam. "Hey, you can come too. From what I hear, you're back on the market. Or are you still in mourning?"

Before Miriam could answer or duck the question, a thundering sound drowned out any possible conversation. It was Barbara Rush's boyfriend Jeffrey Sorenson's seaplane, flying over the beach at low altitude, with an enormous sign hanging from its tail that read: "Amanda, will you marry me?"

There was great commotion on the beach. Catcalls. Hurrahs. Applause. Everyone turned toward the person of the hour: Young, probably just over twenty. She was soaking in the attention. I'd say she'd been in similar situations before. Local beauty queen, perhaps? Prom queen at the very least. She smiled and cried from emotion, squealing: "Oh my God! Oh my God!" as if she hadn't expected it and wasn't prepared. But obviously she'd been getting ready for that moment all her life. It was seven in the evening. The setting sun, warm and low, was the red bow that tied up that perfect moment. Then he appeared: Alex. Around the same age, mounted on the back of a majestic white draft horse. All the inhabitants of the island, who had been scattered all over different parts of the beach playing around, now gathered and, as if they'd rehearsed it, formed a passageway that led from him to her, adding to the feeling of collective catharsis.

There they all were, bunched together. All the mixed-up pieces of my treasure map. *It's not a treasure; it's a sentence. And that key you always carry around as if it is an amulet, the Master Key, isn't going to open anything good. It leads to the void, darkness, a black hole that's going to suck you in, and you'll never get back out. What are you doing here, Alice?* That wasn't my voice; it was Chris's.

The first thing I noticed was a very high-pitched whistling in both ears that pulled me backward furiously, unleashing a wave that dropped from my head to my feet.

Tachycardia. Dry mouth. I clutched Ruby so my maternal instinct would drive away my panic.

Alex leapt from the horse and knelt in front of Amanda, who kept repeating, "Oh my God!"

Where is Olivia? I don't see Olivia. I want out of here, off this island. My vision went blurry.

Alex took out a box with a ring. Amanda brought both hands to her mouth in a gesture of surprise.

I put my hand in my bag. I always kept a Xanax on me now. My hands were trembling. I couldn't find it, even though I'd put it in a special pocket—together with the Master Key—so that I would know where it was in case of emergency. But my arms ignored me. All my extremities went rigid.

"Amanda Elizabeth Younker," Alex pronounced ceremoniously, like a prince in a fairy tale. "You'll need to answer the question from the hydroplane before the gas tank runs dry."

To which she replied immediately with a shriek, "Yes, of course! Yessssss!!!"

"I'm leaving," I said to Miriam, handing over Ruby. "Sorry, my little one . . ."

I faded to white.

———

Miriam took care of the girls. I insisted I was all right, that the heat had gotten to me—even though it wasn't very hot. The emergency triumvirate—Ben the paramedic, Margaret the chief of police and Gail the chief of the volunteer fire department—wanted to take me to Cape Cod Hospital in Hyannis. But Mark, who must have intuited that my problem was more psychosomatic than anything else, interceded, as though bringing Ruby into the world gave him jurisdiction regarding decisions related to my person. In the end they took me to the police station, where they kept an emergency kit—defibrillator, Duralone, adrenaline, atropine, IV fluid, a blood pressure cuff—to make sure I was OK. I had a red rash across my chest. Once they'd discarded anaphylactic shock, Mark, who had come along with us, offered to stay with me and take me home when I stopped looking so pale. That way Ben, Margaret and Gail could go back to the picnic. They were worried about the level of alcohol consumption at the party. "There's always some joker who wants to start a brawl. It happens every year," Chief Margaret said. Mark invited me to his dental office, right out front, where we would be more comfortable.

The blood pressure cuff beeped. Mark had taken my stats again. I was lying back in the chair and still felt nauseated. It was the second time I'd been there, and neither time had to do with my teeth.

"Eighty over sixty, still really low. Is this the first time this has happened to you?"

"Hardly. I'm very prone to fainting."

"No, I mean is this the first time you've had an anxiety attack."

"No, this was just a drop in my blood pressure . . ."

"Alice, I pulled a baby out of you. You can trust me. Anyway, I've been taking Zoloft for three years; I can recognize an anxiety attack from miles away."

The rash on my chest was starting to burn, a sign that I should give in to the evidence.

"My God, how embarrassing, doing that right when he was asking her to marry him."

"Don't worry, we'll say you had an overdose of mushiness. Everyone will understand. Those kids were born with the object of becoming the happiest and most perfect couple on the island."

It caught my attention how new everything in his office was, almost as if he hadn't used his equipment yet.

"You must not have many patients here, huh?"

"No, this is a front business. I don't whiten teeth; I launder money," he joked. Then: "I go to New York once or twice a month. I have a clinic there with a partner. A week of endodontics with rich people on the Upper East Side goes a long way. Plus, it's nice to get out of here once in a while. Islands can get really claustrophobic."

Mark told me he was from Cedarburg, Wisconsin, a small, fairy-tale village close to Lake Michigan. His father was the only dentist in town. A homey, easygoing guy who caught salmon in the lake in his free time and made cheese and beer in his garage. He always wanted one of his two sons, Mark or his older brother, Paul, to take over the business and carry on the family tradition—his own father had been a dentist as well. But Mark didn't want to be a dentist; he wanted to be a doctor, the kind that saves lives, a surgeon or something like that; and he wanted to get out of the village, which he found suffocating, idyllic as it was. So he felt a great relief when it became clear that Paul had the family vocation in his blood. Years later, the night of the prom, Paul, who had already been accepted to the pre-dental program at the University of Illinois, was in a car accident with his girlfriend, Samantha, and two other couples. The driver of the limo they'd rented, who later turned out to be drunk at the time, lost control of the vehicle, ran off the road, and smashed into a tree. Three of the occupants died. Paul survived, but he was blinded in the accident and suffered grave burns on his face and parts of his body when he tried to pull Samantha from the burning vehicle, where she was trapped among the twisted metal. He fell into a severe depression after the accident.

It was terrible for Mark. He loved his brother like crazy and wanted to make him feel better. He wanted to become his eyes, so his brother could live things through him. Maybe that's why, a year later, when it was time for him to graduate, he changed his mind at the last minute and, instead of studying premed at the University of Michigan, he decided on the pre-dental program at the University of Illinois, where his brother had planned to study. There was little point in that praise-worthy gesture, because four years later, just three months before Mark graduated, his brother, who had gotten hooked on painkillers due to chronic pain from his burns and the loss of his girlfriend, killed himself with a lethal mixture of alcohol, tranquilizers, muscle relaxers and antidepressants. Their father followed him just five months later after a massive heart attack. They closed the father's business; his mother went to live with her sister in Key Biscayne, Florida; and Mark left for New York, where he hoped to resume his plan of being a surgeon, but he still had to pay back the $60,000 in student loans he'd received to pay for his education. So he started working part-time at a dentist's office while he did a master's in clinical endodontics.

"Conclusion," Mark finished his brief account. "What did I want to avoid? Being a dentist in an idyllic, suffocating village. What did I end up being? A dentist in an idyllic, suffocating village. Huge step, no doubt about it."

I smiled while I thought, *What does that remind you of, Alice?* I already felt a lot better. Finally, the shaking in my hands and the tickling feeling in my head had gone away.

Before taking me to Miriam's house in his golf cart to pick up the girls, he gave me several Valium.

"It works better than Xanax for anxiety attacks."

The whole time, I had the feeling that Mark had managed to get me alone for the sole purpose of hooking up. No, I stand corrected, of flirting, of giving off signals without committing to anything. But maybe if I hadn't been witness to that pained portrait of his marriage, if I had seen him and Julia saying sweet nothings to each other, I would have taken his flirting as a simple gesture of solidarity among residents. A good neighbor, with a certain knowledge of medicine. Period. So I decided not to overthink it, considered it a mere projection that had nothing to do with emotional or sexual desire—to which I was completely numb—but with the need for a good-looking, secure and engaging man to notice me and take care of me. It wasn't longing for Mark; it was nostalgia for Chris.

THE DOOR TO the attic was stuck. It must have gone so long without being opened that the wood had swollen from the humidity. A hard push with the shoulder. Ow. Another. And it opened. I heard something scurrying off, scratching wood as it fled. *Mice*, I thought. I wouldn't kill them. I'd patiently hunt them down and take them outside. Since my incident with the cuckoo looking at me as if it were Chris at that intersection, I had turned sensitive toward the fauna surrounding me. I didn't believe in reincarnation—at least, not before then—but I thought that Chris's spirit could inhabit any creature in the animal kingdom, so I wouldn't even kill a fly or a spider or any unpleasant pest. The only ones that didn't get a reprieve were cockroaches.

The attic was dark, with a wooden table in the center, an old chalkboard that had been poorly erased and a broken chair. Sheets were nailed to the window frames to keep out the light, which gave the attic the feel of some dreadful crime scene.

I pulled down the sheets, and light and dust filled the room. More noise from frightened feet looking for a hiding place. *Easy, little mouse, I won't hurt you. I just want to evict you, but the nice way.*

When I turned around, I screamed: rabid-looking teeth were threatening me. A raccoon was standing between me and the door, ready to defend to the death what it considered its den. *Only one of us gets out alive*, it seemed to be saying.

I had never heard Olivia scream so loudly or at such a high pitch. She had just come to see what I was doing upstairs. Her shriek caught the raccoon so much by surprise that it took off, escaping the girl, in my direction.

Its claws dug into my left forearm. *God, it's pissed*, I thought. But instead of frightening me, it made me react. I got mad. A loose chair leg. A blunt, well-aimed blow. Pow. *Chris, I hope you're not inside this raccoon.*

We had to bury the animal with all the honors. Olivia felt she was to blame for its death. When she saw it inert on the ground, the first thing she said was, *Oh, how pretty, it's so puchi puchi . . . Is it going to wake up now, Mommy?* Great, there we go, another trauma for the kid. We dug a hole in the yard; we buried it; we put a cross there with its name inscribed: *Puchi Puchi.*

––––––

The attic was going to be my center of operations, but first, I needed it completely clean. *Speaking of, what are you going to use it for, Alice? To paint. Look at the view: trees, vegetation creeping up toward the edge of the sea, land and water, green and blue, facing east to enjoy the sunrise, the clouds, the dunes, the sailboats, the birds . . . You can't take refuge in a dark basement like in Providence or say you don't have views that inspire you. No more excuses. How long has it been since you've painted, Alice? Why did you give up your dreams of being a great painter? No, I didn't give up, but my great references let what was nearby inspire them, almost without leaving home. Wyeth and Hopper would have painted marvels without moving from the basement. Right, so why haven't you tried? Why didn't you manage to make that fit in with your wonderful life? Was your life wonderful?*

I decided to take Diego Sánchez Sanz's picture up there. I was uncomfortable looking at it in the living room. Too big. In my bedroom? In the hallway? No point. I didn't like it anywhere. It was the image. Not the one portrayed there, but the one it brought back to me. The abysmal distance—at all levels—between that moment and the present.

I set to work on the attic, using bleach and ammonia to clean every corner and burn away all the thoughts that kept me from my objective.

I liked the chalkboard—it was big, majestic, intelligent, as if it had memorized and stored away all that had been written on it. That chalkboard would be my ally, helping me organize my thoughts, my discoveries. There was a little box with broken chalk in various colors. I chose white. I stood back a few feet and looked at the board. It seemed very important to me to meditate on what was going to be the first thing I wrote, as if I would be marking out a path I couldn't stray from. I thought. What did I want to find out? What was my objective? If I had to sum it up in a single phrase, what would it be?

———

WHAT WAS CHRIS DOING ON THE ISLAND?

OLIVIA LOOKED AT the seaplane as if it were the epicenter of a tornado. The children boarded, excited for their first day of school.

Oli was still leaning against the car door, with no intention of moving.

"It's like taking the bus," I told her. "But this bus goes through the water and flies."

"I don't like it. It's scary."

"But you're not scared of airplanes. We went to Alaska in a plane, and you loved seeing everything from up high."

Mark pulled up in his golf cart with Oliver. We exchanged a brief glance, and by his smile, I could see he understood the situation.

"Why don't we go back home?"

She was about to burst into tears, and I was about to throw in the towel.

"When you come back from school, I'll be here with Ruby waiting to take you home."

"I don't mean that home. I mean our real home."

That hit me right in the gut. I felt like a bad mother for dragging her there in my delirium. But she had liked the idea, I had consulted with her, and she had said, *We're going to live on Treasure Island!* But she was still young and didn't know the repercussions of such a decision. *And do you, Alice?*

Mark came over with Oliver, who looked embarrassed.

"Hi, Olivia. Did you know Oliver was scared too the first time he got in the hydroplane? Isn't that right, Ollie?"

Oliver nodded, scratching his freckly face.

"But he likes it a lot now," Mark continued. "You're the only kids in the whole country who take a plane to school. Isn't that cool?"

"No, it doesn't scare me. I already went to Alaska in an airplane, and that's far away," Olivia said, braver now that the boy was close by.

"Well, come on, Ollie," Mark encouraged his son. "Give Olivia a hand, and you can go on together."

Mark took Oliver's arm and stretched it out toward Olivia's. One, two, three, four seconds of uncertainty until the pilot started up the hydroplane's motor. From fear, Olivia took Oliver's hand. Mark pushed them softly.

"Good golly, it's Ollie and Oli. Go ahead!"

The children ran, a little embarrassed but also excited.

As we waited for the airplane to take off, I thanked him again for throwing me a line. He asked me if I was doing better; I told him yes, that for now the Valium pills were untouched. He was glad, we said goodbye, I got in my car, and as I left, I could see him in the rearview mirror following me with his eyes.

———

That same morning, I went out to run with Ruby in the sport stroller. She loved it and moved her arms as if she were asking me to go faster. I couldn't have asked for a sweeter baby, seemingly adaptable to any circumstance or life event, as if she knew she had already been through her worst trauma—losing her father before meeting him—and now everything would go fine, without any big upsets. Pure joy. I didn't feel like running; there were too many boxes to unpack at home and in my head, but it would help me to wake up, get acclimated, and take a look around to get a sense of the layout of the place without anyone stopping me or asking questions. I was surprised at the quantity of dogs there. That justified the existence of a vet on an island that didn't have a doctor. And more than the quantity of dogs, I was surprised by the dog culture, how social life revolved around dogs. In Shoreline Park, there was the Bark Park, where dogs could run, leap, splash and play while their owners talked over coffee. Did they ever talk about Chris? I was bothered by the feeling I was missing relevant information. Four months had passed since Chris's death. I had read about it and seen it happen hundreds of times on the news: in investigations, the more time that passes, the harder it is to recover clues.

———

I caught the ferry to Hyannis and went to the Animal Rescue League in Brewster. I had grown up surrounded by dogs: two German shepherds from the same litter, Jack and Jill; a beagle, Clifford; a Jack Russell, Hawkeye; and a poodle (my mother's), Cotton. But now I felt a little guilty, as if I were being unfaithful to Chris, because he was allergic to dogs. That's why we'd never had one. Bringing a dog into the house was like pushing him away a little bit.

Walking through the rooms of the shelter was a mix of being in a candy store and on death row. Terrible stories looking for a happy ending. It was very simple: the ones that didn't find a family to adopt them ended up dead. So I looked for a dog that would have the worst chances in this unnatural sorting process. I wanted to take home every dog I approached. Their pleading gazes, their crying, their need to be loved and to love broke my heart. Abandoned dogs, lost dogs that no one had claimed, dogs that had been in an accident, sick dogs. Before I got to the third cage, I had already started to cry. The employee took a quick disdainful look at me, as though thinking that for all my crying, if I didn't find a purebred I'd head straight for the pet store. But no, I was set on picking a dog as abandoned as I was.

And there it was, in a corner, its head resting on its front paws, as if it had already been through the drill many times and had lost all hope.

"What's with that one?"

"Which?"

"The black one lying down."

He looked like the dumbest or smartest dog of all. I caught him looking at me sidelong, and when we made eye contact, he looked away. Clever strategy.

"That one is five years old, over the hill."

Oh no, he isn't, I thought. *He's waiting for his opportunity to escape from here. Just like me when I decided to go live on Robin Island.*

"What breed is he?"

"Breed? Ha!" the guy said, confirming his suspicions that I was a yuppie fraud. "A mutt. Anyway, he's actually a she."

Stiff black hair with three white spots on her back and one on her face. Very thin, ribs showing, with long, drooping ears.

I opened the door to the cage. The dog didn't even move. I knelt down to her height. I had Ruby in the baby carrier.

"Excuse me, you can't open the cages," the employee warned me.

I didn't pay attention. Ruby, who was always marvelously opportune, awoke. The dog raised its head, defensive.

"Excuse me, miss."

The dog sniffed at Ruby's little nose and tickled her. She smiled and stretched out her hands, grabbing one of the dog's ears. The dog let her and licked her. Then she lay down again, as if not wanting to get too attached only to be let down again.

"I'm serious, miss, would you please . . ."

"I'll take her."

———

My plan was perfect. Olivia would come back from school, flooded with contradictory emotions. But when she got home and saw the dog, she'd be happy, she'd name it, and this would be her home, and the island would become our natural habitat. I'd felt a great weight pressing down on my chest since she had told me she wanted to leave. Well, I had wanted to leave several times myself.

That afternoon while waiting for their children, some of the parents were chatting among themselves. Others remained in their golf carts absorbed by other things, making use of those last moments before the children arrived with their homework to gobble up their parents' time.

I saw Julia and felt the impulse to go over. But there seemed to be a warning signal in her look: *Keep away*. The fact that Olivia skipped out of the hydroplane, running toward me, saying goodbye to Oliver, Ginger, Tracy, Ryan, Britney, and a few others, gave me back one of the points I had lost as a mother.

When she got to the Cherokee, Olivia walked around it in a circle, counting the wheels. One, two, three, four.

"Olivia, what are you doing?"

And then she did it in the opposite direction, counting them again. One, two, three, four. Then she got in the car.

"Yep, they're all there; we didn't lose one on the way," I said without giving it any particular importance, thinking it must be some game she'd learned in school. "How'd it go, honey?"

When I listened to her hurried, delighted tale, some of the anguish that reigned over much of my life was replaced by a milder sorrow—which I was thankful for, since it was easier to handle. I was a teacher. I should have been giving classes, making the first day of school memorable for lots of frightened children. Making memories, creating adventures. Molding character. Discovering virtues and smoothing out defects. Preparing them for life.

———

Half an hour earlier I had left the dog alone in the house, attached to a pretty leash that was now destroyed. In brief, this was the message she seemed to want to send to the world, to us: *I deceived you*, accompanied by a malevolent laugh. She had shit and pissed all over, which she hadn't done in the car or on the ferry or when we got home or after I fed her and gave her water or after a short walk up the street or after playing in the yard. She was holding it in for a higher purpose. The great final battle, annihilation and destruction. Cushions, shoes and remote controls destroyed. Unopened boxes that the dog had decided it was time to unpack and drag out their contents all over the place. The Tasmanian devil reincarnated in a midsized dog that looked at us very serenely, with floppy ears and her tail between her legs, knowing that she hadn't behaved well. And worst of all: she had the Big Smelly Bear in her jaws, one arm torn off and one eye MIA. Surprise!

"Smelly!" Olivia shouted, and leapt at the dog with the same determination and absence of fear as a mother protecting her baby from an evildoer.

———

Two hours later, Olivia was shut up in her room, still glum. I went in with Big Smelly Bear, now better, his eye and arm freshly reattached. I imitated Smelly's voice: "Hello, Olivia, look, I'm good as new. What a scare we had, right? But it wasn't the dog's fault, it was me, I started playing with her, and things got out of control."

The dog peeped timidly through the door. She seemed genuinely sorry, a little angel coming over slowly.

"Look who's coming to ask for forgiveness . . ."

"I don't want a dog. You told me you were going to buy me a pony." She hammed it up, hugging Smelly tight.

I was about to tell her I'd never promised her anything of the sort and that I hadn't inherited the promises made by her deceased father. But it didn't seem appropriate or right.

"It's not a dog. It's a pony. Look at her closely. A black-and-white pony. A precious pony. Look at her."

I got on my knees, crouching down behind the dog. I grabbed her front legs and lifted them up, as though she was rearing back and neighing.

"Giddy up, pony, giddy up!"

Under normal conditions, Olivia would have cracked up and told me: *Let me, Mommy, it's my turn now!* But this time, nothing.

"We can't have dogs, Mommy." She cut me short, and I smelled what was coming next. "Daddy gets sick from them."

I know, Oli, but Daddy's not here. That would have been the logical thing to say. But how could I say something like that to my daughter?

"She's a good girl, Oli. She's going to bring us lots of love and happiness. And I promise you she won't hurt Smelly again. She was scared because it was her first day in the house. Just like you when you went to school."

"I didn't tear up the school and eat some kid's arm."

"We're going to name her. What do you want to call our pony?"

"She's not a pony."

"What if we call her Pony, then? Do you like it?"

"No, because she's not a pony."

"OK, fine. But we have to call her something, whatever kind of animal she is. Come on, choose a name you like."

"She's not a pony."

"I know, Olivia, you've made that very clear."

"No, that's what I want her name to be."

"To be what?"

"Shesnotapony. That's her name."

It was the first sarcastic comment she made in her life.

———

To top things off, it turned out Pony had social phobia. She didn't like to be around other dogs. So our walks through Bark Park were an unmitigated disaster.

After a few days of living together, I understood she hadn't tricked me, hadn't sucked up to me, hadn't carried out some elaborate scheme to escape her mortal fate by presenting a different image from what she was, she had just become a puppy again. She had to learn everything over, good and bad. She had erased all the suffering she must have gone through in the course of her five years. A defense mechanism. Like a person who forgets a trauma to be able to go on living.

YOU REALLY WANT to solve this issue you've got on your hands? It's simple, Alice. Take a photo of Chris, one you like, more or less recent, one where he's recognizable. The one you keep in your wallet, for example. Scan it, blow it up and put underneath:

Do you know this man?
Reward for information.
Respond to Alice Dupont.
(The redhead who set foot on the island and gave birth)

Print out a hundred or two hundred copies, paste them up all over the island, and that's that. You'll see, you'll get immediate results, and you'll stop feeling paralyzed.

I am looking at the photo of Chris I always carry with me. My favorite one. Recently I have hardly looked at it because it submerged me in nostalgia and loneliness. But I needed to feel it and have it close. That photo for me was my ground, meaning, necessity. I had taken the photo of Chris during a trip we'd made to Charmingfare Farm, a petting zoo in Candia, New Hampshire. He was looking enrapturedly at Olivia, who had gone off on her own to feed a little goat. She got scared and laughed when the animal tried to bury its muzzle into the bundle of hay she held in her hand. She went over, laughter, bleating; she stepped back, shriek, bleating. And of course, once the test was over, she wanted us to take the goat home. Later she rode a pony for the first time in her life. On the animal's back, with her father holding the reins at her side and me taking photos, Olivia wouldn't stop saying: *I want a pony, I want a pony* . . . And of course, her father promised her one.

That night, in the cabins at the petting zoo with their odor of stables, I got mad at him for promising her things we weren't going to be able to give her. Then I told him there was a slight delay—a little out of nowhere. I went to a pharmacy and bought a pregnancy test as well as two scented candles. We lit them in a little makeshift love ritual, invoking Venus, the goddess of love, beauty and fertility, because we both wanted another baby. The test came out negative. We went back home, and Chris left for a week on one of his supposed business trips. Was he on the island? I'd say yes. But I couldn't trace anything concrete for that date. When he came back, we made love, I told him I still hadn't gotten my period, we had dinner, and we repeated the pregnancy test—this time without any rituals. It came out positive. *Come on, remember, Alice. Did you notice anything weird when he returned? When you fucked, was it just because it was time to do it, the kind of sex you give in to because if you don't, it will arouse too many questions, insecurities and doubts that will take up more energy than twenty minutes' physical effort (which has a bonus included)? Was it one of those fucks? Because obviously you had fucked like that, who hasn't? And the foreplay? And the cuddling after? And the happiness about the pregnancy? Was there some shadow of anxiety? Come on, Alice, waste your time looking for answers that will make the questions multiply; feed into your chaos. Why won't you just keep things perfect? Everything was perfect, and that's that. It was perfect because you made it perfect. And you could do that again. That's it. Rest. You need rest before climbing back to the top. Alice, you were a mountain climber of love. You can reach the top whenever you want. Go up, not down.*

    I returned the photo to my wallet, and instead of the wanted poster, I made this one:

Private classes at your home.

Painting and visual art.

For all ages.

Individual or group lessons.

Discover your artistic side.

Reasonable prices. First class free.

ALICE

48 Shelter Road

email: paintingwithalice@gmail.com

I didn't need it. The money, I mean. At least not for now. All I wanted was to get into their homes. Everyone's. And go through their private dirty laundry. Because the really important things happen behind closed doors. Anyway, I was up for it. The school year had started, and I had the itch. I felt a kind of inner resentment every time I dropped Olivia off at the hydroplane.

I printed a hundred copies. I went from one establishment to the next. I asked permission nicely; they always gave it. I put notices in windows or on doors, and I left some loose ones on the counters, at the same time checking out possible homes for the Master Key—that was the only tangible thing I had to hold on to—while I gathered information, useful facts about the owners, their families, their respective occupations.

Dime Bank. Conrad, the manager. Single or divorced, still to be determined. A bulldog, overweight and struggling to breathe. I opened a checking account, paid for a safe deposit box—the key didn't look anything like the Master Key—and chatted amiably with Conrad, asking if the children in the photo were his, and he said, "No, they were his nieces and nephews." I tried various ways to seduce him to find out if Chris had an account there and left asking myself what happens to the money in a checking account if you die.

Le Café. Mindy Bishop. Married to Matt Bishop, owner of Bishop Oysters. I had an espresso and bought ground coffee from Colombia.

Post office. Lina. Her husband, Martin, maintained the water tower. I rented a PO Box, and wondered whether Chris could have had one. Why would he? The Master Key didn't fit in any of those boxes either.

Grocery store. Cung and Michelle Nguyen. They have fifteen-year-old twins, Leyna and Han. I bought dark chocolate to fend off the anxiety, fruit and vegetables to compensate, and a big bowl of Ca Kho To, a Vietnamese soup of caramelized fish slow roasted in a clay pot, which Michelle had made following her grandmother's recipe.

O'Gorman Liquors. Jodie and Keevan. Children to be determined. Dog, Tootsie. I bought a bottle of Russian Valley Pinot Noir.

Burr's Marine. Sales and rentals, leisure boats, golf carts and electric bicycles. Rodney Burr. Father of Alex, Amanda's fiancé. The people from the proposal at the Labor Day picnic. I rented a golf cart and an electric bicycle, both for a year, though Rodney insisted it would work out better for me to buy it or rent to own. *A year, Alice, whatever you don't find out in a year, you'll never find out.* The Master Key didn't fit in the golf cart ignition or the electric bike.

Nursery. Lorraine and Peter Southcott. Two children, fifteen and ten. A boxer dog. I bought an African violet.

Presbyterian church. Father Henry. Widower with five children. Twenty-dollar donation.

McCarthy Realty. Miriam. Daughter, Chloe. My beloved neighbor. We chatted about her ex and what a son-of-a-bitch he was while I thought about how to get my hands on her files. I needed to find out if Chris owned any properties. Absolute priority.

Police station. Chief Margaret. She asked me how I was making out and gave me her personal cell number and said not to hesitate to call if anything came up. She liked to keep busy. In part because Robin Island had an almost nonexistent crime rate, just trifling little acts of vandalism. Miriam had stressed that to me when I was considering moving to the island with the girls. Since the ferry was the only way of getting there—and it stopped running at nine at night in the summer, at eight in the spring and fall, and at seven in winter—it was like a residential neighborhood on the peninsula, but protected by the Atlantic Ocean. Chief Margaret boasted of having the most marvelously boring job in the world. Even so, she said she never let down her guard. I left thinking it was impossible that Chris's presence on the island could have gone unnoticed.

Veterinary clinic and pet store, Family Pet Land. Frank Rush. Father of Barbara, girlfriend of Jeffrey the pilot. Owners of the horse ranch Horse Rush Farm. I bought chew toys for Pony and a guppy, which Olivia had been itching for. *Why do you want a fish at home if we're surrounded by fish?* I asked her. *You've already got a pet, Pony.* And she said: *Shesnotapony isn't my pet; she's your pet.* There was no convincing her. She called the fish Flint, in honor of Captain Flint from *Treasure Island.*

Karen's Petite Maison. Karen and John. Son, Rick. Cat, Dingleberry.

I gave her an African violet, though I'm sure she would have preferred a bottle of white wine. I noticed the office with the computer where the record of guest registrations was stored. I'd have to find out if Chris had stayed there.

Pharmacy. Gail. Certified nursing assistant and chief of the volunteer fire department, whose brother was one of the ferry captains. I bought diapers for Ruby and met the woman who was so glamorously eating a hot dog at the Labor Day picnic and whose husband was in a coma. The one with the young, gorgeous babysitter niece who was probably already pregnant. I had a brief conversation with her. She told me her name was Jennifer, and I encouraged her to sign up for the classes, but she told me that she didn't see herself painting, that she wouldn't know where to find inspiration. I quoted a phrase of Edward Hopper's: "Great art is the outward expression of an inner life in the artist." But it didn't seem to have any effect.

———

In the meantime, I started painting an enormous mural in the attic, a cave painting. Alice, the troglodyte, painting the island on a thirteen-by-ten-foot wall, with the priceless assistance of the Street View feature on Google Maps—which only covered the main roads—and my journeys across the island, cell phone in hand, taking photos left and right, with Olivia, of course, who thought the whole thing was a game. So while she painted ships, clouds, seagulls and other things on the periphery of the island, where she didn't interrupt my labor, I mapped out all the streets and the main points of interest: the lighthouse, the ferry, the Wampanoag Indian tribe's totem pole with the robin on top, the beaches, Haven Creek—a little stream that bisected the island— the mill that looked straight out of a Van Gogh painting, Kissing Tree Mountain. A giant game board, where little by little I would place the pieces/houses/people who were going to battle. Me against them all. Me going after the phantom king, Chris. And his queen?

But despite the fact that the island's dimensions were small and that by now I could close my eyes and trace out its perimeter from memory, I still found it completely unmanageable. That's why I decided the time had come to make a list of suspects. People I could center my attention on a little more than the rest. I thought that everyone I met was hiding a secret relationship with Chris. And that couldn't be. It made my head ache and sent me into a paranoid spiral that could never turn out well. I needed to pin everything down a bit. Write it on a chalkboard. Give it a place.

Suspect 1: Miriam, recently separated, fighting with her ex, with a one-year-old girl. Young, pretty, nice, with big boobs, which Chris loved. Did he have something to do with their separation? And that girl, Chloe, were her eyes honey-colored like his?

Suspect 2: Julia Ponsky. Depressed. Tyrannical relationship with her husband, Mark, who also travels regularly to New York. Could his trips to New York coincide with Chris's to the island? Was her depression due to Chris's disappearance/death?

I knew they were dicey justifications, lacking consistency, and that my reasons lacked weight. That everything was based on conjectures, not clues. And that more than suspects, they looked like rejects. That it couldn't be something so obvious, so visible at first glance. But it's also true that when I began writing my list of suspects on the chalkboard, my headache passed, and I felt a twinge of delight in my belly, which didn't strike me as appropriate at all.

GOING OUT RUNNING on the island in the mornings at the beginning of autumn was an experience as useful as it was liberating. In
the beginning I never ran the same route twice, because my course was
designed to help me get the lay of the land. Once I had a grip on it, I
developed a pattern, choosing the most attractive route, the one that
made me feel best. I always wound up in front of the lighthouse. I'd
stop there, catch my breath, drink water, make sure Ruby was all right
in her stroller, usually sleeping with her arms around Pony, and then
head back home. At first I tried to get Pony to run with me and get a
little exercise, but it was impossible. She was stubborn, and anywhere
that wasn't home or the pet store seemed hostile to her. She'd lie down
flat on the ground, and good luck getting her to move an inch.

"Are you looking for the island's emergency exit?"

Mark caught up to me from behind. His words didn't frighten me.
They were swathed in the roar of the waves and the light wind from the
southwest. I was observing the pile of eroded rocks at the base of the
lighthouse. A miniscule island. It had the shape of a skull. The waves
and the passage of time had carefully sculpted the eye sockets, nose,
jaw, cheekbones and chin. A skull from a pirate ship. Was I the only
one who saw it?

"Have you noticed the rocks on the . . ."

"They call it Monkey Lighthouse."

Wow, and I thought I was super-special, seeing something no one
else had.

Mark had gone out for a run as well. Again, I noticed the agreeable
scent of his sweat.

"What's with you, you never work?"

"Of course I do. I'm on call twenty-four hours a day. You want to
see my office?"

"I've been to your office twice."

"No, not my practice. I have a separate office as well."

———

It was literally called *The Office*. A sailboat with a vintage air, but it was also modern, of mahogany, thirty-six feet or so from stem to stern. Mark only went to his practice to see his patients; he hated to be there waiting, taking calls or doing paperwork; he found it asphyxiating. That's why his base of operations, the place he went every morning, was his boat, whether he took it out or not. It was equipped so that he could live there comfortably. More than his boat, it seemed like his home.

Once I'd climbed aboard with Ruby and Pony, Mark stowed the stroller, undid the moorings, and we left the port—using the motor, without letting out the sails. He didn't even ask me if I wanted to go. I understood that once we were in there, he was the one who called the shots.

The sea was calm, the wind warm. Occasional clouds. We stuck to Nantucket Sound. I had Ruby in my arms. Was it to defend myself against the fear that was creeping in? *Is it fear or desire, Alice?*

I decided to ask him how he'd met Julia. I couldn't help but feel uncomfortable, thinking that we were doing something inappropriate. It seemed like a logical question and discreet way of cutting off any possibility of sexual tension.

They had first met at his office in New York. Julia went there for an emergency visit because she had cracked a molar while sleeping. She had bruxism, ground her teeth when she slept, which she hadn't realized until then, but that explained her aching jaw and head when she woke up each morning. And she was going through a precarious phase in her life. Her first novel was going nowhere, which she blamed on her emotional chaos at the time. She was seeing a colleague from the Comparative Literature Department where she taught. David Drouin was much younger than her and had already published his first novel, and both these things were a source of pressure. He was the enfant terrible of the department. Undisciplined, tormented, capricious, spoiled, an alcoholic, an occasional heroin user, but tremendously talented, charismatic, fragile, a tormented soul. So he had everything he needed to become one of the great cursed writers of contemporary North American literature, because it seemed his plans included not living past thirty. Julia told all this to Mark during that first emergency visit to his office, as if she'd gone to a psychologist instead of a dentist. Mark smiled at her, and after giving her the anesthesia, which she barely noticed, he said: *Now you're going to have your mouth open at least an hour without talking. So I'm going to offer a reflection for both of us: Why are we always set on being with the wrong person?* Because Julia wasn't the only one in a toxic relationship. Since the death of his brother, Paul, Mark had had serious problems with commitment. He had a theory that what ended up killing his brother wasn't the blindness or his interrupted career or even the unbearable pain he suffered after the accident. It was losing his one great love, Samantha, the girl he'd gone out with since he was eleven. That's why Mark was so afraid of the Samanthas in life and avoided them almost consciously. Because all the love they devote to you, all the light they bring, can turn into the worst blindness, the deepest darkness from one day to the next.

He finished reconstructing her molar and helped her get her smile back, in part, and before she left, he asked her if she'd come to some conclusion after that hour of reflection. She answered: *Yes. From this day forward, you're going to be my dentist, because you didn't hurt me. I'm not used to that, not with dentists and not with life in general.* And then she added: *And you? What conclusion did you come to?*

Mark answered: *Not to hurt people, because I don't like people to hurt me.*

Julia left David Drouin that same day, started going out with Mark, got past her writer's block, decided that there was no need to subscribe to a life of torment to be creative, got pregnant, thought about aborting, decided that Mark was really good for her and that she couldn't imagine a better father for her children, finished her magnificent first novel and had Oliver. More or less in that order.

For his part, Mark started going out with Julia, got accepted to a master's program in implantology, freaked out when he found out Julia was pregnant, thought about telling her to get an abortion but didn't, hooked up with a chick from a bar and lost his erection for the first time in his life, took it as a sign, got back with Julia, asked her to forgive him for being weird the past few weeks, told the story of Samantha and his brother, Paul, told her he thought she was his Samantha and he wanted to have the kid and finished the master's in implantology. Then Oliver was born. More or less in that order.

I smiled despite my nausea. We'd been out for almost an hour, and I had started to feel queasy. I didn't say anything because I was embarrassed to admit it. I excused myself and went to the bathroom. I looked at his desk. Agendas, papers, laptop. But before I could think of doing anything, I felt a sudden jab of nausea, this time in my mind: *What are you doing here? You think this is your way of "fitting in" on the island? Going out with the husband of a famous writer. Someone probably saw you get on the boat. Now everyone on the island knows. You've got the scarlet letter tattooed on your forehead now. Are you leading him on? Giving him signs? Go back. I have to go back. Now. Immediately.* Crying. Ruby.

When I went out, Mark was cradling her in his arms—it seemed so tender to me. His back was turned. It reminded me immediately of Chris doing the same with Olivia. A sharp ache, between pain and poignancy. I was about to burst into tears. To throw myself into his arms. To jump into the sea. To vomit. To something.

"I think Ruby's hungry," Mark said.

"Yeah, it's that time."

Silence. Uncomfortable moment. I took Ruby. *Where can I breast-feed her?* Before I could think of a response, I took out my breast and started feeding her. Nothing seemed less sexy to me. That would certainly cut off any possibility of flirting.

Mark looked away calmly, without brusque movements, to make it clear that he wasn't uncomfortable, but that he wanted to give me my privacy. He turned the boat around, and we went back to the port, without talking the entire way back, each of us caught up in our own thoughts.

CONSIDERING MIRIAM SUSPECT number one was almost a way of exonerating her right off the bat. It was impossible I'd hit the nail on the head right away. I liked her; I needed her on my side on the island. That wouldn't keep me from rooting around in her life, of course. The one had nothing to do with the other. I mean, she *was* a suspect, but there wasn't some big question mark floating over her head like a helium balloon. She had something like diplomatic immunity. Besides, to get to know about her life, I wasn't going to have to make any great effort; almost right away she made me into her escape valve during her nasty separation. What began as a strategy to get information out of her ended up, little by little, becoming the closest thing to a friendship I could allow myself to have at the moment.

"Hurricane Sandy ruined a fair amount of property on the island. Mike and I saw a ready opportunity to do business here. We found interested investors, we bought a dozen places at bargain basement prices, and we set up the agency. Mike rehabbed them, and I sold them for three or four times the original price."

"So you hit it big, in other words."

"Don't doubt it for a second," she said. I laughed.

"And calling your dog Sandy . . ."

Now it was her turn to laugh.

"No, silly. Sandy showed up on the island after the hurricane. No one had seen her before. I found her frightened and starving, and I brought her here. She didn't have a chip or any kind of identification."

"And you sold all the houses you bought?" Translation: Did you sell one of the houses to Chris?

"No, no way. There's still a few left. In this particular case, time is a factor that works in your favor. Demand almost always outstrips supply. You have to know how to play your cards right. Plus, since I started the agency, I've been managing lots of properties for people who don't live on the island. Mainly land or places purchased as an investment. In general, there's not much movement, though. This is a small place."

As I listened to her in the office of McCarthy Realty, I didn't stop scribbling notes in my mind: *I have to get into their files . . . Documents, notes, purchases, sales, rentals . . . She keeps everything in two filing cabinets . . . Miriam must have known Chris . . .*

Miriam took out a little box with a diabetic kit inside.

"Do you mind if I inject my insulin now?"

"No, not at all," I answered, despite my phobia of needles. "How long have you been diabetic?"

"They originally diagnosed me with gestational diabetes; you can't imagine what a treat that was. Goodbye to anything you crave. It was awful for me because on top of the pregnancy, I was watching my marriage go to shit. But I held out like a champ for my baby's health." While she injected her stomach, I looked away. "But it turns out that after I gave birth—supposedly that's it, it only lasts the time of the pregnancy—it won't go away. And in the meantime, all this shit with Mike, and my glucose levels go through the roof, and the pills I'm taking don't work anymore, and more shit, more stress. Thirst, nausea, having to pee all day, losing weight. More shit. Hyperglycemia. Blurred vision, tingling, fatigue. To the hospital, and it's type 2 diabetes."

"To me, it sounds more like type ex diabetes," I said, and we laughed.

————

McCarthy Realty was housed in a small reddish stone building with big windows full of photos of properties for sale or rent. I had already been inside on various occasions and had glanced at the two locked filing cabinets. The back door led to an alley where Miriam always parked her car. The lock was standard, and she never used the deadbolt. I trusted I could get it open with X-ray film. That would be my first big mission.

Dark athletic wear. So they don't see me. What is your excuse? I'm out running, the girls are asleep, and this is my brief time to clear my head. A mile there and a mile back. Brief, well, not exactly brief. But you have to go running; there's no other option; that's the only way not to raise suspicions. Black tights, black shirt. Nothing that will attract attention. We're on an incognito mission. A flashlight? The one on the phone will do. Make sure it's charged. Yep, all in order. The lock picks? Got them. Girls asleep? Sound asleep. Baby monitor? Yes, with a two-mile range, best one on the market. Sounds iffy. Should have tried it first. Abort mission? No, it's getting done tonight. Chris's X-ray, the one of his head, the one that shows the injury from the accident. How macabre that you held on to it. Tonight Chris is coming with me to break into the real estate agency. So what about Pony? You can't take her; she's too unpredictable, too jumpy. But if you leave her alone at home with the girls, she'll definitely cry and wake them up, and then you're screwed. Give her a tranquilizer? No, how cruel, drugging a dog. Leave her outside? Worse, she'll start barking, wake up the whole neighborhood. What do I do with Pony? I'm taking her. You think she's going to run a mile there and a mile back? No way. Don't look at me like that, Pony. Wait, I can't leave the girls alone. How crazy. Especially Ruby. She's an extension of me. Granted, she's good and she never cries and she almost always sleeps seven hours straight after her last feeding. But maybe she sleeps that deeply because she feels me close by. Maybe if I go, she'll wake up and cry and wake up Olivia. No, if I go, I have to take her with me. Abort mission? No, the golf cart. We'll go in the golf cart. If they catch me, I'll say that it relaxes the baby, that she won't stop crying and that I've taken her out for a spin. And Olivia, are you going to leave Olivia alone? Forty minutes max. Two miles. A baby monitor. It's absolutely impossible for anything to happen. If they catch you, they'll take away custody. Oh shit, now don't say that. Are we going or not?

––––––

I, who had been so careful not to wear anything that would attract attention, ended up in a golf cart with headlights, driving around a baby and a dog. Luckily, I didn't cross paths with anyone. Beginner's luck. First I passed by the agency. When I got to the end of the street, I turned around and then went into the alley.

It was surprisingly easy to get the back door open—I had tried the same maneuver at home for hours. I slipped the X-ray between the frame and the door, then slid it downward. One, two, three times, and *clack*, the door opened.

The light from the streetlamp—the only one still lit on Grand

Avenue—filtered softly into the agency. I made a rapid attempt to locate the keys to the filing cabinets. It was likely that, with the trusting atmosphere on the island, Miriam kept them in some container along with rubber bands, pens, pencils and clips, or in one of her desk drawers, but I couldn't find them. I tried the Master Key, just because. Obviously, that didn't work either. Whatever, I was prepared. I took out my phone and opened the YouTube app, where I had a video set up and ready to play: "How to Open a Filing Cabinet without Keys." It lasted one minute and fifteen seconds. It was a preteen boy, eleven or twelve years old, with a reedy, singsongy voice, giving an in-depth explanation of all the steps that had to be followed:

"This type of filing cabinet is the easiest. So easy, even a kid could do it. Ha, ha. Here we go: take the pick, in it slides, and you'll notice there is a little play inside. Turn the pick in the direction you would to open the cabinet with a key, and when it stops, hold it and leave it in that position. Then you put in a second, thinner pick or a wire or a paperclip, and you start to move it, like you're picking your teeth with a toothpick, even though my mom says it's bad manners to do that in public. And so on until you find the exact spot, and then the lock opens. *Clack*. See? Easy as pie."

The fifth time I played the video while trying to open the lock, I started to get really irritated and to curse that little pissant nerd and his bullshit. And since service is bad on the island, the video stopped and started jerkily: "Taaaaaake the pick, in slides, you no t ha a lit play insiiiiiiide." To top it off, midnight fell and the streetlamp went out. And almost at the same time, I realized that the baby monitor's signal didn't reach this far. Something could happen to Olivia, and I wouldn't know. I mentally reprimanded myself, got up and aborted the mission. The dense hatred I felt for that eleven- or twelve-year-old kid who made it look so easy made me kick the filing cabinet. I dented it a bit; Pony barked nervously; Ruby woke up scared and started crying. I locked myself in the bathroom of the agency to calm her down, so no one would hear us. Then she stopped crying and smiled, and I left. *You aren't going to last long on this island, girl . . .*

———

The DeRollers, Gwen and Dan Sr., a pleasant African American couple, were the mayor of Robin Island and the owner of Dan's True Value Hardware Store, respectively.

"It's enough to make you mad. My wife is the one who wears the pants in the house and out. And I'm here in the meantime selling screws and live bait. On this island, the ones that really run the show are the women: my Gwen, the mayor; Margaret, the chief of police; Gail, the chief of the volunteer fire department; and Julia, the famous writer who put the island on the map. Lots of people come visit because they know she lives here. Weirdos. You see that, Alice? All women, all mothers. There's a reason they've been calling it Mom's Island since the old days. You know the story?"

"No, Dan, I don't."

"They'll tell you soon enough. Don't think you'll hear it from me, though, because every time someone does, the legend gets bigger, the curse falls harder on the men of Robin Island," he said jokingly.

Dan had a model of filing cabinet identical to the ones from Miriam's agency. She must have bought them there.

"I need a sprinkler, a hook for hanging a picture, a folding ladder, two or three steps, some pruning scissors, a regular plunger, and . . . and . . . let me think, I might be forgetting something . . . Oh, and a filing cabinet, that one right there will work."

I didn't need any of those things. I just said them as I saw them on the shelves. It was all part of my tactic to throw people off and my recently discovered paranoid streak.

"Well, I can give you everything but the filing cabinet. Miriam reserved it. Hers is messed up. It won't open." *Gulp.*

———

Three days went by until they delivered the filing cabinet that I ordered from Dan Sr., and in the meantime I had my first encounter/run-in with Julia.

"Did they take all of them?" I asked Gail when I saw that the advertisements for my painting classes had disappeared from the pharmacy.

"It was Dan DeRoller Jr.," she answered me. "He wants to be your only student in the class and says he's going to be Picasso."

Dan and Gwen's son, Dan Jr., was sixteen and had Down Syndrome. When he was born, they gave him only four days to live. His parents homeschooled him. He was my first student and had called me himself, without asking for permission. He was adorable.

"Wow, and I was getting my hopes up . . . I'll leave more, OK?"

Gail assented softly while putting several bottles of gummy vitamins on a shelf. Before I left, I went to the book section. On a rotating shelf I saw the two novels Julia had published, *The Funeral Dress* in paperback and *If You Came Back Home* in hard and softcover. I took a hardcover copy, opened it, and read her brief biography on the jacket:

In 2009, Julia Ponsky was introduced to the general public with her celebrated first novel, *The Funeral Dress*, which became an instant contemporary classic and a sales phenomenon, remaining on the *New York Times* bestseller list for several weeks. Translated into more than twenty-five languages, it was selected by the American Library Association as one of the most important books of the year, and named Book of the Year by the *New Yorker*. Hailed by *Granta* as one of the best novelists under forty, Ponsky is a frequent contributor to *Vanity Fair* and *Harper's*. After graduating from Princeton she received an MFA from Columbia, where she became a professor in the Creative Writing Department. She currently lives with her husband and son in Robin Island, Massachusetts.

If You Came Back Home is her second novel.

I looked at the author photo: pretty, beaming, confident. She had the air of a Hollywood star, the kind who wins Oscars, like Jennifer Connelly. I lowered the book, and there Julia was, standing right in front of me. A pulse of heat radiated up to my cheeks.

"Oh, um, hi . . ."

"Hello."

"I'm Alice."

"I'm Julia."

"Right . . ."

She shook my hand.

"How embarrassing," I had to confess, because it was evident that any attempt to cover up my feelings would make me look even more idiotic.

"I'd be embarrassed if you read it."

She snatched the book away from me so smoothly that it took me a moment to realize I didn't have it in my hands anymore, like a magic trick.

"I didn't want to publish it. My editors made me, because of my contract. Gail is dedicated to putting it out there. Right, Gail?"

Gail looked over the top of her glasses.

"It's the one that sells best," she said, going back to her business.

"Because I come here every week to buy them."

"I'd be delighted if you'd sign it," I said, looking at the copy she had taken from me, as if it were mine since I'd seen it first.

"If I sign it for you, we'll never become friends. Not that I want to be your friend, not yet. But maybe in the future. And you can't be friends with an admirer who collects autographs. Every time I sign a book, instead of feeling closer to the reader, it puts up a fence." And without waiting or looking for a reaction to her words, she added: "I'm a little weird; don't pay any attention."

Julia grabbed the four remaining copies of *If You Came Back Home* from the shelf.

"Put these on my tab, Gail," she said as she walked out.

Why did that woman intimidate me so much? *Well, her biography is pretty impressive. She's done important things, unlike you.*

That same night, in bed, I started reading Julia's book—I bought the e-book on Amazon. I didn't make it past page twenty-five. Not only was I tired, but the book seemed like a drag.

———

You and I are going to be best friends. Pony looked at me disconcertedly, maybe jealously, because I was talking to a rectangular metallic structure with two drawers, each with its own handle. Finally, the filing cabinet had arrived. Once it was set up in the attic, I took the picks and turned off the light to work completely in the dark. Pony whined. Weren't dogs supposed to be able to see in the dark?

In two and a half hours, I managed to get the filing cabinet open with the two picks, without looking, in even less time than the eleven- or twelve-year-old kid in the video. Suck on that. I wanted to make my own video and post it because I was actually pleased with my progress. Title: "How to Open a Filing Cabinet in the Dark without Keys, and Even Quicker Than the Repulsive Eleven- or Twelve-Year-Old Kid with the Singsong Voice."

In the effusion of the moment, I thought: *Why don't I do it now? It's midnight. It's Tuesday. There's a new moon. It's starting to get cold*—which frightened Olivia; we were in for a hell of a time. *There won't be anyone there. Indulge your impulse. You're on a roll. You're starting to get a handle on the situation. Come on, take off for the agency.* And so I did.

———

I opened the filing cabinet on the first try. The purchase and rental contracts were arranged by date. I looked through all of them back to 2012, the year when Miriam started the agency. There weren't really very many. Could that be all of them? Mine was there; it was the first, or the last, depending on how you looked at it. Yeah, that must be all of them. There wasn't so much to buy or rent on the island. Miriam had already told me that. I did an initial sweep, searching like a madwoman for the name Chris or the last name Williams. Nothing. I tried again, looking for the name of Chris's business, WTT. Still nothing. And since I knew myself, knew that later that night, already back home, or the next day, I would be absolutely certain that I had gotten nervous and overlooked some detail and wouldn't want to break into the agency again because that would be tempting fate, I decided to take photos of all the files. Of the cover of each folder and the first page of the contracts. I took them with me to the bathroom in the back part of the office. I was afraid someone outside would notice the light from the flash. *Good thinking, Alice. See, you're learning quick. You've really got a knack for this.* Even Ruby and Pony behaved impeccably, as if they'd learned from past experience.

I left the agency, and when I reached the main street and was in my golf cart again, I had to slam on the breaks not to run over Frank, the vet and owner of Family Pet Land. He was in the middle of the road, looking at me with wide-open eyes, like a frightened animal, blinded by the headlights.

"Frank, you scared me!"

"Why?" he asked, without understanding anything. Then I realized he was in his pajamas. He had been driving his electric car. It was up on the sidewalk, badly parked. The first thing I thought was that he was drunk. Then, that he was maybe a sleepwalker.

"Rose, it's time to go home."

Rose? Who is Rose?

"Frank, I'm not . . ."

"Not you, not you . . . But it is you, it's always you . . . And that's just great that you give yourself to all the little animals on the island. And that you work ungodly hours. But, honey, it's time to go home . . ."

Then I remembered Rose was his wife, the one he had lost many years ago. Frank wasn't drunk or sleepwalking. It was something much worse, something irreversible.

"Of course, Frank, let's go home," I said, playing the role of Rose.

"Come on, get in the car."

"No, honey, I'm going in the golf cart. We'll see each other at home, OK?"

He didn't answer me. I could see he was confused. Lost, looking for something, not really knowing what.

He got in his car and, with full command of his motor skills, took the road back to his house.

I wanted to follow him, to be sure he made it safely to Horse Rush Farm and to tell his daughter, Barbara, what had happened to her father so she could take charge of the matter. But I couldn't risk exposing myself. The worst thing is I hoped that Frank was experiencing an episode of senile dementia so that the next day he wouldn't make any comment to his daughter that would give me away.

To confirm that he didn't remember, I went to Family Pet Land the next day to buy food for Pony. When he saw us come in, he greeted us effusively:

"My favorite girls, Alice, Ruby and little Pony. Come here, Pony, pretty girl, take a treat from Uncle Frank . . ."

Alice? Ruby? Pony? Perfect control of the situation. Was he lying last night? Was he faking an episode of Alzheimer's? Had Frank caught me red-handed?

I left the store disconcerted and worried. Miriam saw me from the sidewalk in front of her agency and ran over to meet me. *Oh God, they've caught me. Frank told Miriam.*

"Hey, Alice," she said to me, worried. "What's going on? Have you seen yourself? We're friends, right? So why don't you tell me things? Why are you trying to hide something so obvious?"

Miriam looked at me very sternly while I held back the urge to cry, but above all, to confess.

"You look really rough," she continued. "You obviously didn't sleep a wink. And don't tell me it's Ruby's fault, because she sleeps like an angel. And, hey, if you don't want to talk about what you never talk about, I understand. I'm not going to pressure you. But at least let me pamper you a bit and take you to lunch. Because even if you don't think so, you deserve a prize for coping with everything so well."

Whereupon I started crying, though Miriam never found out the real reason.

"I WANT TO be Puchi Puchi for Halloween, Mommy," Olivia announced with conviction.

The story of Olivia and the raccoon I had killed didn't end with his burial with full honors. Two nights after the tragedy, Olivia said to me: *Mommy, when I saw Puchi Puchi, I didn't scream because I was scared, I screamed from happiness because I thought it was a present for me.* And a week after we adopted Pony: *I wanted Puchi Puchi as a pet, not Shesnotapony.* One day, when Pony had finally started to understand she needed to attend nature's call in the yard, Oli caught her peeing on Puchi Puchi's grave. She screamed at the dog hysterically and chased her with a stick as if she were profaning Oli's father's tomb. Obviously, from then on, Pony decided that the best place to take care of her needs was my bedroom, the living room, the bathroom or the kitchen, in that order of preference. How was it possible that my daughter had fallen so in love with a savage, rabid animal and had so much contempt for one desperate to smother her with protection and love?

So Olivia went trick-or-treating in a raccoon costume, an homage to Puchi Puchi, going from door to door with her little pumpkin-shaped basket. Which struck me as interesting. The door-to-door part, not the candy. Looking, trying to glimpse what they had inside the houses, even if just from the front door. A few friendly seconds to get a sense of the place. Ruby was a kangaroo, and I was dressed as the Corpse Bride. Why had that struck me as a good idea?

First house. The Wilkins. Christina and Donald. Retired.

"Hi, I'm Puchi Puchi!"

"Honey, I think you can just say trick or treat."

Another house. The DeRollers. Dan Jr. opened the door, delighted to see us, and kissed the three of us as if we were his sisters.

"Hi, I'm Puchi Puchi. Trick and treat."

"*Or* treat. Trick or treat, Olivia."

Next house. The Hurlbutts. Tina and Josh. Both on their second marriage. Tina runs the daycare. Josh, no idea. Three children. Jodie (nine?), Karen (twelve?), and I don't know the boy's name (fourteen?).

Another house, another, another.

I started getting queasy. Too many people, too many untold stories, too many unknowns. I toyed with the Master Key, which I kept in my pocket with half a Xanax and half a Valium. Both wrapped in foil, easily distinguished by their shape. I didn't want to take them; I wanted it to be enough knowing they were there.

Until I moved to the island, I wasn't aware that it was hard for me to establish cordial relationships with people. I had grown up in a controlled, stable, unchanging environment, with the same friends from daycare through high school. My world was closed and recognizable. An island. And inside, it was sweet, fun, good. But when the ground fell out from under me, and I had to start from zero, I realized the effort it took for me to relate—perhaps because I wasn't looking for friendships, but for suspects. It drained me, trying to keep up the circus all day, the smile, the mask, the disguise. Something similar probably awaited me in the romantic realm, although it was too early to think of reigniting my love life. But the mere thought of going through what I had with Chris . . . again?! Our relationship had been forged over a slow flame, for over eighteen years, if we start from the time I began loving him in secret like a good teenager in heat. Go back to enjoying/getting used to/tolerating the scent, the touch, the kisses, the sex, the manias, the traumas, the defects—mine and someone else's? And sharing moments, tastes, favorite places, foods. Letting someone into our lives—mine and my daughters'? Having more children? Changing my name? It seemed totally unfeasible.

Another house. Mark and Julia. Olivia was slack-jawed when she saw Oliver dressed as a pirate of the Caribbean, looking like Johnny Depp himself. No trick, no treat, no nothing. Julia didn't come out. Mark barely looked at me. He just gave a slight, prefabbed smile when I said to him: "Today must be your favorite day of the year, millions of people acquiring new cavities."

Another house, another, another. And the inn. Karen's Petite Maison. Karen opened the door dressed as the evil queen from *Snow White* with a glass in her hand that looked like the holy grail, undoubtedly with wine inside.

"Hi, I'm Puchi Puchi, trick or treat." Weariness was starting to get the better of Olivia, which relieved me.

"What's this?! A raccoon and a kangaroo! Somebody needs to call animal control!" Obviously she was already tipsy.

And then her husband, John, appeared in his football uniform, complete with hip protectors, shoulder pads, cleats and helmet. The Virginia Cavaliers. My heart skipped a beat. John swung Olivia up in the air. "I'm going to eat this raccoon for supper!" he said while taking her inside. The same university as Chris.

"You don't eat raccoons!" Olivia giggled offscreen. No, it couldn't be. It had to be a mere coincidence. John was much older than Chris—though bald guys like him could throw you off as far as their age. But not even that thought managed to quell the burning in my head. *Smile, Alice, come back. Fake it. Disguise. Twenty seconds more and you'll be out of here.* I discreetly slipped half a Valium under my tongue so it would absorb more rapidly and outpace the torrent of blood threatening to drain out of my head.

"I know, he looks pretty silly in his football uniform. He thinks he's still twenty years old and forty pounds lighter," Karen said when she saw my frightened face.

John returned with Olivia in his arms. I looked away, having already seen what I needed to see. I just wanted to get home. I was incapable of forming normal, neighborly niceties like: *What position did you play on the team, John? What year did you graduate?* Fortunately, I was the Corpse Bride so they couldn't see my pallor under the makeup.

––––––

There were three boxes labeled *Chris's Things*. An entire life fit into just three boxes. But there weren't any clothes in them. When he died, his sports clothes—especially his sweatshirts, T-shirts and shorts—had gone into my closet, no matter how much Suz, my best friend from high school, who was always hanging around Chris before we started going out and had always been in love with him, insisted that getting rid of them was a necessary healthy step to get over the loss. *I'll take care of it, if you like*, she told me one day, very helpful. And I thought, *Right, what you want is to have his clothes for yourself.* She was one of the first people I suspected when I saw her crying so ostentatiously and fainting at the mass we held in his honor. But before she regained consciousness, I had already dismissed that possibility. Chris hated the cheerleaders at school. Never in his life had he even gone out for ice cream with one of them. *You know why I started playing tennis when I was a little weakling? Because there weren't any cheerleaders*, he said drolly.

I spent a while staring at the boxes, gathering courage. Olivia called to me from her bedroom in a troubled voice. Her stomach hurt from all that candy. She vomited in the bathroom while I held her hair. Pony did the same, almost simultaneously, all over the bedroom floor, provoking my daughter's rage, because she'd been robbed of the spotlight. When both were calm and asleep, I finally opened the boxes.

The main thing I was looking for were Chris's yearbooks from the University of Virginia. Maybe I'd find John and some note or comment of the kind friends usually write. I hoped they hadn't ended up in the trash during one of the top-to-bottom house cleanings we used to like to do, to try and live less encumbered. Operation Dead Weight we used to call it. It's not that Chris disowned his university years, but he didn't like to cling to nostalgia or look back, always straight ahead, new projects and interests.

I found two yearbooks, from his freshman and senior year. Almost immediately, I remembered the reason the others were gone. Chris had kept the first because he liked marking where events in his life started and ended. And the last, because it was when the Virginia Cavaliers tennis team won the NCAA national championship, with Chris finishing the season ranked third and reaching the finals of the US Open Junior Championships. The first and the last. The rest didn't interest him; he said there wasn't much history there. Or maybe there was too much he wanted to hide? Because our *parenthesis* was his third year.

I had never looked at the yearbooks before. I felt they were something private, reflecting adventures and stories I hadn't shared in the first person. I remember what a tough time he had his first year, so far away from me. At the end of the first semester, he even thought about applying to Brown to be closer, though the tennis team and the program were both worse. But I didn't let him. Those kinds of concessions always end up coming with a price tag. What I really wanted was for him to be in the best possible place for him and for his career.

I started flipping through his first yearbook. Straight to the sports section, to football. Nothing, John wasn't there. Not in the last year either. I went back through the yearbook from his first year. The whole thing this time, page by page. No results. And again through the last year's. When I was almost convinced that their going to the same university had been a coincidence, I found him. The first time I'd missed him, he was practically unrecognizable. He had hair—a nineties style cut—an angular face, and a moustache. He was handsome, strong and wiry. Fifth from the right, in the first row: *John Rushlow, Defensive Coordinator, alumnus and former Cavaliers teammate, 1984–1988*, it read at the bottom of the photo. He was on the team's coaching staff, pictured with the head coach, proud to come back to the team he loved.

I looked over the first yearbook for the third time, to see if I might have missed him, but there was nothing. So they hadn't been there together all four years, just part of the time, and when John was an alumnus and his only relation to the university was with the football team. What was the real probability that they'd known each other? Chris wasn't part of a frat; he hated them. He wasn't much of a partier; he was there for tennis and his future. Football season ran from fall to winter and tennis season was in the spring, so the possibility of their crossing paths was almost nil. But the more I thought about motives and the statistics in order to discard the possible link, the more I felt John fit naturally into the category of suspect and that I wasn't shoehorning him, as I had Miriam and Julia. In fact, I considered scratching them off the list and leaving just John as my number one suspect. But I didn't, because I wanted to feel I was getting ahead instead of moving backward. I felt desperate because this opened a whole range of possibilities I hadn't considered up to then.

Then I searched Google: *lactating mother wine negative effects*. There was a certain consensus that, with moderation, not exceeding eight ounces, there was no risk involved for the baby. So I had a glass and a half—I measured the amount scrupulously—from a bottle of Pinot Noir to celebrate my little find.

Before going to bed, I looked into Olivia's room to be sure she was sound asleep. Something caught my attention: she had organized all the candy by size and color, making squares (if the candy was square or rectangular) or circles (if it was round). Now I understood what she had said to me while she was throwing up: *I only ate the ones that didn't go together, Mommy, the ones that were left over.* I had originally thought she was suffering from hyperglycemic delirium, and I reprimanded her mildly for gorging herself. Her stuffed animals were also laid out on the floor from smallest to largest, against the wall, like a lineup of suspects at the police station. I changed the order of a couple of the animals and ate three pieces of candy to break the geometrical perfection.

The next day, when I found my bedroom completely trashed, my first reaction was a blend of panic and paranoia. Clothing thrown on the bed, open closets, drawers pulled out. *I'm busted. They've come to rob me. To snoop. For what? Chris's boxes. Someone knows you're on their trail. They're on the hunt for you. You need to run; you and your daughters are in danger.* Once my little melodrama was over and I'd made sure Chris's boxes were intact, I was enraged, initially attributing the disarray to Pony. But as far as I knew, the dog didn't have the ability to open drawers and dump them out. So who then?

I found Olivia in her room, painting calmly, her back turned to me. I stood in the doorway and knocked a couple of times softly to get her attention. She didn't react. Then I knew it was her.

"Olivia, what have you been doing in my bedroom?" I asked her, not letting my anger get the best of me. I only called her by her full name when I wanted to scold her. That was enough for her to know she'd done something wrong.

She didn't turn to look at me and didn't stop painting. She just said: "You change where my things are; I change where your things are,

Alice." I think it was the first time in her life she called me by my name. A clear provocation, like, *Two can play at this game.*

I was ready to punish her and make her straighten up my room when I realized her dolls were again ordered by height and her candy in almost perfect geometric shapes. But not just that. The books were also ordered perfectly by size and the drawings according to dominant color. I returned to the idea that we might have a genius in the family, to dispel my fear that she was becoming a textbook case of obsessive-compulsive disorder.

IT MIGHT SEEM that I lived for the sole purpose of trying to find out the answer to Chris's presence on Robin Island, but really the better part of my time was taken up by Ruby and Olivia. My first occupation and preoccupation was being a mother. How did I do it, then? How did I make time to do all the snooping I was doing? Sincerely, I don't know. When Olivia was born, I only had energy for her. I couldn't concentrate on anything else. The first six months, I was plunged into an overflowing current of feelings and responsibilities. I was immensely happy, but exhausted, overcome, and my hormones were through the roof. I lived with permanent jetlag, unable to even sit down to read a book or watch a movie, let alone paint. When Olivia was asleep, I slept; I unplugged. When she was awake, I was awake, with her, for her. Nothing fit into my world that wasn't breastfeeding, diapers, boogers, burps, looks, fingers, cooing, bottles, crying, smiles, rattles, first purees, vomit, kisses, lots of kisses and love.

So when Ruby was born and I decided temporarily to abandon my *mission*, it was because I thought I was going to enter a phase of life like the one I'd already lived through. Even more so, since Chris wasn't there to help me, spoil me, take care of me, and I was in the midst of mourning, emotionally numb and deeply traumatized. But against all expectations, my grief, combined with the uncertainty and anger provoked by his secret/lie/mystery, ended up fueling my determination. It was as if I had made a partition in the hard drive of my life, a parallel universe to maternity.

I was mulling over this as I sat in the waiting room of the psychologist's office. I then wondered why I had taken so long to make an appointment for Olivia. I had tried so hard to deny the evidence of her strange behavior and growing obsessions, concluding they were the logical consequence of losing her father. I wouldn't forgive myself if this was something irreversible that would mark her for life. But then a powerful opposing force convinced me that it was absurd being there and that the girl would be perfectly fine and that this was a waste of time and money. Luckily, before that notion drew me out of the waiting room, the psychologist came out to greet us. Dr. Ruth Poulton specialized in treating children and had an office in Sandwich, next to the Montessori school. I chose her after an exhaustive quest on the internet with the search terms: *Best child psychologist in Cape Cod.*

I went in first with just Ruby, who was sleeping. The therapist wanted to speak to me before meeting Olivia. I glanced at the diplomas hanging on the wall: Middlebury College in Vermont, graduate studies at Bowdoin College in Maine, certificate in childhood development from Saint Joseph's College, also in Maine.

"Tell me in your own words, Alice, how would you describe Olivia's problem. Why did you decide to bring her here?"

"When her father died, she seemed like she was OK. Really sad, of course, but more or less able to handle the situation. The summer passed calmly. She had fun, played, ate and slept well except for occasional nightmares. The only thing was she had a slight aversion to cold. But it didn't turn into anything else, not even now, when it really is getting cold." *See? If she's fine, what are you doing here?* "But since we moved to the island, little by little, she's started acting a little obsessively, as if her routines were turning into compulsions."

"Why did you move to Robin Island?"

"I needed a change of scene. I thought it would be good for the three of us."

"I understand. Obviously it's a marvelous island. Can you tell me something about those routines/compulsions?"

"Order. Her dolls, her books, her candy, her toys are all arranged in her room by height, color, shape . . . and she's gotten into the habit of counting things out loud. The wheels of the car every time she goes out, the steps on the stairs when she goes up . . ."—*She's a kid; she's learning to add. It's normal, Alice, not a disorder. She's a genius! Ask the doctor to give her an intelligence test and that's that. You'll see how it'll turn out.*—"I tried to get her to learn the piano, I bought her one, in fact, but she's not interested in playing music because she says the songs are out of order; they skip from one key signature to another for no reason. She likes to play scales, from *do* to *te*, low to high. And you can't get her to do it any other way."

———

For the half hour Olivia was inside with Ruth Poulton, to calm my anxiety over whatever the psychologist might *find out* about her, I looked for John Rushlow on Facebook. I found him and considered friending him, but that would mean he'd have access to my posts—even though I didn't write anything. I'd been tempted to erase my old account, but that would have led to such an uproar in the family that I decided to leave it as it was—Chris's cemetery. Because there were dozens of posts that I hadn't read, let alone answered, offering condolences and good wishes after the terrible event. I always liked to leave my wall open for people to write things. Serious mistake. And even though you can adjust your Facebook profile however you like, I decided it was better to make a new one, with my maiden name, and just put up photos from the present, with my kids on the island. An island profile, far away from the rest of my existence. That way I could make contact with the other neighbors and snoop around naturally and safely. Then I thought it would make more sense—and be less suspicious—to add Karen rather than John, since I'd had more contact with her. And that was how I discovered that Karen and Mark were cousins, which surprised me because I didn't remember ever seeing them interact or mention one another.

When Olivia came out, Ruth asked me to come back in by myself. She showed me a picture my daughter had drawn with crayons. She had asked her to draw *now*, what the word meant for her just then. *What a spacy thing to ask a kid*, I thought. It seemed that Olivia had understood the concept perfectly. She, her sister and her mother were in the center of the paper, all holding hands, floating in the air; underneath, an island (a green and brown oval) surrounded by the sea, the lighthouse (a red and white stick), the mill (a brown circle with an X in the middle for the blades) and something that looked like Puchi Puchi the raccoon. There were boats—one of them a pirate ship—whales, fish and a few seagulls to round it off. And a cross in the sky nailed to a threatening dark blue, almost black cloud. Undoubtedly her father's tomb. She had painted us suspended in the air, with me holding on to—or pulling—my daughters' hands. In limbo. Yes, *now* looked a lot like now. By the way, not a trace of Pony.

Ruth didn't comment on the drawing, at least just then. She just pointed to the crayons Olivia had used.

"She didn't select the black crayon because it was more worn down than the others. She grabbed the rest and used them just enough so that each of them measured the same length and the tips were the same rounded shape. And when that was finished, she was done with her *now.*"

"Right . . ." I said, with the adhesive tape of guilt muzzling me.

"I think it's possible she has obsessive-compulsive disorder. We call it OCD."

"Is it because of her father?"

"Everything seems to suggest that."

"But it's been more than five months"—173 days, I count them—"and until recently, she hadn't started doing . . . weird stuff."

"Sometimes these things remain latent and then come to the surface. Anyway, it's important not to call them weird or bad, or punish her or make her feel uncomfortable about them. She's just trying to bring some order to her life. To the exterior at least. Because there must be a great deal of chaos inside."

I didn't say anything because my voice would have cracked and I wouldn't have been able to keep from bursting into tears. Was I the one who needed to go to a psychologist? Was I mentally ill? And worst of all: Was I passing it on to my daughter?

"Children in general mimic a great deal of what they see, what they live through. And it's clear Olivia is an intelligent girl, sensitive and empathetic. These are things that need to be followed up on, and we have to take it one step at a time, but she's probably following a model of conduct similar to someone close to her, someone who has a big influence on her life."

"I don't waste time drawing with crayons until they all have the same length," I defended myself, thinking she was alluding to me.

"I imagine not. With age, our mechanisms become more sophisticated . . ." And before I could bare my teeth, she added, very softly, "Sorry, Alice, I don't want you to feel attacked or guilty. That really isn't my intention. I'm not suggesting you have OCD either. Just as I told you it's important that Olivia not feel bad or guilty for what she's doing, neither should you. I know you have a lot to deal with right now, and I'm sure that the well-being of your daughters is your top priority. But you also need to worry about yourself. Olivia is a healthy, happy girl, and she's going to be even happier and healthier. In the past six months, she's been through the most traumatic and painful thing a person can experience: the death of her parent. Along with that, her new sister was just born. She has had to reconfigure everything about her surroundings. What she's doing is simply an attempt to control it and manage it in an appropriate way. To channel her fears. She'll be fine, you'll see. But for that to happen, you need to be fine too."

While Olivia, Ruby and I were waiting for the ferry at the Hyannis terminal, I felt a force tugging at me, something that wanted to pull me away, take me back to Providence. Forget everything for my daughters' good, and my own. It was true that Olivia wasn't going to get completely well unless I got well too. And there was no point in pretending—which I did frequently—because she could tell; she could sense it. And me? What did I need to get well? Closure. To solve Chris's mystery/secret/lie. I needed to know the truth. I didn't know if what I was doing, and what I was going to do, was the right thing or the best thing. It almost surely wasn't. But I did know it was the only thing that would help keep me afloat and capable of hope. And maybe I was deceiving myself, but that deception at least gave me the necessary positive vibrations to transmit to my daughters.

Anyway, I wanted to be completely sure, before we got on the ferry to go back home, that that's what we were doing: going back home.

"Hey, Oli, I've got a question. Now that you've been on the island for two months, do you like it?"

"Yeah, of course."

"More or less than when we came?"

"More, because I met Oliver and I like going to school in the hydroplane even though it scared me at first."

"So where do you like living better, Providence or Robin Island?"

"Can you take an island somewhere else?"

"What do you mean?"

"Like could we take the island to Providence and put it all together? So I have my friends from both places together."

"No, islands don't move. I'm afraid you have to choose."

"If we go to Providence, can we leave Shesnotapony on the island?"

"No, Oli, if we leave, Pony goes with us."

"Then Robin Island. But there are three things I'd like to change."

"OK, well, tell me what the other two are, because I already know one is Pony."

"The other two things I'd like to change are, I want Puchi Puchi to be alive and Papa too. And for them to live with us."

A pinch in my soul. My heart ran and hid.

"Yeah, me too, Oli . . ." I said as I hugged her. "And if you ever decide you want us to go back to Providence, you tell me and we'll go. Deal?"

"Deal . . ."

I kissed her on the cheek.

"Mommy, are you still sad about Daddy?"

"Yes, honey. Very much."

I could see that Olivia was trying to hold back her tears, maybe because I was too.

"You want us to cry for Daddy now?"

"Sure," I said, unable to hold back any longer.

So we cried together, and then, yes, we went back home.

WHILE I TRIED to mentally sort out what I'd found out about John Rushlow and decide how to proceed without hurrying things, I reined in my impatience by opening a new line of investigation. Once I'd decided Chris hadn't bought a house on the island, my mind turned immediately to the possibility that he had bought or rented a boat and a space at the marina. Could the Master Key open the main cabin or some other part of a boat? I didn't have any memory of Chris knowing how to drive a boat or even having any special interest in the sea. But supposedly he hated Cape Cod, and there I was, living on an island by the Cape, because he had been sneaking around there for more than two years. So any certainties were under quarantine until further notice.

Burr's Marine wasn't as easy to get into as Miriam's real estate agency. It was a modern building with large windows that featured brand-new leisure boats on display. The interior was protected by motion sensors and alarms. Impregnable, in other words. Anyway, even if Chris had bought a boat, he may not have bought it there. He could have bought it at another dealership or secondhand from a private individual. What was clear was that if he spent time on a boat on Robin Island, he would most likely have moored it at the port.

Pat Heise was the owner of the marina, Heise Harbor Waterway and Boatyard.

"Hello, Mr. Heise."

"Hiya, Alice. Call me Pat; don't make me feel old, please."

I told him that since I'd come to the island, I'd gotten the itch to have a little boat of my own. Something simple to take my girls out for a ride in the bay. Pat was very helpful and nice to me. In his office he had a chart with an outline of the port and all the numbered berths, each with a red, orange or green pin. I saw that red and orange were for different types of rentals, and green was for open berths. I memorized a few positions and their colors to confirm the layout in situ. There were no filing cabinets: instead, there was a locked closet that I presumed must contain the contracts, documentation, etc. And a computer, of course, which was undoubtedly protected with various passwords as well. Plus, rear access was blocked off by a number of locks and a wrought-iron bar across the door. The main door had double locks. So Chris's X-ray wasn't going to cut it.

Pat explained I'd need to take a class if I wanted to get a captain's license, but I could take it online and it was really easy. As far as the marina went, it depended on the type of boat, but from what I was telling him, he figured it would be around $1,500 a year.

"If you're just getting started, it's best for you to begin with something small, without spending too much money. You can find second-hand boats in perfect condition for a really good price. In fact, I've got several here for sale or for rent. Would you like to see them?"

"Now?"

"Yeah, now. Unless you got something to do."

"No, no, sure. Perfect."

Pat showed me several types of boats with names I didn't know: pontoons, zodiacs, semi-rigids and fiberglass. The prices ranged from $10,000 to $20,000. All of them were small, designed for fun or for taking a quick spin. Not for living in. Pat had taken my requirements too literally.

"So, Pat, these are all great, but could you also show me some bigger boats? The kind you can spend a couple of days in, where you can sleep, cook, you know, live in. Not for now, but just to get an idea."

He showed me other, more commodious ones. Among them was the one belonging to Stephen, Jennifer's husband, who was in a coma. Not because it was for sale, but just as a curiosity—for the sake of gossip. Jennifer hadn't set foot back in it, but she still paid the rent scrupulously. For Pat, that was a little macabre, not getting rid of the boat, keeping Stephen alive . . . Not to me. I would have done the same. To tell the truth, I was, in a certain way. I was keeping Chris alive as well.

"And this poor thing is homeless as well," he told me, pointing to another boat. "A Rio 800 Cabin Fish. Thirty feet. Complete bathroom, bedroom with a queen bed, external shower, a sofa that converts to a double bed, sink, stove and fridge. A really nice fishing and leisure boat."

"Why's it homeless?"

"Well, the owners disappeared. They haven't been here in almost a year."

Owners? A couple? Almost a year? How long ago did Chris die? I always kept scrupulous count of the days that had passed, but suddenly I didn't know what day it was. A hundred seventy something. *No, it hasn't been almost a year. It's been half a year, more or less. But Pat, when you say almost a year, is that really almost a year or a way of saying several months have passed?*

"I called them. Nothing. No one answers." I had Chris's voicemail on. If Pat had called, he would have left a message identifying himself and warning about the outstanding debt. But of course, Chris could have had another phone. "Now, if I'm honest with you, it's not that I'd wish anything bad on them, God forbid, but far as I'm concerned, it's for the best. If they don't appeal or pay up in eighteen months, then it's my property. And I'd give you a good price on it, of course."

He went on showing me other vessels but I no longer listened. What was the boat called? You will know it by its name. *The Call of the Wild*, like the Jack London novel, one of Chris's favorite books when he was a teenager. It's about a lazy domestic dog that lives in a mansion in California and is kidnapped and sold as a sled dog in the freezing backlands of Alaska during the Gold Rush, and it has to make use of its ancestral instincts to survive in a savage, hostile world. That seemed closer to my reality than to Chris's lie.

———

That night I went back to the port. I repeated the same MO: golf cart, Ruby, Pony, baby monitor in Olivia's bedroom, nerves, adrenaline, guilty conscience, excitement and remorse. The complete package. Limit: thirty minutes.

I left Ruby in the golf cart, sleeping in her basket. Pony moaned a little when I jumped onto the boat. I tried the Master Key in the cabin's lock. It didn't fit. I used a small, unidirectional LED flashlight to peek in one of the windows. I didn't see anything. Nothing that wasn't the boat's interior. Nothing that could identify the owners. No personal element in sight. I then looked through another window and saw a photo of a dog, an Alaskan malamute in an oval frame, with the word *Buck* written underneath, like the dog in the novel. It couldn't be Chris's; he was allergic to dogs. Unless he had lied to me about that, too, which, really, who knows? I looked closer and saw that there was dog hair on the cushions.

When I left, I felt the slight urge to celebrate my non-discovery. It comforted me to dismiss things. Far from frustrating me, it made me feel I was furtively getting closer.

———

Since Halloween, I had run into Mark a number of times. Almost always taking Olivia to school and picking her up. Julia very rarely went, and when she did, she stayed in the car. If I didn't know she was depressed, I would have thought she was an unbearable diva. But maybe she was an unbearable depressed diva? I chatted with Mark as much as a person could chat for three or four minutes, usually with some other father or mother in the middle. About whatever vegetables, fruits and fish were in season, what the children had done wrong or right, sports and the weather.

Another time, we saw each other while shopping at the Shoreline Park market, and he told me that if I ever needed more *provisions*, making clear reference to Valium, I knew who to turn to. *By appointment only*, I said, smiling.

Well, you can always come by The Office. *No advance notice required there.* Was he propositioning me? But suddenly, instead of holding my gaze for that nanosecond that would have confirmed it, he glanced over at some kabocha squash and went over to snatch them up before they were gone.

It disconcerted me, the constant push and pull. Cordial, distant. Close, cold. Now I want to; now I don't. I can, but I don't want to. I like you, so I'm pulling away. You pull your breast out to feed your baby on my boat, that means you don't like me; I don't make you uncomfortable; I don't interest you. Bye. Sometimes he made me feel special, like there was a connection; other times he was just normal, with a good neighbor's friendliness, and that's all. Not that I wanted to hook up with him—I couldn't handle the thought of it—but finding out he was Karen's cousin opened a cranny I could creep into to find out more about John and his possible connection to Chris.

———

One day we ran across each other running in the morning. We were going in opposite directions. He had his headphones on; I had on mine. We smiled and waved. I went on. Ten seconds later, I flinched when he touched my back. He had turned around and caught up with me. Without stopping, I said I couldn't hear him. I took off my headphones.

"What did you say?"

"I said I don't like your route. I know everyone has their own way and that's sacred, but the path you take is pretty lame. I had to tell you like the good neighbor I am."

"Right. Well, thanks a lot, neighbor; that's very friendly of you. Will you tell me what's wrong with my route, then?"

"Well, it doesn't pass by the prettiest place on the island."

"Oh yeah? Where's that?"

"Where you almost gave birth, where we met: Kissing Tree Mountain."

"I prefer skirting the ocean coast and looking at the sea to the interior. Anyway, how do you know my route? Have you been following me?"

"If I followed you, it would be really boring. You can't really call what you do running; it's more like someone with a walker."

"Are you trying to rile me up so I'll race you?"

"I guess so."

"Ready when you are, then."

"How about now?"

"I've already been running half an hour."

"Me, forty-five minutes."

"I've got a baby carriage and a dog."

Mark stopped me. He took Pony out of the carriage and cradled her in his arms.

"Now we're even," he said. "Up to Kissing Tree Mountain. One, two, three, go."

And he took off without waiting for a response. It took me a few seconds to react. Still, I smoked him.

Kissing Tree Mountain got its name from Nathaniel Haven, a merchant from a sugar company on the island of Barbados. In 1652, he bought the island for 1,500 pounds of sugar from Thomas Mayhew after a leptospirosis epidemic killed off the entire Wampanoag tribe, and the first thing Haven did upon reaching his new domain was climb to the top of the highest point with his seventeen-year-old fiancée, Grizzel, to scan the terrain and decide where he would build their home. After choosing a creek with potable water at the southernmost point of the island—Haven Creek, which would carry his name forever, and at the mouth of which was a beautiful Dutch-style mill—they kissed under the sumptuous oak and carved their initials there inside a heart. With time, what was no more than a little hill came to be called a mountain to give the place more significance, and all the islanders and occasional visitors would pass through there to attest to their love.

Since we moved to the island, I had been there only once, with Ruby and Olivia, who of course asked me to carve her and Oliver's initials inside a heart. *Now you and Daddy, Mommy. Come on!* I did it to keep from irritating her, with a bit of nostalgia and lots of love, as if I were carving into my own skin with that knife, because I thought that maybe Chris had been there, carving his initials with those of another woman on some corner of that tree tattooed with other people's loves.

Mark arrived with his tongue hanging out and Pony on his back, legs splayed, happy for someone to carry her and give her attention.

We stayed there silent for a moment, listening to the sea, the gulls and a red-tailed hawk that felt it was more special than the rest. It really was beautiful seen from up there; with a 360-degree panorama, you could look down on all parts of the island. *Chris, where are you? I know you're there. I know that right now I'm looking at some place you've been going to for over two years.*

Mark told me the story of Nathaniel Haven, which I didn't know, and how, after his death, his two sons, Nathaniel Jr. and Giles, each inherited half the island, divided where the family home at Haven Creek lay, and how a civil war broke out between the two of them to determine the borders of their property and assign exclusive use of the creek, instead of sharing it like the brothers they were. The struggle was resolved with the mysterious death of both brothers from a strange illness. Legend says that their mother, Grizzel, weary from the constant, violent confrontations—which their father would never have tolerated—poisoned them with *Abrus precatorius*, a plant that grew in the sand near the beach, the seeds of which contained an alkaloid called abrin. Ingesting a single seed can kill a child. And according to Grizzel, that's what they were: spoiled children. From that moment on, it was the three women—the mother and the two widowed wives—who raised their families, creating a true sense of community and making the island into a prosperous, neighborly and peaceful community. Since then, Robin Island was known popularly as Mom's Island in honor of Mama Grizzel, who, by the way, was a redhead like myself. That was the explanation Dan Sr. had refused to give me. But for me, at that moment, it was Dad's Island. Chris's Island. And little else.

We were sweating. The northwest wind was kicking up, and it was getting cold. We turned, went down the mountain and ran separately, both to our own homes. Only right before our paths forked off did he say, at full stride, "I'm still waiting for you to come visit me at *The Office*." He went on running without waiting for a response.

———

That same afternoon, when I went to the hydroplane to pick up Olivia, I found him talking to Lorraine, the owner of the nursery, about her Baby Blue geraniums. Whether she had noticed holes in the stems. Not even a furtive glance. Whether the plants were a little translucent. I came closer. Lorraine was afraid it was a damned budworm. He must have seen me by then, out of the corner of his eye. Those damn worms live inside the stalk and feed on the sap. "Hey," I called from the distance. He should come by the nursery later and she'd give him a special insecticide to take care of the pests.

He waved to me quickly. "Thanks a lot, Lorraine, we'll see if I can save my little girls."

Why am I so affected by what he says, or doesn't say? Because you're attracted to him, Alice. You don't know how much or in what sense, but the fact is, you feel bad about it, because you just lost your husband, because he's married and has a kid, because it's been a long time since you've really looked at a man except for Chris and because he came to your rescue in the middle of your crises on the island—twice, when you gave birth and when you had that anxiety attack on the beach—and we all know how things like that bring people together. It's unnerving and distressing but also stimulating. And obviously he's been sending you signals. He clearly likes you. Is he playing with you? I don't know. I don't think so. Probably he's got his own personal battle as well. Anyway, if you need an excuse to justify your attraction, just think that Mark can serve as a bridge to John. And from John to Chris.

———

"I get the feeling you need some of this."

Before going to Mark's *Office*, I passed by the nursery to buy a bottle of insecticide for the budworms affecting the geraniums. *Wow, looks like we've got an infestation*, Lorraine said. It was an excuse to go see him and make clear that yes, I was there, so close I could hear the conversation, and knew that he decided to ignore me, but as he could see, I didn't hold it against him.

Mark looked at the bottle. He seemed confused by everything: my sudden visit and my knowledge of his drama with the geraniums.

"Thanks," was all he managed to say.

"Why are you nice to me sometimes and then you suddenly stop?"

I was so tired of my internal debate that it came out soft and affectionate. Easy.

"I think to answer that question I need to open a bottle of wine."

"Just open it?"

"Well, open it and drink a glass."

I smiled. I was also in the mood for my daily eight-ounce dose.

Between the first and the second glass of wine, I asked Mark if he was close to his cousin Karen.

"Julia can't stand Karen. And Karen can't stand Julia. Which came first, the chicken or the egg? Who knows."

"I've never seen you with John either."

"When you get to know him a little better, you'll see why."

"Don't scare me, I'm going to have dinner with Karen at the inn next week."

Since we had moved to the island, I had invented all sorts of friendly excuses to put off her invitation, but after finding out about a possible link between Chris and John, I decided to accept. It was the perfect occasion to carry out a plan I'd been mulling over in my mind for some time.

Between the second and third glass of wine, Mark finally spoke to me for the first time about Julia and her depression. Everything came out after a single question, which up to then, for the sake of discretion, I hadn't dared to ask: *What's with Julia?* A question that Mark latched onto. It was obvious he needed to cut loose.

"Sometimes I think she's depressed because I let her be. I've taken over her role in the family. I handle everything, so she can wallow in her misery without there being any consequences. And maybe there aren't any, at least with Oliver, because with him she's really caring, of course, and more or less normal. But . . ." He paused. "You know? I think it's a lie. I don't think she's depressed or in a creative crisis. Because I know she's writing. She shuts herself up in her office for hours and hours. I hear her typing on her laptop. And believe me, it's been a long time since she's written much in the way of emails. She even broke things off with her editor and agent after the second novel. It's like she was reinventing herself, changing. That seems good to me. But I don't understand why she doesn't share it with me. Before we used to read what she had written during the day together every night in bed. She'd come in; she'd hand me the sheets of paper, usually three or four pages. I'd read them; I'd comment, give my opinion. And if I liked them, she'd be really happy, and . . . just that. And if not, then I'd have to cheer her up, and then . . . you know, *that*. Now that *that* is ancient history."

"Have you asked her to let you read what she's writing?"

"No. That's not the kind of thing you ask for. With Julia, there's a thin line between showing interest and badgering. It's very much her thing."

"But you don't want to take a look, even secretly, without her knowing?" *Don't project, Alice.*

"No. In part from respect and in part . . . I'm not interested. It doesn't make me curious . . ." He poured his third glass of wine and refilled mine, which was half-empty. "And you know the worst thing?" He drank. "I'm here blaming my wife when I'm the one who's been losing it." He drank. "Apathetic. Distant. Without wanting to . . . *you know, that.*" He drank. "Maybe I'm the one who's depressed. Maybe I infected my wife." He drank. "I listen to myself and it makes me want to bash my face in." He finished the glass. "I think I'm trying to make you feel sorry for me."

"Why?" I asked him, but I knew the response perfectly well. And he knew that I knew. We stayed there looking at each other. I felt bad. I didn't like that. "Making people feel sorry for you never works," I said to him. Though in this case it had, a little bit. And I knew that he knew.

———

Back home, I asked myself why Mark hadn't answered the question that had led to the bottle being opened. Even so, I figured it didn't matter. I hoped that when I went to the hydroplane to pick up Olivia the next afternoon, I would find him again talking to Lorraine about the bud-worm and avoid seeing in his face the reflected guilt, shame and barely masked discomfort of my own desire.

FOR A MONTH, I'd been giving the occasional painting class, generally to kids with parents who wanted to keep them busy for an hour so they could do their own thing, while still feeling like good parents for helping develop their children's artistic gifts. I thought that being inside their houses would help me unravel the mysteries they hid inside. Wherever I was, my eyes always wandered discreetly over the shelves, looking for locks where the Master Key might fit. It was something I did constantly, compulsively, involuntarily and obsessively. But soon I realized that no matter how much I cozied up to people and gained their trust, no one was going to just come out and reveal their deepest secrets. I needed to listen when no one thought they were being heard. That's how you find things out.

I decided to take the ferry to Hyannis and pay a visit to Night Eyes, the spy shop run by the loquacious Antonio from Malaga. Before the dinner at Karen's Petite Maison, I needed certain provisions. Once again the insistent theme to *The Pink Panther* greeted me at the entrance.

"Blondie! Happy see you again."

I wasn't wild about the fact that he recognized me so quickly and effusively. I would have preferred a conspiratorial wink, like, *Your secret is my secret.*

"How can I help this time?"

"I want to record conversations."

"Ours? Good idea. Nice thing to make memory for kids."

I tried to laugh at the joke, I really did, but nothing came out.

"I'm going to tell you thing, Grace. You have perfect skin. That very good. But also symptom of not laugh enough. Why be pretty if you no laugh things in life? Your husband no make you laugh, Blondie?"

"Antonio, I already told you, I'm not blond. And my husband's dead."

I wanted to hurt him, to humiliate him. That kind of rancor and rage were absolutely foreign to me. In my former life, pleasantly free of threats and tests of survival, emotions like rage and contempt had never been necessary. Now, however, I was starting to develop them. Rage had begun filtering through my nervous system and emotional makeup, gaining ground on sorrow and anguish. Not necessarily a bad thing, but it had more to do with Chris and his lie/secret/mystery than with Antonio and his little jokes.

"Grace, I already tell you me colorblind. And very sorry about husband dead . . ." Then he blurted out, as if it were a single word, "You-wanttomarrymeBlondie?"

That took me off guard, luckily, and made me laugh.

"No, seriously. I'm really sorry. Apologize for me stupid," Antonio said as he took out a small contraption that he seemed to have had hidden for me from the first day he met me, as if he knew I would come back for it. It was a black box the size of a thumbprint.

"This is what you need: miniature GSM bug." He showed me the different parts while explaining how it worked. "Put in telephone SIM card. Hide microphone where you want record conversation that make you nervous. You call phone number of SIM card from your phone or computer with program included in kit, and ready, you listen and record."

I bought four. I still didn't know if I had the bravery necessary for that kind of invasion of privacy or the consequences that would come with it if I was caught. But I wanted to be ready.

———

In the Cape Cod Mall, there are stores for the main cell phone companies: Sprint, AT&T, T-Mobile and Metro PCS. I bought a unit at each of them, with prepaid SIM cards, no contracts, and of course, I paid in cash.

And then, back to Robin Island with my stash, listening to a channel of eighties hits on the radio, eating pepperoni pizza and singing at full volume "Missing" by Everything But the Girl, while I cried, but without getting sad, during the chorus: "I miss you like deserts miss the rain . . ." Little self-indulgent moments are necessary in the heat of battle.

———

As I plugged the SIM cards into the contraptions, numbering each one and writing down the corresponding phone numbers, I thought of putting a nom de guerre on each of those little rectangular black boxes, which looked similar to matchboxes. Peons? No. Soldiers. No. Little guys? Maybe. Cockroaches? Perhaps.

Then I placed Velcro on each one so I could mount them on any surface I wanted. I'd try the first one out in my house, where the only one who could catch me was Pony. Before hiding it under the sofa, I sprayed it with a dog repellent.

The doorbell rang while I was still stretched out on the floor, my arm reaching under the sofa to which the microphone was firmly attached.

"Oli, open the door; it must be Summer!" I shouted.

Summer Monfiletto, Jennifer's niece, the one who had the eye of the entire male population on the island and part of the mainland as well. The one everyone suspected was pregnant. The pioneer bug would hear nothing but a bored teenage babysitter while I went to the dinner-trap at Karen's Petite Maison to meet Keith, her mega-rich brother, owner of his own island.

It's hard to describe what it was like dialing that first number from the computer in the attic, which connected to the microphone and activated it. A fuse to a bomb, and I didn't know when or how it was going to explode. Probably in my own face. Anyhow, it was a special moment, even exciting, putting on the headphones and listening clearly, despite the location of the mic, to the following conversation.

SUMMER: What's your dog's name?

OLIVIA: Shesnotapony.

SUMMER: Shesnotapony. What kind of name is that?

OLIVIA: The one she deserves, because she's not a pony, no matter how much my mom says she is. She's a big liar. Are you a liar, Summer?

SUMMER: Depends.

OLIVIA: On what?

SUMMER: On what you ask me.

OLIVIA: Is that a lie?

SUMMER: No.

OLIVIA: Are you sure?

SUMMER: No.

OLIVIA: Can we play like you're my pony?

SUMMER: Sure.

OLIVIA: Is that a lie?

SUMMER: A little. But it's your lie.

OLIVIA: I like my lie.

SUMMER: Then I'll be your pony.

The joy I felt at recording that conversation was small compared to the jealousy that beset me that I'd never had such a simple, deep, existentialist conversation with my daughter. Or had I? Regardless, at that moment I decided what I was going to call the bugs: snitches.

———

Though I was going to the dinner with a clear mission, or maybe for that reason, I wanted to run out from the moment I entered. In fact, that was something that happened to me a lot recently. The situation was as embarrassing and uncomfortable as it was routine and relaxed. A family dinner with a guest. We're going to make her feel cozy and at home. We're going to see if she's got the right pedigree to hit the jackpot of her dreams and celebrate becoming a widow so young.

When Karen introduced me to her brother, Keith, who was dressing a salad of tomatoes and escarole from his own garden, I thought he was like a classic Hollywood actor. Handsome, elegant, polite, sober, tall, desirable, manly, clean-shaven, his hair parted on the right, with a bit of a forelock.

"My brother had a girlfriend for fifteen years; I don't even want to say her name, the gold-digging slut," Karen blurted after introducing us. "All I'll tell you is she was redheaded. I'll leave it at that. Keith always had a weakness for redheads."

Before I could react, Karen left us alone in the kitchen to break the ice, which had the opposite effect, until Keith said to me, "Right now, you must be thinking, *My God, why did I ever come here?* But you'll see, it'll be nice, maybe even enjoyable. John and Karen love to hog the conversation. And they go over the top when they have guests like you. Just look at it like you're watching a TV series. *The John and Karen Show*. Live! I want to apologize ahead of time for anything rude my sister comes out with, because you can be sure it'll happen more than once."

"So, how are things going?" Karen came into the kitchen. "Well, is it just me or did the temperature in here go up a few degrees?"

Keith looked at me as if to say, *See? I told you.* I relaxed immediately and was able to focus on how and when I would carry out my plan.

———

As Keith had predicted, John—whom I hadn't seen since Halloween—hoarded the conversation during dinner, talking about Rick and his upcoming choice of colleges.

"Yale, Georgetown, Charleston, Boston College, Stanford, Brown, the Naval Academy, Old Dominion, Saint Mary's and Harvard. All of them have been in touch with us. The top ten at last year's National College Sailing Championships. And we can choose any one of them we want."

I could sense how the hair stood up on the back of Rick's neck and his teeth gnashed every time his father talked about his life in the plural. A toy in his father's hands. Clichéd phrases with a suffocating subliminal message:

I just want you to have the best life possible (*I'm going to relive my life through you*).

I want you to have a bright present and future (*following my orders*).

Don't make the same mistakes as your old man (*I never managed anything worthwhile in my life and that's got me frustrated*).

Sometimes I'm hard and demanding, I know, but you'll thank me for it (*You'll harangue your kid when you have one and will do the same thing to him that I'm doing to you*).

There's no limit for you. You're going to be an Olympic champ (*I envy you. You're better than me. I'm pushing you; I'm encouraging you. I love you; I hate you*).

I love you, son (*You're mine and all mine*).

———

Karen was drinking wine, a lot of it, and once in a while, she'd say, "Don't smother the poor kid, John." But with much less interest and emphasis than when she offered you more mashed potatoes with gravy to go with the venison stew, which was delicious, I must admit. I had ingested my eight ounces of wine—maybe a little more—and was happy not to have to focus on the conversation.

Keith and I exchanged occasional glances. With his comfortable silences and understanding gazes, Keith was making an excellent impression. I was curious to know why he didn't have a partner.

I don't know when John broke into our conversation to tell me it was thanks to him that Keith had gotten rich. It had to do with a patent on semiconductors. An idea that, according to John, he had given to Keith one drunken night and that Keith had expanded on and materialized and then sold, to a multinational in Silicon Valley that produced processors and microchips. Keith ended up with millions of dollars plus 10 percent of the company's stock and a position on the board—whose meetings he only had to attend twice a year—as well as an ironclad contract and who knows what else, which gave him all the free time in the world to cultivate tomatoes on his little island.

"And I didn't want anything. ANYTHING. He offered me a piece and I said no. He was the one who deserved it; ideas don't count for anything; they belong to everybody. What matters is the guys who grab hold of them and make them happen. Out there—in the war—you never know what's going to happen, and it's good to know my wife and kid have their backs covered by Keith in case anything ever happens to me."

"We should be so lucky," Karen said, already too drunk. "Just kidding, babe. I'd be the saddest widow around, promise. But anyway, with you being a materials engineer, I doubt we have to worry about that."

John didn't care for this comment either and censured her with a tense, curt silence. Keith broke it by opening another bottle of wine he had made himself, from some sauvignon blanc grapes he had imported from Chile. I used the pause to excuse myself, go to the bathroom and put my plan for planting the snitch into action.

———

I felt my heart racing as I turned the doorknob of the master bedroom. *If they catch you, say you were looking for the bathroom and you got mixed up . . . Sure, I was looking for the bathroom while digging around under the bed. No, not under the bed. We all look under the bed sometimes. What's this? A bottle of vodka . . . Leave it; get out . . . Rick's trophy case . . . Why are they here, shouldn't they be in his room? It's true, the kid pilots that boat and wins everything for his father . . . Inside a trophy? No, I need a heavy piece of furniture. Something that doesn't move and isn't going to be moved. That giant armoire with the rivets. It must weigh a ton. Get up on the chair. Wedge your hand into the hollow part up top. Gross, it's full of dust and grime. They never clean there. Perfect. That's the spot . . . Come on, run . . . I hear noises . . . No, those aren't noises; that's the idling sound your brain makes . . . Could I be schizophrenic?*

Before walking out, I managed to briefly look at a series of photos on top of the dresser, set out chronologically, in their respective frames. A baby photo of John; one of Karen; John's family; Karen's family; John in the eighties as a football player for the Virginia Cavaliers; Karen with her brother, Keith, at their parents' silver wedding anniversary; John in his naval uniform; Rick as a baby; the opening of Karen's Petite Maison; Rick's first regatta championship. *How easy it is to sum up the appearance of a life*, I thought while I went out into the hallway and to the bathroom—really this time.

I could hear John in the distance explaining to someone, probably himself, the importance of a materials engineer, that when he was stationed on the submarine *Seawolf* he was in charge of fiber optics, which might seem stupid, but in fact those were the veins of the submarine, and if there's any little problem that doesn't find an immediate solution, nothing works. NOTHING. Lot of good the Tomahawk missiles would do in that situation.

As I descended the stairs to return to the dining room, I stopped in the vestibule by the door. Would I have time for one more escapade? The door to the reception office was open. I could see a table with a desktop computer and could hear the fan of the CPU, which was on. I decided I wouldn't go in, that it was tempting fate. But then I heard Karen cut John short.

"Dear, really, we're thankful for the enormous sacrifice you make for the family, the country, really, but . . . That's not the reason we're here . . . Keith, say something to Alice, OK? Why are you so quiet, apart from the fact that John won't let anyone talk? It's because you like her, right? Whenever you liked a girl back in school, you'd fall silent. She's pretty and tactful, right? Invite her to your island and your yacht."

Given the drift of the conversation, I postponed going back to the table. I crept into the office almost without thinking. The screen was black. The conversation continued.

JOHN: Well, to me, a widow with two girls seems fishy . . .

KAREN: So? What better place to come heal your wounds?

JOHN: Sure, but . . . she's weird. I get a feeling like she is escaping from a . . . I don't know . . . a shady past. There's something she's not telling . . .

I moved the mouse a little: *Welcome to Karen's Petite Maison.*

JOHN: Maybe she killed her husband; you tell me . . .

KAREN: Shut up, don't give me any ideas . . .

I clicked on the Reservations tab. *Enter password*, it asked me. *Of course, what did you expect, genius?*

KEITH: Well, I have to admit, she's the best girl you have introduced me to, no denying it.

The commentary pleased me. So much that, although it wasn't in my plans, I got brave and took out another snitch. Luckily I had brought two just in case.

JOHN: All right, then, we've finally awakened the beast inside you... Hallelujah.

Where do I put it? Come on, quick. The cuckoo clock, behind the clock. Get on the chair. Careful, it's got wheels. Can you make it? It's really high. I'm going to try. Get on your tiptoes. Fast. What good's a microphone going to do you here?

JOHN: What's taking her so long?

RICK: Maybe she was smart and escaped.

I could say that what made me lose control, push the chair away, slip, grab the cuckoo clock on an impulse, and fall with a crash, smashing the clock against the floor, was hearing Rick's voice for the first time that night. But that would just be an easy way to excuse my stupidity.

A confused silence. A *what was that?* from Karen. A scraping of chair legs on the floor. Hurried steps of two people toward the racket.

When Karen and John peeped into the vestibule by the door, I was already gone, far from the office, with a bruised hip that barely let me move, standing paralyzed at the foot of the steps, as if they had caught me coming back from the bathroom and had frightened me.

"I think the noise came from that room," I said, pointing to the office, as if I didn't know what was in there.

I was clutching the snitch in my left hand and had broken a nail. While they peeked into the office, I hid the snitch in my pocket. I thought I was going to faint from the blow, the pain, the fright. *No, not again, Alice.* I felt my hair to see if it was messy. My mouth tasted of metal. I was bleeding. I didn't know if I'd hit my head. My vision was a little blurry. I wanted to get out of there. I needed to get out of there.

"Grandpa's cuckoo clock!" Karen shouted, enraged as she ran out of the reception office. She looked around for the Persian cat, which was perched on the column of the balustrade. "Dingleberry, I'm going to kill you! Come here!"

And she ran off after him. John stood there looking at me. He had caught me. *Faint, Alice. Right now, it's best if you faint.*

"Dingleberry," he huffed. "Could there possibly be a more ridiculous name for a stupider cat? But I'm thankful, because I can't stand that damned animal waking me up every hour anymore."

He turned and went back to the dining room. All the bad things disappeared, and I laughed to myself. I felt like I was in a video game. I was getting hooked, and wanted to keep playing. How many extra lives would I have? Because I'd just used one, that went without saying.

I WOKE UP with a certain eagerness because the recordings from the snitches were waiting for me. I was curious to know what they'd captured. I don't know why I imagined that when John and Karen were alone that they would start to argue and upbraid each other for the way they'd each behaved during dinner. But no, in their bedroom silence reigned, mitigated only by the murmur of the TV. They fell asleep almost immediately. A half hour later, they both started snoring as one. They left the TV on all night on some shopping network.

So I focused my attention on the snitch in my living room. I downloaded the audio recorded onto my phone and slipped it into an adjustable armband I used when I ran, put on my ergonomic headphones and hit Play.

While I opened windows, aired out the house and picked up cushions, books and toys scattered over the floor:

SUMMER: Come on, Olivia, it's time to go to bed.

OLIVIA: No, some more cartoons.

SUMMER: You've already seen three episodes of *Dora the Explorer.* Your mother said two at the most.

OLIVIA: But it's got to be an even number; otherwise, I have nightmares.

———

While I hung the clothes on the line in the garden (I don't like dryers; I love the scent of clothes that have dried outside):

SUMMER: Come on, this time I'm serious. Bedtime.

OLIVIA: Just one more, please.

SUMMER: You said they have to be even. We've already seen four. And we're not going to watch six...

OLIVIA: But six is my favorite number...

While I raked up the leaves—curiously, everyone hates it, but I find it relaxing—and Pony ran around leaping into the piles I made:

SUMMER: You tell me now that seven is your favorite number, and I'll tear your little nose off.

OLIVIA: No, seven isn't my favorite number, because it's everybody's favorite number. And Mommy says that the luck that's in numbers has to be shared with other people. That's why I chose six, and because it's my age. But when I turn seven, it'll still be six. When I turn eight, I might change it to eight, because then I'll be done with all the luck six has. And now I'm going to bed.

While I expressed breast milk with an electric pump:

Ruby crying.

SUMMER: What is it, precious? Don't cry, little baby. Come here, come over here. You want me to sing you a song? You want? Let's sing a song together. A good one.

She taps her cell phone and plays "Wrecking Ball" by Miley Cyrus.

No, not Miley Cyrus, please. Don't spoil my daughter's mind: she's still really little.

Summer sings.

Ruby stops crying.

Don't stop crying, Ruby, bawl, don't succumb, be strong.

SUMMER: "All you ever did was break me... Yeah, you wreck me..."

Ruby laughs.

————

I sighed while I looked at Pony. She was moaning.

"So what's your problem, what are you whining about?"

She was sitting on her hindquarters. Her eyes homed in on the little glass fishbowl. Flint, Ruby's yellow guppy with the bug eyes, had gotten tired of going round and round and not getting anywhere. He was lying flat on the surface of the water.

"Not again, Flint . . ." This was the third time it had happened. I huffed. Then I looked at Pony. "So are you crying because you're sad or because you want some food?"

Pony looked at me, and I swear she answered: *Both.*

————

While I was on my way to Family Pet Land to look for a guppy to replace Flint III without Olivia realizing it and going through another death-trauma:

> **SUMMER** (*on the phone*): I'm a little fed up, to be honest... I have no idea how much longer I've got; I don't want to count; it freaks me out... Sure, but you've got to understand that right now, like, I can't go back... My mom? No idea. I'm telling you right now. I don't talk to her... Yeah, I can already see my belly... How the fuck do I know what I'm going to do when it gets bigger; get off my back, shit! I called you to vent, not to get a lecture... Sorry, it's just that my hormones are going nuts... Ha, ha, ha! I'm not always such a slut! You're the one who's a slut!

————

"No, not that one, the one closer to the left," I corrected Frank, who had the little net in his hand, trying to fish the guppy I was pointing to out of the tank. There were dozens of them.

"But they're all the same, Alice," he complained.

"No, they're not all the same, they look the same, but they're not. No, not that one either; the one next to it, right beside it."

Exasperated, Frank passed me the net.

"Here, get it yourself."

I took the net and went directly for Flint's clone.

"They last shorter and shorter each time," I complained.

"Because you pick wrong. If you let me pick . . ."

I cornered the sly guppy I wanted, and Frank put him in a plastic bag with water. Done. Rest in peace, Flint III. Long live Flint IV. Welcome to the Dupont household.

———

When, three days after recording Summer's conversation, I received a call from her aunt Jennifer, I thought I'd been caught. How? It didn't matter. With my recent paranoia I could come up with hundreds of responses a second to justify my unfounded certainties. Even when she told me she was calling because she'd finally made the decision to take painting classes, I still thought I smelled a skunk. *Careful, Alice.*

What most struck me about Stephen's room was the light. There was an enormous, south-facing window overlooking the beach and the sea. The dunes seemed to have combed themselves for the occasion, and the sea appeared unusually serene. You could breathe in the peace there. I'd imagined a sicker scene, colder, like a hospital. An inert body connected to tubes, noisy machines pumping oxygen and fluid. Monitors registering vital signs. But Jennifer had taken care to camouflage it with light, life and scents. It smelled good, like a baby, like talcum powder. Burt Bacharach was playing, "I'll Never Fall in Love Again"—very appropriate for both of us. Later Jennifer would tell me that he was Stephen's favorite composer, that they were both from Kansas City, and that Bacharach was even born the same day as Stephen's father in 1928. When her relationship with Stephen was already on firm ground—and they'd gotten over the fact that he was twenty years older than her—he surprised her with plane tickets to Sydney, where he brought her to the famous opera house to see a Burt Bacharach concert. When I saw Stephen, I immediately felt a healthy envy. If only I had Chris like that. Something to hold on to. *But what are you saying, Alice? This is horrible, a real limbo, not what you're going through.* What would have happened if Chris had remained in a coma?

Would I have done what I was doing? Or would I have been compelled to wait patiently for him to wake up, and then ask him, *Hey, honey, there's something that's been going around and around in my mind: What the hell were you doing on Robin Island?*

Stephen didn't give the impression of being in a coma, it was as if he was taking a pleasant nap or just had his eyes closed, listening to his favorite music and meditating. His perfectly trimmed white beard and his fluffy white hair added to the overall sense of calm. I felt that there, in that room, everything was OK. I had a strong urge to weep and embrace him.

"Remember that when we met, you told me that to paint, you had to find your inspiration nearby?" Jennifer said. "For me, nothing is closer than Stephen. And don't look for some in-depth explanation, because there isn't one."

I took her advice. We started off working on volume, learning to balance out dimensions. The most basic thing. In pencil.

"How long has he been like that?" I asked, once we had established some trust and the question would appear reasonable and not malignant and nosy.

"Three years."

More or less the same amount of time Chris had been going to the island. I looked around while I toyed with a snitch between my fingers. On top of the bookshelf seemed like a good place. Jennifer must spend a good part of each day up in that room, judging by the quantity of everyday objects filling it with life: wildflowers, plants, skin care and masculine hygiene products, books on the nightstand, CDs and CD player, a laptop, a tablet, a book of Sudoku puzzles, a TV, etc. I was sure she talked to her husband a great deal. She'd tell him the news, read novels, share memories with him, preferably the good ones, so he would want to wake up, but she'd also need a sounding post, and it was clear no one else played that role, not on the island, anyway. Did she have unfinished business with Stephen, just as I did with Chris? And if so, would she get it all off her chest, express it, whether as a confession or a reproach? I would bet Jennifer felt a little guilty for her husband being in that state, just as I sometimes asked myself what I had done wrong with Chris to make him have a secret/lie/mystery that took up such a big part of his life.

"Is his condition irreversible?" I should have asked it another way so it would sound less harsh. "I mean . . . is there any possibility that . . ." I said clumsily in an effort to repair the damage.

She shook her head softly.

"Brain dead . . . which means I don't need to talk to him and read him books at night, but I still do anyway . . ." she said with a bitter smile.

"You've got a knack for drawing. You sure you've never done it before?"

"You say that to all your students, sweet talker."

"No, seriously." I smiled. "You've got a fluid way of sketching. You hold the pencil very delicately. You don't struggle with it, that's very important."

"I was bored in school, especially in econometrics." *A subject from business administration, the same thing Chris studied.* "And you know who my boring teacher was? Stephen."

"Forbidden love . . ."

"Not exactly. Until I graduated, he didn't speak a word to me. Plus, he told me later he passed me even though I didn't deserve it because he didn't want me to come back and dispute my grade during office hours. He was scared he wouldn't be able to control himself."

"So how did he take the first step?"

"He didn't. I did, without meaning to. At a graduation party, someone had the brilliant idea of making a chocolate cake with marijuana without telling anyone. Ten minutes later, I was knocking at the door of Stephen's apartment on campus, high as a kite, shouting that I didn't understand how he could ignore me that way. I went out like a light right after seeing what I was sure were dragons. He wasn't even home. He got there twenty minutes later and found me curled up on his doormat with vomit everywhere. He didn't want to call emergency services and get me in trouble. He made me drink a quart of milk and left me sleeping on the sofa. When I woke up, there was fresh coffee and toast. He wasn't there. A week later, one day before leaving campus forever,

I gathered my courage to overcome the terrible embarrassment I felt. I made a chocolate cake, without marijuana, naturally—I hadn't had any since—and I took it to his house. I left it on the doormat where he'd found me. I didn't want to see him; I just wanted to leave the cake and a thank-you note. Two weeks later, he wrote me an email that said: 'No worries. Take care. PS: The cake was delicious.' *Take care*, what a bunch of bullshit, I thought. Four days later, I answered him: 'Whenever you want, I'll give you the recipe. Take care.' Half an hour and a glass of wine later, I wrote him again: 'Or I can make you another one.' An hour and two glasses of wine later, I wrote him again: 'And we can eat it together . . . if you want. Take care.' Five days later, he answered: 'Yes, I want to. Take care.' I loved those *take cares*."

I was surprised how easy this was. I was worried, my heart pounding, trying to figure out where to put the snitch, and she was trusting me with her love story right off the bat. Maybe there was no need to spy on her. Maybe being her friend was enough.

"At which university did this precious pre-love story take place?"

"Dartmouth, the Tuck School of Business."

"So, what happened to Stephen?"

I was carried away by the euphoria and thought it was an opportune question, until Jennifer answered, "Hey, you're not as gossipy as Karen, are you?"

"No, I'm sorry, my apologies, I didn't . . ."

"It's a joke, stupid," she said to calm me down. And then she said something that made the blood rush out of my head: "Stephen had a cerebral infarction."

Knot in my throat. Gooseflesh. Dry mouth. *Isn't that the same as a brain aneurysm?*

"We were out for a ride in the boat, and while he was raising the sail, he felt a sharp pain in his head. Soon afterward, he started vomiting and passed out. The boat was adrift because I didn't have the least idea how to pilot it . . ."

"Damn, I'm sorry . . ." was all I managed to say. Cold hands. Queasiness. Tachycardia.

"He didn't have any risk factors. It was hereditary. His father died of the same thing, but since he was a chain smoker, a drinker and had high blood pressure, no one thought about the hereditary aspect till it happened to Stephen."

Didn't the doctor tell me what happened to Chris was something congenital, or did he say hereditary? Is congenital the same thing as hereditary? At that moment, I didn't know. Tingling. Trembling. Sweat. I couldn't get a word out, not even to playact. Jennifer realized it.

"You've gone pale. These things upset you, don't they?"

My neck forced itself to nod.

"So you're not going to ask me the million-dollar question? The one all the island must be asking?" I looked at her, trying to convey that I didn't know what she was talking about, even though I did have an idea.

Tell her you understand. Tell her your secret. The truth behind your lie. Cry. Be sincere, Alice. Dispel your cloud. Maybe she has the solution to everything. And if not, she's going to understand you. No one more than her. And she'll help you. You'll see.

"If you don't mind, I think I'll take that tea you offered me earlier," I said, getting a grip on myself somehow. I wanted to show Jennifer that I wasn't going to judge her, that what she was doing was fine if it was what she needed.

"Green?" she asked with a smile. She was thankful for my discretion. Was she testing me?

"Yeah, please."

I was left alone with Stephen. I didn't plant the snitch. It seemed dirty to me. A lack of respect toward the trust she had shown me. But then I remembered Chris had told me that when he was just seven, he had passed through a phase of thinking he was adopted. It was all the fault of his cousin Kenny, who told him that he had been adopted and that meant that Chris had been adopted too. Why? Because both his mother and Betty, Chris's mother, had a gap between their two top teeth, the ones in the middle, and Kenny's sister, Susan, and Chris's sister, Tricia, had teeth just like their mothers'. But the boys didn't; neither of them had a gap between their top front teeth. Conclusion: they'd been adopted. And of course, since Kenny was two years older, Chris believed every word of it and went back home in tears. His parents then convinced him that he hadn't been adopted. But could his cousin Kenny have been right?

That memory and the whistle of the teakettle with the boiling water broke the spell Jennifer had cast, awakening me from the hypnosis of her presence. The room suddenly seemed suspect. Stephen's long fingers, his thin hair. What color were his eyes? What size shoe did he wear? How do you do a DNA test? Things I asked myself while climbing up onto a chair to plant the snitch on top of the bookshelf.

When I got home, more clearheaded now, I remembered the coroner had told me what Chris had was congenital. And that maybe, only maybe, had he inherited it.

I opened my computer's Internet browser and searched Google: *How to do DNA test*. There were 31.5 million results in .42 seconds. I clicked on the first result that wasn't sponsored, and it showed the proper procedure for collecting samples—outside the lab.

Later I read for a few hours, all sorts of articles about infarctions and brain aneurysms. I found that the number of patients whose aneurysms were due to hereditary causes was around 10 to 20 percent and that one of the most frequent causes of cerebral infarction was the rupture of an aneurysm. For all those reasons, I thought I should get my daughters tested right away—and that Stephen had just earned the right to be considered suspect number four.

THE BEACH IS deserted. The reeds are dancing to the sound of the northwesterly wind. The sand makes little whirls on the dunes. It's not too cold, even though it's the end of November. A man is standing on the shore, hypnotized by the sea. I can't see his face. I don't need to see his face. His hair is disheveled and frizzy from the salt breeze. He's barefoot, with khaki pants rolled up a few times. The waves break with a wild beauty. The receding surf traces furrows around the soles of his feet. I come over slowly, as if I want to surprise him or am worried I'll frighten him. I'm naked, except for a baggy turtleneck sweater that hangs almost to my knees. I think I just made love to the man, and the sweater is his. The neighing of wild horses. A seagull suspended in the air. Peace is what I feel. Love for the man. That's why I don't want to scare him away. I reach him. I have a snitch hidden in my hand. I look for a place to hide it without his realizing.

OLIVIA: Mommy...

ME (*whispering*): Shhh... be quiet...

In the back pocket of his pants. I can slip it in there if I'm careful. That's a good place.

OLIVIA: Mommy...

ME (*whispering*): Not now, Olivia, go...

I manage to slip it in. I take my hand out very slowly, and just when I'm going to take a step back, Chris, because the man is Chris, turns brusquely and grabs my arm forcefully.

165

———

Olivia screamed when she saw me sit up so suddenly. She had taken hold of my arm, not tightly, but in my dream it felt like a lion's claw. Ruby woke up, and Pony crawled under the bed. Both were whining.

"What is it, Oli? You scared me . . ." I said while I calmed Ruby down.

"Why did you tell me to leave?"

"What? Huh? I was dreaming, Oli. What's going on? Why are you awake, honey?"

"I had the ugly nightmare again."

Olivia's ugly nightmare was worryingly similar to my own. She was up on her father's shoulders. They were running, jumping, playing, laughing. *Giddyup, horsey!* Olivia shouted. Faster, faster, until they took off, galloping up into the sky. Higher, higher, until they reached the clouds. And when they crossed through them, her father disappeared. Olivia could walk on the clouds, which she liked a lot, but she was sad because her father wasn't there, and she got scared, and she cried, asking for him, and she was afraid because the world was very far away and it looked very small down there, and suddenly she stepped in a puddle—actually she had peed—that turned into a hole and she fell into it. And just before she smashed against the ground, she woke up, soaked in urine, crying and frightened.

Obviously, I hadn't told her about my dream. The similarity between our dreams was startling—and slightly gratifying. Two nightmares from the same fear.

"Come on, get in bed with me and Ruby, honey."

"No, Shesnotapony's here."

"Believe me, with you in the bed, she's not coming out."

Pony had learned to stay a few feet away from Olivia. Pony had imposed a restraining order on herself, for her own good.

"I don't trust her; let's go to mine."

"Oli, yours is way smaller and it's got pee in it."

Olivia accepted grudgingly. She got in bed and rolled over all the way around, then repeated the same thing in the opposite direction.

"Oli, what are you doing?"

"Scaring off the nightmares."

"Well, scare off mine while you're at it."

"No, you have to scare your own off. Do it, turn."

As if we had changed roles and I was the little girl who was frightened and needed to believe her mother, I did what she said. I rolled all the way around once.

"Now the other side. If not, it doesn't work."

I turned in the opposite direction.

"There you go. Nice job. Good night, Mommy."

"Good night, honey."

It worked. We slept all night, our arms around each other. The three of us, in the fetal position, cuddling like little Matryoshka dolls. The warriors deserved rest.

———

The next day, I got my first letter in the mailbox. It was a wedding invitation. Alex and Amanda's wedding, the two people from the proposal during the Labor Day picnic that gave me the anxiety attack.

I called to confirm our attendance after making a decision: I would buy more snitches. Lots more. At Night Eyes, of course. Where I also acquired, as if to divert attention from my excesses, a telephonic voice changer I saw in the display case next to a sign that said: "Professional Voice Changer. 14 different tones! Easy to use! Was $399, now $299." The usual impulsive purchase that I had no concrete plan for at the time.

———

I laid out all the listening devices on my desk, an enormous lacquered blue table—better suited to a dining room than anything else—of old pine. A vestige that hadn't made the cut when the previous owners moved out, it had become my center of operations. Olivia caught me slipping the SIM cards into the devices.

"Mommy, what are you doing? What is that stuff?"

Until then, it hadn't occurred to me that I was starting to hold on to too many things nobody should see, especially my daughter. Until then, it was all just boring facts that would pass unnoticed before a child's eyes: names, detailed family relations, addresses, jobs, photos of houses, places. List of suspects and questions. Telephone numbers, Post-its, notebooks. For Olivia, the attic was the place where Mommy did her boring things, except for the map painted on the wall, where I would occasionally let her add seagulls, a sailboat, a sun, a moon. But it couldn't go on like that. I had to make it clear that this was Mommy's place, that she couldn't come in without permission. No, that she couldn't come in, period.

"What are those little boxes?"

"Those boxes are to scare off raccoons like you."

"I'm not a raccoon."

"Oh no? We'll find out right now." I picked up a snitch. "Puchi Puchi . . . I invoke the spirit of Puchi Puchi . . . Oh, Puchi Puchi, up in heaven, tell me if Olivia is a Puchi Puchi like you. Puchi Puchi. Puchi Puchi," I chanted while I slowly approached Olivia, who was hypnotized, believing everything. "Attention: Puchi Puchi is going to make an announcement. Puchi Puchi tells me that Olivia is . . ." Dramatic pause. "A raccoon!"

"Noooooo!" she screamed, running off in terror and laughing.

"Out of here, raccoon! Out of here!"

I grabbed a board and painted the following.

An homage to Grizzel Haven. The place where Mommy does her things. A little private parcel necessary to find a little peace in a house governed by the needs of the little ones. Something that didn't look suspicious, and that any adult would understand, respect and applaud.

But it still needed something else. I went to Dan's True Value, Dan DeRoller Sr.'s hardware store.

"Hello, Dan."

"Hey, Alice. How can I help you?"

I thought about going on a tangent and asking for a bunch of things before what I really needed, but what I needed was so simple, there was no point in preambles or distractions.

"I need a padlock."

"What kind of padlock?"

"To put on a door."

"And what's behind that door?"

"Something that a small, simple padlock can take care of."

"OK, so we're not talking about the Declaration of Independence."

"Well, a little, yeah. It's my own declaration of independence."

"Oh, now I get you. I have just what you need."

He took out a medium-sized lock. Normal, the kind you can get anywhere. But with one particularity, at least for me. The key to the lock was exactly like the Master Key. Same brand, same type of key. Standard-sized and a popular brand, but it made me certain that Chris had bought it there. That didn't solve anything, just confirmed what I knew before. The big difference now was that I was convinced, with utter clarity, that I would eventually end up finding the lock that the Master Key would open.

AMANDA AND ALEX'S wedding took place on the Sunday of Thanksgiving weekend, during the first snowfall. As if that were just another element of the design scheme, a dreamy white passage to the Presbyterian church, Our Lady of Grace.

Olivia, Ruby and I had just returned to the island the day before, after spending a few days at my parents' for Thanksgiving.

The wicked tongues of the island—almost all of them—said the bride and groom had to push the wedding earlier because she had gotten pregnant. That she was due at the beginning of spring. But of course, since they were the perfect couple, the crown prince and princess of Robin Island, a slur of that kind seemed like sheer blasphemy.

The first chords of the "Ode to Joy" sounded, and everyone stood up.

"If another horse rides up, I'm getting up and leaving," murmured Miriam, who was sitting beside me with Chloe.

I had come, of course, with Ruby and Olivia, whom I'd had a drama with that very morning because when she looked out the window and saw a coating of snow everywhere, she started crying. "What's under it?! We don't know what's there, Mommy. I don't want to go outside. I don't want to step in it . . ." I calmed her down, reminding her how much she'd always liked the snow and ice-skating. And after I had swathed her from head to toe in winter clothes, she dared to go out with me to make a snowman at the foot of Puchi Puchi's grave. I had to leave Pony shut up in the house so she wouldn't bother Olivia. We started to pile up balls of snow: the big bottom, a smaller one, and finally the head. Then we put a scarf on him, a cap, two buttons for eyes, a carrot for the nose and branches for arms. Olivia was rather disturbed by the result.

"What is it, Oli? You don't like it?"

"It's scary."

"What do you mean? It's like a nice, big doll made of snow. Do you want to give him a name?"

"No . . ." she said, taking two steps backward, her eyes remaining fixed on the snowman, as if she feared it would pounce on her.

"Well, if you don't like it, no problem; we will get rid of it."

But before I could do anything, she said: "No, don't kill him!"

"Oli, stop with the nonsense; it's snow. Snow isn't alive."

"Yes, it is alive, because it moves; it falls from the sky." She didn't give me time to dismantle her argument, because she added, "Maybe Daddy sent it. Maybe he's inside it. Snow comes from heaven, and Daddy's in heaven. Don't kill it."

And she ran off inside the house. *What happens when the temperature goes up and the snow melts?* I thought. To top it off, Pony had shit in Oli's bedroom, causing more screaming and crying. Olivia didn't want to leave the house or go to the wedding even though Oliver and her other friends would be there. So I ended up resorting to what you always resort to in these arguments: bribery.

"Let's go to the wedding and I'll give you a present."

"Fine. I want a pony. A real pony."

"A pony in the summer; it's too cold outside now."

"No, because it will sleep with me in the bedroom."

"Oli, you can't sleep with a pony. Ponies live in stables."

"Well, send Shesnotapony to the stables."

And so on for an entire hour. I let her use my iPad Mini with retina display, because you could see the cartoons better and especially because she could FaceTime with Oliver.

————

Mark was a few rows ahead of me, on the other side of the main aisle. Julia beside him, completely absent, her gaze lost up ahead, as if she were witnessing a funeral. Mark couldn't avoid turning to glance at me from the corner of his eye.

Very close at hand, in my pocket, I had a Valium. I didn't want what occurred at the picnic to happen to me again. To see all the island gathered together raised my level of anxiety considerably. The now-familiar tingling and burning in my head reappeared, together with my abiding fear of fainting, as was now customary in these stressful situations. When I found out my phobia had a name, asthenophobia, I calmed down because I felt less weird, part of a group. Just as finding out that same morning that there was also a name for fear of the cold, cheimaphobia, and of the snow, chionophobia, had diminished, if only a little, my level of worry about Olivia. Irrational fears we use to cover up, like a second skin, to protect us from aggressions, to isolate us and to make us lose a bad part and a good part, probably more of the second, of life. But I had never managed to control it, and after Chris's death, it had exploded.

The first time I fainted was during a lacrosse game in elementary school, when I was nine. In a strange twist of luck, my protective mask fell off just as a teammate was passing me the ball. It hit me in the eye and I collapsed. When I woke up, the game was already over. We had lost 3–2 after being up 2–0. *See? If you faint, you lose,* I must have thought with my childhood logic. And now, however much I told myself, *Alice, may your defeats catch you while you sleep. That's better, right?,* it did me little good. I suppose it had to do with my exaggerated need to maintain control. That's why I had limited my world to a micro-circle, with the least possible number of variables. And there, right before my eyes, I now had more than three hundred variables. Infinite possibilities that just begged for a couple of Valium. But I was fine; I felt it wouldn't overwhelm me. Flustered, yes, but the fact I knew almost half the attendees helped. When I say know, I mean their names, jobs and where they lived. Every night I spent at least an hour going over and studying the notes I'd gathered for my particular dissertation: "Anthropology of Robin Island: A Study of the Human Specimens and Their Possible Relationship to Chris Williams." One or several of the people there had the answer to my first question: *What was Chris doing on the island?* In my three months there, I had realized it was impossible to pass unnoticed. Discreet, yes. Distant, yes. Reserved, yes. But invisible, no. Impossible.

If you could choose, Alice, who would you like to be the guilty party? Where would you like Chris's map to lead you? What spot would you like the X to mark? Which one of them would you like to possess the treasure chest that the Master Key unlocks?

Reverend Henry, an affable, sensible man, was not much given to rambling, and the ceremony proceeded without too many corny asides. Two snowmobiles, decorated with the names of the bride and groom, substituted for the typical wedding limousine—as if they'd known all along it was going to snow.

"Please let them crash; please let them crash," Miriam whispered as she saw the newlyweds exit hand in hand, leaving behind a trail of rose petals as if they were being escorted by a flock of robins.

Had they rehearsed that too?

———

The entire island attended the wedding. No one was going to miss the event, whether from duty or prior commitment. The wedding banquet was celebrated in climate-controlled tents at the home of Alex's parents, Maggie and Rodney Burr, owners of Burr's Marine.

While the event stretched on, everyone left their homes and, as could be predicted, left them unlocked. Amanda's father, Doug, who ran the ferry, had also invited all his employees to the wedding, deciding that the ferry wouldn't operate that day. So even access to the island was limited, as if it were a private party, safe from tourists, who were unlikely anyway, given the cold. That meant I'd have access to all the houses for a limited time. I had made a list of the most important places to plant my snitches. I came up with twelve where I had already studied the entries, windows, possible alarms, pets that might get hysterical . . . I had them laid out on a map and had timed how long it would take to go from one to the other in the golf cart. The total time, allowing three minutes to plant the snitches, was fifty minutes. Too long to go unnoticed? Maybe, but it would be months before I'd get an opportunity this good again. So it was up to me to make do. The best time to begin the mission: between the second course and the cutting of the cake—no one was going to go home without sampling the wedding cake. I would take off, telling Miriam I was going to feed Ruby somewhere discreet, and asking her to please keep her eye on Olivia, who would be eating at the kids' table. Twenty minutes later, I would send her a message saying that Ruby had thrown up on my dress when I burped her and I was going to go home and change quickly. That would justify the time and my absence. I hadn't counted on the complication of the snow. That was something that would undoubtedly slow me down and oblige me to modify things on the fly, setting my priorities by location to minimize the loss of time.

———

The image was picturesque and comic, to say the least. A golf cart with snow chains, crossing snow-covered streets, skidding all over the place. Me at the wheel in my deep-blue evening dress with the crisscross V-neck and a white three-quarter length down jacket, with Ruby attached to me in her carrier.

Besides setting out the snitches and making sure that Ruby stayed warm and asleep, I also carried the Master Key in my purse in case I came across any lock that it might fit.

My invasion route, in order:

- **Chief Margaret's house.** Basement. Not because I suspected anything, but she was the chief of police. She had a police radio in the basement, turned on twenty-four hours a day, rattling off all the fire and police notices in Barnstable, Dukes and Nantucket counties.

- **Jodie and Keevan O'Gorman's.** They own the liquor store and live on the second floor above the shop. I went in through the back door, again using Chris's X-ray. I put a snitch in the living room, and before leaving I saw a bowl with various rings of keys. Could the keys to the store be there? They were, on a leprechaun-shaped key ring marked with the handwritten word *store*. Long live Saint Patrick. I put a bug under the counter.

- **Conrad the bank director's home.** Two snitches. Bedroom and living room. I wanted to see if Chris had opened an account or rented a deposit box.

- **Julia and Mark's house.** Two snitches. I tried to place a snitch in Julia's office, but it was locked, and Chris's X-ray did me no good there.

▶ **Jennifer's house.** Hard for me to enter in every sense of the word. Because I respected her a lot and because it was locked. But Summer had left her bedroom window open—to air it out and get rid of the unmistakable scent of marijuana. Unbelievable, the girl was smoking in the middle of her pregnancy. I got in by climbing up a ladder. After planting the snitch in Summer's room, I went down to Stephen's room, approached it slowly, trying not to make noise, as if I was afraid of waking him up from his coma. I slipped on some latex gloves and took out a cotton swab I had in a paper envelope. I put it in Stephen's mouth and swabbed for twenty seconds, with medium pressure, on the inside of his cheek. Then, with the other side of the swab, I did the same with the other cheek. The idea was to pick up skin cells as well as saliva. I put the swab in the envelope—they insisted you couldn't use plastic—and sealed it. I reveled—just a little—in my prowess as a detective. Before leaving, I begged Stephen's pardon for the bother and kissed him on the forehead, thinking it would bring me good luck.

▶ **The DeRollers'.** Two snitches, master bedroom and Gwen's office, where she normally conducted her business as mayor.

▶ **Family Pet Land.** One snitch. The day before, I had taken Pony for a checkup and opened the lock on one of the back windows. I wanted to keep an eye on Frank, especially after the episode that night when I surprised him—or he surprised me—coming out of the real estate agency.

Since time was pressing, I decided along the way to put off planting the snitches in Miriam's office and home until another day. She had given me a key to her house not long before, because we were such good neighbors and even better friends, according to her. I hadn't done the same, of course.

I passed by my house, changed into a long-sleeved dress with a pattern of poppy flowers. I touched up my makeup a bit and put on deodorant because I had sweated a lot, despite the cold. Before returning to the banquet, I visited my final stop: Karen's Petite Maison. I went straight to the office, I cooed to Dingleberry, gave him a treat, just as I had to the multiple pets I'd come across at the various houses. I put the snitch in the desk, toward the base, in the hollow between the frame for the drawers and the strip of wood along the bottom. Easy. But there seemed to be a curse against me in that room, because when I got up, I tore my dress on a loose nail. Dingleberry looked at me in seeming satisfaction, as if it were an act of poetic justice. I had to go back home. That was another twelve-minute delay.

When I came back to the wedding banquet, they'd already cut the cake and passed it out. Fortunately, I had missed Amanda and her father dancing earlier to the tune of "Eternal Flame" by the Bangles.

As soon as I came in, completely numb in every sense, with Ruby in my arms, I scanned the room until I found Olivia. She was leaping around to "Gangnam Style" by Psy with a number of girls, trying to get Oliver's attention, but from shyness or indifference he wouldn't get on the floor. Watching my daughter dancing like that so relieved me that I wanted to go over and join her.

I saw Miriam arguing with Mike, who was standing in front of her—Chloe was sitting in her lap—hands on his hips, slightly bent over, threatening, drunk, spitting bits of saliva while upbraiding her for something I couldn't manage to hear. I thought about not going over, to keep from getting in the middle, but his irritating attitude and the euphoria I felt obliged me to intervene.

"Is everything OK?"

Mike looked at me with disdain, biting his lower lip.

"Yes, everything's fine," Miriam said, not scared, at least not obviously. "Mike was just going. Right, Mike?"

Mike took his beer, finished it in one swig and walked off. As he passed by, he grazed my shoulder in a way that was as soft as it was calculated, so I could sense his contempt but couldn't accuse him of aggression.

Had he always been so unpleasant? I couldn't believe he and Miriam had ever been together. This was something I had already told her before, given our newfound trust. She had never tried to justify herself,

but when she started to tell me all that had led her to her current situation, she'd get lost, drag her feet or turn elusive. Apparently, as time
went on, the peevish postadolescent, full of potential, that she'd fallen
in love with had become a frustrated pseudo-adult without much of a
future who had wasted the better part of his life. He had started drinking again and messing around with drugs, hanging out with a gang of
undesirables that made him feel less worthless and then "everything
went to shit," as Miriam said, and she left it there. But I didn't. There
had to be something else, definitely, and I was going to find out.

When Mike walked off toward the bar, Miriam started to tremble
and turned very pale.

"That motherfucker made my blood sugar drop . . ." she said, or
tried to say, rather, because all she managed to get out, dragging her
words, was: "That mmm-fucker may mmy bloo . . ."

Hands quivering, she fumbled till she got the kit out of her bag. She
had put in a quick dose of insulin, a bit bigger than normal, because of
the copious meal along with sweets and wine. But she had miscalculated.

"Get sugar purse, please . . ." she told me while she measured her
glucose levels. Forty-four. It had dropped through the floor.

I took a few packets of sugar out of her bag. She always kept some
on hand. I opened them and she gulped them down.

"Don't let him see me, please. I don't want to give the asshole the
satisfaction . . ."

I calmed her down, saying he was off laughing with his pals, far
away, and no one could see what was going on. I gave her a little of the
Coke that was on the table. We waited. Quiet, without talking. I had
never seen her in such bad shape.

"It did take you a while to get back . . ." she said, coherent now,
when she had her color back. "You did it on purpose. I'm sure of it. My
hypoglycemia is on your conscience now."

I laughed and answered, "So, how long does it take you to pick a
dress that isn't even the one you picked the first time? Forever, right?"

"Well, I like the one you chose."

It was a red skater dress with a pleated skirt, Karen Millen.

My phone vibrated—I had it on silent. It was a message. From Mark.

Just so you know, when you left, I missed you, and I got jealous thinking you were with someone else.

I thought that was out of place and lacking in respect. Obviously, he'd had one too many, like almost everyone. I looked at him. He turned his back to me. He was four tables over to my right. Two minutes later, another came through.

Sorry for the previous message. It was totally inappropriate. I love your new dress. Did I ever tell you I like you?

That one almost bothered me more. Well, maybe bother isn't the right word. It affected me more. The first one was clumsy flirting; the second was edging into romantic territory. Still innocent. The beginning. It scared me more than a little. He still wouldn't look at me. Julia was beside him, still inert, with a glass of champagne in her hand. Was he writing all that with her right next to him? I didn't like that either, too audacious. A third message arrived.

I'm a little drunk, don't pay too much attention to me.

OK, great, Mark, don't write me again. It's fine, let it go. Everything's OK. But no, he wrote me again:

Meet at my office later?

I didn't go. I was exhausted after the day's intensity. That day and the two hundred that preceded it. I wanted to put the girls to bed and activate the snitches. Try them out and make sure they worked correctly. I realized that I hadn't been able to put one in Mark's boat. It would have been a good opportunity to round off my plan. But that proposition wasn't an innocent invitation. I knew what I'd be going for if I ever went.

LISTENING TO THE conversations on the snitches was really frustrating. Most were just background noise. Impenetrable. I couldn't pay attention to every sound, every phrase. It drove me mad. It was hard, not to say impossible, to do it and raise my kids at the same time: crying, pooping, diapers, breastfeeding, vomit, playing, housekeeping, cleaning, shopping, meeting the school plane, homework, more playing, eating, sleeping and all the rest. Until I decided it wasn't my mind that needed to listen to and process all the information, but my body. Letting the words flow without paying them any attention while I went on with my life, as if they were the street noise, the music you listen to through your headphones. Anytime the word *Chris* popped up in any conversation, my body would react automatically. For sure.

Maybe for that reason, to stem that mind-boggling feeling, I decided to bring my impulse buy into the game. The problem is that the voice changer turned out to be a bit of a fiasco. The fourteen super-professional tones it promised just changed the pitch of your voice. And it always sounded a little metallic, unreal, digital. With the women's voice tones, it was still somewhat credible and didn't give me away, but with the men's voices, any little slip and it started to sound like a parody, a joke you'd play on a colleague pretending to be the bad guy from a superhero movie. It only really worked in a brief conversation with background noise, so it would blend in with the other sounds. I downloaded various park and city noises, far from what you'd expect to hear on Robin Island and would play them when I made my calls.

The following are transcriptions of the most significant conversations the snitches had picked up so far and of my experiments with the voice changer. In chronological order.

Voice changer. Mode: Man—Frequency 13.
Day 203. 17:00 hours.

John Rushlow's phone rings. He picks up.

John: Yes?

Me: John?

John: Yeah, it's me. Who is it?

Me: Chris.

John: Chris? Chris who? Your voice sounds really weird.

Silence.

John: Hello? There's a lot of noise. Are you there?

I hang up.

Snitch at Jennifer's house. Summer's room.
Day 204. 20:30 hours.

Knock at the door.

Jennifer: Open the door.

Summer: Wait.

Jennifer: Summer, open the door right now.

Summer: Wait a sec!

Pounding on the door.

Jennifer: Open!

Summer: I'm coming!

Pause. The door opens.

Jennifer: What is that smell?

SUMMER: Nothing. I don't smell anything.

JENNIFER: It stinks all the way down to the kitchen. It smells like marijuana.

SUMMER: How would you know?

JENNIFER: Summer, don't play with me.

SUMMER: It calms me down, and if I'm calm, the baby's calm. It can't be bad.

Smack.

JENNIFER: You smoke again and...

SUMMER: And what? What are you going to do? You can't do anything. Anything.

Door slamming.

Summer cries in her room. Jennifer cries in Stephen's room.

Voice changer. Mode: Man—Frequency 10.
Day 205. 10:00 hours.

The phone rings at the bank branch.

CONRAD: Good morning, Dime Bank, how can I help you?

ME: Hello. I would like to know my checking account balance.

CONRAD: I'm sorry, I can't hear you well. You'd like what?

ME: My balance. To know my balance.

CONRAD: Your balance? Give me your account number.

ME: I forgot it.

CONRAD: Who is this? I don't recognize your voice. And where are you? I hear cars. Are you sure you've got the right number? This is the Robin Island branch.

ME: OK, sorry.

I hang up.

Snitch at Family Pet Land.
Day 206. 03:22 hours.

Shopkeeper's bell.

FRANK: Rose, where are you? Come on, hurry, let's go home. Rose, I know you're here. God knows why you want to be cooped up here all day. Rose? (*Pause.*) Rose?

Silence.

FRANK (*alarmed*): Rose, don't scare me, come out now wherever you are...

Silence. Doorbell.

FRANK (*walking off*): Rose?!

Voice changer. Mode: Man—Frequency 12.
Day 206. 13:11 hours.

John's cell phone rings. He picks up.

JOHN: Yes?

ME: Hey, John.

JOHN: Hi, who's there.

ME: Chris.

JOHN: Again? Chris? Chris who? What do you think, I know every Chris in the world?! What's all that noise in the background? Hello? Are you there? Why is your number hidden?

I hang up.

Snitch at Jennifer's house. Summer's bedroom.
Day 206. 21:30 hours.

Knocking at the door.

JENNIFER: Summer, could you open a moment, please? (*Pause.*) I
brought you something to eat. You've been shut up in there for two
days. You have to come out and get some air. Open up... (*Pause.*) I
wanted to ask your forgiveness; I didn't mean to hit you the other day.
I'm sorry, really... You have to be more responsible. This isn't a game.

The door opens.

SUMMER: I know. I'm sorry too... But I read on the internet it's not bad
to smoke, that it's not any worse than taking pills for a stomachache. I
swear I read it. Plus, it's organic marijuana, without any pesticides or
anything. It cost me a fortune.

JENNIFER: Summer, don't start again...

SUMMER: Fine, fine, I won't do it...

JENNIFER: Thanks, babe. Give me a kiss?

Kiss.

JENNIFER: I'm sorry I lost my cool.

SUMMER: If you want, I can give you a little marijuana. It's really good
for that...

Jennifer laughs very hard despite herself.

Voice changer. Mode: Woman—Frequency 3.
Day 211. 13:00 hours.

CONRAD (*on the phone*): Good afternoon, Dime Bank, how can I help you?

ME· Good afternoon. So... my brother died a year ago.

CONRAD: Gosh, I'm sorry. My sympathies.

Me: And well, I'm still getting his affairs organized, and I see he had an account at your bank.

Conrad: Aha...

Me: I'd like to close it and transfer the funds.

Conrad: Sure, but without wanting to be rude, I can't take care of something like that over the phone. You would have to come in person with a death certificate and a letter of testamentary from the court showing your appointment as executor of the estate.

Me: Right...

Conrad: Anyhow, what was your brother's name?

Silence.

Conrad: Hello?

I hang up.

**Voice changer. Mode: Man—Frequency 11.
Day 214. 14:20 hours.**

John's mobile phone rings.

John: Yes?

Me: Hey, John, this is Chris Williams.

John: Chris Williams?

Me: Yeah.

John: Are you the one that's been calling these past few days?

Me: Yeah.

John: Why are you using a voice distorter? You think I'm a moron?

Silence.

JOHN: I'm in the military. I'm going to find you, and when I find you, I'm going to knock the shit out of you. For trying to pass for Chris Williams. Because you're not Chris Williams. Because the Chris Williams I know is dead. And I know you know.

I hang up. I take out the SIM card. I break the phone and destroy the voice changer with a hammer. I burn it all.

Snitch on Mark's boat.
Day 215. 10:50 hours.

MARK: You've never told me about yourself.

ME: We have talked about you, though.

MARK: You talk to me about your daughters and not much else.

ME: There's just not much to tell.

MARK: Come on, already, Alice... I feel like I don't know you.

ME: Maybe it's better like that, right? Easier.

MARK: I don't know, it could be...

Pause.

ME: Fine. One question, ask me one question, whichever one you want, and I'll answer, with complete sincerity.

MARK: Just one?

ME: Is that your question?

MARK: No, shit. No, OK, no...

I laugh. He laughs.

ME: A well-chosen question can do a lot.

MARK: Fine, I'm working on it... (*Pause.*) Let's see... It's just I have a lot of them...

ME: I'm sure all of them eventually boil down to one. The mother of all questions. I'm telling you from experience...

MARK: I can't concentrate... It's not coming.

ME: See?

MARK: What?

ME: Maybe you just don't have anything to ask me. Maybe we're not talking about me because you don't want to.

MARK: Maybe.

ME: Maybe you don't know me because you don't want to.

MARK: Maybe. But maybe what's happening right now is I can't concentrate because I really want to kiss you.

Silence. I hear the sound of my cheeks catching fire.

MARK: In fact, my question could be: Do you want to kiss me as much as I want to kiss you? Because I'm not going to ask it. Mainly because I'm afraid you'll say no. So no, that won't be my question.

Silence. I hear the sound of desire hiding behind fear. Or the reverse.

MARK: What are you doing on the island?

Silence. I hear the sound of my wish to run off.

MARK: That's my question. That's the question I keep coming back to every time I have a question to ask you. I always ask myself what brought you here and now to me. But I suppose the answer to that question could change every day, every moment, because I also ask myself that question, and I almost always change the answer, because it depends on something as fickle and contradictory as our longings, our frustrations, our needs, our shortcomings, our fears, our desires... But if you're here with me right now, it has to do with one thing: that you've come to live on the island.

Silence. I hear the sound of my wish to run off... run to him.

MARK: So I repeat the question: What are you doing on the island?

Silence. I hear the sound of my kisses.

Two hundred and fifteen days had passed since Chris's death. Seven months and a day. And six months and a day since I'd given birth. I never stopped asking myself if enough time had gone by. Enough time to not feel so guilty and dirty. Perhaps that's why, before we kissed for the first time, I held back a little; Mark probably didn't even notice. But I wanted him to give a last push before our lips came into contact, so in the future I could blame him for everything that would end up happening with us. Something like, *You started it!*

I'd planted the snitch that recorded this conversation just a few minutes before, when Mark went out on deck to rescue a bottle of white wine he had tied to a rope, to chill in the sea, which was now at forty-two degrees. *The perfect temperature*, he said.

I would have liked the first time to have been less lovely or for the conversation that got us there to have been less meaningful, less emotional. Not that the situation was idyllic. The boat moored in the marina, in a cabin bedroom, during office hours, with the curtains closed, in daylight, with Ruby and Pony conveniently asleep in the main cabin. But looking back, I think I would have preferred to take him up on that mistimed invitation he sent me at the wedding. I think I would have felt less dirty.

Before I went to the boat, I already knew what would happen. That's why I tried to arm myself with reasons that would justify it. Hiding behind the idea that it was part of my research. Perks of the job. A necessary step to create a tie and bring Mark under my power. Sex as a strategic bargaining chip. Desire, need, power, chemistry, seduction. *That's not a justification, Alice, it's a reality. You're going to plant a snitch. You need information. Although you've never done anything remotely similar, you're changing. You're going somewhere else. You're learning things you need to learn, learning to know yourself outside yourself. And for that, you have to find Chris first. That is the end, Alice, and what you're going to do is just one of the means.*

Without a doubt, what I liked best about that first time was that he fell asleep after his orgasm. A moment of intimacy unrelated to seduction. Of comfort and closeness. But besides planting a snitch, I had gone to take advantage of any negligence on his part and snoop around in his suitcase, look over his agenda, get inside his laptop and try to find the dates for his trips to New York to compare them with Chris's trips to the island. I got up, trying not to wake him. He was hugging me from behind. The same way we had reached orgasm. Without looking into each other's faces. Maybe from shame. And that's how we'd stayed, spooning but not too close, not completely embracing. I softly pulled away the hand he had wrapped around my waist, put on my panties, and went into the main cabin, heading straight for the desk, but when I saw Ruby and Pony still asleep, reality hit me in the face. Regret. I felt obscene and muddled walking nearly naked through the cabin. So much so that I decided to abort the mission. *Or maybe you want to screw again and you're looking for an excuse.* I wanted to get out of there immediately and shower. It was twelve in the afternoon. Night would have softened it all. In the light of day, it was too cruel to digest.

Mark peeked out, in his underwear and T-shirt, looking as regretful as I was, or more. Especially because, for the first time since I'd met him, I saw him vulnerable. I saw the boy as well as the man, clever and dumb, smug and sensitive. All together. I felt that in that very instant, I could ask him anything and he would respond to me sincerely without hesitation. I felt I wanted to go back to bed with him, because I hadn't really done it. I had done something else that seemed the same but wasn't. Something that has to do with what you want the other person to feel, but not your own desire.

"Sorry, it's just that between the sex and the wine . . ." he said to justify his postorgasmic nap.

Don't worry, it's typical male behavior. Almost like being unfaithful to your wife. So much anger. Toward him, toward Chris—for imagining him in a similar situation—or toward myself?

"No worries," was all I said.

Ruby started to moan because she sensed I wanted to get out of there without saying another word. Thanks, my little one.

SETTING OUT THE snitches had thrown me off track. Rather than give me the chance to listen, it had made me deaf. An explosion of noise that had caused an intense ringing in my ears that covered up everything else. I had opened up an infinity of roads that led me away from what was concrete. The only concrete thing I had at the moment was the paper envelope with Stephen's DNA sample.

I opened the browser and typed into Google: *Paternity test Massachusetts.* There were 780,000 results in .48 seconds. Once again, I clicked on the first one that wasn't sponsored. They promised various sorts of kits for a price of around $400. After taking a look, I saw one of the sidebars: "Solutions for Deceased or Missing Persons." I clicked on the link. Another tab showed the different options for finding out if two people had some degree of blood relation, giving the different locations of labs that did analysis. *Find the one that's closest to you.*

Though there was a DNA lab in Hyannis, I decided as a precaution to choose one farther away, in Mashpee, which was also close to the psychologist's office, so that I could go over while Oli was in therapy.

It was very discreet. A sign read: "Clinical Analysis Laboratory." Nothing obvious that might scare away clients looking for privacy. Even so, before I entered, I felt jittery, as if inside the lab I'd face the FBI, a SWAT team and social services ready to take away my daughters. But no, there was only a very kind nurse, who must have seen the distress on my face and sensed that I wanted to get it all over with as soon as possible.

After filling out the form, I turned in the two samples I had with me: Stephen's and Chris's. I had been digging around in his boxes of clothes, looking for a hair, not just any hair, because it was essential that the root was still attached—so I had read. Chris's hair was short and blond, impossible to mistake, and I looked desperately with a magnifying glass through all the hats and sports clothing of his that I still had. Nothing. Until I found a piece of gum stuck to one of his pairs of tennis shorts. *The bitter taste of defeat*, Chris used to say. *But it's not a manner of speaking; it's the damn truth. When I'm losing, I start to taste something stale in my mouth. I hate it. Once, during a game, I was down one set and I was losing the second. There was a kid chewing gum in the audience, so I asked him for a piece, and he gave me a stick of hot cinnamon gum. I hated that flavor, but I would have drunk gasoline before going on with that nasty taste in my mouth. And what happened? I ended up flipping the scoreboard, and, since then, I've been addicted to hot cinnamon gum. Obviously, it doesn't always work; otherwise, I would have been number one in the world. But it's gotten me out of a bind more than once.* And now that chewed-up, dry gum was on top of the counter in the laboratory, in a self-sealing bag. The receptionist looked at it unsettled.

"Let me get this straight, you want to know if the swab is the father of the gum." She laughed. "Sorry, I can't help it."

I couldn't help laughing either.

"It requires a special treatment. We have to send it to CSI, but in Las Vegas; they're much better than the ones in Miami and New York, which I don't trust," she added, smiling.

Then she told me there wouldn't be a problem with the saliva sample, but that the gum was another story. Much more expensive and the accuracy percentages much less trustworthy.

"Because, look, I understand that if you've brought me the gum, it's because there's no possible way to get something more solid for the test. But"—she paused—"if you want to know if the gum is the child, there's something much easier. Does the gum have sons or daughters? Because you can always do a paternity test between a grandparent and grandchild. And if it comes out positive, that's an obvious tie between the gum and the saliva sample. So the question is, without being nosy"—she paused—"does the gum have a son or daughter we can get a saliva sample from?"

Ruby laughed. I didn't. I was about to say no, that the gum didn't have daughters—and certainly not one that was in my baby carrier—to sidestep the humiliation. But no, I succumbed to the evidence and she took a saliva sample from Ruby. One more anecdote she could tell another customer.

The results would take between three and four weeks, and would arrive confidentially by messenger.

———

We'd been living on Robin Island almost four months, and I had more or less kept my mother at bay, trying to make her understand that they couldn't come to visit every weekend. At least, not at first. That I needed to have the feeling of starting from scratch. Independence. Of course, none of that even entered my mother's mind. So when we got to Providence on Christmas Eve and I set foot in the front yard, which she'd decorated spectacularly with a Santa Claus in his sleigh weighed down with presents and pulled by reindeer climbing up the façade, I had to endure the outburst of reproaches while Olivia counted the reindeer three times (*Yes, Oli, it's nine, same as always*).

"It's just, honey, I don't understand," my mother told me later. "Well, not just me, not anybody." She raised her voice. "George, you don't understand either, do you?! Out there, alone in the middle of nowhere . . . What have we done to you? I feel terrible, as if the tragedy were my fault. As if we were bothering you . . . I don't know, you running off like that . . . I didn't say anything at the time or at Thanksgiving because I respect your loss and your pain. But it's been forever since you left. And you're still all closed in on yourself, and I'm getting more and more worried. I can't even sleep at night." She raised her voice again. "I can't even sleep, can I, George?! We've suffered from the loss as well. He was like a son to us. Wasn't he, George?! We've cried since we lost him, we still do, and we pray for him and even more for you, of course. Because I don't want to lose you, too, honey. In moments like this, you have to lean on your loved ones. Now are we or aren't we? Your loved ones, I mean. Because sometimes you make me doubt it. And what is this about you taking back your maiden name?"

"It's not my maiden name, Mother, it's our family name."

"I don't understand why. It's going to look like you're rejecting your dead husband's last name."

"To whom?"

"To people, the family, Chris's family, all the people who are coming here for dinner tonight."

"And you, is it going to look like that to you, Mother?"

"Well, a little, yes, honey. What's the point in lying to you? A little, yes." I looked at my father, who was setting up a second table where the children would sit. She looked at him: "And you're not going to say anything? I'm tired of always playing the bad guy. Both of us agreed to try and convince her this was madness and she needed to come back home. And you just stand there like a nitwit . . ."

My father stopped what he was doing and gave her a serious look. Nothing aggressive, simply formal, reverent, like a literature professor before starting to talk about Shakespeare.

"Marie."

"Yes, that's my name. I thought you had forgotten it because you never talk to me."

He walked over to her.

"I love you, Marie. I really do."

He kissed her on the forehead, then turned around and went back to his work. My mother got flustered and was taken completely off guard.

"See? That's why I forgive everything. That's why I've been in love with him for almost fifty years now. You scoundrel, you dirty scoundrel."

"So that's all it takes to disarm you?"

I walked over to my mother, imitating my father. I kissed her on the cheek.

"Mom, I love you a lot too."

"No, it's not going to work for you . . ." but before she finished the phrase, tears were streaming down her cheeks. "OK, fine, it's working. You see how little it takes? Scoundrels, that's what the two of you are."

I went out for a run to clear my head after my mother's harangue and change the memory card in the Bushnell Trophy Cam I had camouflaged in the cemetery. There were 9,792 new photos in a little over four months. I had something to occupy me while I was there.

I thought I'd gotten over my aversion to receiving sincere and deeply felt condolences from my family. But when I saw a van arrive from my bedroom window with my grandmother Brigitte, my uncle and aunt, my three cousins and their four children, I realized that no, I wasn't yet ready to receive their effusive gestures of affection and worry. Christmas and being in Providence made the absence of Chris even more ominous.

Before going down for dinner, I stilled my urge to go back to Robin Island by poring through the first of the photos from the camera in the cemetery—without obtaining any results—while I listened, for the fourth time, to the conversation Mark and Julia had had earlier in the day, at noon. I knew it almost by heart.

JULIA: What are you doing?! What are you doing?!

Julia slams the laptop closed in one violent go.

MARK: I was curious. You say you're not writing, but I hear you typing every night.

JULIA: Typing isn't writing. Typing is something anyone can do. Writing, no. And if you're curious, ask.

MARK: Would it have mattered?

Silence.

MARK: I only read a little bit, but I really liked what you wrote, sorry, typed.

Silence.

MARK: It was hard to read, it moved me, but that's exactly why it's good.

Silence.

MARK: I really liked that you called the protagonists Paul and Samantha.

JULIA: You've never disrespected me this way before.

MARK: Remember the thing I told you when we met, when you came to the office for an emergency? I said to you: Why are we always set on being with the wrong person?

Silence.

MARK: You also told me that day you didn't like for people to hurt you, and I told you I didn't like to hurt people either or for them to hurt me. But now, I'm not so sure we're not hurting one another. Maybe I'm not your Paul. And you're not my Samantha.

Silence.

MARK: It's shocking how you've turned the tables. It makes me the responsible one for this goddamn situation... You want me to leave? You want us to separate? Tell me what you want to do. Anything but this, because it's unbearable. It has been going on too long...

Silence.

MARK: At least put on a different face. Just for tonight. Until your parents leave, so they don't pelt you with questions. We'll just pretend we're a normal, stable couple. One night. OK?

Silence.

JULIA: OK.

The argument sounded far away. It had taken place in Julia's office, and the snitch had picked it up from the bedroom. A snitch that I thought didn't work because it never captured any voices, only occasional noises. Until I realized that they didn't share a bedroom. Julia slept every night on the sofa in her office, after typing for two or three hours with barely a rest. More than writing, it seemed she was running away. That was what Mark had told me.

Going to Providence a few days after sleeping with Mark helped deactivate the possibility of another encounter, convincing me it had been a one-time thing that would never happen again. The physical distance would make us realize how dangerous and improper it had been. I didn't want to be a married man's lover. Well, I could tolerate that, so long as I told myself it was a sacrifice for the cause. But what was inconceivable to me was falling in love with a married man. I wasn't going to allow it.

Still, however much I tried to cover it up, it was impossible for me to get him out of my mind.

Olivia came into my bedroom looking pallid and upset, holding on to Big Smelly Bear.

"Mommy . . ."

Pony crawled under the bed, begging forgiveness for existing.

"What is it, Oli?"

"I feel really dizzy. Is the earth moving?"

I crouched down, set her on my lap, and put my cheek on her forehead. She was quite hot.

"The earth is always moving, honey."

"Yeah, but more."

"No, it always moves the same."

"No, it moves more here than on the island."

I laid her down on my bed and stretched out beside her. I could have stayed there that way all night.

"Did you say hi to your cousins?"

"Yeah. There's four of them."

"Why do you like to count everything?"

"Because numbers never get lost."

"What do you mean, they don't get lost? What are you talking about?"

"I give things numbers so they don't go away."

"Where would they go?"

"I don't know, somewhere else. If you put a number on them, they stay."

"You count people, too?"

"Sure. Everyone's got a number."

"And me? What number am I?"

"You?" *Say I'm one, honey, please, I'm begging you.* "You're number four, Mommy."

"What do you mean, four?!"

"Yeah, because when I was born, I saw the doctor first, then the two nurses, then Daddy, then you."

"You started counting as soon as you were born?"

"No, silly, you showed me the video of the birth a little while ago, remember?"

"Oh, yeah, that's right . . . But then I should be number five. Doctor, two nurses, Daddy, and me. I'm the fifth."

"No, because Daddy's not here anymore. I didn't count him in time, and he ended up without a number."

When I was about to try and explain to her the importance of giving her father a number and say that his number should probably be one, she vomited in the bed. I took her to the bathroom so she could get the rest out, and while I held her head, my hand on her forehead, I thought I was doing the same thing as her. I had counted almost everything from the day Chris died, but I hadn't given him a number either. In my list of suspects, he should have been number one.

Before going down for dinner, after I finally got Olivia to sleep in the bed, after changing the comforter, I thought that I was wrong, that it wasn't a question of giving Chris a number—not for her and not for me—it was a question of no longer numbering things.

————

There were bunk beds in my childhood bedroom, for when some friend came to spend the night, though I always thought they were for my little brother, who never came. I longed for a little brother with all my might, and I wanted a brother, if possible, instead of a sister. That was something that played a key part in Ruby's conception. I had always missed not having someone else in my home. Someone to teach—maybe that's why I ended up being a teacher—to share secrets with, toys, fights and small everyday adventures. I never understood why, with my mother being a traditional housewife, we weren't a big brood like in *The Sound of Music*. When I was a girl, and I asked constantly why I didn't have a little brother, my mother would smile at me and tell me it was because I had come out so perfect that there was no reason to keep trying. As an adult, I figured it had something to do with premature menopause, because when my period came when I was eleven, my mother didn't have any pads in the house. It didn't seem strange to me at the time, but it did as the months and years passed and I went on being the only one who used pads or tampons.

That *You came out perfect* got stuck, or better said, nailed, in my mind. I suppose that all my life I've been trying to be at the top, to be doubly good. To be worth two children. Now that girl with the impossible task of touching perfection twice over was committing a crime while lying in her bed surrounded by her daughters and her dog, all of them asleep. She was listening on her phone, with the headphones on, to another conversation between Mark and Julia.

JULIA: Here. Read.

Noise of paper shuffling. Pause.

MARK: Are you sure?

JULIA: No.

MARK: I'm really sorry about what I did.

JULIA: I'm not. The mere fact that you took the time to figure out the password to my laptop makes me happy now.

MARK: Your birthday. July 9, 1979. Too easy. You should change it to something a little more elaborate. Less obvious. For example, instead of 7979, you could put the year first: 7979.

Laughter.

JULIA: Where have you been?

MARK: What about you?

JULIA: You really liked what you read?

MARK: A lot.

Pause.

JULIA: Can we go on faking a little longer?

MARK: What?

JULIA: That we're a reasonably happy and stable couple.

MARK: Now that everyone's gone, there's no need to.

JULIA: Yeah, there is a need.

Pause. Kissing.

Bodies falling into bed.

Moaning and panting.

I felt something between pride and disgust. Pride at being partly re-sponsible for that truce. Disgust for having done what I had done, and for being jealous. In that instant, I decided I would never sleep with Mark again. That was the first of many times I made that promise.

———

I knew I was going to find my father in the living room, in his easy chair, sitting next to the drink cart in silence, alone, holding a thick glass with two fingers of whiskey neat. It was his time. Silence was probably one of the things he enjoyed the most. Sometimes when I was a girl and I would wake up from a nightmare, I would get out of bed, go down-stairs, see my father sitting there beneath the tenuous light of the old floor lamp, his back to me, observing the darkness through the window without moving, and that was enough to calm me down and make me feel that everything was in its place, and I could go back to bed without exchanging a word with him. But that night, I needed a little more.

I sat on the sofa, curled up and covered myself with a patchwork wool blanket my mother had crocheted.

"Here." My father passed me the glass of whiskey, like a doctor pre-scribing a medication, and you don't ask what it is, you just take it, no questions asked. "I haven't drunk from it yet."

My father liked to feel he was in control, that he wasn't giving in to anxiety or necessity. That he could have something as irresistible as that eighteen-year malt whiskey in front of him and be able to resist it. He was the most patient person I'd ever known. If not, he probably wouldn't have been able to put up with my mother, who was a powder keg. Or for that reason precisely, in order to tolerate her, he needed to become a Zen master.

I waited for him to serve himself another glass. Then I toasted the air and I drank.

"You're really distant, honey."

"I'm not distant; I'm reserved. Like you."

"That's what I usually say so they'll leave me alone when in reality I'm being distant. Like you . . . Remember when Jack the dog died?"

"Not too well, I was really small. How old was I, four?"

"That's right. You were sad for many days. You didn't even want to play with Jill because you were scared the same thing would happen to her."

"Yeah, that rings a bell."

"You know how you got over it?"

I shook my head.

"Painting. I gave you your first set of watercolors. You learned to use them without us really even telling you anything. You know what the first thing you painted was?"

"A portrait of Jack," I remembered immediately. I started laughing. "Just a second, Dad: Are you comparing Chris to a dog? Are you asking me to give Olivia some watercolors so she can paint a portrait of her father?"

I said it without any malevolence, but my father didn't seem to like me making light of the situation. In part because he always chose meticulously when to intervene in my issues.

"I'm not comparing Chris to Jack. I'm not saying Olivia needs watercolors. All I'm trying to tell you is that I think Olivia needs something that inspires her as much as painting did you. And that probably it's something simple, something within arm's reach. Give it to her, the way I gave you the watercolors."

Then he took his first sip of whiskey and smiled at me, noticing my silent tears.

ON THE WAY back to Robin Island, my head still pounding with the litany of reproaches from my mother about what she had considered far too short a visit resounding in my ears, I made a stop at Night Eyes, the spy shop. I left Olivia in the car with the iPad Santa Claus had brought her, relieving me of the promise I'd made.

"Hey, favorite blonde! What bring you here?" Antonio's effusiveness and quirky English were comforting despite the place's ambience of secrecy and espionage.

Almost a month had passed since I had hid the snitches. The good news: not even a single slip-up that could expose me. The bad news: I hadn't made it far in my investigations. I always had the slight feeling that the snitches were really just little soldiers sent out to be sacrificed for the sake of their older brothers. The ones who disembark first, rush to the front lines, and do the dirty work. Of course, one of them could find glory and carry out his mission with honors, sure, but the majority were only good for cannon fodder and making a sweep of the terrain. The snitches were my way of gaining confidence, of showing myself that I could get into people's houses with something small, easy to place, and impossible to find. Because I knew very clearly what my real objective was. It wasn't just listening. It was listening and seeing. Spy cameras.

"Hi, Antonio. I need to see."

"I know. You completely blind because you no see my beauty."

"Cameras, Antonio. I want cameras."

"Ah, power of images. Impossible make comparison."

Ruby started complaining, not too much, just enough to remind me it was time to breastfeed her.

"Grumpy baby," Antonio said. "Like mother, like daughter."

"She's hungry. Just a minute now, babe." I calmed Ruby down,

cradling her in my arms, while I went on with my business. "I'm looking for a miniature camera, pinhole lens, wireless, with an internal battery, motion sensor and streaming signal retransmission, with a range
of more than a mile."

"Well, well, well . . . I see you done homework, Blondie . . ."

"Have good teacher," I said, imitating his delivery.

"Hope I learn English as fast as you learn spy."

When Ruby realized that her mother wasn't going to satisfy her desires, she raised the volume of her complaints. I had on a T-shirt for lactating mothers, with a horizontal slit that opened up to nurse discreetly,
so in a matter of seconds Ruby was feeding. Although it was impossible
for Antonio to see anything, his fantasy took over.

"Third date and you already show tit. Maybe a little fast, Blondie . . ."
he said, his eyes fixed on a breast he couldn't see.

I laughed.

"The camera, Antonio . . ."

"Ah, of course, Blondie. How long you want batteries last?"

"Uh, well . . . forever?"

"Same as me with this moment . . ."

*Antonio no longer asked what I wanted things for or cracked jokes about
it. He had learned not to pull too hard on the thread of our trust. He asked
me basic questions I had answers for. I had spent a long time on the internet
looking at different types of cameras, but I also wanted someone to consult
with, to perfect my plan. Interior or exterior? Interior. Distance between
the camera and signal receiver? Three miles, minimum. Open space or with
walls in between? Walls. With sound? Yes. Lighting conditions? All types,
something adaptable. Price? Not a worry.*

Of all the models he took out, the most appealing one—which
had already been on my list of favorites—was an IP mini-camera with
a pinhole lens. Ninety-degree vision angle, CMOS sensor and a resolution of 626 × 582 pixels. It was motion activated and could be on
standby up to a year with a 3.7-volt lithium battery. It also had a night
vision mode. It was so small, it could be hidden inside anything, which
was fundamental to my purposes. It had an integrated microcomputer
that connected to the internet through a fixed IP address, and it could

offer real-time displays or record what was happening even if you were thousands of miles away. Price: $599. For the moment, I only wanted one. *One camera never enough. Cameras like eyes. Need two to look better at things.* So I bought two. My Christmas gift to myself.

––––––

As soon as we got off the ferry and had passed the totem pole, Olivia got her color back and smiled. I took that as a good sign, that she had missed her home, her things and Oliver, always Oliver. Maybe she had gotten sick in Providence because everything there reminded her of her father. Now I just had to get her to quit counting every damn thing in the universe.

Before we went home, we had lunch with Miriam at Le Café. *I missed you, neighbor*, she said to me. *Missed you too*, I said to her, and it made me feel good to actually mean it. Once I'd made sure she wasn't going to leave me hanging at the dinner party for Karen's forty-fifth birthday, just for a few friends and her brother, Keith—another setup, in other words—I stopped in at Dan DeRoller's hardware store to pick up an order I'd made over the phone: slats for picture frames, twenty-three by fifteen inches, and a ten-by-thirty-foot roll of raw canvas—a little thicker than the type I like to use—and two cans of acrylic paint to prime it. I like to build the frames and stretch my own canvasses. It's a ritual that precedes the act of painting, maybe to help dispel the fear of the void that comes from staring at a blank canvas. In fact, I primed them with three or four layers of light gray. White put me off, blinding me and blocking my ideas.

I wasn't going to do a painting. Well, I was, but then the painting was going to become a decorative clock. Earlier, on the internet—this was one thing I could get that way—I had bought all the parts necessary to make a wall clock: a noiseless quartz pendulum mechanism; an hour, minute and second hand; and roman numerals.

I had taken a number of photos of the façade of Karen's Petite Maison, which was a Second Empire Victorian. It looked a lot like *House by the Railroad*, the Edward Hopper painting that was said to be the inspiration for Norman Bates's house in *Psycho*. So, given the resemblance to the Hopper, I decided to paint the house, in imitation of the great master.

My objective was to create a painting-clock to give to Karen as a substitute for her grandfather's antique cuckoo clock, the one I had accidentally destroyed. A birthday present with a surprise inside. The camera I had just bought would be hidden inside, capturing her office from a small hole near the number twelve.

The painting ended up much better than I'd imagined. I suppose that since it was made-to-order, in an imitation of someone else's style, and it had to be done quickly, the pressure had inspired me. In just a few days, I did what was probably one of the best paintings I had ever done in my life. Now I had to poke holes in it to arrange the clock mechanism and stick the numbers into the canvas with the help of Olivia, who made no bones about criticizing the chaos of the Roman numeral system.

I left the most delicate part, the most important part, for the end: inserting the camera. But that was fairly easy too. Once it was stuck with Loctite and duct tape to the back of the canvas—to protect it from potential clawing by Dingleberry—I looked at the picture very closely, at the little hole the camera peeked out of, to be sure it was barely perceptible. There was nothing left but to seal the picture from behind to safeguard my trap. I took extreme measures. I made a reinforced wooden frame—no plywood here—with a hole in the middle to be able to manipulate the clock mechanism, set the hour, change the battery, but without a chink where you could make out or reach the camera. I screwed the top onto the frame and placed a metal slat over it so the screws would be out of reach of any screwdriver. I shook it energetically like a drunk who's lost her judgment—like Karen, in other words. Perfect. Everything was in place. Now I just needed to find mine. That was going to be more complicated.

———

"Well, my goodness, how amazing, Alice!" Karen said enthusiastically when I handed her the present. "What an artist you are! It looks like that painter who paints those depressed people."

"Hopper," I said.

"That one!"

"Well, I wanted . . ."

"I love it. I'm going to have to sign up for one of your classes."

"Well, it's not as special or valuable as your grandfather's clock, but I wanted to do something for you . . ."

"What are you saying, I like this one much better. This is exclusive; it's mine. Come on, help me hang it up."

At first the image looked pixelated and jumpy. I cursed all the money and especially the effort I'd put in, which added to the perennial feeling since I'd moved to the island that I was being an idiot and that everything was going to turn out badly, regardless of what path I took. But the distortion lasted only for a moment, as if the camera was reawakening after a long period of inaction; then the image resolution was clear and fluid. The fact that the islanders had agreed not to erect any cell phone towers—despite the bad coverage that guaranteed—meant that the signal was clear and potent, without interference. Kudos to the local government and their commitment to preserving public health and the environment.

Karen looks directly at the camera, at the clock, while she makes sure it's securely attached to the wall behind the desk. A few steps back and a broad smile. Me behind her.

KAREN: Beautiful, just fantastic. (*Her face changes, she turns to me.*) But wait a second... This isn't some kind of trick?

ME: Trick, why? I don't know what you're talking about.

KAREN: Why'd you bring it to me now?

ME: Well, it is your birthday. It's your present.

KAREN: So why didn't you wait to bring it to me the night of the dinner?

ME: I don't know, just...

KAREN: Don't tell me you're not coming to dinner. Is that why you're here now? Is this some kind of trick to weasel out of it?

ME: No, I just didn't feel like giving it to you in front of everybody, what if you didn't like it... So I thought that...

KAREN: Don't give me the run around. Are you coming or not?

ME: Obviously I'm coming. (*That's part of my plan. I have to be there.*) I wouldn't miss it for anything in the world.

The office was empty and the camera was on standby. It came on a few hours later, when Karen was vacuuming. Then when Dingleberry got on the table to nose around and finally fell asleep next to a document tray. Minutes later, Karen came in with a glass of wine in her hand to answer the phone.

KAREN (*Picks up.*): Karen's Petite Maison, how can I help you...? Of course, tell me what date you had in mind... Valentine's Day? Good choice, let me look...

Karen moves the mouse and the screen turns on. She types three numbers on the keyboard.

Pause. Rewind. Zoom in 200 percent. Play. Three numbers: 128. Pause. Rewind. Play. No, it was 108. Pause. Rewind. Play. Yes, it was 108. That was obvious, because Karen's inn was at 108 West Neck Road. *Blessed eyes, how I've missed you.*

––––––

"Girls, what do you think of Alice's gift?! Isn't it the best?! Watch out, now, with this present, Alice is now at the head of the race for Keith . . ."

Karen was completely looped. *Forty-five, girls! What a bitch! Forty-five sounds too serious, doesn't it?* That, and the absence of John, who had gone to the Groton naval base in Connecticut a few days before, gave her free rein to cut loose with her own particular spectacle: something between a nightclub standup comic and someone hawking self-inflating mattresses on a shopping network.

Luckily, apart from Keith, she had also invited Miriam, Jennifer and Barbara, whom I'd barely had contact with. Now I had the chance to get to know her better, and I didn't have to deal with Karen's harassment on my own.

"Hey, so this dinner is secret, it stays between us; otherwise, everyone else will find out and get their panties in a wad. But I said to myself, I want this dinner to be intimate with my brother, Keith. Fun with single girls. And you all are the cream of the single-women crop on this island. Well, sorry, Jennifer, you're not there yet, but you know, no reason not to start playing the field, know what I mean?"

I saw the remorse on Jennifer's face at having accepted the invitation. We all had a similar expression on our faces, even Keith—although he always did a little bit. I had insisted that Jennifer come, because she seemed to really have her hands full with the Summer situation. Their constant arguments and reconciliations were exhausting; they razed everything in their path. I figured it would be good for her to get out of that oppressive atmosphere. Plus, with alcohol flowing freely, who knew if she might let her hair down and spill her guts. Her or any of the rest of them.

"I'm not single either, Karen," said Barbara, who looked the least uncomfortable of anyone there. "Jeffrey and I are still together."

"Well, that's not what I've heard. A little bird told me that they've been seeing your pilot in and around the island with a girl from Martha's Vineyard. A sugar mama. He's no fool, your boy."

Barbara turned red as a tomato. She'd been busted.

"OK, so we're taking a little bit of time for ourselves, that's all." She wanted to dodge the issue.

Why are they taking some time for themselves? I wondered. *How long has that been going on?* A burst of pettiness rattled my body. How little I knew. Everything was still completely out of my reach . . .

"Yeah, sure, 'taking a little time for ourselves.' That's what they always say. That's one of those euphemisms or whatever they're called." Karen's mind was getting cloudy, and she was starting to slur. "You need another man that can make you fly higher than Jeffrey with his air taxi. Keith doesn't just have a yacht; he's got a helicopter. Did you know that?"

This was like an episode of *The Bachelor*, with the four of us as contestants. Number one: Miriam McCarthy, from the real estate agency, recently separated, with a precious daughter, Chloe. Contestant number two: Jennifer Fay, with a husband in a vegetative state and an unruly niece pregnant by God knows whom. Contestant number three: Barbara Rush, from Horse Rush Farms, a beautiful veterinarian with sky blue cat eyes, almost single, looking for another pilot who can make her fly high. And, last but not least, Alice Dupont, artist, widow, with two daughters, Olivia and Ruby. There they are: a blonde, a brunette, one with black hair and a redhead. Which one will our golden bachelor Keith Zarpentine choose?

Keith, without John there, was more relaxed and a more active participant. Plus, Karen hogging the conversation meant that there was less time for her to play cupid with her poisoned darts, and we were all thankful for that.

"Three siblings. Karen, Katherine and Keith. KKK. What kind of parents do that? What kind of subliminal message are they trying to send to the rest of the world? KKK."

Keith laughed. "Well, the truth is, our father, may he rest in peace, was always a little racist." And he added, as if it were an unconfessable secret, "He was in the Tea Party."

"Don't talk nonsense, being in the Tea Party doesn't mean you're racist," Karen interrupted.

"No, you're right, it means being a goddamned intolerant conservative."

It was the first time I'd heard Keith curse. He clearly had unresolved issues with his father.

"So, what, you're a Democrat now? You can't be that filthy rich and be a Democrat; it's incompatible. I'm sorry, little brother. So choose. Filthy rich or Democrat? Miriam, Jennifer, Alice or Barbara? But then, with all the bedrooms you have in that castle of yours, you could put them all up. Maybe you should convert to Mormonism . . ."

Karen's laughter. Silence.

"I think we need more wine . . ." I said, getting up and taking the empty bottle. "The rest of us, anyway . . ."

"Right, let the wine flow, the elixir of truth. A bunch of wet blankets, that's what you all are . . ."

I had decided not to do it during dinner. That was pushing my luck too far. Too unpredictable. Too many people and too many variables, and with Karen bubbling over like a volcano, something unpredictable was likely to happen. So when I went to the kitchen. I passed by the office without stopping. Better to do it another time, another day. A visit to Karen's—maybe while she was out shopping or at the liquor store, since she spent a good bit of time there choosing the finest vintages— and then I'd take advantage of her absence to bring the operation to fruition. But I was possessed, intrepid, on a roll and half-drunk. So on my way back, with the bottle already open, I went into the office. The voices were still audible but muffled.

"One thing, Jenny," Karen asked. "Was your niece's pregnancy something she wanted or was it more of an, oops, surprise . . . ?"

"I think it would be best if you asked her."

I woke the computer up. Karen kept pushing.

"Are you going to tell us who the father is? Here she is, all summer, going from house to house. So pretty, so ripe, so nice. It's inevitable that people talk and all kind of rumors start spreading."

"Started by you, in the majority of cases." That was Miriam.

I went to the inn's main menu and I clicked on *Reservations*. It asked me for the password. 108. In. Ha.

"Your niece is an adult . . ." Keith said.

"Yeah, exactly eighteen years old . . ."

"Right, so she's old enough to do as she likes and make her own decisions."

"Oh really, little brother? Should I have invited her to dinner too?"

I went to the reservation history and removed my phone from my jacket pocket. Instead of taking pictures, I decided to take a video of the screen while I scrolled down with the mouse, going through the reservations for the past three years. I didn't look at the names; I could do that later at home. When I wouldn't have to fake it if I found anything.

"If I had her living in my house," Karen was saying just then, "at least I'd want to know who the father was."

"It's her life and that deserves respect," Jennifer responded. "And anyway, who's to say I don't know who the father is?"

"Ah! That's what I like to hear. Now you're getting hot under the collar. You do know who it is, then."

I put the computer to sleep and walked out. Dingleberry didn't move an inch, sleeping there in the document tray. It was the first time I had been in Karen's office alone without incident.

"So what's your deal, you went to pick the grapes yourself?" Karen blurted as soon as I walked in.

"No, I was about to go. Karen, it's your forty-fifth birthday, and as you said, it's a complicated age. We know it's going to be hard for you to cross that line, but you should let us cross it with you, don't throw us overboard. We love you, and we really appreciate you. So please, let us sing 'Happy Birthday' now, and we'll enjoy this marvelous chocolate cake you've made."

I said it with a sober, superior air completely unusual for me. Undoubtedly, I was still high from my recent victory. Karen, who wasn't accustomed to anyone stopping her in her tracks—we just put up with her, and that was that—started crying like a little girl, half-embarrassed and half-moved by my words. She asked us all to forgive her and then began flattering us, saying how lonely she felt almost all the time. She said she'd never say those kind of rude things again and would stop being a nasty little gossip. We sang "Happy Birthday," she blew out the candles, we opened a bottle of champagne, and for the first time since I was on the island, I felt comfortable surrounded by a group of people.

———

I downloaded the cell phone video onto the laptop in the attic. While I looked through the reservations, I listened to a conversation between Summer and Jennifer.

SUMMER: Where's my stash?

JENNIFER: You said you weren't going to smoke anymore.

SUMMER: Yeah, but it's mine, give it back!

JENNIFER: Don't shout, please.

SUMMER: Why not? Maybe it'll wake him up. Wake up, Uncle Stephen!

JENNIFER: Summer, we're getting along now; don't spoil it, please.

SUMMER: Then give me back the weed.

Sound of a chair scraping. Jennifer has gotten up.

JENNIFER: Have you been drinking?

SUMMER (*laughs*): It's the holidays, you gotta celebrate… Plus, there's a study in Denmark of more than sixty-three thousand pregnant women that shows that it doesn't affect the fetus. I saw it on the internet.

Summer laughs more. Jennifer slaps her.

And then I saw it.

March 8, 2013. Chris Williams.
One night. Room 202. Comped.

I paused the video. I lost my sense of time. I might well have spent more than an hour without moving, looking at what I'd found. Just one day. He'd spent one day at the inn. Never before, never again.

Comped? They had invited him there. Was it John who invited him? Or did he run into him by chance when he was on the island? Why didn't Chris tell me? Why had he never talked to me about John? What reason would he have for not doing so? Room 202? That was the suite, the room on the second floor. The biggest one. With a Jacuzzi, the works, Karen had said. Had he gone alone or with someone?

Just like Olivia, I had to take refuge in numbers to escape my state of shock.

March 8, 2013. Fifteen days after my thirty-first birthday, which we had celebrated with a romantic night at the Chandler at Cliff Walk, a hotel in Newport, built on a cliff with spectacular views. Did I notice anything strange? No.

March 8, 2013. Presumably his first time on the island. Chris died on May 13, 2015. Two years and sixty-six days, 797 days later. Had he been coming and going to the island since that day?

THE YEAR WAS finally ending. At last. I wanted to declare it the worst one of my life, as if that way I could say that box had been checked off and another one couldn't come along and push it aside. But it was also the year Ruby was born. I couldn't put a stigma like that on my daughter. I couldn't let that thought take up space in my mind and through some treasonous lapse be conveyed to my daughter.

The important thing was to finish the year well and start the new one even better. With my daughters, with our new life. Something intimate. Generate a current that could channel things into their proper place. I woke up excited. It was a beautiful gray day, silver really, not too cold, as the days before had been. Perfect for taking a bike ride to the promenade along the beach. The Williamses had given us a tandem tricycle, something stable for taking along the girls. *I'm going up front, Mommy, that way we can race and I'll always win*, Olivia said when we tried it for the first time. But now she didn't seem at all enthused about getting on it.

"I don't want to go to the beach," Olivia said. She didn't like the sand either. Impossible to quantify. "I've got plans with Oliver."

"What do you mean, you've got plans with Oliver?"

"He told me to come to his house to play. I'm talking with him over FaceTime."

She showed me the boy on her tablet, and he turned red when he saw my face appear on his screen.

"Oli, you can't bother people on New Year's Eve."

"His mom said it was OK," she said to me, and then to Oliver, "Didn't she?"

Julia, appearing quickly behind Oliver, made a gesture that combined consent and resignation. A comical wink I'd never seen her make before.

"See? She said yes!" Olivia celebrated.

My cell rang. New message. From Mark. The father apparently says yes too. He's going to be at *The Office*.

No, that wasn't the plan. I wasn't ending the year like that.

Second message from Mark:

Come see me.

No. I was going to end the year doing something productive. Third message from Mark:

That way we can end the year doing something productive.

Those messages made me feel rejection and joy in equal amounts. I rejected him and I wanted him. *Who do you think you are to play with me like that?* Since I'd come back from Providence, we had neither seen nor written each other. Meanwhile, I continued to witness how what had begun as a matter of decorum in front of the family on Christmas Eve had turned into a real reconciliation. Once again Julia was joyful and enjoyable. She let him read what she wrote, and he loved it. They slept together. And even—this was almost the most important thing of all—they had started laughing together again. I was still going back and forth between relief, which little by little erased the guilt that clung to me, a certain pride as I felt partially responsible for their reconciliation and, of course, a bit of envy and jealousy. But I told myself it wasn't for Mark; it was because I missed the kind of companionship being part of a couple brought with it. Anyway, I had considered the story over, until I received his three messages at ten in the morning on December 31. Everything was much uglier than a hot-and-bothered message in the middle of a humdrum night. To top it off, it suddenly started to snow, with all that meant for Olivia.

While I organized some alternative plan to try and keep from falling into temptation, I caught Pony's eye as she lay there on the floor next to the radiator, and she seemed to say: *You know what you're going to do; you already know. You're going to cover it up, like, "Oh, let's take Ruby and the dog for a walk." And all of a sudden, like it was the last thing on your mind, you'll walk us past the port, and we'll see the lights on in Mark's boat. Plus, it's snowing harder and harder. And well, since no one's looking, you'll go in for a bit, but just a little while, until it clears up. And hey, that's fine with me, Alice, because I hate going for a walk, I hate leaving the house, and just like Olivia, I hate the snow. So take a shower, put on a few drops of that perfume he likes so much, and let's go ahead and wrap this farce up.* Pony told me all that, very inconsiderately, I swear.

———

It didn't make things easy for me in the least that Julia was so nice when I dropped off Olivia. Since our run-in at the pharmacy, we had crossed paths from time to time on the island, out shopping, dropping off or picking up the kids, taking a walk . . . A friendly glance, a smile that never quite formed, a distant greeting, a hello, a see you later . . . But this time she smiled warmly, shared with me a light that had previously been absent, asked me about Christmas, how things went, did we spend it with family. She offered to watch Ruby and Pony so I could enjoy a few hours to myself—*What's the difference between two or three kids, or one or two dogs*, she said—and she told me I smelled good, that she loved my perfume, asked what it was. White Musk from the Body Shop. And finally she invited me in to have tea. *Say yes, Alice; you can have that tea and avoid temptation. Grab this opportunity to get close to her and push yourself away from him, because she's the one who's been keeping a secret. Say yes.* I turned down both offers appreciatively. And however much I pretended not to, I knew why. I told her I'd be back in a few hours, and I went to Mark's boat, taking more turns than necessary, as if I was afraid she was following me, as if I was trying to get lost and avoid the inevitable.

Mark had opened a can of Russian caviar a patient from New York had given him and had made Valencian Water, a cocktail with a base of champagne, orange juice, vodka and gin. I was the one who had told him about the cocktail, which I got hooked on when I was in Spain. I was surprised he remembered. A nice detail. We toasted to the New Year.

He was unusually animated as well. He looked contented, was

chatty and told me outrageous stories about his New York patients. For a while, I thought that he might not even want to sleep with me, that he just wanted to chat, that all that idle yakking had been to set the stage for telling me how well things were going with Julia, and that all this was a kind of farewell to thank me for services rendered and to be sure that everything was good between us and that we could go on being friends. That would have been fine with me. Well, that's what I told myself. Because, if all that would have been fine with me, why didn't I suggest it myself? But Mark didn't say anything whatsoever about Julia, and after three Valencian Waters—I had barely tried it—and polishing off the caviar, he told me he had missed me, and without waiting for a response, because he knew he wouldn't get one, he kissed me. We kissed.

"You did it again."

"What?"

"You stopped."

"What do you mean?"

"Yeah, right before our lips touch, you stop yourself. Just like you did the first time."

"I did?" I bluffed.

"Yes."

"I don't think so."

"Yeah, you did. Look, we're going to kiss again. On the count of three, we'll both come close at the same time."

"OK."

"One, two, three."

We kissed.

"See? You did it again."

Yeah, I'd done it again. And this time, it was against my will.

"Do you regret giving me each kiss?"

"Maybe a little."

"For me, it's the opposite."

"How's that?"

"I regret it after I give you each kiss. Because of how much I like it."

Then I did kiss him. I think.

———

"Who's going back to my house first? You or me?" Mark asked after waking up from his obligatory postcoital micro-nap with his arms wrapped around my waist.

"The least suspicious thing would be for us to go back together."

"Yeah, holding hands." Mark laughed. "If you don't mind, I'll go back first, I'm going to need a few hours for the oyster stew. When you leave, make sure the hatch is locked."

I said OK. Mark got up and started dressing.

"Maybe you should shower first. I smell perfume."

"I love how you smell."

"Julia does too. She just told me."

He didn't like me mentioning her name. I could see he was bothered and about to ask me what the hell I was up to. I think I did it on purpose. He was so relaxed, and it pissed me off. I wanted him to feel at least a little bad so that I wasn't the only one.

"You know what? You're right. I'm going to take a shower . . ." he said, not wanting to spoil the moment, and he stepped into the little shower in the cabin.

He closed the glass door. I went out to the main cabin where Pony and Ruby were sleeping placidly, as usual. I took my cell out of my pocket and went straight to Mark's laptop. When I'd showed up at *The Office*, he was in the middle of writing an email. He didn't close it or turn it off.

I went into his calendar app and did the same as in Karen's office, taking a video of every month from January to June. All the appointments and trips to New York.

————

I left twenty minutes after Mark. I took the chance to feed Ruby and look over the video that I had taken of Mark's computer. I knew the dates of Chris's trips by heart, so I could tally them up without the need to look at my notes. Mark went to New York twice a month for four or five days, so it was likely that some of the dates would overlap. But it seemed as if they had agreed to travel in alternating periods. Only a few of the trips coincided, and even then, not on all the days. Anyway, there I was assuming that, if Julia was committing adultery with Chris, it would be on the dates when Mark was away, even though Mark himself was committing adultery with me right there on the island, while she was taking care of my child. What kind of bullshit investigation was this? What was I after? What a shit day. Ridiculous. I was doing everything I'd told myself I wouldn't do. And not just that day.

As I was leaving the cabin to go onto the deck, I stopped short when I saw something in the distance that caught my attention: activity. Although it was two in the afternoon on New Year's Eve, with not a soul on the street and all the shops were closed, there was a fishing boat unloading merchandise. *Make sure you get some fresh fish today; tomorrow no boats will be going out*, Ray Schepler, the fisherman, had told me the day before. And now he had his raincoat on and was unloading crates with two other men I didn't recognize. They must be members of the crew.

Then a van arrived from WasteWorks, Mike's waste management company. He got out, wearing jean shorts and sandals with white socks, as if it were summertime. He opened the sliding door in the side of the van and put a few crates inside.

"Dude, you're gonna get sick," Ray said to Mike.

"I'm gonna get sick if this shit is as bad as that fish you sell."

"Shut up, asshole. I only deal with the freshest merchandise. Fresh as your balls in this cold."

They both laughed. Mike gave him a fat envelope. Only when the van was gone did I realize how dumb I had been not to record the entire thing with my phone. The first really relevant thing I had found out had been a complete stroke of luck, and to top it off, I hadn't recorded it. Hell of a detective I was turning out to be.

———

We had dinner with my parents over Skype. *Honey, for this, it would have been much better being together.*

Mom, I'm hanging up.

No, no, OK, let's celebrate in peace.

That's what I'm saying.

At eight, we did a version of counting down to the New Year. Olivia pounded a casserole dish with a ladle while we screamed: *Ten, nine, eight, seven, six, five, four, three, two, one. Happy New Year!* Then we had to repeat it because Olivia said we had to get to zero. So we did it again. *Ten, nine, eight, seven, six, five, four, three, two, one, zero. Happy New Year!* But that was no good either because Olivia wasn't wild about counting backward; it made her sad. We had to count forward. To me, that made all the sense in the world. *All right, come on now. One, two . . . !*

Nonononono, from zero!

Oh, of course. Come on, now. Zero, one, two, three, four, five, six, seven, eight, nine, ten! Happy New Year for the fourth time! Great, yay!

Again, Mommy, again!

We did it three more times until we all finished, with a ringing in our ears from Olivia's thwacking on the casserole dish. We toasted to 2016 with juice.

––––––

An hour later, I managed to put the little counting beast to bed.

"Lights, iPad and Olivia, all three things in sleep mode now."

"Okaaaaaay . . ."

Olivia turned off her iPad, opening and closing the protective case twice. One, two. She left it with the edges perfectly aligned with the corner of the nightstand. She rolled over, then rolled over again in the opposite direction.

"Oli, why don't you try one night, just one night, not doing it?" The curious thing was, since the first time we did it together, I had gone on doing it every night. It wasn't perfect, but it worked. "That could be your New Year's resolution." And mine, while we were at it.

"What's a New Year's resolution?"

"Well, when the old year is over, we decide to change some things we don't like, or that are bad for us, so we don't do them in the year that's starting."

"But I like it. And it's good for me."

"I'm just asking you to try, so you'll see that nothing will happen and that the world's not going to end."

"So I can't ask for another resolution?"

"You don't ask for a resolution; you make one."

"It's not like a wish?"

"It's like a wish. A wish that you have to grant yourself."

"So I can't ask for Daddy to come back?"

Jabbing pain in the heart.

"No. You can't ask for that, sweetie. It has to be something you're capable of doing. Like not rolling around and around in bed. Or being nice to Pony. Or when someone says bye to you, not getting scared. That would be a good resolution for you."

Pause. She seemed to be reflecting on my words.

"I don't like those resolutions."

Another battle lost. I gave her a kiss and turned off the lights, leaving on the Peppa Pig nightlight.

"Bye, honey. I love you."

"No, not that."

"Till next year, honey. I love you."

"No, not that either."

"See you tomorrow, honey. I love you."

"See you tomorrow, Mommy. And don't close the door all the way."

I shut the door until it was left open the exact length of my palm. First the fear of the cold. Then the OCD. Now she was in a phase where she couldn't stand anyone saying *bye* to her because she was afraid she wouldn't see that person again. Her father had said *bye* to her the last time she saw him. *Bye, my princess, my love*, he said to her. And she answered him with a simple, *Bye, Daddy, goodbye*. Now, months later, that memory had lit up and had turned into a new fear. I had realized it for the first time two weeks before, when I went to pick her up from school and she was taking leave of Lori Mambretti, the teacher who was in charge of going with them in the hydroplane that week. She had run off, and as she did, she had shouted: *See you tomorrow, Miss Mambretti. Goodbye, Olivia.* She turned around, still running, went back to the hydroplane and shouted once more as she ran away: *See you tomorrow, Miss Mambretti. Goodbye, Olivia.* And again. And again. It seemed like an innocent game played by a child with too much sugar running through her veins. She only stopped when Lori had finally had it and said, *See you tomorrow, Olivia.* And a few days later, she had gotten sick at the Christmas party on the last day of school when she realized how uncontrollable the situation was as she tried to take leave of the dozens of children and their families. She got dizzy, but everyone chalked it up to the heat in the auditorium and the bear costume she was wearing. They had acted out "Goldilocks and the Three Bears." She was the Mama Bear, and a happy one, especially because Oliver was Papa Bear.

When I told the psychologist, she tried to explain to Olivia that saying goodbye wasn't necessarily definitive. A kind word you exchanged with the people you came across. But right now, for Olivia, the world, her world, was so fragile that a single word could change everything. That's how my daughter felt. That's how I felt. *And then he told you: "Goodbye, my queen, my love." And you never saw him again either*, Olivia reminded me when I was trying to understand why she had prohibited the word *goodbye*. If I had ended up rolling around and around in my bed—once for each side—how did I know I wouldn't end up avoiding the word goodbye for the rest of my life too? How many aftereffects awaited me still?

————

Miriam had invited me to spend New Year's Eve at her house. And Karen at the inn. And the DeRollers, Father Henry, Frank Rush, the Burrs, the Nguyens, the O'Gormans and practically everyone I had run into on the island in the past several days. I cordially turned down all the invitations. In part because I felt guilty, remorseful. I was spying on them, on many of the people who had invited me into their homes so effusively. I wasn't authorized to go into their houses. Punishment. It was remarkable how the more care and concern people showed me, the deeper my feelings of solitude. So I had decided that to exorcize it, the best thing was to be alone. I wanted to immerse myself in solitude, to face the monster. That night was the right one to do so.

The absence of a companion had plunged me into an internal dialogue so intense, so constant, that it made me fear all sorts of psychotic ailments. I was tired of spending the day with myself, of talking with Pony to justify myself. Tired of looking at that picture by Diego Sánchez Sanz and feeling like I was pulling further and further away. Who was that woman? I no longer knew. Now I only recognized myself in the shadows, on the dark side. I had done everything you shouldn't do in circumstances like mine. When you fall into the sea, without anything to grab onto, you have to lie on your back and float, without wasting energy. Instead, I had been splashing in the water, desperately trying to keep myself afloat, and now my strength was ebbing. My body was starting to weigh me down. I was drowning in my own psyche.

I had three snitches active right then, simultaneously radiating conventional ways of celebrating New Year's. A skein of noises, laughter, clinking glasses, shrieks, songs, partying, TV. All mixed together, whirling around, joining the storm in my mind. A perfect storm.

Bail out, Alice.

Not till this is solved. How do I only have four suspects? How many months, and only four suspects? It can't be.

Disconnect.

I'll take care of this right now.

Mike, for being a drug dealer and a dickhead and for trashing the life of the only person on the island I consider to be a friend, I declare you suspect number five.

Ray Schepler, for being a drug dealer, liar and not always giving me the best cuts of fish, I declare you suspect number six.

Summer, because even though you're spoiled, unbearable and grating, by the dates, you could have Chris's baby in your belly, so I declare you suspect number seven.

Jennifer, even though you are the kindest woman I've come across in my life, you've got something weird going on with your niece, not to mention Stephen, your husband in the coma, so I declare you suspect number eight.

Stephen, for . . . ah, no, Stephen's already a suspect.

Karen, because of whatever it was you did with Chris in Room 202 of the inn and because I'm sure you drink so much to forget him, I declare you suspect number nine.

Conrad, because I'll bet you opened the checking account for Chris and now you're going to keep his money, I declare you suspect number ten.

Chief Margaret, because . . . because you're Chief Margaret and that's enough, I declare you suspect number eleven.

Frank Rush, because I don't trust your episodes of dementia or Alzheimer's are what they appear, I declare you suspect number twelve.

Barbara Rush, for taking a break from Jeffrey the pilot and for your lovely sky blue cat eyes, I declare you suspect number thirteen.

But wait, couldn't he have gone to the island with someone else? A secret getaway for him and another woman. How did I not think of that before? I can't believe it.

Cousin Keegan, because you're still single and because you cried at the dinner table remembering Chris, I declare you suspect number fourteen.

Suz, my best friend from high school, secretly in love with Chris and head of the cheerleading squad, because even though Chris hated cheerleaders, I can't trust anything anymore, I declare you suspect number fifteen.

All the girls who were at the University of Virginia between 1998 and 2002, especially those from the year 2000, when we broke it off for six months, I declare you as a group suspect number sixteen.

Twelve more suspects at the flick of a pen. Much better. Surely the solution is here. Everything's here. I have to solve it.

You're going in a spiral, Alice. Pull out.

Solve it already. Now. Because if not, they're going to catch you. They're going to send the police and social services to the house. They're going to take away custody of your daughters.

You're in a tailspin.

You're not Moby Dick, or Captain Ahab, or gentle Ishmael.

Defocus your eyes and look at the map.

There is no map.

X marks the spot.

There is no map. There is no X.

You have no ship or crew.

You're looking for a treasure that doesn't exist. The Master Key doesn't open anything.

There's not even a minute left before the New Year. Hold on. It's almost over.

Close your eyes to see it better.

The countdown's starting. Count forward, Alice. Go.

Ten seconds to solve everything.

Ten!

Stephen is Chris's father or secret brother.

Nine!

Chris finds out he's in a coma and goes to visit him. The first night he sleeps at the inn, but then the visits become more regular and he stays at Jennifer's house.

Eight!

Jennifer keeps Stephen alive because she likes having Chris around.

Seven!

Then Chris meets Summer and screws her and leaves the poor girl pregnant.

Six!

Before or after he meets Miriam, too, and of course, he also screws her and ruins her marriage. So that makes Chloe his daughter too.

Five!

Then, one day when Mark isn't there, he runs into Julia on the street, no, on the beach, walking, they see each other, they laugh, and he screws her too. Right there in the dunes.

Four!

So every time Chris goes to the island, he screws some chick.

Three!

And so all the kids born in the last two or three years are his!

Two!

Solved! See how easy it was?!

One!

Map, X and treasure, found.

Zero!

Happy New Year!

PART THREE

ROBINSON CRUSOE

Thus, we never see the true state of our condition till it is illustrated to us by its contraries, nor know how to value what we enjoy, but by the want of it.

The true greatness of life was to be masters of ourselves...

That the height of human wisdom was to bring our tempers down to our circumstances, and to make a calm within, under the weight of the greatest storms without.

Grief was the most senseless, insignificant passion in the world, for that it regarded only things past, which were generally impossible to be recalled or to be remedied, but had no views of things to come, and had no share in anything that looked like deliverance, but rather added to the affliction than proposed a remedy.

—Daniel Defoe, *Robinson Crusoe* (1719)

THE BEACH IS deserted. The reeds are dancing to the sound of the northwesterly wind. The sand makes little whirls on the dunes. It's not cold, even though it's January 1. A man is standing on the shore, hypnotized by the sea. I can't see his face. I don't need to see his face. His hair is disheveled and frizzy from the salt breeze. He's barefoot, with khaki pants rolled up a few times. The waves break with a wild beauty. The receding surf traces furrows around the soles of his feet. I come over slowly, as if I want to surprise him or am worried I'll frighten him. I'm naked, except for a baggy turtleneck sweater that hangs almost to my knees. I think I just made love to the man, and the sweater is his. The neighing of wild horses. A seagull suspended in the air. Peace is what I feel. Love for the man. That's why I don't want to scare him away. I want to embrace him. I want to run up to meet him. Do it, what's stopping you? Trap the moment and preserve it forever. He's yours. You're his. Run. Two people cross my path. Where did they come from? Who cares. Now I'm closer. Twenty people. They turn their backs to me. I dodge them. I don't see Chris. Thirty people. They all love Chris. Forty people going toward him. Fifty. I almost can't move forward. Sixty, eighty. I drag myself across the sand, begging them to let me through. A hundred people. I make it to the shore and see Chris's footprints, but he's not there. I get up and howl his name to the sea. *Chris!* I can hardly breathe, because the whole island is there behind me. *Alice*, I recognize the voice. It's Ruby. Even if she doesn't talk yet, I know it's her voice. *Alice*, she repeats. Don't turn. It's a trap. Why doesn't she call me Mommy? *Mommy*, she says. I turn. Ruby isn't there. Neither is Olivia. Or Pony. Or Chris. All the people who aren't us are there. My daughters aren't there; they've taken my daughters. I try to shout their names, but my voice doesn't come. Chief Margaret unholsters her revolver. *Chris is ours*, she says before she shoots me.

225

———

I fell; I lost consciousness, like in a lacrosse game I played long ago, when they hit me in the eye with the ball. When I woke on the shore of the New Year, I thought hours had passed, but people were still celebrating and toasting. I heard fireworks coming from the beach. The first thing I thought of was my daughters. That relieved me. Then the noise was gone. In the end, there was a bit of calm waiting for me after the storm. Enough to get on my feet, feel terra firma, and realize where I was and, above all, that I had the wrong book.

You're a shipwreck, Alice. A shipwreck on an island. On Robin Island. You're Robinson Crusoe. It's not about finding a treasure. It's about survival.

Curiously, New Year's Day fell on a Friday.

———

I got up and went over to Diego's picture. I turned it around. I didn't want to see any more of myself. But that wasn't enough. I didn't even want to feel my presence. I took it down to the garage, and there it stayed, leaning against the wall. All $20,500 worth of picture wedged in among junk and boxes. I had the feeling I was saying goodbye to myself. But it didn't bother me. I was relieved.

———

Olivia woke up, peeped out the window, saw there was still snow in the yard and started crying.

"What's going on, honey?"

"There's snow."

"Of course there's snow. There was snow yesterday."

"But it's New Year's. We changed years, right?"

"Yeah, of course."

"But everything should be new."

I considered explaining to her that it wasn't the first year of her life, that she should know how this worked by now, that it's not starting from zero, it's continuing. But strangely, I identified with her attitude since I too felt paralyzed, disoriented and blocked, as if I had forgotten how to walk through life and distrusted the white blanket that was covering everything.

"Oli, last year there was also snow on New Year's Day, don't you remember? We were skiing in the mountains."

Of course she remembered, and that's probably why she didn't like this new beginning. Because a year ago, there were three of us—well, four, since I was already pregnant—in Wachusett Mountain, in northern Massachusetts, where Olivia put on skis for the first time and learned to make a wedge turn.

For some reason I started wondering how many mistakes I had made since Chris's death. I remembered how cold it was in the funeral parlor room when I'd agreed to let Olivia see Chris in the casket. In trying to avoid one trauma, I'd created another. My first error, without a doubt, had been not telling anyone the truth. Being incapable of saying that Chris wasn't at Yale, that he'd had an accident on US 6, during his drive along the Weweantic River. And my last mistake . . . What had been my last mistake? Drinking too much wine last night? No, my last mistake was the same as the first: not telling anyone what I was doing. The moment I sat down in front of anyone with a bit of common sense and told them what I was up to, the house of cards would collapse, everything would fall in under its own weight. The parallel universe I was living in would vanish, and I would come back to reality.

While considering how to address Olivia's latest episode of chionophobia, I suggested she go downstairs to watch her daily dose of *Dora the Explorer* on TV.

Her shout a few moments later shook my entire body.

"Mommy!!! There's a man in the living room!"

I rushed downstairs, looking for a blunt object to defend my daughter and my home. All I found was a toy train.

"Get out of here!" I shouted, brandishing the train. One of the cars detached.

It was Frank from Family Pet Land. He was sitting on the sofa in silence, looking at us disconcertedly, without understanding what all the fuss was about. He had a briefcase in his lap. A portable record player from the sixties, a Victrola.

"Frank? What are you doing here?" I asked while I hugged Olivia, who was crying again. "It's Frank, Oli; you know him."

"Hey, sweetie," Frank said, smiling at her. Olivia seemed to calm down.

"Frank, you scared the hell out of us."

"Sorry, I should have called. But I didn't want to wake up Rose."

"Sure . . ." I said, not very sure how to get out of the situation.

"Who's Rose, Mama?" Olivia asked.

"Rose is Frank's wife."

Frank laughed.

"I wish. She's my girlfriend. Is she up yet?"

Olivia was going to say something, but I covered her mouth.

"We'll go see if she's up. We'll be right back."

I thought about calling Barbara to see if she would come pick her father up, but seeing Frank sitting there, calm and affable, lost in his own world, made me think of my own father and above all of the last conversation we'd had. *All I'm trying to tell you is that I think Olivia needs something that inspires her as much as painting did you. And that probably it's something simple, something within arm's reach.*

Until then, I hadn't dared to go near Horse Rush Farm because I knew that as soon as I did, Olivia would become crazy with excitement and complain all the more about how I needed to buy her a pony. I knew that sooner or later it would be inevitable. Anyway, Barbara had made a good impression on me at the dinner at Karen's Petite Maison. She told me we could go to the farm whenever we wanted so Olivia could feed the horses and even ride a pony. Barbara had three. Perhaps it was time to buy Olivia a pony or a horse. She was little and light. She could be a great Amazon. Better to jump obstacles than to devote herself to counting them.

I told Frank that, against all odds, Rose had decided to get up early that day and had gone to the farm, that they must have crossed paths on the way and that I would happily take him over there. I got Olivia, wrapped her in several layers of clothes, gloves, a hat and a scarf. She complained a lot. I got mad. I put her in the car against her will, grabbed Ruby, and then we went with Frank to the horse ranch. My final wildcard, my last ace in the hole. If this didn't work, I was throwing in the towel.

When Olivia opened her eyes—she'd kept them shut the whole way in protest—and saw the horses in the snow, she was mute for a few moments until finally she looked at me and asked me with a beaming face, "Mommy, are we still on the island?"

"Of course, Oli."

"Why didn't you ever bring me here?!"

The complaint didn't go any further because just then Olivia saw a precious white pony with black spots that seemed to have been placed all over its body by a haute couture designer.

The ace in the hole had worked. But unfortunately, the pony in question had an owner and wasn't for sale or for rent or anything. Barbara was enormously grateful to me for taking care of Frank, after searching for him for two hours. She quickly grabbed the reins of the situation, put a saddle on Panda the pony—that was its name, for obvious reasons—and helped Olivia to hop on. "I'm sure the owner won't show up here today," she said, winking. I knew that as soon as Olivia got on the pony, she'd never want to get off. The good thing was, Olivia wasn't cold anymore. Or rather, she no longer cared about the cold.

The bad thing: a pony cost between $5,000 and $6,000, and the board was $600 a month (or $7,200 per year). But after the expenses I'd incurred to get where I was right now, it didn't seem right to use money as an excuse.

The really bad thing: there weren't any ponies for sale. Snow White, Panda's mother, was pregnant and would give birth in the spring. So we'd have to wait, which wouldn't make Olivia any easier to handle for the rest of the winter. But Barbara winked at me again and said: "No problem, she can go on riding Panda. Hardly anyone comes around here until spring." The farm was only open to the public in the spring and summer, when they organized camps for the kids and guided horseback rides on the island. In fall and winter, she maintained the stables and trained horses for their owners.

Olivia didn't stop smiling for the whole ride. She barely spoke, as if she wanted to savor every second. I also didn't hear her counting, though sometimes, when other people were around, she did it silently.

As Barbara held the bridle, controlling the pony's pace, she told me about Frank's Alzheimer's.

"They diagnosed him a couple of months ago. For now, he just has occasional episodes. He gets disoriented, especially at night, when he wakes up and doesn't know where he is. Normally he goes to the clinic. He's usually good during the day. It's weird he showed up at your house . . ." She immediately realized something. "Unless . . . Wait. Where do you live? No, don't tell me. Forty-eight Shelter Road, right?"

I nodded.

"That house belonged to my grandparents on my mother's side over fifty years ago. When my mother was a teenager, my father used to go there to visit her. They'd listen to music together on my mother's portable record player. Elvis, Jerry Lee Lewis, Ritchie Valens, Johnny Cash."

Mystery solved.

"And thanks a lot for not chewing him out or making him figure out his mistake. The neurologist told me it's best to just treat it like it's normal and be caring."

"It's nothing. It must be embarrassing enough for him when he gets the sense something's not right, without adding to it by rubbing his nose in it."

In fact, a little before arriving at the farm, Frank came back to normal—or to the present—and told me: *Alice, it was high time you came to the farm.* How intricate the human mind is. Or on the contrary, what a basic mechanism: when everything starts to disappear, it grasps the fundamental, the heart, his eternal love for his deceased wife.

"Don't you worry, I'll keep an eye on him," I told Barbara to ease her fears.

"Great, well, every time my father sets foot in your house, which will be frequent, it's one free pony ride for Olivia."

"Yes, yes, let Frank come to the house every day!" Olivia shouted blissfully.

———

Finding out Chris had spent a night at Karen's Petite Maison, probably his first night on the island, had been a milestone for me. But it did nothing but make the next question more urgent: Where did he stay the rest of the times he came to the island?

Therefore, the first chance I had, I snuck into the inn, because Karen had caught the ferry to go to the hairdresser in Hyannis. I wanted to take a look at Room 202, where Chris had stayed. I took Ruby with me. I left Olivia doing homework with Wendy, one of Reverend Henry's daughters, who was in her last year of secondary school and made a mint as a private tutor. Not that Olivia needed help with her homework. On the contrary, Wendy challenged her with more advanced math problems. Something fundamental for keeping her obsessions up-to-date.

Room 202 is undoubtedly the prettiest one in Karen's Petite Maison, but three years had passed since Chris was there. What did I hope to find? Maybe I just wanted to stoke up rage, imagining him there with another woman, in the Jacuzzi on the balcony, enjoying the sunset over Pleasant Beach.

Besides, that expedition helped me to discover how—presumably—John had figured out Chris had died. After going over the whole house in search of yearbooks or photos from the University of Virginia, I ended up finding the quarterly journal from the university's alumni association in the magazine rack in the bathroom. And there it was, in the copy from the third quarter of 2015, in the obituary section:

> Chris Williams, alumnus. Class of 2002. Deceased at thirty-five years of age. Graduated cum laude in business administration. NCAA national champion with the Virginia Cavaliers tennis team. Ranked third by the ITA. US Open Junior Tennis Championship semifinalist. Our sincerest condolences. Our prayers are with the friends and family of this authentic Cavalier.

I was happy to see the obituary was so normal, one among many, with no personal data, no family photos, no mention of my name.

My telephone buzzed; I had it on silent. When I saw it was Karen, I instinctively looked for somewhere to hide. Under the bed. *I'm busted*, I thought, then realized she couldn't have caught the ferry back so soon. Since I didn't pick up, she sent me a message:

Alice! Just a reminder—today is the residents' meeting at city hall.
Don't ditch me when I need your support, things are going to heat
up!!! I hope you haven't forgotten! OK, time to get these damn gray
roots dyed.

I quickly answered her message:

Of course I'm coming! See you later. And give those four gray hairs
of yours hell! You're such a drama queen.

Once a month, there was a residents' meeting at city hall, where
subjects proposed beforehand by the island's inhabitants were discussed.
In general they dragged on and seemed more like an excuse to eat,
drink and band together, criticizing the other surrounding islands. But
that day, it was about a subject that had already raised a ruckus before:
the installation of closed-circuit television cameras. One side favored
having the island monitored for security purposes—So *our women
and children can rest at ease without fearing for their safety.* The former
mayor had started the fight, insisting that the island wasn't bucolic just
because, that it was bucolic because people made it that way. Things
needed to be controlled. He lost the battle by a slim margin, and ended
up quitting his job and leaving the island. That's how the new mayor,
Gwen DeRoller, and Chief Margaret were elected: they insisted that
trust built trust, that since we all knew each other here, it was precisely
that feeling of community that brought security, because we all covered
each other's backs.

"Sure, great, but then I go and find out my son's smoking marijuana,
and I want to know where he got it from, who gave it to him? How
did the drugs make it onto the island?" said Karen, the one who had
brought the debate back up. "Because if I don't, my husband will find
out his own way, and believe me, the consequences will be much worse.
For my son and for whoever gave it to him."

Various voices, pro and con, followed. *You think that's going to keep
them from dealing drugs? This community is fragile and vulnerable; we
have to protect it. Many of us are here precisely to escape the paranoid world*

out there. Exclusivity means feeling protected. Exclusivity means feeling free.
An ounce of prevention is worth a pound of cure. Yeah, then what's next?
Putting cameras inside the houses? Because once we've started . . . Throughout the controversy, I thought about how much it could have saved me
if there had already been a system of cameras on the island, but I also
thought that it would have been my punishment, or else my liberation,
because I wouldn't have been able to do anything I was doing.

"And you, Alice? What do you think of all this? Because I'm bored
with hearing the same arguments all the time," asked Miriam, who was
sitting beside me and was from the pro-CCTV faction. Did she want
to run Mike off?

All of them looked at me as if the decision depended on me, as if I
was the person who had to clear up the dispute once and for all.

"I haven't been on the island long. I don't feel it's my place to take
sides on this issue. I'll accept what the majority decides," I said, even
though I had no doubt that I favored no, both for conviction and for
self-interest.

"Coward, red, anarchist, agitator. If I knew it, I wouldn't have
pushed you to come," said Karen between her teeth, without a trace of
ill will.

Later she would confess to me that deep down, it didn't matter to
her. She just wanted to rile up the meetings a bit. *I was on the debate*
team in my high school, and it gets me going, she said.

Especially when you've downed a few glasses of wine, I thought.

The proposal was knocked down on this occasion as well, the ninth
time in four years, with twenty-nine votes against, twenty-five for, and
two abstentions: one from Mayor DeRoller—who was firmly opposed,
but said it was her job to enforce what the others decided—and one
from me.

Once the session was adjourned and we were all eating, I caught
sight of a bulletin board announcing the annual Cherry Blossom Art
Fair from March 7 to 14, with photos from the previous year. The fair
supposedly coincided with the blossoming of the cherry trees, celebrating the end of the harsh winter, though in reality this did not usually
take place until late April or early May. But the year the fair was first or-

ganized, 1977, saw record temperatures in March, and the cherry trees blossomed early. The event was mentioned in lots of tourist guides, and the exhibition booths were highly prized. Everyone on the island had the right to set one up, but if you were from somewhere else and wanted to set up a booth, you had to pay a subscription fee and go through a selection process the year before.

I saw there was a $7,500 dollar prize for the best stand and decided I was going to win. I had a little over two months to prepare. Not that I needed more motivation. It was time to change strategy, come up with more ambitious plans that would produce results, dig even deeper into the intimate lives of the island's inhabitants. And the fair would be the key.

"Are you going to do a stand?" Mark asked me as he approached. I tensed up.

Since sleeping together for the first time, we'd made a tactical decision to keep a certain distance in public.

"Probably," I said, trying to look intriguing.

"So what are you going to sell?"

"You'll have to wait till March to find out."

Just one second sharing a fond glance was enough to cause me to throw my first New Year's resolution in the trash.

————

It didn't last as long the other times. There were fewer words, fewer prologues. It was more sexual. More animal. Less inhibited. And though I was angry with myself for doing it—for not being able to invent some *official* excuse that would justify the encounter, given that I'd already gone through his agenda and put a snitch in his place—of the three times we'd slept together, it was undoubtedly the best. And that disconcerted me. I guess until then, I thought of Mark as little more than a pawn to be sacrificed—and enjoyed—on the game board of the island, among other reasons because I had experienced, for the first time since Chris's death, something akin to a surge of love.

————

"Tell me the truth: you no come here to spy other people. Come here to spy me."

"You got me, Antonio. Your English is getting better . . ."

"Thanks, Blondie. Happy New Year."

Could Antonio be my man Friday? He was sufficiently eccentric, distant, enthusiastic and seasoned to keep from judging me.

"I need more cameras."

"There's a word for people like you: spy junkie. Every time need more, dose more frequent. Careful, Blondie, spying more addictive drug than heroin."

"Antonio, I don't think it's a great business strategy to make your customers feel bad for buying your products."

"Right, Blondie. How many fixes are we talking this time? One? Two?"

"Let's just say I'm going to become your best customer."

"You best customer from moment you come into store." I smiled. And after a pause: "You no nursing baby today? Ask me, look like she very hungry."

———

On the way back to Robin Island on the ferry, I felt like an arms trafficker with several grenade launchers and bodies in the trunk. I had two twenty-seven-inch monitors from Best Buy, signal relays, routers and the fifty cameras I had bought at Night Eyes. They were different brands, because Antonio didn't have enough of the same kind in stock. But hey, though at the end of the day, some were better, some were worse, all served the same purpose: winning first prize at the Cherry Blossom Art Fair.

MY GOAL HAD been to show up at the fair with fifty spy clocks. I felt productive, creative and fulfilled making the clocks in series, ten at a time. But when I was wrapping up the first batch, I realized how stupid I'd been. I was taking it for granted that only the people on the island would buy my clocks. But the fair was known throughout the region, and people came from the surrounding towns and islands. What good would it do me to have a clock in a cabin in Woods Hole? That setback made me feel stupid. Very stupid.

I shattered the clock on the floor. Not that it had really turned out so well.

———

While I tried to piece my plan back together, I took refuge in Mark. We started to see each other often. Almost every day. Once it was established that those encounters weren't part of any of my lines of investigation, I let myself go. The excitement of the forbidden won out—just a little—over guilt. And the excitement of the new did the same—once more, just a little—over penitence. And though that battle of contradictions didn't give me rest and was still far from being resolved, I decided to open a new sexual chapter in my life. Because, yes, I wanted, I needed to center it in the terrain of the sexual, to try and keep my emotional life in check, because even if I was still in mourning, rays of light began to filter through with the need to love and be loved.

Despite the spark and the excitement, our encounters were marked by the hurry, the timetable and the narrowness of the place. It couldn't be otherwise. I set the frequency. I was the one who had decided to go almost every day. It seemed as if I were speeding everything up. As if I wanted to wear it out as soon as possible. To stop doing it, I suppose, to lose the urge, to exhaust the novelty. But the more I did it, the more

I liked it, the more I got hooked. I was plunging headfirst into the eye of Hurricane Mark. In the end, everything came down to the fact that I felt very much alone. I needed his warmth more than the sex. Maybe that was why I couldn't help but feel a little used—and jealous? And yet, strangely, the more we saw each other, the better he felt—and this I heard through the snitches—being with Julia. They were rediscovering each other after a long period of absence. Often I surprised myself by listening to them make love. I was absorbed, unable to silence the snitch. He didn't tell me he was better, that he had lowered his dose of antidepressants. Nothing. As though now his relationship with her was the one he had to hide and deny. As if I had become the wife instead of the lover.

But that wasn't Mark's problem, it was mine. I lived my life through others.

————

"Hey, Frank. I want to give you a present."

"Me? Why?"

"Because you treat me and my girls and especially Pony very well."

"Sorry, but I should be the one giving you the present, you're my best customer."

"I'm happy to be. Here, take it."

I gave him his gift. It was a spy clock shaped like a guppy for the wall.

"How pretty. It's Flint, right?"

"Yeah. For you to put in the vet clinic. It would look great above the counter."

"I love it. Thanks so much."

Though I still hadn't resolved what I was going to do about my clock strategy at the Cherry Blossom Art Fair, I kept on working, advancing, because time was tight. Besides, I was worried about Frank. His Alzheimer's episodes were getting worse. He had come to my house a few more times. Olivia went crazy every time he showed up at the door—*A free ride on Panda!* When he came, I didn't call Barbara or take him back to Horse Rush Farm right away. I just let him stay. We had practically adopted him as Grandpa Frank. He usually showed up on the weekends. According to Barbara, that was when Rose's parents had let him pay his visits to their house. He always came with the portable record player, though it had stopped working a long time ago. Olivia loved playing at being Rose. Eating pancakes with Frank, which is what they did when they were kids. It's not that Frank was in another world, another reality. He was in limbo. You could see he wasn't totally lost, that there was a push and pull inside. He was in a place as comforting and recognizable as it was false and shadowy. He was fighting not to vanish completely, but he didn't want to leave, or he didn't know how. The boy was reborn; the adult suffered. Seeing him sitting there in the kitchen, looking at the fork as if it were the first time he had seen one in his life and he was trying to find the purpose of it, provoked an intense mixture of sorrow, tenderness and identification, because I was also trying to figure out things as basic as knowing whether my life had been a big lie.

Barbara was afraid he'd hurt himself during one of these episodes, that he'd have an accident at the wheel or in the clinic with all the veterinary equipment. She even considered encouraging him to retire or making him do so, but she knew that would spell the end for him. That's why I gave him a spy clock, to keep an eye on him. And frankly, because I was a little bit tired of seeing nothing on the monitor but the fishbowl in reception at Karen's Petite Maison. I had debated between calling it a fishbowl or a cage every time a signal came through. Until one day I looked closely at Flint, who was turning around and around obsessively in the water, trying to find a way out, and I decided on fishbowl. Now, after finding out Chris had spent a night at the inn and without John there, Karen's fishbowl was as boring and unproductive as watching Flint. Plus, it was frustrating to watch her drink so much. I started to seriously question whether I should intervene with that issue. But how? Our friendship wasn't that close, and she herself recognized now and then how plastered she'd gotten the night before, asking people to forgive her and laughing at herself. She did it so naturally, so aware of her actions, that it threw you off, and you'd think: *Well, we're all old enough to know what we're doing. Take a look at yourself, Alice. You should be starting Spies Anonymous; you could be the association's first member. Hi, my name's Alice, and I'm a spy, not a real clever one, but a spy.*

———

And then the messenger arrived with the results of Stephen/Chris's DNA test. It came in a hard cardboard envelope, very thin, very discreet, without a return address. I had waited for it impatiently, almost as impatiently as I waited for John to come back from his deployment on the submarine. And yet I was surprised I didn't get nervous, that my heart didn't speed up at all. Was I getting used to this life on the border between illegal and extralegal? I didn't even do any special ritual before opening it. It came; I opened it; I looked at it. There were three pages with all sorts of explanations and data. But only one phrase mattered to me:

Probability of genetic link: 0.00001%

I don't know if I was irritated or relieved by that infinitesimal possibility. Because in one sense, I would have loved it if Chris and Stephen were related. That they were family, which would make me family too.

But curiously, the result that I thought would push me into helplessness, actually reoriented me. I lived in fear of getting stuck in a dead end, waking up one day with no more threads to pull on. But in this case, having discarded such a solid clue made me feel I was getting closer. It drove me; it activated me. Now I really did have to explore the whole range of possibilities, set up new fishbowls to make room for the lives of the other little fishes.

So I decided three things:

1. To make two of each type of clock. That way I could put the ones that didn't have cameras on display, without being afraid the ones with the spy cameras would end up in the hands of the wrong person. And if I was interested in spying on the buyer of a certain model, I would give them one already wrapped, which I had kept under the counter. All that would naturally mean twice the work.

I couldn't lose even another second. Not even to beat myself
up, because this was an idea so obvious I shouldn't have needed
almost a month to hit on it.

2. Not to hook up with Mark again.

3. To call my stand Alice in Wondertime. Because it was my time.
   My moment. And I was going to grab hold of it.

FOR THE FIRST time since Chris's death, my physical weariness overtook my spiritual weariness. The aches in my back overtook the aches in my soul. And I was thankful for it. It was much easier to bear. I'd had to lose many hours of sleep to make the clocks in time, and during the day, I erased myself from the map of the island. Anything that didn't have to do directly with Olivia, Ruby and, to a lesser extent, Pony, vanished for that month and a half. I arrived at the opening of the Cherry Blossom Art Fair with a total of seventy-two clocks, two of each type of the thirty-six models I had designed. Despite the exhaustion and the rings under my eyes, I was ecstatic. I had done it. Of course, that meant I'd had to leave some victims in my path.

"Why won't you ever accept any help?" Miriam had asked me. She was very hurt by my absence. "I offer to lend you a hand with your clocks. You say no. Fine, I get it. It's your thing, your art. I respect that. Then I offer my assistance setting up the stand. Nope. Then to help you get the public's attention—that's what I do, I sell things—that way you don't have to be by yourself all day at the fair, or I say we can take turns, without a commission or anything, out of friendship, because I want to be with you, spend some time together and laugh. Nope, not that either. So I don't know, it weirds me out, because I think, well, maybe you don't want to be my friend. You make me feel like a nagging neighbor. And shit, it hurts my feelings. Because you mean a lot to me. I sold you the house for less than I could have gotten because I felt a connection with you from the day we met; you transmitted something really nice to me. I saw your strength and your vulnerability. And now, look at us, here we are, having our first spat, and that's always an important step in any relationship, but this is the thing, I'm talking nonstop, and I don't know what's going through your head. Because you barely share anything with me."

The next day, I went to her house with a clock—a spy clock, obviously—shaped like a crescent moon, smiling and surrounded by stars, each of which was a number.

"Happy first fight," I said, timidly passing her the clock.

"You think you're going to talk me off the ledge with a clock shaped like a moon because you know I'm a Cancer and I'm prone to lunacy?"

"Yeah, I do. Because today's a full moon and you're feeling more sensitive."

"See?" she said, bursting into tears. "You know me really well. But do I know you?"

Pause. Then I started up. Following her lead.

"I don't let you help me because, since my husband died, I don't let anyone help me. And I really don't let anyone into my life. You're the person I've let get closest to me, without a doubt. And that might not mean much to you, because it isn't much, I know. But for me, it's a lot. It means a whole lot. And of course you're my friend. Although, let's be honest, you're also a bit of a pain. But you know what? I'm glad you are, because knowing you're there and that I can count on you helps me so much. And I also felt that connection when I met you. If you hadn't given me that special price on that lovely house and you weren't my dear neighbor, I probably wouldn't have made such a radical decision in my life. And by the way, I'm a Pisces with Cancer rising and the full moon affects me a lot too. A lot," I said, bursting into tears.

We hugged, crying together. Then she asked me, "Does this mean you're going to let me help you set up your stall?"

"No."

———

I sold most of the clocks during the first few days of the fair, and I got all kinds of praise and even an offer from a really fancy shop on Martha's Vineyard where I could have made a juicy profit—I was selling them for between seventy and a hundred dollars. The good thing was lots of neighbors on the island I was interested in had already bought or ordered one. So my cameras were going to be adopted and my fishbowls would find lots of homes.

———

Julia and Mark were holding hands and walking among the different stands at the fair. But as they approached mine, Mark started to straggle, who knows whether because he wanted to avoid a three-way meeting or because he was looking at a cane two stands farther down.

"Hi, Alice."

"Hi, Julia."

"Did you do these yourself?" she asked, admiring the clocks.

"Yes."

"They're lovely. I'd take all of them."

"Thanks."

Why did the compliment mean more coming from her? I even turned red. Julia focused her attention on a clock shaped like an elephant's face.

"This would look good in Oliver's room."

"If you take it, I'll give you another one at half price. For your office." *Easy, you're making it obvious.* "Or for wherever."

"The one made of the old book covers seems designed just for me."

In fact, she was right.

"They're real antique book covers that I found at a flea market," I said, acting like it was nothing.

"Well, to hell with it, I'll take two."

"No, no, wait!"

Olivia showed up, holding Oliver's hand. Well, they weren't exactly holding hands, more like Olivia was clutching his arm and dragging him along.

"Oliver gets the Puchi Puchi clock so he can have the same one as mine."

A while back, Olivia had caught me making a clock shaped like a raccoon.

"That one's for me, Mommy. Puchi Puchi is for my bedroom," she'd said.

"No, honey, those are for the fair," I'd told her. But then I thought: *Wait, maybe it's a good idea. Putting a camera in her room would let me observe her in private and get to know her obsessive-compulsive patterns better so I can help her. But no, how could I do that with my own daughter?*

How could I spy on her? No, I couldn't do it. And what if she caught me? She would never forgive me. If I was incapable of respecting my daughter's privacy, if I couldn't manage to help her overcome her neuroses without needing to control every one of her movements, what kind of mother did that make me? No, I couldn't put a camera in the Puchi Puchi clock. She was another victim, like me. So I finished the Puchi Puchi clock without a spy camera and took it up to her room.

"Where do you want me to put it, Oli?"

Olivia had looked around her bedroom, trying to find the right place. Without saying anything, she picked up one of her crayons. She got up on the bed and drew a tiny dot in what she swore was the exact center of the wall. I was even afraid to hammer in the nail because any tiny deviation could start a drama. Maybe my daughter was destined to be a great mathematician, or an astrophysicist like Stephen Hawking, with a vision of space that went beyond black holes. When I finished, I looked at Olivia's disconcerted face.

"What is it?"

"It's not right."

"No, Oli, I nailed it in where you said to."

"I mean the clock. It's not right."

"Why?"

"One needle is bigger than the other."

"It has to be like that. The short one tells you the hour and the long one the minutes." She didn't look especially convinced. "Should I set it for you?"

"No. I always want one on top and one on bottom."

"Don't you want to always know what time it is? Don't you want to hear the clock go tick-tock?"

"No. The big one on top and the little one on bottom."

"You want it to always be six o' clock?"

"Puchi Puchi time," she said with remarkable firmness.

"All right, then. Puchi Puchi time it is. That's how the clock will stay forever."

And now Olivia wanted Oliver to have a replica of her clock—which had a spy camera inside—in his room. I absolutely did not want to sell a clock with a camera in it to any child. It didn't seem . . . *Were you going to say ethical? You really have nerve to use the word* ethics. *No, not ethical. It doesn't seem decent to me. Right, because all this other stuff is decent.*

"Isn't it cool? Don't you want to have the same Puchi Puchi clock as me? You want it, Oliver?"

Oliver shrugged, incapable of contradicting Olivia. *Sucks to be you, kid.*

Well, I could always keep the camera unactivated, but it irritated me having to waste one of my fishbowls.

Julia seemed to be enjoying the situation. Recently she seemed to be enjoying everything.

While I was wrapping the two clocks in bubble wrap, Mark showed up with his recently purchased cane in hand, destroying my theory that he wanted to avoid any possible uncomfortable situation for me or him.

"Look at this beautiful cane. It's made of hundred-year-old walnut and has a hand-carved marble handle." He did a few tricks, rolling it in his fingers like a majorette.

"Honey, what do you want a cane for?"

"It gives me an air of dignity, don't you think?" he said, leaning on it like an English lord.

"Yeah, right, tons of dignity . . . I bought two clocks from Alice. You pay; I'm out of money."

"That's all you want me for, to get money out of me."

"Honey, I make ten times what you do in a year," she said, amused, yet not wishing to offend, before kissing him.

I wanted to vomit witnessing that everyday scene. I'd already heard much of the same in their private life through my snitches, but seeing them live and direct, acting silly and saying sweet nothings, was unpleasant and made me sad, because it reminded me of Chris and me. And now there was Mark, looking like a doting husband, amused and in love with his wife and his life, while he was carrying on an affair with me. Could Mark be a mirror image of Chris? Was he showing me his MO, the path to discover Chris's double life?

"Will we see each other later?" Mark asked me.

It took me a moment to respond. I was alarmed, as if I had forgotten that Julia had just left to look at scarves and Olivia had gone off to play.

"You've really left me hanging lately," he insisted. "Are you avoiding me?"

"I'm not avoiding you. I've been really busy."

Since I'd gone back to making the clocks and had promised myself not to sleep with him again, I had only given in once. It was the day of my thirty-fourth birthday. February 21. Of course, I didn't tell him it was my birthday; I didn't want him to feel important. But I needed to celebrate. Because even if I'd spent the morning with Olivia and Ruby taking Panda out for a ride at Horse Rush Farms and then making a special meal that Miriam and Chloe came over to share with us, I felt a knot that I thought Mark would be able to untie. The worst thing is that he did. I felt good during the hour we spent together late that night on the boat. And I didn't like that. I only wanted him to fuck me and get it over with. Throw off the baggage and tension. But it gave me— or made me feel—something that up until then I'd only gotten from Chris: protected. I needed my corner, my shell, my place in the world. Everything ordered. I needed to curl up once in a while and embrace someone I loved, and for that someone to embrace me and love me. All that had happened, maybe just for a few brief seconds, but it was enough to trip all the alarms, make me get up and dash out of there with a flimsy excuse—*I have to stop in at the pharmacy before they close blah, blah, blah* . . . Was I falling in love? It frightened me so much I cut off any possibility of another encounter.

"Did I do something wrong?"

"No, you didn't do anything wrong; it's the opposite; you're doing everything right. One look at you both and I can see that."

I couldn't help that little note of spite. He must have realized it, because he smiled at me softly, relieved. As if in reality, he had only been worried about my possibly losing interest and not so much about the fact that we hadn't slept together in three weeks. He clearly loved seeing me jealous.

"They're a hundred and fifty dollars," I said. If Julia had paid, I'd have let her have them for $120.

———

In the middle of the flurry of activity before the fair, as if I didn't have enough fish to fry with the scrambling, the stress, the excitement, the long hours, the clocks and the fishbowls, one of the snitches wanted to reassert itself before being forgotten and succumbing to the attraction and the power of images, and captured the following conversation in Summer's bedroom:

> SUMMER (*crying hysterically*): Fuck, what is this? It's disgusting! Aunt Jenny! What's happening to me?!
>
> JENNIFER: Relax, Summer. Your water broke. Everything is fine. I'm going to call Ben to get the ambulance boat ready.
>
> SUMMER: It's so gross! It's worse than in the movies.
>
> JENNIFER: Summer, come on, now, breathe, everything that's happening is totally normal. Your due date was more than two weeks ago. The gynecologist saw you the day before yesterday and said you had already begun dilating a bit. Come on, let's go to the car, can you walk?
>
> SUMMER: No, dammit, we're not going to make it to the hospital! It's falling out of me; I can feel it!
>
> JENNIFER: The contractions are still spaced out. There's plenty of time to get to the hospital.
>
> SUMMER (*breathing haltingly*): Slap me. Slap me, Aunt Jenny; I'm hysterical; my nerves are taking over; give me one of those slaps of yours, please.
>
> *Pause. Slap.*
>
> SUMMER (*sobbing more calmly*): Thanks.

Four days later, Summer and Jennifer were back with the baby. During a pause at lunch, I closed the stand and went with Miriam and the girls to visit them, with a spy clock as a gift, naturally.

OLIVIA (*giving Summer the clock*): It's a whale clock, and it's from me and Miriam and Chloe and Ruby and Mama.

SUMMER (*absently*): Thanks.

Jennifer can barely conceal the strain on her face. It feels more like a funeral than a birth.

MIRIAM (*whispers to Jennifer*): I think she's starting to be aware of how unaware she was.

JENNIFER (*doesn't like the comment*): She's tired, that's all. It was a very long labor.

The baby starts crying. She's hungry. We leave.

When they're alone:

JENNIFER: You need to feed the baby.

SUMMER: No, it's going to mess up my boobs. I read it on the internet.

JENNIFER (*with great patience*): Summer, it's healthier for her. It helps her build her own natural defenses.

SUMMER: Defenses against who? Against you? Then I'll take some too.

JENNIFER (*with zero patience*): Feed her! Now!

The constant arguments were interspersed with brief truces when they had some visitor, and it was all smiles as they kept up appearances. Well, more or less, because Summer didn't bother to fake too much.

Visit from Alex and Amanda, who is now visibly pregnant, which corroborates the theory that they moved the wedding up for that reason.

AMANDA: Oh, I'm so ready to have mine.

SUMMER: Take mine, that way you can have some practice.

Visit from Karen.

KAREN (*drunk*): She's just precious... Has her father come to see her?

SUMMER: Yeah, he's coming now; he's right around the corner. Wait and I'll introduce you to him.

Jennifer's face rebukes her.

SUMMER: No, I'm just kidding. Her father's dead.

Dead? Did she say dead? I hit Pause and rewound the video.

SUMMER: Her father's dead.

Again.

SUMMER: Her father's dead.

Again.

SUMMER: Dead.

I grabbed the calendar. Summer gave birth two weeks late, which meant she was supposed to give birth in February. So she could have gotten pregnant around Day 0 AD, coinciding with Chris's last journey. Did I really consider it a possibility? Sure, why not, it could have happened. Why wouldn't Chris sleep with an eighteen-year-old beauty with a slim, well-proportioned, voluptuous body; blond hair; and emerald eyes? The Chris I thought I knew would never have. Never. But now that person was very far away. Lost. Dissolved.

———

To round off the week of the fair, as if the birthing season was being officially inaugurated, Barbara called us to tell us that Snow White, the pony, was about to foal and we could come there if we liked.

I thought the delivery would take place in the stables, in a closed room, but no. It was in the middle of a field. *Where the mama pony chooses*, Barbara told me.

"Come on, Olivia, come over here. Don't be afraid. We're going to help Snow White," Barbara said to Olivia. She took her hand and guided her very attentively through the process, making her feel she was the one who was doing all the work. "See how it's already starting to come out? Grab here; grab the baby pony's legs. Hard. Now pull; pull and don't be afraid."

Rarely have I seen Olivia so happy and excited as when she pulled the pony from its mother's body with her own hands. Seeing its little head peep out still wrapped in the amniotic sac filled me with warmth as I remembered how Barbara helped me give birth to Ruby. Closing the circle.

"Is it a boy or a girl?" Olivia asked while she walked around the pony, counting its legs. Yes, four, not one was missing.

"Girl," Barbara answered. "Yours is a girls' family."

"Girl! Great!"

When the foal was on its feet, Olivia celebrated by giving it a hug, not worried about dirtying herself with the viscous mix of fluid and blood. A good step toward getting rid of her cleanliness compulsion.

"Can I ride her now, Barbara? Can I?"

"No, not yet. You have to wait a little bit, but you can give her a name in the meantime."

Olivia started jumping around nervously, as if she needed to pee, while she spouted off one name after another and rejected them all for various reasons. *It's too bad she can't be Puchi Puchi because there already is a Puchi Puchi, but she's like a Puchi Puchi too!* It wasn't at all difficult for her to name things. In fact, it was one of her pastimes/obsessions. But this time, she was more serious. It was her pony. It was going to be hers for all its life. She couldn't just choose a name at random. It had to be something special, something unique, something . . .

Suddenly, Oli stopped, as if her battery had run out, without warning.

"Sunset," she said. "Her name's going to be Sunset."

I don't know if she was conscious that just then the sun was falling behind the mill, as though embracing it; that when she said it, it was almost six in the evening, the hour she chose to have on her clock for-

ever; that the pony was the same coppery color—except for the mane
and the legs, which were white—as the clouds framing the event. A
moment I would never have experienced if her father hadn't died and
we hadn't ended up on the island. A moment neither she nor I would
ever forget. It made me feel light and satisfied as I rarely had been, as if
everything fit together and made sense, and it made that new world we
both needed to hold on to finally come together.

I WON THE prize for best stand at the Cherry Blossom Art Fair, as I had predicted. I would invest the $7,500 in the purchase and maintenance of Olivia's pony, since I didn't need the money. I had an even better prize: my two twenty-seven-inch monitors that showed my forty-eight cameras. Forty-eight fishbowls in thirty-four houses. To see the spectacle of monochromatic daily life—I had set them all to black-and-white to make the image more fluid—was a kind of small miracle. I never thought I'd make it so far. Soon euphoria gave way to anxiety because even if I was only reaching a small percentage of the houses on the island, around 25 percent, that constant flow of information was unfathomable. If I wanted to watch everything that was happening, I wouldn't have time for anything else. I had run too much and now my heart was pounding. I had taken too big a leap. The feeling that I was falling, which had been with me since Chris's death, intensified at times. *You don't have to see it all, all the time*, I repeated to myself without knowing where to look. *Little by little, you'll start getting a handle on the situation, be able to distinguish what's important.*

Curiously, the first few days I always ended up turning my attention to the familiar, to the first camera I put up, the one in Karen's Petite Maison, and the second, Frank's in Family Pet Land. Watching Karen do the same thing as always—drinking and not much else—calmed me down. What at first made me feel frustrated, as though I wasn't getting anywhere, now calmed me, made me feel at home. Besides, not much time was left before John's longed-for return.

And watching Frank was like gazing at the horizon to rest your eyes after spending a long time at the computer. It was another way of being alert. It wasn't about looking for clues or a suspect. It was about taking care, worrying about a specific person and his health. I didn't mind running off to Family Pet Land in the golf cart in the middle of the night to try and prevent him from eating the can of cat food he had just opened and spread ceremoniously on a bagel, ready to enjoy it as if it were pâté. I suppose that humanitarian effort made me feel good, or a little less bad. Because contemplating all those fishbowls and keeping my conscience clear was mission impossible. So Frank, with his mishaps, his recently acquired taste for cat food, and his Rose here, Rose there, served to justify this whole scenario I had set up.

Another thing that helped me to control my vertigo was scanning the fishbowls in search of possible locks where the Master Key would fit. I took screen grabs of the different rooms to blow them up and look at details. Focusing on something as concrete as that helped placate my overflowing mind.

———

For the first few weeks after the art fair, the list of suspects multiplied by three. Which I think was a response to my need to justify that large layout of fishbowls rather than the appearance of real, solid evidence.

Carrie Anne Kowalsky, single twin sister of Mindy Bishop, owner of Le Café, lived in Hartford, Connecticut, but came regularly to the island to "visit" her sister, really to drag her hookups there. She stayed in a little cottage connected to the Bishops' house, but it was private and had an open-air Jacuzzi. While looking through Chris's WTT contracts, I found one from three years ago to renovate the courts of the Hartford Tennis Club. That turned Carrie Anne Kowalsky into suspect number seventeen.

Suzette Tompkins, the island's marvelous Pilates instructor, tried out for *The Voice*. I saw her recording an audition video at her home:

Hi, my name's Suzette Tompkins, and I live on Robin Island, a little island almost no one knows between Martha's Vineyard and Nantucket. I'm twenty-eight years old and I'm a Pilates instructor, but my dream has always been to be a singer. My idol is Taylor Swift. That's why I'm going to sing "You Belong with Me." Here goes.

She did it well, to tell the truth. And while she sang the song, I remembered that the last person Chris had started following on Insta-

gram was Taylor Swift, even though he'd never shown the least interest
in her or her music. For all that, I considered Suzette Tompkins suspect
number eighteen, even if she didn't make the cut for the show.

Mike kidnapped Sandy, Miriam's dog. He went into her house while
we were at our weekly Pilates class, and when she got back, the dog was
gone. No trace of her. Chief Margaret, in collaboration with Mayor
Gwen DeRoller and the fire brigade, set up a search party to find Sandy.
A group of volunteers split up and combed the island without success.

"Mommy, what are we looking for?"

"Sandy, Miriam's dog."

"Is that why Miriam's sad?"

"Yes, Oli."

"I don't want Miriam to be sad."

"Me neither, honey."

"I have a good idea, Mommy."

"If you're going to suggest we give her Pony, the answer is no."

"How did you know?"

"Because I'm a witch and I can read your mind."

"Really? What am I thinking right now, then?"

"Now you're not thinking; now you're counting the posts on the
wooden fence around the Burrs' house."

"Wow, you really are a witch!" she said, at once frightened and as-
tonished.

I had a recording that put the blame on Mike, but for obvious reasons, I couldn't use it. Even so, I suggested to Miriam that Mike might
be behind it, and Miriam herself already suspected as much: she had the
sense he was going to use the dog as a bargaining chip in the custody
battle over Chloe. But Chief Margaret went to interrogate Mike and
affirmed that he didn't know or care anything about the matter. *Sandy
showed up from out of nowhere; she probably disappeared the same way.*
Mike wouldn't allow WasteWorks to be searched without a warrant,
so that was out of the question. What worried me most was that he
might have killed the dog. More than once, I'd tried to put a snitch
or a fishbowl in WasteWorks, but it was more or less impenetrable.
Mike had cameras watching the exterior. The only way to get inside, I

thought, was to get intimate with him, and I wasn't willing to go that far. For now.

———

Three weeks after Summer gave birth, I took Olivia and Ruby to pay her another visit. It was already the fourth time I'd gone. I had tried to take advantage of any lapse or absence to get a sample of the baby's saliva, but I hadn't gotten lucky. I'd also started gaining her trust to see if she would reveal something about the child's supposedly dead father. No luck. I usually tried to go when Jennifer was out getting groceries. Summer was much more docile without her there. She let down her defenses and showed herself as she really was: a lost, frightened girl who had just given birth.

"Are you sure you don't mind taking her for a walk?"

I had offered to take the baby out for a walk for a few hours. That didn't seem remotely necessary to Jennifer, because she was there to do that. In fact, she spent more time with the girl than the baby's mother did. Summer just breastfed her (in the end, she'd negotiated with Jennifer to do it three times daily; the rest of the time, it was the bottle) and stayed shut up in her room. But I told Jennifer that she too could use a little rest—she really looked exhausted. It was as if both of them were suffering from postpartum depression.

"No, of course I don't mind," I said to Summer. "You've spent months looking after my kids, and you've done great. Just rest. Talk to your aunt. And when I say talk, I don't mean argue; I mean talk. I'll bring her back in a few hours for her three o' clock feeding." Oops—screwup, I wasn't supposed to know that one of the feedings she'd negotiated was at three in the afternoon. What a slip. Bad. But Summer was so out of it she didn't even notice. "By the way, have you named the girl yet?"

Summer shook her head. Her eyes grew damp.

"Don't worry, it'll come to you. There's no rush."

I thought that by this time, I would be used to doing bad things and wouldn't judge myself or put myself down so much. But no, because when I took a discreet saliva sample from her in the light of day in Shoreline Park, I felt like my blood wasn't flowing right, as if I were

playing hide-and-seek. Nor did it help that there was the remotest possibility that the baby belonged to Chris.

"Can we call her Olivia?" Olivia asked.

"She can't have the same name as you, honey."

"But it's a really pretty name."

"Yeah, but for everyone else it'll be a pain."

"Then Olivia II."

"That's enough with your numbers, babe."

"Mommy, can you have more babies?" she asked me point-blank.

"Of course."

"With Daddy?"

"Olivia, I think the three of us are good for now, aren't we?"

"Yeah, for now, sure. But if you want to have one later, can it be
with Daddy?"

Pause. What to tell her?

"No, Oli, it can't be with Daddy."

"Oh. OK," she said, trying to mask her disappointment. One more
for the list?

————

Before stopping in at the DNA laboratory in Mashpee, I left Olivia in
her weekly therapy session. After she'd gotten over her suspicion during
the first few appointments; she loved being able to talk, as she put it,
about *her things*. It made her feel like an adult. Ruth, her psychologist,
had told me Olivia frequently had a hard time at school because she
couldn't suppress her obsessive-compulsive behavior. She was embarrassed that people saw her counting things, and sometimes she didn't
go out to recess, staying behind instead to line up the desks and chairs,
which she said were super-disordered, or cleaning the chalkboard because the traces of leftover chalk bothered her. The good thing is that she
seemed to have stopped adding compulsions to her repertoire. The birth
of Sunset, starting horseback riding classes with Barbara and fantasizing
about growing up to be a great Amazon had yielded fruit, no doubt
about it. It was a huge help for her to have a goal in life, something to
grab onto. Now, little by little, we had to *negotiate* so she would let go
of some of her compulsions and realize that the world wouldn't end.

———

I thought that Conrad, the director of the bank branch, had died. One Friday night, he fell asleep in front of the TV eating tortilla chips with peanut butter. Nothing out of the ordinary. The next day, he was still asleep on the sofa. Nothing out of the ordinary there either. But he hadn't gotten up by one in the afternoon, either, and his dog, Chubs, had eaten the peanut butter straight from the jar and had licked Conrad's face, and he hadn't reacted. Was he or wasn't he breathing? It was hard to tell, but he wasn't making a sound, and Conrad was a heavy snorer. I had his number. He had given it to me some time back, saying, *When you feel like it, we can go out one weekend and take the dogs for a walk and see each other without a conference table between us*, but I had never called him. Until then. He didn't pick up. *What do I do?* I thought. In fact, if he was dead, there was little I could or should do. I called a second time. And finally he woke up. He didn't have time to get the phone. I was glad. He seemed to be OK, a little groggy, but OK. What could he have taken to pass out like that for fourteen hours? He shouted at Chubs for eating the peanut butter. He made brunch—waffles with strawberry syrup, scrambled eggs and bacon—took a shower and called me back.

"It was so nice to see you called, Alice. But I was worried, I thought maybe something had happened. Everything OK?"

"Yes. I was just seeing if you wanted to go walk the dogs. But maybe it's a little late at this point . . ." I said, trying to get out of it.

"What do you mean too late?! Give me a break. It's the perfect time. We can see the sunset together."

I couldn't say no. It was inevitable that spending so much time looking at the inhabitants of the fishbowls, I would start to worry and feel responsible for their well-being.

The walk with Conrad was agreeable. He clearly appreciated the company, and I felt good and bad. Good for having agreed to take the walk, and bad because I hadn't done it before. Plus, he turned out to be a first-rate mimic. He cracked me up with his chronological rundown of the US presidents and their best-known phrases and blunders. Just when he was about to start on Bill Clinton and his memorable "I did not have sex with that woman," we ran into Mark and he saw me laughing. He couldn't cover his expression, *You traded me for that tub of lard?* At least that's what I thought he was thinking. And since we were there, I took advantage of that obligatory walk to ask Conrad, as if I just happened to be curious, what happened to the money in a checking account when a person died and no one claimed it. He said if there were no other account holders or beneficiaries or it was impossible to contact them, the money was left in limbo. *There's more than thirty billion dollars unclaimed in the United States. It's crazy.* He told me there was a webpage, MissingMoney.com, where you could look for it. I went on there as soon as I got home and put in Chris's name and mine, without results.

A few hours after he saw me walking with Conrad, Mark sent me the following message—corroborating my theory that he'd gotten jealous:

Let's go to New York together one weekend. I miss you.

I got mad when I read it. *You've got some nerve . . . You want everything: home, wife, kid, dog and lover. The true American Dream. If you're good with Julia now, go to New York with her. And by the way, you should thank me for it, because hey, things were pretty rocky when I met you both . . . So please, enjoy your wife and your perfect life and leave me in peace!* I said this to myself to snuff out my desire to go to New York with him. It worked. Halfway, but it worked.

What I didn't know was that his message had a bomb attached to it. I only realized when it exploded.

Mark and Julia's bedroom.
17:30 hours.

Mark comes out of the shower. He has a towel around his waist. Julia is standing next to the dresser, looking stern.

JULIA: Who'd you invite to spend the weekend in New York?

MARK: I don't know what you're talking about.

Mark realizes Julia has his phone.

MARK: What are you doing looking at my phone? Why the fuck did you take my phone?

I ran for the prepaid cell phone that I used exclusively for Mark. It was in my bag on silent. I looked to see if anyone had called. No one had. I had to think back to recall that I'd deactivated the voicemail.

JULIA: For weeks now, you've been the same as before.

Mark puts on a white shirt even though he's still wet. He's nervous.

JULIA: It's happening again.

MARK: What's happening again?

JULIA: You're avoiding me; you're not present.

Why didn't he erase the message? He did it on purpose. He wanted her to catch him. It's the only explanation I can see.

MARK: I'll remind you that what happened last time was your fault.

JULIA: Oh really. So what's this, then, your revenge? No, sorry, the consequences of your revenge...

Mark puts on underwear and jeans, as if he's ashamed of arguing naked or he wants to be dressed in case he has to dash out.

JULIA: Who'd you send the message to?

MARK: Give me the goddamn phone!

JULIA: You'd rather I call and find out?

MARK: Give it here!

JULIA: I've got the number memorized.

Julia tosses him the phone calmly, without violence. But Mark still fails to catch it, and it falls onto the carpet, without suffering any apparent damage.

MARK (*making sure his phone is all right*): I sent it to a colleague.

JULIA (*quoting from memory*): "Let's go to New York together one weekend. I miss you..." To a colleague? You think I'm an idiot? You don't even have the number saved.

MARK: Well, great then, you've caught me; now you've got material for your novel. Run, go write.

What are you after, Mark? Getting her attention? Paying for what you've done? Purging? Revenge? On her? On me? How can you be such a moron?! Both of us are morons!

Mark leaves. He's barefoot, with a pair of sneakers in his hand. Julia stays by herself. She grabs his phone and dials a number.

Don't call, Julia.

She stops before making the call. She finally gives up.

Half a Valium.

I erased all the messages. I took the SIM card out of the phone. I was going to break it. I stopped. What was the point in breaking it? It was better to keep it, better to keep the situation under control.

Mark didn't dare call me or message me for the next forty-eight hours. I was thankful for that, because, enraged as I was, I didn't think I could have held back from throwing all I'd seen back in his face. I didn't understand his cool, evasive attitude. It stunned me to see him acting like a completely different person from the one I knew. Was he playing a game with me? Just like me with him, I supposed. When I saw him with Julia, I got jealous. But there was something else that bothered me more: I didn't like to see this gruff Mark. It pushed me away. That was good, right?

In any case, leaving aside all the emotional connotations, the important thing was finding out what Mark meant when he said, *I'll remind you that what happened last time was your fault.* What had happened last time? The only thing that brought me slightly closer to Mark and his attitude was finding out that he hadn't brought about Julia's crisis/depression, whether it was personal, emotional or creative. It had been Julia herself who seemed to have stepped into that morass and who had provoked their marital crisis. Could it have something to do with Chris? I doubted it, but . . . Why hadn't Mark told me anything about it? Why hadn't he justified his own adultery? But on the other hand, I liked it that way. It's not very flattering to tell a person that you're hooking up with her out of pure spite.

———

Julia went to Le Café every morning. The name didn't need to be more original because it was the only café on the island. She would sit with her laptop at a table by the window that looked out onto Grand Avenue and write for hours. I could see her through the fishbowl in the café. The owner of the café, Mindy Bishop, had ordered a clock shaped like a steaming cup of coffee from me and had put it on the wall just over the counter, where she had the first dollar the shop had ever earned in a frame. It gave me a bird's-eye view of the interior and the customers.

I went in and acted clueless, as if I hadn't gone there deliberately to see her. I went to the counter, waved to Mindy and asked for a mocha to go.

"Hey there, sister," Julia said to me, still typing, barely looking up from her computer.

"Oh, hey, Julia, what's up? I didn't know you came here to write."

"I'm not writing. Banging keys isn't writing."

Angry, Julia slammed her laptop shut. I got scared, thinking she was going to confront me, that she knew Mark's message was for me. Julia must have noticed my reaction, because she smiled to calm me down.

"Today's not a writing day. It's better not to force it. When it doesn't come, it doesn't come."

"So what do you do when it's not a writing day?"

"Feel bad, question myself and trade in my coffee for a glass of wine. You in?"

"I'm in."

"Mindy, can we get a couple of glasses of white wine?"

Mindy was putting out her homemade cupcakes.

"I don't have a license to sell alcohol."

"So . . . ?" Julia asked, motioning around to show we were there alone. "Two glasses of that Chardonnay you keep in the fridge, please."

From that day on, from that wine on, my meetings with Julia in Le Café became frequent. I liked her, she was easy to talk to, to get close to and to wheedle information out of. But above all, I think I was doing it because the closer I felt to her, the further I pulled away from Mark, keeping temptation at bay. As if there were a rule in my mind that forced me to take sides: one or the other. Mark or Julia. Not both.

I DON'T KNOW if leaving the island barely a month after installing all the spy clocks was torture, a relief or a mix of both things—I was still getting my bearings with all the fishbowls and all the activity—but it was Olivia's spring break. And anyway, I could connect through my laptop or even my phone.

Olivia wasn't crazy about taking time away from Panda, Sunset and Oliver either, so she spent the entire trip to Providence counting telephone poles on the side of the road. She would reach a hundred and then start over, after making a mark on the back of her hand with a pen. She had learned to multiply before she could write.

As soon as we got there, we went to Holy Name Church, my parents' Catholic church, to a recital of the senior choir my mother took part in—in fact, she had started it. While they sang "Wir wollen alle fröhlich sein" by Michael Praetorius, I started to feel a tickling over my body, especially in my hands, and my ears began ringing slightly, as if my blood sugar was low and I was about to collapse. For a few seconds I chalked it up to not having set foot in that church since Chris's burial mass. Then I thought it might have to do with the fact that, despite the praiseworthy effort, the sweet gesture and how proud I was of my mother, they weren't singing too well. But no, I didn't think it was any of that. In any case, those symptoms passed immediately when Olivia called my attention. She was extremely pale.

"Mommy . . ."

"What is it, honey?"

"I'm sick to my stomach . . ."

"Again, babe?"

Olivia nodded.

"The recital's almost over." I took her in my arms and set her on my lap. "You know, counting posts like that in the car, it's normal you'd get sick."

But it had been a few hours since we had arrived, and she hadn't shown any prior symptoms. Her nausea didn't have to do with the 8,464 posts she had counted, just as mine didn't have to do with the out-of-key voices.

———

I put Olivia to bed early. Her symptoms were a carbon copy of those from the previous Christmas. Nausea, slight fever, a little asthma, itches and a rash on the elbows. Clearly psychosomatic. It was as if, just like me, she felt the response to our ills lay on the island.

She fell asleep while I stroked her hair. It relaxed me to make abstract figures in her fine blond strands, just like Chris's. He too had loved for me to stroke his hair while we watched our favorite television series.

My father was standing in the doorway observing us. I didn't know how long he had been there. He was very quiet. From the time of my arrival, we had spoken very little, among other things because my mother hogged the conversation.

"You remember your great-grandfather Ernst?"

"From the merchant marine?"

"That one."

"Not much. Just the stories you and Grandpa Vince told me."

"I used to love to go to the port and see him off and watch him set out on those huge ships to distant lands. He worked in the engine room shoveling coal into the firebox. But the thing is, every time he came back after spending months on the open sea, the same thing happened to him."

"The same as what?"

"The same thing that's happening to Olivia. It's called disembarkment syndrome."

"The island isn't a ship, Daddy."

"Maybe it is for her." Pause. "And maybe for you too; you're looking pale as well." Pause. "A ship in the middle of the storm, adrift."

"Daddy, we come and go on the island constantly. Couldn't it simply be that Olivia has allergies with spring starting?"

"Yeah, could be," he said, not wanting to force the conversation any further.

His message had reached me loud and clear. For a moment I felt like a spy being spied on. As if my father had painstakingly followed my every move since Chris's death.

"Dad, didn't Grandpa Ernst end up killing himself?"

"Yes," he muttered on his way out of the room.

———

I couldn't sleep. My legs were in agony, and whenever I stopped paying attention, I would clench my jaw. Unresolved nerves ran through my whole body. Mark, Julia, Summer, Jennifer, John, Karen, Frank and the rest. I felt they were calling for my attention. I had them trapped in my mind, like those residual images that remain a few seconds on the retina after you close your eyes. *Withdrawal symptoms, Alice.* And almost without realizing it, I found myself in my father's office in front of my laptop, with my browser open to the page that asked for the password to access the streaming signal from my spy cameras. I typed in and erased the password several times: *PuchiPuchi2015.* Trips back and forth for penitence. *Alice, we're on vacation, but you haven't taken a break. Three hundred and thirty-two days without stopping. So it's fine if you rest for a few days. Five days, just five days. It'll do you good.*

I closed the laptop and went back to bed, rolled over once, then again in the opposite direction. It halfway worked.

———

Well, I'm on vacation, but . . . maybe I'll take a look at the photos? At least I can glance at the new batch of photos on the camera in the cemetery. That's not on the island; it's here. That's allowed, right? That next morning I was left alone when my parents took the girls to Roger Williams Park Zoo and I decided not to go. For me, it was a trial by fire to be completely alone and not succumb to my addictions. I wanted to put myself to the test. Show myself I could. *Fine. Allowed. There were 2,722 new photos. That's all? It has been three months, and that's all the photos? Is the camera broken? No. It had been wintertime, no one goes there then.*

In just four hours, I managed to look at all the photos. Nothing.

Now what? Occupational therapy, that's what I needed. *How long since you painted? I mean painted for you? How long?*

I sat on the porch, in front of a white canvas, with my oil paints and brushes. I always kept a painting kit in places I considered home, in case inspiration struck or the need arose, as in the present case. But before I could make a brushstroke, six messages in a row came through on my phone. They were from Mark:

Hi, it's me, Mark.

New number, just for you.

I'm at *The Office*. I'm going to stay here a few days.

Things aren't good with Julia.

Come whenever you want.

Come...

My legs started shaking. Maybe that withdrawal I was suffering through, which I attributed to being a spy junkie—a term I had scorned when Antonio said it—had something to do with Mark? *Hi, my name's Alice, and I've been without Mark for forty-nine days. Hi, Alice.*

Absence intensifies love or loneliness, or both. Observing Mark's behavior with me made me ask myself if maybe Chris had pulled away from me to love me more. If the island was the place he came to miss me. During our reunions, there was always more ardor than on the normal days. The ones I missed now. I missed the ardent days too, don't get me wrong. But less.

I stayed there looking at the white canvas. I put a little black on the palette, took a thin brush, spread the paint, lightly daubed the hairs of the brush and signed the lower right-hand corner: *Alice, 2016.* Was that my world now? A small square, box, compartment, blank, empty? Where were my dreams of being a great painter?

I got another message. It was my mother this time.

We're coming back home. Mega drama with Olivia. Everything OK
now.

Olivia was asleep when they arrived. I went out to meet them and
took her in my arms. She didn't wake up, but I noticed how she grabbed
onto my neck and smelled it. She felt safe now. I was heartened by that
tiny gesture. It frightened me to think that she had gotten sick in my
absence, that she needed me and depended on me as much as I did on
her. A powerful, selfish and not particularly healthy feeling.

As soon as they'd arrived at the zoo, Olivia ran off toward the area
with the red pandas. She greeted the panda family and named them.
Well, numbered them. *Hello, Panda Number One; hello, Panda Number
Two; hello, Panda Number Three; hello, Panda Number Four; hello, Panda
Number Five.* Then they could go on to enjoy the other animals. At
lunchtime, they bought food from a kiosk and took it to the red panda
area because Olivia insisted on eating near them. *She ate too fast, almost
without chewing, no matter how often I told her to pay attention to me.*
Olivia was in a rush because she wanted to play with the red pandas. Especially with Number Five, the smallest one, but when she went to look
for him, he wasn't there. He had disappeared. She threw such a tantrum
that my father went to find the guy in charge to get him to explain to
Olivia that Number Five was fine, that he hadn't left, hadn't gotten sick
and definitely hadn't died, which was what Olivia was afraid of. But
before that happened, Olivia started to choke. She couldn't breathe.
My mother went hysterical. A man with his three kids took charge of
the situation: he was a doctor. *I thought he must have been divorced. Very
handsome,* my mother observed in the midst of her anguished tale. He
examined Olivia, made sure she hadn't aspirated, that her respiratory
pathways were clear. But Olivia kept getting worse. He took her in his
arms. He ran off with her to the zoo's medical services. Just before they
arrived, Olivia vomited, then she got better: her color came back, her
breathing became normal, and the scare was over. *The doctor stayed until
he was sure everything was fine. I thanked him and asked for his name and
address to send him a token of thanks for his help, but really I was thinking*

he could be a good match for you. He was really handsome, right, George? Before they left, Olivia insisted on making sure Number Five was OK. She wasn't satisfied with what the zoo employee told her; she had to go see with her own eyes.

Look, see him there eating bamboo? You scared my granddaughter very badly, Number Five, my father upbraided the panda.

So that's it, indigestion, my mother concluded. *You want me to give you the doctor's number? His name's Donald. I talked to him about you; I said you were very pretty. And he answered, "If she's your daughter, I don't doubt it one bit." How charming, right? Oh, and he confirmed it: recently divorced. He had the kids for vacation. Yes, I asked him about it. Don't look at me with the same face as your father, dear. I did it for you.*

My diagnosis was a bit different from hers. Olivia had had an anxiety attack. What could be circulating so virulently and recurrently in her little body? Her tale about the incident at the zoo turned out to be much more concise, direct and devastating.

"What happened to you at the zoo, honey?"

"I got sick because I couldn't find Number Five. I thought he had left. Like Daddy. But then he came back and that's the end."

I tried to convince myself that it had been a simple summer storm, the kind that soaks you unexpectedly but doesn't have any real consequences—especially for her. But I couldn't stop thinking of how the last time we'd gone to the zoo had been with Chris. A year ago, also during spring break. On that visit, Olivia decided that the red pandas were her super-favorite out of all the animals in the world. She didn't name them because she wasn't yet obsessed with order, but we did have to go back and eat next to them. Was she repeating the same ritual to see if her father would turn the corner to pick her up and carry her off on his shoulders?

———

Again I found myself in my father's office, in front of the laptop, debating whether to take a peek at my fishbowls or not. In reality I had them set so that whatever movement happened in front of them would be recorded. So there was no risk of missing anything. It was better that way. Leaving them to record a few days and then going over the material, fast-forwarding through the video, to see if anything interesting happened. I'd save a lot of time. And that was the thing that bothered me the most: despite knowing all that, I could hardly restrain the discomfort that was eating me up inside. *Just a little look. To make sure all the fishbowls are working right, then off to bed. No, hold on, it's like your father's whiskey. You have to be the one who feels you're in control of it and not it of you.* But before I could log in—and I was going to do it—I heard Olivia's whiny voice.

"What are you doing up, sweetheart?"

"I had a nightmare with Puchi Puchi, Number Five, Panda, Daddy and Oliver. They were all in a cage at the zoo. I was counting them, but I never could finish, because I would mess up before I got to five and I would have to start over."

"Well, it's over now, honey. Here, drink a little water; you're dehydrated; you've been sweating."

I gave her the water, dried the sweat on her forehead and changed her pajama top, which was damp.

"Mommy, am I crazy?"

I got a knot in my throat and my eyes teared up when I heard the question.

"No, honey, of course not. Why do you say that?"

"At school they say I'm crazy because I do weird things and that only crazy kids go to the psychologist. Beth Yoxhimer said it, and so did Eric Aver, Gordon Howie, Sandy Karstetter and Steve Poppler."

She had listed them in alphabetical order by first name. That didn't help to relieve my sorrow.

"You're not crazy, Oli. Don't pay them any mind. You're very sensitive, and you're still a little sad about what happened with Daddy. That's normal. Don't worry about it. Next week, we'll go see Ruth, and you'll see, she'll tell you the same."

"I don't want to see Ruth."

"But you love going to see Ruth . . ."

"I want to see Oliver."

"When we go back to the island, we'll see him."

"No, I want to see him now."

"Honey, we're almost three hours from home. And it's night. We can't go now."

"FaceTime hasn't connected since we left. I haven't seen him in three days."

"Well, it's OK; you will."

"Is he dead?"

"Who? Oliver? Of course not."

"When Daddy died, we went to the island." I think that was the first time she had verbalized that her father had died, at least so bluntly. "Did we leave the island this time because Oliver died?"

"No, baby. He hasn't died. And we didn't *leave* the island either. Oliver's at home. He's on break."

"I don't like breaks." She didn't say it like a hysterical child but with deep grief. "Let's go see him."

"Listen, don't talk nonsense or I'll end up getting mad." I decided to get hard with her and see if that pulled her out of the vortex. "I told you we can't, and that's that. Now go to bed."

Silence. She stayed still, without saying anything, staring straight into my eyes. I thought it had worked. But she didn't close her eyes; she didn't even blink.

"I close my eyes and I see him dead, like when it happened to me with Daddy."

WHEN JOHN CAME back, it didn't catch me by surprise. I had it down on the calendar, April 14. I was expecting it.

I had done my homework. I had cameras or snitches in the office, bedroom, kitchen and main room at the inn. Also, during various expeditions, taking advantage of Karen's absence—and when I say absence, I mean just that she was three sheets to the wind, barely conscious—I had tried the Master Key in every imaginable lock without any result. I had found photos of John in his student days and when he was a football player, as well as during his time as an assistant coach. Chris wasn't in any of them. I had also found photos of John, Mark and Keith on a boat, fishing and posing with a smile along with a bluefin tuna that was six feet long and over four hundred pounds, which did nothing but make me yearn to be on Mark's boat. Shadows, all shadows.

John was quiet those first few days back, serious, out of sorts. Karen barely talked to him. It was clear this was an important exercise in containment and moderation. She told me that it was hard for John to reconnect with the world after being shut up in a submarine for four months. He needed time. Time he spent exclusively on getting Rick ready for sailing season—to the boy's misfortune. He took him out of school early, with the blessing of the principal, who was a close friend. He didn't want anything to compromise his selection of colleges and his ultimate objective: the 2020 Olympic Games in Tokyo.

In any case, there wasn't a single mention, gesture or action that could tie him to Chris. Maybe I had placed too many expectations on John? What did I hope would happen when he returned? Once more, I had the feeling that I had been deceiving myself, grasping with all my might onto his tangential connection to Chris. To his return. To keep the speeding train of my investigation from running off the rails, I supposed. To know that there would be at least one stop along the way.

John's return. That was my handbrake. Now I had the feeling that I had just blown through that station. And now what? Where did I go? How much fuel did I still have in the steam engine of my obsession?

———

"How long have we known each other?"

"A little more than seven months, I think."

"I'd say fifteen days. Since we met each other here one day and switched the coffee to wine."

"Yeah, that's true . . ." It was a fact that our complicity had grown exponentially in that café, which was almost always empty except for us.

"So I guess enough time hasn't passed . . ."

"For what?"

"To tell you I had an affair a few years ago."

I tried to keep my face and body from reacting to the wave of nervousness I felt on hearing those words. Affair. A few years ago. Chris?

"Affair? Did I say affair? How awful," she rebuked herself. "Like I was Nicholas Sparks. Which I would have liked, to be honest . . . I was hooking up with another guy for almost three years . . . And you know how Mark found out?" I shook my head. "Reading my last novel."

"But the novel doesn't say anything about infidelity."

"That's exactly it: I tried so hard to keep from writing about it that finally it became too obvious. And to top it off, the novel ended up being an insubstantial piece of shit," she said, not hiding her anger. "Lots of times I ask myself to what extent I provoke the things that happen to me to have material for my novels . . . I think I'm afraid of easy cohabitation. The anesthesia of the middle class. It's fine to write about it but not to fall into it."

"Then I don't know if this is the best place to look for stories."

"This is the perfect place to look for stories. The more calm there is on the surface, the more lava there is underground about to erupt. What a shitty metaphor. Don't ever let me write that in a novel. Though now that I think of it, I believe I already did . . ." She was beating herself up the way I did. That made me feel more normal. "Anyway, watch out."

"What do you mean?"

"All I see and hear might end up in one of my novels."

———

The DNA test results arrived by courier.

Ruby and Olivia II
Probability of relation: 0.00001%

I'm glad, really glad. But it doesn't end here, Summer Monfilletto. By hook or by crook, I'm finding out who Olivia II's father is.

Why this sudden commitment, if it didn't have anything to do with Chris anymore? Because I was curious. No, it was much more than that. I had a need to know.

JENNIFER AND SUMMER had agreed to a ceasefire and an end to hostilities, though communication was practically null. Summer just breastfed Olivia II three times a day. That was her only responsibility with the baby; the rest of the time she spent watching reality shows on TV and putting cream on her breasts so she wouldn't get stretch marks. Jennifer took charge of the baby all day. It seemed strange to me that she almost never took her out on the street. She didn't socialize; it seemed as if she wanted to hide the baby from the rest of the islanders. She had always been very retiring and evasive, but now, with a baby in the mix, it was much more noticeable.

The conversation that intrigued me most was a phone call from a friend of Summer's—maybe the only one—from outside the island:

SUMMER: Disgusted, girl, I mean I've got the urge to get up and go God knows where... So you're going to flip out, but the thing is, being shut up in here, you go stir crazy. And all this time and breastfeeding the baby so much... So I don't know, it's like, even though you don't want to, you end up caring about the thing. I don't know, it's like something weird happens in your head. I even thought about keeping her. That's what I'm saying... What do you mean she's not mine? I gave birth to her. The baby's mine if I want her. Jeez, you're always so negative. I tell you my shit because I don't have anyone else to talk to about this, and instead of supporting me, you're pouring salt in the wound.

Everything indicated she was going to give the baby up for adoption. To whom? Or was she a surrogate mother? For whom? Both questions pointed straight to Jennifer.

———

I had been following John's steps all over the island. I was on guard day and night in case he made any strange moves or left Robin Island. I even decided to bump into him one day. Sometimes seeing and hearing a person just through the fishbowls was dehumanizing; it made them un-real. I needed to interact with the characters without the glass between us. *Characters? When did you turn the people into characters?*

"Hey, Alice, what's up? They told me you were a hit at the Cherry Blossom Art Fair," John said to me. I had run into him in the pharmacy.

"Yeah, it went well."

"You've filled my house up with clocks. They're pretty, though, no doubt."

"How were things for you in the submarine? Where did you go on maneuvers?"

"Can't say. That's classified information. Well, look, now that you're here, I'm going to give you something and save myself a stamp."

He went through a backpack with a navy logo and took out an en-velope with my name and address on it.

"An invitation. Keith's going to have a blowout party for his fiftieth birthday."

"Oh yeah, Karen mentioned it. How nice. I'm looking forward to going," I said.

"Well, we'll see if you get lucky this time. You know what I mean, right?" he winked at me.

"Yeah, I know. We'll see . . ." I said, pretending to be shy.

————

"And Mark?" I felt obliged to ask Julia during our usual morning coffee at Le Café.

At that point his absence was more than obvious; it would have been weird not to ask. Julia might take my discretion as a sign of respect for her privacy, but she could also find it suspicious. And although she'd memorized the phone number I used with Mark, she had never dialed it. But he had gone on sending me almost daily messages.

Hello?

Are you there?

Did you change numbers? My message is showing as unread.

Yes, you've read it.

Fuck, Alice, at least tell me what's going on.

I deserve an explanation.

No, I don't deserve an explanation. I'm sorry I lost it. I just really want to see you.

Bad.

I've decided your silence is a good sign.

So don't answer me, don't write me, that way I'll know you love me, deep down you love me.

I love you too.

I think you're my Samantha.

Would you let me be your Paul?

Samantha was my brother Paul's girlfriend, the one who died, in case you don't remember.

Sorry, I was really drunk last night, I feel alone.

I'm pathetic. I make myself sick.

I'm not like this, at least I didn't used to be. I don't know what the fuck is happening to me.

I'm going to stop writing you. I don't want you to remember me like this. I want to be the man who helped you bring a life into the world.

I want everything to be all right between us. You're one of the few good things on this island.

You've given me and helped me a lot, but I don't need you anymore.

Now, finally, I am going to respect your silence.

Alice, are you there?

I will always be here for you, when you're ready.

Two days without writing you, but I haven't stopped thinking of you.

I'm in NY.

I'd love for you to be here with me.

I think I'm going to get a divorce.

I'm not happy.

Your silence doesn't pull me away from you, it pulls me away from Julia.

It helps me to see things clearer.

Thanks, Alice, for being there without being there.

I'm not trying to be with you anymore. I'm really not.

I'm trying to be with me.

I'm going to throw this phone in the Hudson. I'm getting rid of it.

My message in a bottle for you.

I love you, m.

When I met him, he was full of life, a man sure of himself. Now it surprised me and made me want to reject him when I saw that he wanted me so desperately he couldn't contain himself. Seeing him so fragile and vulnerable. But I had the feeling he was continuing to write me because I gave off something in the distance and in my silence, legitimizing him. Why didn't I answer him or see him to put an end to the matter? Maybe I wanted to have him there? To keep sending me those messages that were so mysterious but so full of feeling? Three days had passed since he'd supposedly thrown the phone in the Hudson. At first I was thankful for his silence, but now I was genuinely worried about him. I needed to know he was all right. Maybe that's why I had asked Julia.

"He's in New York. He's been there all week. But you know, if it was up to me, he could stay."

"Why?"

"What time is it?" she asked, looking at her cell. "Eleven thirty. A little early, no?"

"A little early for what?"

"Mindy," Julia said, "give us two of our usual."

"They're going to end up sending in inspectors, and then you'll see . . ." Mindy complained without much conviction.

"Yeah, sure . . . And don't even think about serving us in coffee cups again—this isn't Prohibition."

She didn't even wait for the wine to get into her veins; she started opening up right away.

"I think that Mark is having or has had an affair. Did I say affair again? I'm hopeless . . ."

I was the one who drank my wine in two sips this time.

"So why do you think that?"

"Because all of a sudden, we're fine. He started looking at me again. Seeing me. Being there again."

"I don't understand." I did. "If being fine is a symptom of someone having an affair, that's pretty messed up, no?"

"Guilt is one of the great driving forces of our society . . . Guilt, fear and vengeance are extremely poisonous, but in the right measure, they're a revitalizing blend."

"That's kind of what your novels are about, right?" I said, just to say something, so she wouldn't notice my nerves.

"That's kind of what life is about, right?"

"I guess so . . ." I smiled and forced myself not to look down or take refuge in my almost empty glass of wine.

"You know what the novel I'm working on now is about? A successful novelist in a supposed creative crisis, because she always draws on what she lives and experiences, but since she's just been through an extramarital relationship with another man, she doesn't dare write about it for fear her husband will find out. But in the end she realizes her husband is having this torrid, passionate romance . . . Did I say a torrid, passionate romance? Good God, I'm awful. To hell with Nicholas Sparks, I sound like Danielle Steel. Which I also wouldn't mind, as far as that goes."

"Well, it sounds very interesting," I said, forcing myself to speak. I was stiff with fear as she approached the truth, of being caught, as if she was setting out a trap for me. Unable to put a brake on my impulses, I asked, "So how does the story end?"

She took her time replying, as if she was celebrating something inside.

"You don't want me to spoil it for you, do you? You'll have to read the book. If I ever finish it . . .'

We laughed, and the relaxed tone of the conversation made any possibility of following up on the theme vanish. I'd be lying if I said I wasn't glad. Very.

Julia smiled.

"You know, someday I'd really like to write about you, Alice."

And by her gaze and the silence that accompanied her words, I thought that what she was really trying to say to me was: *I'm already doing it, already writing about you. This, all this, including Chris, is part of my novel.* And that made me even more afraid.

"HELLO, FAVORITE BLONDE! I missed you," Antonio greeted me, effusive as usual.

Ever since I'd practically plundered Night Eyes with my purchase of fifty cameras, I hadn't been back. Antonio smiled at Ruby, who was in the baby carrier, as usual.

"Hello, little kangaroo, you grew a lot."

It was true. She had also become a great observer. In fact I had started leaving her outside the attic when I went in because I felt she was starting to absorb everything. She seemed hooked on the monitors, scanning the fishbowls, just like me. OK, so she was only a little more than ten months old, but I didn't want her to become too familiar with the attic or feel it was a normal place for her to go.

"I need to hack a computer," I said after the usual greetings.

"What computer? CIA computer? FBI? Pentagon? White House?"

"No, a normal one. Like mine."

"You want hack your own computer?"

"No, Antonio, one like mine. Not mine."

"It was joke, Blondie! Bad joke, but joke." And before I could say anything, he added, "I know, you never like joke. So, you have access normal computer like yours? You can actually be in front of computer you want to hack alone?"

"Uh, yeah, I guess so . . ."

"Well, if you can be in front of computer one minute, it's very easy. Even Spanish can do it."

———

I waited for Olivia to make a perfect triangle with the piece of swordfish she was eating. She had learned to use a knife to make her cuts more precise. She wouldn't eat just any piece of the swordfish: it had to be of uniform thickness, round, without gelatinous edges. Ray Schepler, drug-dealing fisherman and suspect number six, cracked up when I told him I used round metal pastry molds to cut the fish before I cooked it.

"That's it? You're going to leave the rest?" I asked her.

Olivia didn't answer. She looked a little frustrated, as if she didn't know how to keep eating but also preserve the geometric figure.

"I know you're hungry and want to eat more, right? You love sword-fish."

Again she didn't answer.

"You know what you can do with the triangle? Turn it into a rhombus by cutting off the lower right- and lower left-hand corners diagonally."

I brought my knife over to show her where to cut.

"Don't touch it. I already know how to make a rhombus. Wendy showed me."

And in fact she did know. She gobbled up the two just-excised pieces. Then she looked at the fish again, unsure how to proceed.

"And now, if you cut the rhombus down the middle, you have . . ."

"Two triangles . . . I know!"

"By the way, Oli. Would you like to make a deal?"

"No, because you won't keep your side . . ."

"That's not the best way to negotiate, Oli. You want to go back to the horse ranch tomorrow to see Sunset and ride Panda?"

"OK, I accept."

"No. Not just I accept. There's got to be an exchange. It's a deal, remember?"

"In exchange for what, then?"

"You say good morning each day to Pony and put food and water in her dishes."

"Do I have to touch her?"

"It would be nice if you'd pet her, but for now I'll be happy if you don't hit her."

"OK."

"And one more thing . . ."

"No, now it doesn't count, that's a trick. We already have a deal."

"Don't worry, it's something small, you'll love it. It's a game."

———

It was the first time I had had dinner in Julia's house. Though in reality, Oliver and Olivia were having dinner while Julia and I ate oysters from Bishop Oyster Farm that I had bought beforehand because it was part of my plan. Mark was still gone. I wasn't sure whether in New York or exiled to *The Office*. He hadn't written me again. *And tell me, Alice, how does it make you feel that he's stopped looking for you and begging desperately for your presence? You like that?*

Julia, like me, locked the door to her office. She didn't like her space to be invaded. Even in Mark's absence, she kept doing it. During one of our meetings, she explained it was a writer's paranoia, as if she were afraid the words she had written might escape. She kept the key in her purse, which she always left in the entrance, hanging on a coat-tree.

I had calculated that in total I needed three or four minutes. I could step away to go to the bathroom, but the office was on the upper floor, and the bathroom was next to the kitchen. It would be very weird and suspicious. That's where Olivia came into play.

"Look, honey, it's very simple. You remember three months ago, when you messed something up in the bathroom?"

"With the paper?"

"Yes, with the paper, you were wiping your butt and you insisted you had to tear the toilet paper off right where the line was and since you didn't manage to, you kept pulling more and more paper out and throwing it all in the toilet and you used practically a whole roll before you got it right. And of course, you flushed afterward and what happened?"

"I stopped it up . . . and you had to call the plumber. Chloe's dad."

"Yes, Mike . . . You think you could do that again?"

"I learned to tear the paper better. Now I almost always do it right the first time."

"Right, but stopping up another toilet, could you do it?"

"I don't want to see Mike again. He scares me."

"Well, this time you're just going to have to do it."

———

Olivia carried out Operation Stop up the Toilet in the Bathroom Next to Julia's Kitchen to perfection. Ten minutes of chaos, the excuse that an oyster was making me ill, a fleeting visit to the upstairs bathroom after fishing out the keys to Julia's office, a moment of panic when I couldn't find the right key, a second moment of panic when I thought maybe Julia had security cameras inside, a third moment of panic when I put the pen drive with the Trojan in the USB slot of her computer, a fourth moment of panic when I left the office and realized like an idiot I had left the pen drive inside, self-induced vomiting in the bathroom to make my absence seem more plausible, another round of vomiting because of my nerves, and that was that: I had access to the writer's fortress.

When I got back home, I felt invincible.

"Mommy, do you think Julia got mad at me?"

"No, no way."

"And Oliver? You think he might think I'm stupid?"

"No, Oliver was cracking up."

"Yeah, he did laugh a little."

"See? Everything's OK."

"Why did you want me to do it?"

"We agreed there would be no questions. You'd do it and that would be all. That was the deal."

"Are we going to keep doing stuff like that?"

"Not for now."

"I like helping you."

"And I like for you to help me . . . Hey, that thing you said to me about wanting to leave the island . . ." It had come during a temper tantrum, but it had still worried me.

"Not anymore. I was just upset."

"What a fibber you are . . ." I laughed and kissed her. "See you to-morrow, honey. Sleep well. I love you."

"I love you too, Mommy, lots. See you tomorrow."

A roll to one side, a roll to the other.

———

I took advantage of the times when Julia wasn't in front of her computer or in the office to go through all her files and documents. I was afraid when I used the Trojan that something would go wrong and she would figure it out. The first thing I did was go through her emails. I did a search for *Chris*. Nothing. Then for *Williams*. Nothing either.

It took me four days to read the unfinished novel. I started reading with my heart pounding, looking for Chris to be wrapped up in it, hidden or running along in broad daylight through any of its pages, but then I was the one who got wrapped up, trapped, hidden and running through the pages. For those four days I didn't go to Le Café, among other things because I was afraid I wouldn't be able to hold back from saying how much I liked it or asking about the characters or the ending. It was the story of a forbidden love, very intense, but kept hidden, probably the same way she had lived it. It submerged you in a universe of absolute normality and apparent happiness that was nothing more than a thin, delicate layer, a slippery surface that barely let you intuit the inner abyss of the characters. The characters didn't have names, which only accentuated the mystery around the truth they were struggling to hide, the lie of their own existence. As anonymous as they were recognizable.

The fifth day, I went.

"I thought that after almost dying at my house from the oysters you wouldn't want to hear from me again."

"Come on. It was to leave you alone. I've been seeing you here for weeks, and I have the feeling I'm not letting you write."

"You're wrong, and believe it or not, I've been writing a lot since I've been hanging out with you. It's lit a spark. And here's the proof."

She rested her hand on top of a thick, white envelope. I knew immediately it contained her novel. All my grand efforts for nothing. *But what about the fun you had, Alice? That adrenaline rush you felt, right? What do you have to say about that, spy junkie?*

"Is that what I think it is?" I asked.

"I don't have an agent or an editor or a husband. So you're up. Sorry . . ."

"Wow . . . what an honor . . . I don't know what to say. But I'm not a professional. I mean my judgment . . ."

"Your judgment is your judgment, and that's what interests me right now. Here." She handed me a new pencil. "I hope that when you're done reading it, you'll have worn it down to the nub making notes in the margins."

"But, is it done?" I asked to dissimulate and because for a moment I thought that the abrupt ending without an ending was the ending. Aren't almost all endings in life like that?

"Novels are never finished, not even after you publish them. In any case, no, it doesn't have an ending yet. I don't know how to finish it . . . Maybe you can help me."

Then the door opened and Mark appeared. He caught both of us by surprise. And by his face, he must not have expected us either.

"Hi," he said. "I just got back from New York."

"Yeah, I see that," Julia said drily.

"I'm grabbing a coffee."

"Well, you're in the right place."

Mark went to the counter and asked Mindy for a large caramel iced coffee. For the four minutes he was in the café—Mindy took a lot of care with each coffee she served—no one said a single word. I made a gesture to Julia to indicate that if she wanted, I would leave them alone, but she shook her head softly. Mindy gave Mark his coffee. He paid, left the change as a tip, took off the lid, poured in two packets of brown sugar, stirred it calmly, replaced the lid, and walked out, taking a sip.

"Bye," he said.

"Bye," Julia said.

"Bye," I said.

It made me sad to see him. When he appeared, I avoided eye contact. Which made me realize I had missed him. That's why I hadn't answered any of his messages. I didn't want the issue to end. Our issue. I liked having him there. I had forced myself to choose between Julia and Mark, and now it turned out I loved both of them. Which couldn't be. Or could it?

"GIRL, THAT'S ONE hell of a disappearing act you've pulled," Karen rebuked me on the way to her brother Keith's birthday party on Napoleon Island.

John piloted the motorboat in silence, beer in hand, lost in his thoughts. How I wanted to put a Trojan in his head to hack his brain and trace Chris.

"Fifty years. But he's like a good wine, he gets better with age. Very important people from the cultural and political world are coming. So you should really grab hold of this opportunity; if not I'll find him a better potential mate."

Karen kept stressing that we'd make a great couple. Yeah, right, great. Why was Karen going crazy trying to pair her brother up with someone?

Miriam, who was still sad due to Sandy's disappearance, especially because she'd now lost any hope of getting her back, had also chewed me out for my absence. *We have a talk about our friendship, we cry together, we hug, we reinforce our tie, but then you always go off and do your own thing. If I had known that, I wouldn't have sold you the house. You iceberg.* It was true that with all the cameras I had installed in the houses, I had been taking refuge more often in the attic. I didn't need to socialize much to get information. I had to promise Miriam dinner twice a month in exchange for her accompanying me to Keith's birthday. Much as I needed to go, I didn't want to do it alone. We had left Ruby and Chloe at Tina's daycare and Olivia with Barbara at Horse Rush Farm. They'd started the season and opened the doors to the public.

Without a doubt, Napoleon Island was spectacular. It was presided over by a medieval style castle built in 1901. It belonged to the family of Napoleon LeCaptain, a famous architect of the time, who designed numerous churches in Philadelphia and New York, as well as a number of fire stations and several of the first skyscrapers.

Keith's place was enchanting, and he was the perfect host. As soon as he saw me, he took my arm, rescuing me from his sister, and gave me a tour while he told me the history of the island. I thought that living there alone, in that enormous castle, could end up becoming a sentence. A constant reminder that you didn't have a family of your own to fill the rooms. Though, apparently, in his philanthropic guise, he housed all sorts of artists looking for inspiration there without charging them anything.

"Anyway, I don't live alone," he said. He had eight employees who lived at the castle permanently and others who came from spring to fall. "And that's without mentioning Napoleon's ghost. He's my best friend and faithful companion."

That was when I saw Mark. He had a glass of champagne in his hand, standing a short distance from the rest of the visitors, his back turned, on the edge of a small cliff overlooking the sea. As if he had sensed my presence, he turned around slightly to look at me, raised his glass in a toast and drank while he turned his eyes back to the sea without waiting for a response. He looked very handsome. It was clear he'd been going out on the boat because his skin was brown and weathered, and his hair lighter and wavier. He seemed much more relaxed than he had in a long time. And there's nothing I like better than a calm man.

———

Everyone seemed to be enjoying the delicious food, the music and the pleasant weather.

After the cake—Keith refused to blow out the candles, saying it was corny—Miriam decided to take a nap in the hammock by the pool because she was woozy after all the wine. I decided to take a walk around the tiny island, fleeing the crowd for a bit.

I thought Mark had already gone, because I hadn't seen him for some time. That's why it surprised me to find him on the small path encircling the island. *Surprised? You don't suppose you were looking for him?* He was going in the opposite direction.

"Hey."

"Hey . . . I thought you'd already left."

"I wanted to, but it seemed in bad taste to leave before the cake."

"Right . . ."

"Were you looking for me?"

"Huh? No, no . . ." For some reason I felt suddenly shy. "I was taking a walk to help the food and the wine go down."

"Oh, well then, I'll leave you alone."

"If you want to come along, that's fine with me."

"OK, we don't want you to get lost on this huge island," he joked, almost as shy as I was.

We walked awhile in silence. It relaxed me not to feel resentment or sexual tension. Maybe everything between us was over. Or maybe we were both faking it and there were bloody battles taking place inside us.

Then I saw it in the distance, behind a line of firs. A tennis court. Hard court (cement or plastic), blue and white. I stopped instinctively only to start off again, afraid Mark would realize I was on the verge of an anxiety attack. I almost told him we should turn back, that it was getting late, but we hadn't even been walking for five minutes. The tennis court was on the edge of the island. I asked myself why it would be there and not closer to the castle. Did I want it to be one of Chris's courts or not? If I wanted to find out, I'd have to go in and look around, check out the surface, look for that little metal plaque that would identify Chris's business, and that would help explain certain things, or at least part of his tie to the island. But I decided to keep going, to get away from there, to take the trail back. Mark stopped me, however. There, did it have to be right there?

"Alice, I want to apologize to you for my behavior." I didn't know if I was ready to have a conversation just then, much less one of that kind. "We stopped seeing each other from one day to the next, without any sort of explanation. I didn't understand it, and I know it's ridiculous, but I felt used. When it was obvious that I was the one using you. And not only was I using you, but it was working. Everything was going better, especially with Julia. I was afraid if I stopped seeing you, that everything would turn bad again. I got really nervous and stupid, and

I fucked things up on my own. I know, I want it all, and in life, you can't have it all."

The way he made that mea culpa, so calmly and clearly, reminded me of the Mark I liked, the one I had gotten hooked on, which didn't help me control my anxiety. Not that, nor the fact that all of a sudden I remembered that though Chris worked with numerous surfaces and colors of court depending on the customers' preferences, the blue and white plastic ones—I think they were called deco turf—were his favorites.

"Why didn't you tell me Julia had had an affair?" I decided to grab hold of the conversation, since my legs were starting to give out.

"Because when you like someone a lot, you try to hide your defects at all costs."

"Julia having a lover is a defect of yours?"

"Defect, mistake, error, weak point, shit. Call it what you want, but yeah, that's how I experienced it at least. How I experience it."

So it was exactly what I felt a great deal of the time with regard to Chris's lie. I looked inside myself for the error that had made him take cover on Robin Island. Had our love story been too perfect, too plain? Or was I stunned because I had just seen a plaque on one of the fence posts that read, in big letters, WTT? Williams Tennis Tech. Chris's business. Was the tennis court a consequence of his stay on the island?

———

When I got home, I looked through all the files, documents, and construction and maintenance contracts for Chris's courts. Physical copies and data files. There were hundreds. I had kept a copy of all of them. But none was for Napoleon Island, and none bore Keith's name. Had I been mistaken? No, it wasn't possible, unless I had suffered a hallucination. I helped Chris design the plaque myself. And now it was on Napoleon Island, the island where suspect number nineteen officially resided.

———

During my last visit to Night Eyes, before I left with all I needed to hack Julia's computer, the combination of a supreme will to survive, absorption into consumer society, and the need to go on fooling myself and to latch onto any port in a storm led me to fixate on a voice changer. A different model. *Quick and easy. Change tone, reverb, pitch, octave. Fifty pre-*

sets. *Great selection. With an adaptor for all models of smartphone. So good not even your mother will recognize you! Sale. Before: $695. Now: $529.* An irresistible offer, clearly justified because in the moment I decided Chris was going to make a few more phone calls from beyond the grave.

Voice changer. Mode: Man—Preset 14.
Day 354. 11:20 hours.

Keith's cell phone rings.

KEITH: Hello?

ME: Hello, Keith.

KEITH: Hi, who is this?

ME: Chris.

KEITH: Chris? Chris who?

ME: Williams.

KEITH: Huh? I can't hear you well. Where are you? It sounds metallic. Hello.

ME: I'm Chris Williams.

KEITH: Chris Williams? Doesn't ring a bell.

ME: I worked on your tennis court.

KEITH: What?

ME: I worked on your tennis court.

KEITH: My tennis court...? Ah! Chris! Long time no hear! How's it going? Don't tell me I still owe you something?

ME: No, no...

KEITH: So, to what do I owe the... Wait... No way. My brother-in-law told me... Tell me who this is again?

I hang up.

Karen's Petite Maison. Reception.
Day 355. 01:35 hours.

John logs on to Gchat and moments later message from Keith appears
on the screen.

KEITH: Hi. You know, something really weird happened to me this
morning.

JOHN: What?

KEITH: You told me your friend Chris Williams had died, didn't you? The
guy who did tennis courts.

JOHN: Don't tell me. He called you.

KEITH: How do you know?

JOHN: What did his voice sound like? Weird, a little distorted, right?

KEITH: Yeah, like with lots of background noise.

JOHN: That goddamn son of a bitch!

KEITH: Who, Chris?

JOHN: No, no, the son of a bitch who's trying to pass as him.

KEITH: But how do you know all this?

JOHN: Because he was calling me for a while.

KEITH: For what?

JOHN: Nothing, just to fuck with me.

KEITH: But are you sure Chris...

JOHN: Yeah, he died a year ago or something like that. I read it in the
University of Virginia alumni magazine.

KEITH: How weird...

JOHN: Did you ever hear anything from Chris after the installation?

KEITH: Nope.

JOHN: And you paid him everything?

KEITH: Yeah. Everything. But now that you mention it, it was kind of weird.

JOHN: Why?

KEITH: Because he didn't want to bill me for it. He asked me to pay him in cash. Under the table. I don't remember too well why I said yes. That was more than three years ago now...

JOHN: I think this guy, whoever he is, wants to blackmail you or me or both of us...

KEITH: Blackmail us, why?

JOHN: Hey, you haven't told anybody about...

KEITH: No, just my sister. Just kidding!

JOHN: Well, don't say a word if the guy calls you back. Nothing.

KEITH: And what about you?

JOHN: What about me? Have I said anything to him? Are you nuts?

KEITH: No, I mean did you ever have contact with Chris after.

JOHN: No, never again...

KEITH: You sure?

JOHN: What, are you getting jealous now? I love it.

So that explained why Karen was having trouble finding Keith a girl-friend. But there was no other mention of Chris. Did he meet Keith on Robin Island and then get the contract? Or was it the other way around? Was it installing the tennis court that got him to the island? There was only way to find out: going back to Napoleon Island.

Keith was ecstatic—his words—when I accepted his invitation to

meet Napoleon's ghost in person and bring the girls to spend the weekend. I took him a gift, a spy clock in the form of a captain's helm. *It's
just a small thing, though I know it doesn't fit well in a place with so much
history and tradition.*

*What do you mean?! Don't be ridiculous, I love it! It's perfect for my
yacht.*

Keith had designed an elaborate plan of activities for Olivia. On
Saturday he dressed all his employees as pirates, including himself in
the part of Redbeard. He organized a scavenger hunt on the island to
look for a buried treasure. Olivia had a blast deciphering clues, fleeing
in dread from the *bad* pirates, tracing out new routes (with a plastic
bucket in the pool), making friends with Napoleon's ghost to get his
help guiding her through the adventure (the creaks and weird sounds
were his compass), determining the path she needed to follow (the road
that led to the docks), crossing dangerous bridges (over the pond) and
finally finding the secret lair that would lead her to the treasure: a crate
that I would swear was from the seventeenth century and contained . . .
Oh no, how terrible, there's nothing inside! Nothing!

The pirate Redbeard told her, "The important thing in any adventure isn't where you go, but the path and the fun you've had and all
you've learned. The greatest treasure at the end of the adventure is you."

"Well, that's bull," Olivia said.

But it turned out that, when she returned to her room, Olivia found
a box filled with toys and sweets.

———

As soon as I arrived on the island, the first thing I did when I had the
chance was absent myself briefly and confirm that the tennis court really was made by WTT, but I didn't dare ask Keith anything about it.
Instead, I devoted my weekend to examining some of the rooms more
carefully, always with the excuse that I'd gotten lost, because it really
was easy to get lost in there. Though it was also completely normal to
let yourself go and wander through the various chambers, because all of
them had their own story. It was a museum castle. So what was I looking for? I already knew there wasn't a contract with Chris. So why was I
snooping through the rooms, unless I was trying to find an improbable

lock the Master Key would fit? The true source of information was Keith. That was the lock I needed to open. I had to talk to him. Win his confidence, spend time with him, like that very moment, at night, in front of the fireplace in the living room, alone, sipping a Burgundy Grand Cru.

"When did you buy the island? Did you have to do lots of renovations?" I asked him.

He'd acquired it six years earlier, and he'd been living there for four. He had barely touched the interior of the castle. Only what couldn't be seen: the plumbing, the drains, the wiring, etc. He liked its age, the life there was in every room. On the exterior he did a bit more. In fact, there were two big renovations. One before he moved and the other, even bigger, after Hurricane Sandy. I wanted to ask the questions I had about Chris, but they seemed to get stuck in my throat. I only managed to squeeze in a few of them in a natural way. *You play a lot of tennis? That court's brand new, no?* To which he answered that he barely used it; he put it there mostly for the guests. Then on with the story of his renovations. How the Japanese garden was by Yoshimi Kono; how the grounds were planted with Bermuda grass, just like in Augusta where they played the Masters; how the wood on the dock was American white oak; how the pool had been designed by a certain Cipriano, an Italian who imported the glass tiles from the island of Murano. But not a single detail about the tennis court because, in the end, a tennis court is just a tennis court.

THE BEACH IS deserted. The reeds are dancing to the sound of the northwesterly wind. The sand makes little whirls on the dunes. It's cold, even though it's mid-May. A man is standing on the shore, looking hypnotized by the sea. I can't see his face. I don't need to see his face. His hair is disheveled and frizzy from the salt breeze. He's barefoot, with khaki pants rolled up a few times. The waves break with a wild beauty. The receding surf traces furrows around the soles of his feet. I come over slowly, as if I want to surprise him or am worried I'll frighten him. I'm naked, except for a baggy turtleneck sweater that hangs almost to my knees. I think I just made love to the man, and the sweater is his. The neighing of wild horses. A seagull suspended in the air. I no longer know what I feel for this man. I don't know if I want to frighten him, push him away, hit him, kiss him, hug him, love him. I come up beside him and he looks at me. He smiles at me.

"Alice, look for simple things. Life isn't as twisted as it seems."

I slap him. He remains impassive.

"Life is a succession of loose ends, Alice. And it's right that it's like that."

I slap him again, harder. He doesn't budge, even though he's bleeding from the corner of his mouth.

"Why don't you ask me? Come on, ask me. Ask me what I'm doing on the island."

Another smack. Another. And another. Harder and harder each time, more and more desperate. But soon the blows turn to desire, arousal. I kiss him. His mouth has the metallic taste of blood. I like it. It turns me on even more. We fall to the ground without hurting ourselves. We start to make love. The waves caress our feet. He gets on top of me. His thrusting is in time with the crashing of the waves, stronger and stronger as the tide rises, closer and closer to orgasm. I swallow water. I try to slow him down even though I don't want him to stop. The waves drag me away. Just me.

I die from pleasure. I die from drowning.

———

I woke up brusquely soaked in a mix of tears, sweat and vaginal lubrication. I was still coming as I tried to catch my breath.

I was afraid to look at the clock, thinking it would be 12:01 AM. The accursed hour when I received the call from emergency services telling me about Chris's accident. This was the accursed night, the night Chris had died. I finally looked at the clock. It was 5:30 AM. I cried when I remembered the absolute helplessness I'd felt just a year ago at that same hour, more or less, when I saw the sun come up at St. Luke's Hospital in New Bedford, and spoke with my mother on the phone, lying, unable to tell her the truth.

I thought about getting into bed with Olivia, but I didn't want to transmit my anxiety, even if I was calmer now. So I got up, put on one of Chris's sweatshirts and went out onto the porch wrapped in a blanket to cry a little more and watch the sunrise.

———

"How much time has passed, Mommy?"

It melted my heart that my child, queen of numbers, expert counter of things, didn't know that just that very day it was a year from her father's death.

"Exactly one year, Oli."

"And after a year you have to cry?"

"If you need to cry, then yes, of course. Whatever your body asks you to do, honey."

"My body's asking me to change the flowers. Can I do them my way?"

"But you chose that bouquet. It's gorgeous. Why do you want to change the flowers?"

"I don't want to change them. I want to put them in order, because if I don't arrange them my way, then I'll want to cry."

"Whatever, honey, cry, I mean, arrange them however you want."

I had gone to the cemetery with Olivia and Ruby, to have a picnic next to Chris's grave and feed the swans and ducks in the pond without the guard seeing us. It was a beautiful, cheerful day. If not, I wouldn't have taken Olivia. I wanted her to associate that place with something that would assuage the grief of recalling that her father was no longer with us.

"Much better, right?" Olivia asked me.

She had taken apart the bouquet and placed the flowers over the grave to read *DAD*. Each letter with a different type and color of flower. At the florist, she had insisted she wanted three different types of flowers: white roses, yellow daisies and purple irises. And the same number of each.

"Were you already planning this at the florist?"

"Of course, Mommy."

"Why didn't you tell me?"

"Because it was a surprise. I have secrets too . . ."

"Well, I have to admit, your secret turned out very nice, honey. It's a beautiful idea."

Then she took out the adhesive tape she had in her pocket—which indicated that she really had planned everything before leaving the house—and began taping the flowers to the stone so they wouldn't move.

In the meantime, I rustled in the bushes to rescue the photo camera. Useless up to now. I smiled when I recalled the first photo I took in the cemetery. Ruby's carriage and the rake placed beside it to simulate a person's stature. *All the things that have happened in a year*, I thought. I had suffered almost the worst devastation, and yet there I was. I remembered the sorrow and frayed nerves of that moment in the cemetery, setting up the camera. And now that seemed to me as easy and routine as brushing my teeth. Hadn't I done far more complex and risky things? Suddenly, I felt a little like Katniss Everdeen, the heroine of *The Hunger Games*, one of my favorite series. Chris liked it too, and we used to get in bed, each of us with our tablets, and read it simultaneously, page by page. I still remember how mad I got when Chris was on one of his trips and couldn't help it and read the end of the second book. That was expressly prohibited. We could only read it together. I waited for him biting my nails, anxious to know how it ended, and he *cheated on me*. Was that the only way he'd cheated on me? The funny thing is I caught him. When he arrived home from that trip, we had dinner, then a quick fuck, so we could get down to reading, and I caught him. I saw almost right away that he'd already read it. He really was bad at faking. He was quiet, not doing or saying anything, taking refuge in the screen of his e-book. But I realized it. *I've got you! You read the end!* I berated him. *No, what are you talking about?! Shut up and keep reading, it's really interesting!* he said, turning red. I got pretty pissed, not just playing around, for real. How was it possible I could catch him in all those innocent little lies, almost imperceptible, and not the huge lie he was living? Had I not wanted to see?

There were 4,344 new photos, for a total of 18,358. A good batch, given that only a month had passed since the last harvest. *It is spring, which encourages families to visit the graves of their loved ones*, I thought. I was glad to know I had two or three days of work ahead of me to go through all of them, but it was also worrying. I changed the battery and the memory card discreetly before my parents popped up in the distance in the company of the Williamses.

"Mom, we're going to try and make this a nice, upbeat day for the girls," I whispered when I hugged her. "No drama and no painful crying bouts, OK?"

Against all predictions, my mother kept her word. Crying, well, of course she cried. We all cried. But it was a liberating cry, accompanied by laughter and funny stories about Chris. A proper homage. I brought up that thing Chris had said about when he was a boy and he thought he was adopted because he didn't have gapped teeth like his mother, aunt, sister and cousin. All because of his dumb cousin Kenny and the damn gap between their teeth. Betty remembered they decided to show him the video of the birth to get him to chill out, but no matter how diligently they looked through the boxes in the basement, they couldn't find it, and finally they showed him the video of Tricia's birth, because they weren't that far apart in age and a baby's a baby and it's impossible to tell. Chris calmed down and never brought it up again. As much as I laughed at the anecdote, I was still taking note, pestered by the thought of my justified, but now discarded, suspicion of a possible relation between Chris and Stephen, and thinking maybe I had been wrong. What if Jennifer was the one who was somehow related to Chris? I knew good and well that my random hunch had more to do with my wishes than with reality. I would have loved to have a sister like Jennifer. Like Jennifer or like Miriam or like Julia or even like Karen. *Maybe you should give them all DNA tests while we're at it, everyone on the island, what do you say . . .*

I WAS BARELY on photo 625 out of 4,344 when one of the fishbowls caught my attention. A new argument—apparently definitive—between Jennifer and Summer. Jennifer never liked to argue in front of Stephen, as if she didn't want to disturb his comatose peace. Maybe that was it; Summer was playing with an advantage there, and that's why she decided to drop the bomb.

SUMMER: I'm leaving.

JENNIFER: You're going out?

SUMMER: Yeah, off the island. Forever. Bye-bye, Robin Island. This momma's leaving Mom's Island behind.

JENNIFER: What do you mean, you're leaving forever?

SUMMER: We agreed I'd breastfeed the girl for three months.

JENNIFER: No, we agreed to six, and then we negotiated it down to five. And we're not even through the three months you're saying.

SUMMER: Can you show me where we signed that agreement?

JENNIFER: What do you mean, signed? We didn't sign anything.

SUMMER: Exactly . . . I'm not spending another summer here dying of boredom. Give me the rest of the money and I'm out.

JENNIFER: Summer, let's have the party in peace.

SUMMER: You know what it is? The more time I spend with the baby, the closer I get to her. So you choose, Aunt Jenny: Either I bounce or I keep the girl. There's only one life . . .

Almost simultaneously, I saw the fishbowl in Karen's Petite Maison go out. Karen was talking on the phone with a swimming pool maintenance company so they would come clean hers for the summer. The image went black and the audio cut out completely. The signal was gone. I made sure all the connections were good. Everything was in order. The camera had burned out. It wasn't the first to do so. Sometimes the signal had interference, was blurry, or would give out for a few hours or even days and then come back. It depended on a multitude of meteorological, environmental, structural and fortuitous factors. I didn't think anything more of it at the time. I ignored the flapping of the butterfly wing that anticipated the chaos about to come raining down on me.

———

I reread Julia's novel—this time the printout she gave me—to try and find some clue about Chris. But once more, just after starting, I found myself trapped, forgot my purpose and abandoned the notebook and pencil.

An hour and two glasses of wine into our meeting in Le Café, Julia stopped suspecting every positive comment I made.

"I love how the people don't have names. It makes them more enigmatic and more recognizable at the same time."

"At first they had them: the protagonists were named Paul and Samantha, like Mark's brother and his girlfriend. Samantha died in an accident on prom night. Paul had gone with her."

Of course I knew the sad story of Paul and Samantha perfectly, and I already knew the characters had been called that at first because I remembered the argument Julia had had with Mark when she caught him reading her novel at Christmas.

"So why did you decide to take away their names?"

"Well, I could lie to you and tell you something artsy, but the truth is that it was pure spite. I was mad at Mark, and I decided he didn't deserve any homage to his brother or his girlfriend or their perfect love."

"A perfect love can only be a love cut short, that's what she says in the novel."

"Good memory."

"You think that phrase is true?"

"I don't know. You?" Before I could say anything, Julia corrected herself. "Sorry, how tactless. That wasn't my intention. I'd forgotten that . . . How stupid. I'm sorry."

"Don't worry, it's nothing. Me, I don't think the phrase is true. At least I need to think it isn't true."

"But there must be something you didn't like."

"Yeah, there's one thing I couldn't stand: not being able to read the end. How does the novel end?"

"I don't know; I'm blocked. That's why I gave it to you. It's been two weeks since I've written a line. Sometimes I think the best ending is not having an ending. But I think that's just a lazy lie to justify myself. So don't ask me if it's finished or how it's going to end, Alice. You tell me how you want the story to end."

———

When I returned home, I scrolled through the photos from the cemetery on my laptop. The majority of them were passersby visiting other graves, the guard making his rounds—sometimes walking, sometimes on a bike, sometimes in a car—the gardener and the occasional animal passing by. It was like a photo essay, a study of life through death. I thought that a great painter of the everyday—Norman Rockwell, Edward Hopper, Andrew Wyeth, or even Diego Sánchez Sanz—would have used those photos as a mirror into society to make a powerful and expressive collection of pictures, always with the same setting. Starting with the first photo, of Ruby's carriage with the rake inside. That would undoubtedly be the first in the series. *So why don't you do it, or try, at least?*

When I was on photo 2,510 out of 4,344, I paused to look at the monitors and noticed that more of the fishbowls had gone black.

I realized that the batteries in the cameras were starting to die. I felt an uncontrollable attack of rage, an inner burning, a horror. Because I knew this was going to happen. Of course I knew. Maybe not so soon, but it was bound to happen. I had thought it wouldn't matter because I was going to solve the mystery before then.

"You told me they'd last a year."

Now Antonio was the target of my anger.

"A year standby, Blondie. Seems like not much standby, cameras and you. You always active."

"I'm asking you, please, don't joke with me."

Maybe Antonio had been scamming me the whole time, anticipating my movements and needs? Making me run up absurd expenses, taking me down a much longer road than necessary, like a taxi driver with a clueless tourist. What if he was the one who had turned me into a spy junkie?

"It no joke . . . Blondie, you no tell me you no think first. Of course you think first. You very smart."

"No, I have the impression you're the smart one here."

"Hey, hold up," he said, seriously. "Don't get aggressive, I no like. You on my good side, I'm good; you on my bad side, I'm bad, Alice."

Why was I blaming poor Antonio? He had always put up with my madness and bad moods with a smile and infinite patience? I was going to let down my guard and ask him sincerely to forgive me, when I realized he had mentioned my name.

"How do you know my name?"

"License plate, Alice. Figure out things much easier than it seem. You should have diversify more. Not always buy here. Beginner's mistake. You know after September 11, law we have to alert authorities when strange behaviors? And your behavior very strange."

I wanted to cry and confess everything to him, tell him everything from the beginning and then offer him any kind of sexual favor. Whatever it was to keep him from turning me in.

"What do I have to do to keep you from turning me in?"

He took two seconds to answer. It goes without saying they lasted an eternity. I started to get queasy and wanted to run out, but running would do nothing in that case.

"Alice, two things: If you don't mind, I rather still call you Blondie. Very offensive you still not know I on your side. And I never turn you in for mistreating me."

"Sorry, Antonio, forgive me, the truth is . . ."

"Eh, eh, wait. You not listen to second thing." This is where I thought we'd turn a dramatic corner and he would ask me for some sexual favor. "Smile a little. Smile for me. A smile, Blondie."

I didn't smile right away, but Ruby did. Her unworried pleasant smile infected me.

"How lovely. See how easy it is be happy when you want to?"

How right Antonio was. But somehow, just then, I wasn't interested in my own happiness.

"I did think this would happen," I said, completely tired of myself. "That sooner or later they'd go out . . ."

"Can I make question? What you try and find out? What you investigating? Why so much time and effort? Maybe you think doing something bad?"

"Every day, every hour."

"Or maybe you doing everything good."

"Antonio, I don't understand you."

"I think you do."

I suppose he meant that maybe all my methods were keeping me from finding the truth. That I was deceiving myself. Maybe. In that moment it didn't matter to me. Nothing mattered to me. Before I could go, Antonio, seeing my dejection, took out a camera from under the counter.

"Wi-Fi connection, HD quality, no interference. Remote viewing and recording. Motion-activated."

"I don't see how it's different from the cameras you sold me before."

"There's a difference maybe you don't know: cable. Connect to plug and bingo, signal forever. Sound familiar?"

Seeing that I didn't react, he added, "Look, do one thing. Today better go home and rest a little. No buy nothing. Think about you and what you want to do with life. I always be here for what you need. But let me make you gift. Let me give you camera."

That was like giving a baggie to an addict at the entrance to Narcotics Anonymous. It revived the burning suspicion that Antonio was manipulating me, that I was his precious toy, his favorite video game, and he wanted to take it to the next level. Anyway, obviously I took the gift.

———

When I was on photo 3,510 of 4,344, I noticed on the monitor that John and Keith were on Gchat. But they didn't mention Chris again. What had he been to them? Apparently no one. A university acquaintance for John, a guy who put in tennis courts for Keith. If he'd been going back and forth to Robin Island for two years, how is it possible John hadn't seen him again? Was he lying? And Chris installing the court without a contract or an invoice, billing in cash? He was very scrupulous about the law. I didn't understand anything. I was furious and wanted to confront them. Punish them for going on with their sexual games and not answering my questions.

On the table, I had the camera Antonio had given me. I wasn't thinking of opening it. At least, not for now. I had to seriously reconsider what I was doing and where I was going.

AND THEN IT appeared. Photo 4,209 of 4,344. I was skipping quickly through the image gallery, barely paying attention, worried because I had lost the signal on three more cameras.

So I skipped over it. From 4,209 to 4,221 until I noticed that the person who had entered on the left side of the frame had passed behind the grave only to end up retracing her steps and standing in front of it with her back to the camera, staying there without moving.

First I went through a phase of denial—which must have lasted two or three seconds—as if I distrusted the veracity of those images or didn't know that person—whom I obviously knew. Then I felt a sudden euphoria, when I realized that my first move, which had been to place a camera in front of Chris's grave, was the one that had given me the most definitive clue up to then, and that the person who showed up there, the guilty party to use another term, was on my list of suspects. I heard the crying of a baby, Chloe, and on one of the monitors, I saw, from the fishbowl in Miriam's kitchen, that she had gotten dizzy, from what looked like hypoglycemia—it had affected her a time or two when she'd been with me—as she was warming up Chloe's puree in a pot of warm water while she cooked something in a pan. Miraculously, she hadn't fallen, because she'd caught the edge of the counter. She tripped and hit the pot with the baby food with her elbow, knocking it on the floor and frightening the baby, making her cry. She stood up with difficulty to go to the refrigerator and get a glucose shot she kept for such occasions, but she didn't make it in time and passed out, hitting her head on the refrigerator door as she fell. Miriam had told me some time ago that her hypoglycemia was especially nasty, that it never showed any symptoms before an attack. On the contrary, she felt magnificent, like a person kayaking through calm, crystalline waters, with the current, not anticipating a waterfall a few yards away—a metaphor I identified with closely. She always kept a couple of sugar packets in her pocket, but more than once, she hadn't had time to get to them. And the only thing she missed about Mike was the calm she felt knowing she had someone with her in case it hit her, particularly when Chloe was around.

I waited. A little, but I waited. I couldn't intervene. I wasn't supposed to be seeing that. I waited to see if she regained consciousness, took something for her blood sugar, turned off the fire and consoled Chloe. But it didn't happen, and when the frying pan started to burn, I ran over there.

I ran an average of six miles a day, and every half-mile I would run full speed for thirty seconds. I was in really good shape. Even so, for the barely one hundred yards between my house and Miriam's, it was like one of those nightmares in which you can't move forward no matter how hard you try.

When I entered the kitchen, the column of fire from the frying pan had caught onto the wallpaper and was devouring the floral motifs adorning it, threatening to spread to the cabinets. I grabbed the frying pan. I dropped it immediately because I burned myself. I repeated the operation, protecting my hand with a washcloth, and threw it into the sink. I put out the flames with water. I cut off the burners on the stove and used the same frying pan to throw water on the scorched wallpaper.

I had to push Miriam roughly because she was blocking the door to the fridge. I knew where she kept the Glucagon, the glucose injection for times like the, I had seen it on numerous visits. I didn't know the proper way to give the injection, but I assumed that in case of emergency, any part of the body would do. I gave it to her in the stomach, which is where they always inject insulin. While waiting for it to take effect, I rolled Miriam over, made sure she was breathing and didn't have her tongue or vomit covering her throat, and felt her head to make sure she wasn't bleeding. Then I went for Chloe, who was still crying, disconsolate. I took her in my arms and tried to calm her down.

"It's over now, Chloe, it's over." I put her in the playpen while thinking that if Miriam died, I would happily keep her. Twisted thoughts always occurred to me in those situations. "Don't cry, baby, it was just a little scare."

Then Miriam regained consciousness. She smiled at me like someone who's awakened from the best and most pleasing of dreams.

"Hey . . ." she mused. "Where'd you come from? You're not here, right? I'm dead."

"The fire alarm went off and I heard it," I lied in a whisper. Chloe had stopped crying and had fallen asleep, overcome by the stress.

"I love you so much, my guardian angel," she said with all the love her weakness permitted.

———

I went back home drunk on the euphoria of having saved two beloved lives. Playing God felt really good. I was always questioning the point of all my spying, and suddenly I felt justified. It had been worth it. Was that my purpose in life?

Being the god of the island, the all-seeing eye, the one pulling the invisible threads that controlled the world, my world, the island. I had made clocks to get inside the houses. Now the island itself had become a clock, and I had access to the internal mechanism that controlled everything.

But then I went into the house, saw the door to the attic open and remembered what I had seen before the accident. I had completely forgotten. The ecstatic sensation, my delusions of grandeur and my otherworldly airs vanished at the drop of a hat. I was paralyzed in front of the door, not knowing whether I should enter or not. What if I was wrong? What if the person in photo 4,209 wasn't who I thought it was? The photos had good resolution, but they were taken from fairly far away. And I hadn't zoomed in to confirm my suspicions; I hadn't had time because Chloe's crying had caught my attention. *Well, go up and confirm it, come on now. What scares you more: if it is or it isn't? But you know damn well who it is.*

Ruby was in the living room in her playpen. She'd stopped playing and was standing up holding on to the railing. It was the first time she had stood up alone. She looked at me in silence, curious to know what I would do, what my next stop would be. It seemed like she was trying to send me a message. As if she had acquired the ability to stand up some time back but had decided to wait and show me on a certain date, at an important moment.

I closed the door to the attic and locked it.

———

Olivia was at Beth Yoxhimer's birthday. I called Julia to ask her to pick her up—Oliver had gone too—and take her home with them. *Of course, no problem. But are you OK? You sound a little weird,* she said. I was speaking slowly because I was having trouble getting the words out and I didn't want to mess up. *Yeah, of course, I'm good. I'll come pick her up later.* And I hung up before she could go on making conversation.

I spent the afternoon sitting in the chair in the kitchen where I had fed Ruby before putting her back in her playpen so she could take a nap, looking in the direction of the attic, as if there were a monster inside that I was afraid would come eat me. Cause, effect. You put out a camera; you get a result. *Photo 4,209; no, better yet, 4,221, the one where she's in front of the tombstone with her back to the camera, not showing her face. That's right, I won't show her face. No one will recognize her. I won't even recognize her. No, from now on, I'm going to ignore her—yes, it's a* her, *a woman. I'm going to forget what I know about her. That treasure chest's not getting opened. That part of the island isn't getting investigated. That mystery isn't getting solved.* I wondered whether it was really so important to know. I shielded myself in my respect for Chris, in preserving his privacy, but it was ridiculous to take refuge at that point. My refuge was Chris's lie. That was my only truth, and it was only a matter of time before I went back to those photos and followed that clue.

———

I abandoned my command post in the attic, avoided peeking at the fish-bowls on the monitors because one of the spy clocks—still active—was in the living room of the woman from photo 4,209. That, not looking, was why I missed an incident that would have grave repercussions. Immediate ones.

I just wanted the day to be finished. But the day was going to finish with me. When a knock came at the door, it was already late at night. I was relieved to see it was Miriam when I looked through the peephole. I opened the door.

"Hey, Miriam."

I was so tired that I didn't notice what she had in her hands until her serious face and the omission of a greeting made me ask myself what was happening. She had a clock in her hand. The clock shaped like a moon that I had given her.

"My fire alarm hasn't had batteries in months. It was always going off . . ."

Dread. Why did I say what I had about the fire alarm? I could have told her I had gone there for salt or just for a visit. I didn't need an excuse to stop by her house, just like she didn't need one to come to mine.

"What are you doing? Was it Mike? Did he tell you to record me, to watch me? Was it him? Are you helping him take custody of Chloe away from me?"

Tell her, Alice. Tell her the truth.

"No, it wasn't Mike," I said coldly.

"Then what? Are you a pervert? Do you get horny watching me? How many people have you done this with? Do all the clocks you sold have a camera in them? Show me where you have everything. I want to see it. You have it inside, right? In the attic. Mom's Island, that's where you've got all of it, right?"

You saved her life; she owes you. And she loves you.

"I don't have to turn you in," she went on in the face of my disturbing silence. "It's enough if I tell one person, just one person, and in a matter of seconds the whole island will know. Is that what you want?"

What comes now is going to be very hard, probably the hardest part of all: the truth. You need an ally, an adult, a friend.

"You're not going to say anything? You're not even going to try and make an excuse?"

"I saved your life and your daughter's," I finally said, putting on my grandiose airs.

"You were spying on me! Me and my daughter! Why?! Tell me why! Whatever you wanted to know, I would have told you. I HAVE told you. I've told you my WHOLE life. Shit, you're my best friend! Why are you spying on me?! Why?!"

Miriam was crying, and I was about to. I needed to give in, but I was fighting with myself.

I don't remember if she slapped me in the face and called me a bitch from hell or if I just wanted her to. I closed the door and leaned back against it. Then I gave free rein to my nerves and started sobbing and trembling, trying in vain not to make noise.

I rushed to the attic meaning to break everything down. Thankful, in part, that it would help me forget what I couldn't forget. Or at least to put it off. Now there was something much more urgent, and that was eliminating anything that could give me away. But when I went up the stairs and saw everything, I froze. It was impossible to shut down the operation in a matter of minutes: the computers, monitors, routers, signal relays, the table set up to assemble the clocks, all the different gadgets I had been accumulating, the chalkboard, the maps, the books, the videos, the notebooks, the notes, the lists. I had left the island full of bodies, of blind fishbowls, of deaf snitches. My house of cards. And a gust of wind had blown it over. Just a gust of wind? The cameras dying out, photo 4,209, Miriam and her accident. Three gusts of wind in a row. I had wasted lots of time and money, for what? To put my life, my world in danger. Everything had gone to shit. My extra lives were used up. Your videogame is finished. Over. Idiot. Moron. Fool. Loser. Out of my sight. Fade to white.

I didn't want anything left, not a trace.

————

I went back over the recording from Miriam's fishbowl. This is what I had missed during my absence from the attic:

Miriam is cooking a pie, probably for me, to say thanks.

She puts it in the oven and adjusts the temperature.

She starts thinking.

She looks at the roof for a few moments.

She gets on a chair to try and reach the fire alarm. Even on her tiptoes, she can't reach.

She gets down and comes back with a little four-step ladder. Now she reaches it.

She takes down the fire alarm.

She gets down.

She takes off the top of the battery compartment to confirm what she suspects: there aren't any inside.

Her first instinct is to pick up the phone. It seems like she is going to call me and talk it over normally, even laugh about it, because there must be some other dumb explanation for how I ended up there and she was just curious. I had probably said something else and she had understood me wrong because she was groggy.

But she stops before dialing.

She looks around without knowing what she's looking for until her eyes focus on the clock on the wall. The lunatic clock, as she calls it.

She goes over as if she doesn't want to frighten it.

Looks at it carefully.

Takes it down.

Looks at it again and turns it around.

The image of the camera goes black as soon as she puts it on the table.

Sound of a drawer opening.

Sound of a hand digging through the drawer looking for a knife.

Sound of a knife unscrewing the top of the clock. It doesn't work.

Sound of another drawer opening.

Sound of a hammer banging frantically on the top, knocking off slivers of plywood.

Silence.

The image comes back.

Shot of Miriam looking into the spy camera she's just discovered.

———

I didn't want to lose Miriam. She had been my greatest support on the island. And though I knew everything was unstable, because my big lie made everything a fiction, I wanted to do right by her. And sincerely, I wanted to make sure that she wouldn't turn me in or tell someone.

I looked at a half-finished clock on the shelf. It was one of my multiple failed attempts, one that didn't met with my quality standards. It was shaped like an electric guitar, but I had abandoned it because I wasn't happy with the way the neck and the frets had turned out, too small in proportion to the body. But now it seemed perfect for what I was trying to do. Now my standards had gone down noticeably because I didn't have time to lose.

———

That year, I had been very afraid, all the time, in almost every way, but I never felt fear for my physical safety. Until that day, when I took that detour. I wished I had a gun, but I knew I'd never win going down that road. If Mike discovered I had a revolver on me, he could justify whatever he did as self-defense. *Your revolver is your clock, Alice. And your bullet is your camera.*

When I arrived at WasteWorks, it was noon and the neon sign reading "Someone's got to do it, right?" was still turned on. I had left Ruby at Tina's daycare. I felt weird without her on my back. Shorn. Unprotected. But I thought she might be a burden, especially as I wasn't totally sure how far my actions would take me or Mike's would take him. Even so, I wouldn't leave there without what I came for.

Mike was the boss and owner, but hey, he hardly ever had to get his hands dirty; he only went on service calls when the two kids he had with him—his cousin Pat and his cousin's friend Junior—couldn't handle it on their own. So Mike had more time for what he really liked: lying on the sofa watching TV in his underwear even in the dead of winter, drinking, smoking, staying up all night and dealing drugs. Since I saw him picking up the goods on New Year's Eve, I hadn't tracked him again. I wasn't interested, to tell the truth. I had enough things to investigate without wasting time on that. Until now.

Since their separation, Mike lived on the premises: he had set up— so to speak—the back room. He'd put in a sofa bed he never closed up—why waste time?—and a seventy-inch LED TV, perfect for any drug dealer worth his salt. Luckily for me, when Mike opened the door and invited me in, he had already downed a few beers.

"What an honor to have you as a visitor, miss. I thought you had blacklisted me because of my ex. Step back, Satan!"

"Well, yeah, I did. But you know, if the house starts to smell like a sewer and I don't really know where it's coming from, I gotta do something about it."

"I find the scent of shit calming. If you smell shit, you can control it. Shit that doesn't smell is worse. And when you least expect it, it swamps you and you drown in it."

"Well, anyway, I'd like you to take a look."

"To tell the truth, I don't know if I feel like it. We can't say you've treated me particularly well . . ."

I was usually very discreet, but with Mike I never hid the disgust I felt when I crossed his path.

"That's why I brought you this. Let's say it's my way of offering you a peace pipe," I said, handing him the electric guitar clock. It still smelled like fresh paint.

"You made this yourself?" he asked admiringly.

"Since I know you're a musician and the guitar is your favorite instrument, I thought you'd like it."

"Shit, Alice, that's cool, right? That's some present . . ."

"Glad you like it . . . Well, I'll leave you be. I'm sure you're really busy."

"No, wait, wait, help me put it up, OK? Choose the best place in my little mansion. You'll help?"

I knew he was going to bite. I was convinced he'd invite me in, especially if I insisted on leaving soon.

When I went in, my eyes wandered discreetly around the room searching for Sandy the dog or at least some clue to show she was still alive. Where could he have her hidden? Was he really capable of killing her?

I decided the best place for the clock was between a stolen Route 66 sign and a neon sign from Foxy Girls, a topless bar in Vegas.

"No sweat, this is perfect, between your hunting trophies," I said, making Mike laugh. He'd already had another beer. I'd turned down the offer. "All right, now I am going . . ."

"No, wait, wait . . . You can't offer me the peace pipe and leave. You don't offer the peace pipe; you smoke it. If we don't smoke, the peace will never be sealed, Alice. And the scent of shit in your house will never go away. You'll see."

Once more, he took the bait. It was pretty gross to me to sit on his unmade bed with dirty clothes all over. Mike came back with a box shaped like a chest. By then he was on his third beer—plus the ones he had had earlier and the night before. I finally said yes to one because I was afraid of smoking on an empty stomach. I know beer isn't the best form of nourishment, but I needed to calm my nerves a bit. I wanted to seem easygoing, for Mike to be relaxed and trust me so he would do what he ended up doing.

"Say what you want about drug trafficking on the Mexican border," he said while he packed marijuana into a bong, "but the border between Canada and Maine, that's a regular free-for-all."

"So you bring it to the island? Like your motto: Somebody's got to do it, right?"

"You got it . . ." he said, laughing at my wit. "But hey, I also deal in local goods. I have a little weed plantation in a hothouse I set up in the garage. Come, see for yourself."

He lit the weed, sucked through a tube and passed me the bong. It had been a long time since I'd smoked marijuana, since my stay in Madrid—at a party so Diego wouldn't think I was a prude. Since then I hadn't tried it again. When I took the bong, my fear of fainting started up immediately. Right then would be the worst time and place I could lose consciousness. I hoped that my racing heart and the adrenaline rush I had at that moment would compensate for my phobia's effects. I breathed through the tube. *Fuck it, God's will be done. If I faint and he rapes me, at least I'll have it on camera,* I thought.

"Good shit." It really was. "Well, that's that, peace pipe smoked." I felt relaxed immediately. It went to my head. I hoped the fall wouldn't be harder and more vertiginous. "So, what other treasures do you have in that chest?"

Though I already had enough material recorded for my purposes, I wanted him to fuck up, to slip in his own shit like the pig he was.

"Well, I've got a little sample here of anything you might want. Gotta try the merchandise, right?" *Good job, Mike, keep talking.* "Perks of the job." He laughed. And opened the box. "Let's see what we got here: coke, oxies, weed, angel dust, blue meth. *Breaking Bad* made it fashionable; it's a disaster the way we flip out with this shit we see on TV. What else? Anabolic steroids; Propofol, the shit that killed Michael Jackson, haven't tried that. And let's see, let's see, ah, my favorite, MDMA, the love drug." He winked. "You down?"

"I thought you were going to make it harder for me," I said, smiling. *You just fell with your whole team, moron,* I wanted to hiss in his face. I was so ecstatic inside I took another hit from the bong.

"Now tell me, Alice, my dear, why would I make it hard for you?"

I don't really know how I managed to get out of there in one piece because I was so stoned I don't remember. But I did. When I got home, I realized that in my purse I had a bag with a baggie of marijuana, two MDMA pills, and a Propofol I flushed directly toilet the drain. I kept the rest as evidence.

———

I edited the video to take out the parts where he named other people on the island. Because after showing me his arsenal, Mike started running down his extensive client list. I wasn't wild about knowing Conrad took Propofol sometimes to sleep—which explained how he'd scared me when I thought he was dead—but just on the weekends when the bank wasn't open, probably to get rid of the void and the solitude he felt; or that Reverend Henry took angel dust now and then because it made him feel closer to God; or that Lorraine and Peter took ecstasy to fuck like animals in heat; or that John, yes John, had bought MDMA from him—Mike thought it was to take it with Karen, but I knew that wasn't the drug's final destination; or that a lot of the kids on the high school sports teams were taking anabolic steroids. He didn't make any of these drug transactions in person, but with time and experience, he had ended up figuring out who was who. *There are people who leave their orders for me in the mailbox at the office, but now almost everything's done through the internet*, he told me, and next thing I knew, he was explaining that WasteWorks's website had a chat area where you could leave comments or ask questions without registering or anything. People made up an anonymous username and made their orders, indicating their favorite pickup spot. For example: *Ecstasy, fifty bucks, Wampanoag tribe totem pole.* He would send the kids in the van with the order, and there, under the plaque, they'd find the fifty dollars. *If the money's not there, we don't leave anything, obviously.* They'd leave the drugs, and through the chat room, they'd let the person know that the order was available. *End of transaction. Boom. Cool, right? Did I set it up good or did I set it up good, Alice?* I was very tempted to tell Chief Margaret what was happening. But the video wasn't for her. Besides, who knew whether she wasn't hiding behind some anonymous username to take who knows what drug, sometimes she looked pretty amped up in relation to the apparent—only apparent—calm and slow lifestyle that reigned on the island.

———

"What the fuck do you want?" Miriam said to me, very serious and hurt, when she opened the door to her house and saw me.

"You know very well I can't stand Mike, and I'd never do anything that might hurt you. I want to ask your forgiveness for doing what I did to you. I'm very sorry, really. I'm sorry I betrayed your trust. It will never happen again."

I should have told the truth and thrown myself, crying, into her arms, and asked for counsel, complicity, comprehension. But all I did was hand her a pen drive with Mike's confession and the video that showed him kidnapping Sandy.

"Here, this is so Sandy will come home and in case Mike ever tries to take custody of Chloe or stops paying his child support."

Miriam didn't say anything, just took the pen drive and closed the door. She did it softly because she must have intuited that what the drive had on it would prove vital to her and that eventually we would clear things up between us.

SO NOW WHAT? I thought. *There's nothing left for me but to face photo 4,209.* But then, as if solving Miriam's problem had cleared up part of the dense fog of my mind, an idea struck me that had all the logic in the world: maybe that visit to the cemetery didn't mean anything. I mean, obviously it meant something, but maybe she was only honoring Chris's memory. An homage paid to him a year after his death by a person who had known him and cared about him. Chris had been visiting the island a long time. Having the kind of gift with people that he had, being as extroverted and nice as he was, he must have made some solid friendships. And besides, why had I assumed she knew I was his wife and Olivia and Ruby were his daughters? I had been hiding it. There was no reason for her to know.

———

Photo 4,209 of 4,344. She had been there the same day as us. The day of the anniversary of Chris's death. A little before. How long before? Hours? Minutes? I hadn't paid attention the hour in the upper-left-hand corner of each of the photos. I didn't think there was anything interesting to find anymore. Just us when we got there. From shock, I got stuck on photo 4,221. I hadn't seen the whole sequence of photos. I hadn't seen her leave the frame. How long had she been there?

She had arrived at 9:56 AM. That meant she took the first ferry from Robin Island, the 7:30. *Nice and early, to keep from running into anyone,* I thought. From 4,221, which is when she stood in front of the grave, to 4,222, there was a time-lapse of three minutes. She stood in front of the grave for three minutes without moving. Between 4,222 and 4,224 she sat on the edge of the grave. At 4,226 she got up to go, five minutes later. She left the frame where she had entered nine minutes later and disappear in 4,223. At 10:05.

I looked over the sequence of photos again, trying not to make too many snap judgments. Trying to keep my cool, struggling to suppress the welter of emotions that piled up at the main exits for my anxiety: head, heart and stomach.

She had left something on top of the stone. Before she got up, she had placed it there. Because her back was to the camera, the gesture wasn't clear, but there was something there that hadn't been there before. It looked like a paper, a card, a note. No matter how much I zoomed, I couldn't make out what it was. Something the wind must have carried off, because in photo 4,254 it wasn't there. Fifteen minutes before we showed up at 4,267, at 11:35—a little more than an hour and a half after she left—and hogged the rest of the photos until I went over to take out the memory card.

Was I sure she hadn't been there before? I started to doubt. In any case, was that relevant? Well, yes, I must have thought so, because I went back through the 18,358 photos again. It took me two days, and I barely slept, using whatever free time the girls left me.

The result was even more disconcerting. Yes, she had been there. On three other occasions in the course of the year. She didn't go over to the tombstone. She walked past it from behind, along the road and sat on a bench in the distance on a bench. It was practically impossible to make out her face. It was normal that I hadn't noticed her. It seemed like she was visiting another grave or simply resting after taking a walk through there. Three times she had sat in the same place, facing the entrance to the cemetery. Was she waiting for me to appear? Why so far away? From fear? Respect? Shame?

Three times. The first for twenty minutes. The second, sixteen. The third, eleven. With an interval of a month and a half between the first and second visit. Two months between the second and the third. Two months and twelve days between the third and the fourth, the last, from photo 4,209, when she left something on top of the slab.

Three days had passed since that paper had flown away. It was absurd to go look for it. A waste of time. Maybe that's why I did it.

———

On my way to the cemetery, I asked myself what it meant that the visits got shorter and more spaced out over time. Was she getting over his death? Her grief? Could she maybe help me get over mine? Four visits in one year. Was that a lot or a little? A lot, obviously. Four times meant much more than a simple gesture of saying goodbye to an acquaintance or even a friend. That created a bond between them as evident as it was suspicious. Especially because she was alone. She was hiding something too. She needed a place to cry alone, and that place was the cemetery, even if it was far away. But how did she know Chris's grave was there? From the bench she was sitting on, you couldn't read the gravestone, so she'd already been there before and had found the grave. The first time she was there must have been before I placed the camera. She had been five times, minimum. I felt a great deal of hatred at that moment. I needed to in order to keep standing and not sink.

The first thing I did when I arrived back at the cemetery was look at the new photos on the LCD screen of the camouflaged camera. Little time had passed, but I wanted to know if she'd gone back. She hadn't.

I started combing the area in a ten-yard radius, looking among the shrubs, bushes, trees and tombs for whatever it was she had left there, like someone looking for a needle in a haystack, though I had already proved to myself that that wasn't something that frightened me, but the opposite. And so the fact that it took just five minutes to find the photo, curiously very close to the tree where I had hidden the camera, left me a little unsettled. It was facedown. The white mat around the back of the photo was dirty, almost blending in with the soil. It was a Polaroid, distorted from the inclement weather it had been through. When I crouched down to pick it up, I knew it was what I was looking for. Turning it over, I saw nothing because it was covered in mud and dried earth. I wiped my finger over it to clean it. The first thing I saw was my face.

It was a family photo. My family. Olivia sitting on Panda's back, wearing a helmet, holding the reins by herself, proud she didn't need any help. Ruby on top of Sunset, while I held her so she wouldn't fall. And Pony looking frightened, because she thought Olivia and Ruby were in danger and were going to fall. That photo was from our last visit to Horse Rush Farm.

After cleaning the front side, I did the same with the back, and I found a handwritten note. *You finally did it, LeCaptain. Your trip was worth it, my beloved Invisible Man.* It was signed *Bresnam.*

That photo was taken by the same person who had left it on Chris's grave. The same one who had gone there at least five times in his honor. Suspect number thirteen. The suspect who became a suspect during my mental torment at the end of the year. The suspect who was a suspect because she had sky blue cat eyes and her dimples made me jealous, and because she was taking a break from her long-time boyfriend, Jeffrey the pilot. The one with the father with Alzheimer's who was like a grandfather to Olivia now. Frank. Panda. Sunset. The one who had gotten lightheaded when I gave birth. The veterinarian from Horse Rush Farm. Barbara Rush. But all those Barbaras I had known had disappeared in one fell swoop. Now all there was in my mind was: Chris's Barbara.

———

That photo confirmed that she definitely knew who we were and had known from the beginning. She had taken it on herself to snap that picture. A family photo. *No, not you this time, Dad.*

And Frank, *Why not, if it's my family?*

And me, *Let him get in, Barbara.*

And Barbara, *No, no. This is a girls' photo. Just girls. The five girls.*

And Frank, *Oh, OK, all right, you should have said so before.*

And Barbara, *Come on, Pony, sit still. Smile. Cheese.*

Two photos. She gave me one, and kept the other, the one she put on his grave.

I could put cameras and snitches in every corner of the farm, go through her house, turn it upside down and look for the lock the Master Key opened, follow all of her movements, even get closer to her. But I knew it would do no good. She knew who I was. Had she known from the beginning? Why hadn't she told me anything? *Oh, hey, you're Chris's wife, right?* But leaving the photo, wasn't that like leaving a visiting card?

Mentally, I went back over our first encounters, straining my memory to figure out if I'd overlooked something. The first time was during Ruby's birth. She was very attentive and took the reins with Mark until she started feeling ill, right after wrapping Ruby up in a towel and putting her in my lap. I had taken it as her being overwhelmed and then the tension draining out of her after what she'd been through, but could it be that she recognized me?

There was one strange thing: she had never come over to greet me or speak to me of her own accord. Had she been avoiding me? It was obvious Barbara didn't make many social appearances on the island; she stayed out on the horse farm, almost like a recluse. Was she running from something like me? Before Karen's birthday dinner at the inn in December, we had barely crossed paths. And afterward? After that came Frank, his Alzheimer's and his visits to the house looking for Rose. That had brought us closer. And the ponies, of course. Panda and Sunset. In that way Barbara entered our lives, and our visits to the farm turned into a habit. Which had done us a lot of good, especially Olivia, however much it now turned my stomach and made me want to vomit. Our meetings were always friendly. Cordial, never intimate. Barbara never asked personal questions. Which I was thankful for because I thought I was the one who had something to hide.

The spy clock I had in the Rushes' house was a painting of horses, hers, running freely on the beach. It was probably one of the prettiest ones I had done. They had hung it in the dining room over the fireplace. And what had I seen through that fishbowl? Nothing relevant. A very close and traditional everyday life. Barbara and her father had dinner together every day, without watching TV or anything, just chatting, talking things over. Once a week, on Sunday, Jeffrey would join in, because even though he and Barbara were taking a break, Frank was like a father to him—he was an orphan—and Jeffrey was like a son to Frank. During those family dinners they talked almost exclusively about animals. It was rare to hear them mention someone from the island, unless it was directly related to their pets. They weren't at all gossipy. And me? Did they talk about me? Or Olivia? Of course they did. But it was always Frank who brought us up, talking about our comings and goings at the clinic and telling stories about Pony. Or about Olivia and the Flint saga. Or one day: *It's funny that they live in the same house as Rose when she was a teenager, where I used to go and flirt with her, listening to records and eating pancakes, always with your grandparents staring us down, of course.* Barbara always listened attentively without wanting to

know more, without showing any particular curiosity. She only brought
my name up once during their conversations. When I bought Sunset.
She was happy because it would be a financial relief for them, not just
because of the money from the sale, but also for the animal's upkeep.
And that was it, not another single mention.

I remembered hardly any of that, because it had barely attracted my
attention. I created that recap after going obsessively over all the recordings from her fishbowl. One by one. Looking for glances, gestures,
uncomfortable silences, hidden words. I didn't find anything concrete,
but there was something general. There was a kind of aura in that
forced distance: maybe I was inventing it, but she seemed to have made
a decision not to involve herself emotionally with virtually anything
that had to do with us. At least at first. Little by little, she let herself go.
Even showing real satisfaction at Olivia's progress riding Panda. But if
you ask me, it was probably all a product of my imagination. I couldn't
trust myself any longer.

————

"Free ride on Panda! Yay!"

I shook when I heard the phrase. Frank had just entered the house.
For a moment I decided to stay upstairs, holed up in the attic, until he
chose to leave. But something inside me needed, to put a word on it,
vengeance.

I almost ran downstairs.

"Mommy, Grandpa Frank's here. Let's go to the farm!"

"Hey, Barbara," Frank said to me. He had confused me with his
daughter more than once. What I had found funny before now made
me sick.

"Frank, I'm not Barbara. I'm Alice," I said drily. And before he could
say anything, if he was going to say anything, "This isn't Rose's house; it's
our house. Rose isn't here. So I'm asking you please to go. Now. Please."

"Mommy, don't talk that way to Grandpa Frank. Let him stay."

"Be quiet, Olivia. He's not your grandfather!"

That dose of reality must have awakened Frank, because he immediately felt embarrassed. He lowered his head like a boy who had peed
in the middle of class.

"Sorry, I . . ." He turned around to leave.

What part does poor Frank play in all of this? I thought regretfully. *Maybe a big one, what do you know?* I answered.

"Wait, Frank," I said, without any real intention of stopping him, knowing he wouldn't turn around. He had left the old portable record player.

"Wow, Mommy, you made him sad," Olivia said, on the verge of tears. But more than sad, she seemed frightened of her own mother.

I reacted immediately. I hugged her and kissed her. She cried.

"Sorry, Oli. I've just had a really bad day."

"Worse than the day Daddy died?"

"No, not that bad, honey. We'll never have a day that bad again. Don't get scared, OK?"

"OK . . . But one thing." I knew perfectly well what was coming next. "Why don't we go to the horse ranch?"

Ever since photo 4,209 burst into my life, almost a week earlier, we hadn't gone near Horse Rush Farm.

"I told you, they're doing renovations."

"My friend Kendall told me she was there last weekend . . ." Pause. "Did Panda or Sunset die?"

"No, Oli, don't start."

The clumsy excuses I was giving my daughter had started to be unsustainable. How was I going to deprive my daughter of one of her greatest pleasures, her best therapy? Because of the fury that was still bubbling inside me, I thought in a nasty way that I wasn't going to give Barbara the pleasure of becoming—even more so—a friend to my daughter, as if I thought she wanted to take her away from me.

I didn't dare go see her because I didn't know how she was going to react. I didn't think I could fake it, pretend everything was normal, be pleasant and friendly as I'd always been. I might break down and start crying, or beg her for an explanation. Any excuse to avoid facing her, facing the truth. But I was starting to run out of hiding places.

AS THE DAYS passed, the fishbowls continued to die. Only four re-mained active. I was running out of lives to observe, and that only raised my level of anxiety. I was becoming afraid to go out, to go shopping or to walk Ruby and Pony. So I found myself shut up at home more and more, only going out when it was absolutely necessary and, if possible, only at times when few people were out. I felt like a ship in the middle of rough seas. The island was rocking beneath my feet, Mom's Island was sinking, and I didn't know what to do to keep it afloat. Well, I did know, but I didn't dare to do it.

Olivia had been having lots of nightmares despite her redoubled efforts at rolling over and over in the bed. I finally had to give in as far as the horse ranch went. I couldn't keep her away from there. Maureen, Kendall's mother, picked Olivia up and brought her back the following Saturday and Sunday. *I'm happy to do it; that way I can stay on Barbara's case*, she said to me. Maureen and her husband, Pat Heise, had been after Barbara for a long time because they wanted to buy a plot of land that adjoined theirs, in order to build a golf course, but Barbara refused. (Which, though I didn't like to admit it, I thought was a good thing.)

A series of linked events ultimately forced me to come out of my shell, the physical one and the inner one. Stephen died. Jennifer un-plugged him. It happened a week after Summer left once and for all, dispelling Jennifer's fear that she might take the baby with her. The baby that Jennifer and her husband had always wanted and had never been able to have. Jennifer didn't need Stephen in order to hold on to life anymore. After many years living side by side with death, she could finally embrace life. She did it with the assistance of a doctor from Cape Cod Hospital and in the presence of Reverend Henry. Jennifer asked me if I could be there with her. I accepted, honored and relieved to have something to pull me out of my vicious circle.

Jennifer placed the baby on Stephen's lap. They had sedated him for the extubation to avoid seizures and unpleasant episodes. Stephen went in a matter of minutes, in peace. It was the first time I had witnessed a death, and despite my familiar fear that I might faint, it was an emotional and powerful experience. Full of love. A lesson in life and overcoming that made me reflect on letting go, on leaving things behind that we can no longer have, people that we can no longer be with, loves that have to remain in the past for us to be able to go on with our lives, move forward and grow and love.

Just after the doctor had certified the time of death, Reverend Henry baptized the baby on the spot: Bertha Stephanie Fay.

Jennifer didn't give me an explanation for why she was keeping the baby, just that Summer didn't want the responsibility, had changed her mind, something like that. And of course, I didn't ask her. She probably knew that I knew. *The father is dead*, Summer had said. It was a clear reference to Stephen. But even without snitches or fishbowls or paternity tests, I could have figured that out. Jennifer and Stephen had always wanted to have a child. Which they had tried to do, without success. What started off seeming like his problem, because of his age, ended up being her problem. Until Stephen had the brain aneurysm on the sailboat and their dream was left unfulfilled. Then Summer appeared, the crazy one in the family, to spend some time away from her problems, and Jennifer got the idea of proposing that Summer, in exchange for a large sum of money, become a surrogate mother, Jennifer's little oven.

———

It had been two weeks since I'd heard from Miriam. Nothing since I'd given her the pen drive with the recording of Mike. Then one day, her fishbowl lit up. Miriam had gone to the trouble of putting the clock in her kitchen back together with the spy camera back in its place, charging the battery, and turning it on. She looked straight at the camera. Serious, as if she were making sure everything was in its place or preparing evidence to turn me in to the police. The overwhelming fear came back, this time even heavier. Until she smiled. And spoke. I didn't hear because the microphone had given out, but I could read her lips perfectly because she only uttered a single message: *Take care of me*. Then she left the clock in its original place.

Minutes later, I saw Sandy the dog running happily around the kitchen. She'd gotten her back. Had she used the video? Yes, or at least part of it, because that same night I discovered that someone had slashed all the tires on the Cherokee, the golf cart and the bikes. In addition to breaking off my sideview mirrors and literally taking a shit on my front porch. I didn't care, because at that point, I was still in a state of shock and had no capacity to react. Nor did I want to file a report. Better to leave things as they were. I wanted to stop the chain of reprisals. Not turning him in was a way of accepting the punishment, showing we were at peace, and if I stopped bothering him, he would do the same. And so it was. I called a mechanic from off the island, to keep from causing rumors or raising suspicions, and had him change the tires and replace the mirrors. Almost $2,000 for my antics.

———

I had stopped going to my daily date with Julia at Le Café. So one day she decided to pay me a surprise visit.

When the doorbell rang, my heart started racing. I thought it might be Frank, or even worse, Barbara. When I saw it was Julia, I thought that, given my recent series of misfortunes, she had come to tell me she had found out I'd hacked her computer or that I was spying on her or that she knew about me and Mark. It wasn't that, but almost.

I invited her to have an iced tea in the garden.

"No progress on the novel?"

I had stopped peeking into her computer to look at her novel. Another result of photo 4,209.

Julia shook her head softly.

"I've lost the story. It's slipping out of my hands. And I feel like I can't do anything to avoid it."

"But why? I don't understand; Julia, the novel is magnificent. Write an ending and be done with it."

"Remember when I asked you for help with the ending?"

"Yeah, of course, I remember, and I'd really like to, but I can't do that."

"You're right. I made a mistake. I don't want you to help me finish. I want you to help me keep going."

What was she talking about, her novel or her relationship?

"Mark's leaving. He's going to take his boat and sail down the East Coast, to the Gulf of Mexico, cross the Panama Canal, and who knows what else. But that's the deal: he's going to be gone for two months . . . before he's gone forever."

"What do you mean, forever?"

"We're splitting up. When the summer's over, he's moving to New York."

Julia started crying. And I almost did too.

"Don't ask me whose decision it was, because I wouldn't know how to answer. Well, yeah, I do know. It's both of ours. We made it years ago, when we tried to be Samantha and Paul. But obviously that ended up being a burden, for me and for him. I hide behind my fiction to complete my reality. He has done the same. The fantasy of finding his Samantha is so great, so unreal, that it can't be a single woman, a single relationship."

She frightened me when she looked up through her tears at me.

"I don't want him to go, Alice. Not because I want us to get back together. I'm not looking for that. I stopped looking for that a long time ago. But . . ." After a pause, she said, vulnerable and small as I had never seen her before, "I'm pregnant."

My head didn't have the resources to process all that information.

"Have you told him?"

Julia shook her head.

"Well, tell him. If you do, I'm sure he'll stay."

"Yeah, I know. And I know he would without blinking. But he wouldn't be happy. Because these concessions, even though you convince yourself when you make them, always come with a price. I know; I know him. And it's not a question of him staying. It's a question of the island not burning him alive. Because right now, that's what the island is doing to him."

That concept sounded familiar to me.

"Why don't you talk to him?" she proposed.

"With Mark? Me?"

"Even though you never talk to me about him, I know . . . that you get along. That you did get along." When she corrected the tense of the verb, I knew she was aware of our fling. Or should I say *affair*, as she did? "When you got to the island, it was really good for him. It was good for us . . ."

For the first time in my life, I wanted to faint. I wanted my phobia to take charge of the situation and get me out of there.

"I don't understand very well what it is you want me to do."

"I told you, help me continue," she answered, composed now, so it wouldn't look like a desperate or impulsive request. Quite the contrary, it was very well considered.

Was she insinuating she knew I was the woman from the messages, the frustrated escapade in New York, his lover? And not only that, but more importantly, that she was fine with it, that she was giving me the green light, that she was getting out of the way. Did she really think the healthiest and best thing for her was for her husband to stay on the island with another woman while she was pregnant?

And me? What was it I wanted? I must not have known very well, because I could barely hold back my almost feverish desire to see Mark. To take refuge on his boat, in his arms and in his love. But I knew that if I did that, it would break me. I would crumble in front of him. And I knew he would have loved that: picking up my pieces and putting them back together, saving me one more time, as he already had before. And I would let myself be saved. But where would that get me? Where would that take us? *What does all that matter, Alice? That doesn't change anything. That doesn't erase photo 4,209 of Barbara. That doesn't solve any of your issues.*

Until one night I couldn't take it anymore, and I went to the port with the intention of seeing Mark on his boat. It wasn't there anymore. He had gone. I cried all the way back home.

I slept in the bed still wrapped in a towel after emerging from the shower, exhausted, and not exactly from the physical effort. I woke up hours later, soaked in sweat, disoriented. It took me a moment to figure out where I was. My stomach was upset, my chest was burning, and I was itching. I'd gotten a rash. While I looked at my chest in the mirror and tried to decide whether to make myself vomit to alleviate my unease, all the different lines of thinking about Barbara suddenly opened up. They started working at full output, like when someone opens the floodgates of a dam that's about to overflow. Phrases of Barbara's that shot through me:

I'm sure the owner won't show up here today.

No problem, she can go on riding Panda. Hardly anyone comes around here until spring.

You just let her ride and then we'll see. It's no problem if she gets attached to the animal. It's not going anywhere . . .

Panda the pony. She was Chris's, I was convinced. In part because just as I had this conviction, the clock on my cell phone struck 12:01 AM.

I SAW BARBARA in one of the stables.

And she saw me.

And by my look, she knew why I was there.

And by hers, I knew that she knew.

"I've been wondering what I would say to you when this moment came, because I knew it would come," Barbara said to me with so much delicacy that it frightened me even more. "I think you should know everything. Because if not, you'll leave here thinking you're stuck halfway. And I think we need to walk through it together, up to the end."

After laying bait all over the island, suddenly I felt as if I was the one who had been caught. Barbara had laid a trap for me that had led me straight to Horse Rush Farm, and now I was afraid she'd devour me. Though I had been preparing myself for this moment for more than a year, I didn't feel up to it. Everything was unreal. In fact I didn't even know how I'd gotten there. How I'd been capable of waking Olivia up, making her breakfast, taking her to the hydroplane, breastfeeding Ruby and leaving her with Jennifer, who was delighted to see her.

I wanted to turn around and go.

I can't. I don't want to.

But Barbara didn't let me turn back. She sensed how hard it must have been for me to take that step, and she didn't want it to be in vain.

"How do you want us to do this? You want to ask me questions?"

My head shook for me.

"Just one," I said. "Then I want you to talk. I want you to tell me everything. As if I wasn't here."

"All right. What's the question?"

Before I started crying, I managed to get out, in a faint voice, "What was Chris doing on the island?"

PART FOUR

THE INVISIBLE MAN

I'm an Invisible Man.

I went over the heads of the things a man reckons desirable. No
doubt invisibility made it possible to get them...

This invisibility, in fact, is only good in two cases: It's useful in
getting away, it's useful in approaching.

—H. G. Wells, *The Invisible Man* (1897)

Barbara

THE FIRST TIME I saw Chris, I didn't see him. He had his back turned, standing next to the mill. I was scared until he turned around, smiled at me and waved like we'd known each other all our lives. I was out for a ride on my horse Nessy, our daily walk. *Sorry, but this is private property.* That was how I answered his greeting. He apologized immediately and started to go. I felt so bad that I said no, no problem, he could stay. *You're not from around here, are you?* I asked him, still a little distrustful. He shook his head and told me he had been dragged to the island by a chance encounter with an old school friend from the University of Virginia, a John something or other, someone I didn't even know. They'd been there together a couple of years, when John was defensive coordinator of the football team. Apparently, this John loved tennis and went to watch him pretty often. Later John had followed his career and was convinced he'd go far in the ATP, until John read he'd hurt his Achilles tendon. John had lost track of him years before. And when John found him that very morning at the New Seabury Country Club in Mashpee, playing with a potential client who happened to be John's brother-in-law—Keith, obviously, though he couldn't remember the name when we were talking—John went crazy, he was so excited, and he proposed a doubles game so they could talk and catch up. But that wasn't enough, because then John invited him for a few beers, and when he was half-drunk, John told him, *This guy here, my brother-in-law, has an island all to himself, and he's redecorating or whatever you want to call it. He wants to put in a new tennis court because his old one is grass, a piece of shit, to put it frankly. So anyway, you gotta strike while the iron's hot, right?* John's brother-in-law asked Chris for his card to get in touch with him and see him another day when he had more time. Then John invited him to take a tour of Robin Island. *You've never heard of Robin*

Island? Better, perfect. Know why? Because it's the best-kept secret in the country. And before he could react, they were on the ferry headed to the island. Chris accepted because his business was expanding and he was trying to put down roots in the states surrounding Rhode Island.

He came over, put out his hand, and introduced himself:

"Sorry, I haven't introduced myself. I'm Chris Williams."

"Barbara," I said to him, shaking his hand, not getting off my horse. I felt safer up there. "So how did you end up here in front of my mill?"

On the way to the port, since he had a good bit of time, he decided to take a walk around and got hooked on the island, enchanted by its landscape and how peaceful it was. He traveled a lot and knew a lot of places, but the island captivated him in an unforeseen way. It was familiar and exotic at the same time, different but recognizable, cozy. "A little like my wife," he blurted out, as if he wanted to avoid having me get the wrong impression, which I thought was charming and actually did relax me. Before he knew it, he no longer had time to catch the last ferry. John's wife had insisted he stay and spend the night in the inn. *A star like you gets the suite with the Jacuzzi*, she had said.

"So instead of going back there and wrestling with all the excess hospitality from John and Karen, I've snuck onto your farm without permission."

Then I got a message from my father saying that our pony Snow White had just given birth.

"I've got to take off, we have a little one coming," I said by way of goodbye. "Oh, and by the way, wander around as much as you want. Make yourself at home. The sunset is spectacular from here."

I liked him, and he liked me. A pleasant first meeting, friendly, innocent.

———

I didn't know how long it was that I went without hearing anything from him. He reminded me of our first meeting, even his name, which I had forgotten, despite the fleeting attraction I had felt. "It's been a month and a half. My name's Chris. And yours is Barbara." He also remembered Snow White and wanted to know how the foaling had gone. I told him very well and that if he was interested, I'd show him the result. It was then that he met Panda. "He looks like a panda," he said.

"That's why his name's Panda," I answered. "The mother's white, hence Snow White, and his father, Batman, is black. He got the best of both worlds."

Chris told me the reason for his visit. Keith had called him a month after the first meeting, finally having decided to redo the tennis court. Chris had just been there, and Keith had proposed he do it in secret, to surprise John, because John loved tennis and would probably end up being the one who used it most. Chris thought it was a great idea because it saved him from having to deal with John. *Poor guy, don't get me wrong, I like him, he's a good guy, but . . . you know, he's a little possessive,* he said as an excuse. While he was on Napoleon Island, Chris had taken an interest in its origins and the life of Napoleon LeCaptain. Keith had told him the strange history of the architect and his dream of making the island a retreat for his family and the coming generations. Chris was particularly fascinated by the pains LeCaptain took to keep it a surprise and how he worked things out so that neither his wife nor anyone in his family would find out about anything. He did it with the help of his friend John J. Bresnam and his boys from the fire department in New York's eighth precinct, whose station Napoleon had designed and built.

Chris told me that the day we met and he first set foot on the island had been complicated, tedious. But that the walk he had taken around the horse ranch had struck him as a well-deserved reward. He had discovered a marvelous place to bring you to one day, you and your daughter, and he'd decided not to tell you about it, because he wanted to surprise you and because your daughter had a weakness for horses in general and particularly for ponies.

"My problem is I have trouble faking. I don't like to lie, in part because you can always tell. Especially Alice. She always catches me. Alice is the all-seeing eye: nothing escapes her attention, and our daughter Olivia has inherited that. They're very similar, too much so. So to lie to her, I'm going to have to lie to myself first, believe my own lie, because if I don't, it'll be obvious."

Then he mentioned Napoleon LeCaptain again and how he'd been a source of inspiration for him. That and my farm, my wild horses, my ponies and seeing the sunset from the old mill that was damaged after Hurricane Sandy passed through. He told me he'd had an idea, a dream, and he just needed to know if it was possible; if not, he'd understand completely, and he'd banish it from his mind. That's why he told me everything all at once, because he didn't think he could keep it all secret much longer without you finding out. I was really intrigued by what he had planned. I encouraged him to keep talking, to tell me what he had in mind.

Chris told me that WTT, his business, was his great professional project, but that for months he'd felt something was missing. He'd been playing competitive tennis since he was six. That had turned him into an adrenaline junkie, craving competition, status, risk-taking, cutting loose, effort, victory, defeat. All that, for him, was summed up in one word: *passion*. He needed to get it back, and he didn't know how until he found himself on the path at the farm, walking among the dunes until he reached the mill, right when the sun was going down. And once he told me that, Chris stopped beating around the bush.

"I don't know if that pony Panda is for sale. I'd love to give her to my daughter."

"She's still really young. She hasn't been weaned yet."

"I figured. I'm not in a rush. The pony's just a part, a fairly small part, of the surprise I have in mind. Because what I really want is to buy the mill from you. Rehab it by hand, without anyone's help, as a personal challenge and because the fewer people get mixed up in it, the better. Do it little by little, in the gaps between my business trips, behind my wife and my daughter's backs. Make it a home. Our castle, our second home, our retreat, like Napoleon LeCaptain did. A place where we can spend happy times and my daughter can ride her pony. Thinking about that, about making that moment happen, inspired me. So if all this really seems viable to you, I'll tell you how I'd like to go about it. I'll need a battalion chief, just like LeCaptain had John J. Bresnam." He paused, then he added: "And that's where you come in. Barb, would you help me to be invisible?"

I wanted to say yes. Of course I did. I didn't see why not, though soon I wouldn't be so sure.

The windmill is hard to get to because the properties surrounding it are private. That makes it a very special place, and since it has a south-facing orientation, you can enjoy the sunrise and the sunset from there. It sat on a hill next to Haven Creek, which empties into the sea. It wasn't for sale. Maureen and her husband Pat Heise had been trying to buy it from me for years, the mill and the land it was situated on, which we barely used. Just the horses went there to graze now and then, to drink water from the creek and eat apples off the trees. They wanted to build a golf course. It was my land, I had inherited it from my grandfather, so I wasn't considering getting rid of it. But his plan struck me as a marvelous gesture on Chris's part and so I thought it over.

I didn't tell him yes, I told him almost definitely no, that I had to consult with my father, which was a lie. I told him we were very attached to that parcel. "I can tell," Chris joked, making reference to the damaged mill. I asked for some time to think it over, which seemed like a less harsh way of doing things. He accepted and told me not to delay too long, so he could get it out of his mind and concentrate his energies elsewhere, though nowhere else was going to please him as much.

Before he left, in case it would help clear up my doubts, he reminded me of a Zen rule that said something like you had to treat matters of vital importance lightly and light matters as vitally important.

———

I didn't share any of this with my father or Jeffrey. Not that I wanted to make it solely my decision, because the decision was made beforehand and it was no. But somehow Chris's sparkling presence had awakened me, making me question things about myself that I hadn't permitted myself to question before. When was the last time I had felt moved that way? Horses were a passion for me; they were my life. But they were also my refuge. Jeffrey said many times in a jocular tone that if only he had a muzzle, mane and horseshoes, I'd pay him a lot more attention. And I guess he was partly right. But we had what I thought was a good relationship. I liked life peaceful and orderly. Stability for me was one of the great pillars of my life. With Jeffrey it was always springtime;

it was never cold, never hot. Love's thermostat was set at seventy-two degrees. But there was something so comfortable that it seemed suspicious. Or at least it started to seem that way to me after Chris came into my life, with his white lies, invisibility and love for you. Chris's heart raced when he saw the sunset from the mill. Mine raced while he spoke to me.

Four days after Chris's visit, I got up and went out to ride Nessy to see the sunrise. When I passed by the mill and saw it clearly, my view unobstructed, I laughed at how much I'd debated the issue. Everything was much simpler. *Treat matters of vital importance lightly and light matters as vitally important.* It was true. I wanted to be John J. Bresnam, the chief of Chris's battalion, to help him be invisible, to help him finally surprise you. And in passing, to do something about the creaky finances of the farm, because between the economic crisis and Hurricane Sandy, we'd been through some difficult years. Besides, I almost never went near the mill, in part because my heart sank every time I saw its sorry state.

I was fooling myself, lying to myself without realizing it. And after that day, I started to go to the mill regularly.

"You just made me the happiest man in the world," he told me, and gave me an effusive hug.

"We haven't negotiated a price yet," I said, calming my spirit and my inner heat.

"Money's not going to be a problem. But don't think I'm a millionaire and try to gouge me. Anyway, if I pay in cash, you'll give me a discount, right?"

Chris told me that all transactions and expenses related to the mill had to be in cash, without touching a cent of his business account or the one he shared with you.

Then I admit I got frightened because I thought maybe it was a money-laundering operation, dirty money from some illegal activity. Chris must have seen it in my face because he rushed to explain to me where the money had come from. When he turned twelve, he decided to start saving a dollar a day. It was mainly his father's fault, because that same day he gave him a hundred-dollar bill, the first one Chris had seen in his life, and said: *This isn't a gift; this is a responsibility. Because someday, you're going to need this hundred-dollar bill. You can spend it on whatever you want. I will never reproach you, believe me. It's yours. It's your decision. All I'm asking is, before you spend it, think about whether the thing you're going to use it on is something you actually need. It's not enough for you to want it; it has to be something you really NEED.*

"Just imagine how weirded out I felt. That bill was worse than kryptonite to Superman. I had nightmares where I'd spend it on something fun, and I'd wake up crying. Since then, I have been obsessed with saving in case something terrible happened and we were stuck with no money and not even that hundred-dollar bill was enough. I set a goal of saving a dollar a day. I always had a good head for saving. Some call it being cheap; I call it being like an ant. My mother gave me two dollars for lunch money at school. I'd make myself a sandwich every morning without her seeing. And so I'd save my dollar. Now I'm thirty-two. For twenty-one years, I've been saving a dollar a day. Twenty-one years times 365 days is 7,665. That's 7,765 dollars."

"So with that money, you want to buy the parcel in front of the sea with a mill that may be ruined but is still historic?"

"No. It's 7,665 dollars plus the hundred-dollar bill. That's 7,765 dollars, Barb."

"Oh, sure, problem solved," I said, laughing.

"No, seriously, I made that promise to myself when I was twelve years old, and I've been working without interruption since I was fifteen. I'm not going to bore you with the endless list of shit jobs I've had. But from my first job, I started raising the amount I saved. I went from one dollar to two. At seventeen, three. At eighteen, five. And then during college . . . Have you seen *The Color of Money*, with Tom Cruise and Paul Newman, where they make bets, play pool and scam people all over the country?" I nodded. "Well, I did the same thing at college playing tennis. I made a lot of money letting rich yuppie kids beat me and then doubling and tripling the bet in the rematch. Then I finished my degree and I started playing as a pro, and let's just say that daily amount went up considerably. And never, not once in my life since I was twelve, did I break my promise."

"So where do you keep all that cash?"

"The hundred dollar bill is in my wallet; I always have it on me. I'm superstitious, maybe even a little manic. I think my daughter inherited some of that. And the rest of it here."

He took a child's Teenage Mutant Ninja Turtles backpack out of his glove compartment.

"They gave me this backpack on my twelfth birthday. A gift from my aunt and uncle. I threw a tantrum because, as you can see, it's Donatello, and I was a Leonardo fan to the death, so I hated the backpack and never used it. It stayed in the loft space in my bedroom until I decided it was the perfect place to keep my money."

"But your wife must know, doesn't she? You've got God knows how much money there."

"No one knows. Remember I told you I had to believe my own lie to be able to get away with it? Well, no one knows this. Not even Alice. Because this"—he pointed at the backpack—"doesn't exist."

I don't know why, but it relieved me slightly to know he was capable of lying, that he wasn't as transparent as he said he was, that he had his dark side. Curiously, that relaxed me and made me trust him more.

"And you've never touched a single cent of it?"

"Not one. Because I knew I'd need it someday, me or someone in my family or someone close to me. I wanted to be sure I was ready for the moment. I don't know why, but I always thought I'd use it to deal with some dramatic event: a medical treatment, a robbery, an accident. But look, no, finally it's going to go to what I hope is the most beautiful gesture of my life. Because in reality, all this has more to do with my wife than with me."

He told me that, since you'd been together, he had seen how you'd been making little sacrifices for him, small stuff, but that came voluntarily from you, obviously. Renunciations that you wouldn't even consider such, because they were just part of life, of maturing, of choosing your path. But in this case, he had the feeling that you had pulled away from your artistic dreams. Alice, he told me, is an art teacher at a primary school, and she loves it and she's happy, but . . . He had his chance to shine as a tennis player. The circumstances were there. It didn't work out, that was fine, but he tried. And he felt you had never tried, that you had been trimming your wings back little by little. Or maybe he had cut them unconsciously, which bothered him to think about. That evening at the mill, he told me about all those painters you had talked about with such admiration and how much that landscape he had before his eyes reminded him of the pictures you loved, and he thought that from there, you could have a real opportunity to try. He already knew that it wasn't enough to have a beautiful and evocative view to become a great painter, that you have to paint from the inside out and not from the outside in. But Chris knew you had a lot inside you that you hadn't yet figured out how to draw on. And when he got here and saw the name of the island, it seemed like a good sign to him. Robin Island. He imagined his robin stretching out her wings and flying around freely. That's what he wanted to give you. Wings. A window for you in the top part of the mill, to look out of, to fly wherever you wanted to. To make your private space. Your studio.

He lifted up the backpack.

"Shall we see if I have enough money in this backpack to make my dream a reality?"

Yes, there was. Enough to buy the parcel and the mill. He knew there was, and I was really happy that there was. In any case he told me later he had an ace in the hole. He was going to invest all the money he made building Keith's tennis court in the mill. In part as a poetic gesture, because it was what had brought him there, and in part because he didn't want it to show up on WTT's books or for there to be a contract. To all intents and purposes, he would make that tennis court for Keith under the table. To convince Keith to pay him in secret, he told him one thing: you want to surprise John, I want to surprise someone else. Keith agreed.

It was a smock mill, around sixty feet high, octagonally shaped, with a brown brick base going up three floors, a two-story wood tower, and a rotating top. Nathan Wilbur, a sailor from Nantucket who'd spent time in Holland, built it in 1752. They called it Wilbur Mill. In 1828 it was in deplorable condition and was sold for fifteen dollars to a carpenter, Donald Herring, for use of the wood, but he decided to renovate it to mill grain, and that was how it got the name Herring Mill. In 1894 it stopped running. And in 1899 it was sold at a public auction, together with all the land that composed Horse Rush Farm, for $1,550 to John Francis Rush, my great-great-grandfather, and so it became known as Rush Mill. It was added to the National Historical Register in 1978. The only condition I gave Chris was that the name couldn't be changed. He accepted. We shook hands and he hugged me. He was happy.

––––––

Chris told me the plan he had come up with to pass completely unnoticed on the island. The idea was for the renovation to seem like it was mine and not his, as if I had hired him to do the work.

"No one can know you've sold it to me till the very end."

He had bought a gray truck, secondhand—a neutral, unremarkable color—to come and go on the island and transport materials. Because if he did it in his Cadillac Escalade, he would draw people's attention. This way he could look like a humble construction worker, which is what he was, deep down.

"And John? What happens if you run into John? What will you tell him?"

Chris was stunned.

"Shit, I hadn't thought about that." But then his smile came back. "Well, of course, I thought of that. But I can't tell you all my secrets."

I was crazy about the idea. The secrecy of it all. I thought it was so funny that, once more, I decided to hide it from my father and Jeffrey. Nothing would have happened if I had told them. They would have kept the secret; they also would have liked that grandiloquent gesture of love. But all I told them was a very rich gentleman from Rhode Island had seen photos of Panda's birth on our website, had taken a liking to the animal and had given us a fortune to buy her for his daughter. Which was partially true. The lie I cooked up was that with the money, I was going to renovate the mill, because Miriam had told me the real estate market was looking up—that was true too—and since I'd been thinking about selling the land with the mill on it for years, I thought I'd get the most out of it if it was in perfect condition. My father trusted me, knew I was a responsible person, and didn't question anything. Like Jeffrey, he offered to lend a hand with whatever was necessary, telling me not to hesitate to ask. But I never did.

———

I could stop here, Alice. Show you the mill, your mill, totally renovated inside and out, just waiting for furniture. But I'd be leaving out a big part of the story. Because that was just the beginning, the first three months. And he came here for more than two years.

———

Chris would come every month, more or less, using his trips to New England to *escape* or even planning fake work trips to be able to stay three or four days—the maximum he could justify without raising suspicions—and push the restoration work forward. I found him a couple of guys on the island to help him clear the rubble. All supposedly under my orders. Orders that Chris gave me beforehand. When communicating with me from elsewhere, he didn't use email or his phone, nothing that could be traced in the electronic world we live in. He resorted to a lost art: letters. I remember them more of less by heart.

Hey, Barb:

What's up? Hard winter? Well, don't worry, there's less of it to go, just five more months . . .

I'll get to the island the tenth or eleventh of this month at the latest. I'll be there a few days. To take advantage of my stay, I'm attaching a list of materials and addresses where you can get them at a good price in case you can't find them on the island. There needs to be more than enough of everything when I get there (that's not an order, it's a plea).

You already know where the money is. And watch out how much you spend—Donatello's got a bad attitude and he might tear one of your arms off if you go over budget.

Did the guys bust down the walls I marked with an X?

I hope they aimed well or else there won't be a mill or anything, and the historic register will take me to court. Yeah, I know, I'm a little controlling and not being there day and night doesn't help.

But I trust you—almost—blindly.

The X, the walls marked with an X, for God's sake! I drew them really big! Oh Lord, I'm having nightmares about the letter *X*.

I wish I was there, Battalion Chief Bresnam. Can I call you Bresnam from now on?

Any request or craving from terra firma? Oh yeah, you can't write me. Sorry . . .

See you soon,
C.

I loved getting his letters, though I wasn't crazy about not being able to write back and answer his digs at me. Communication went in only one direction: from him to me. I carried out his orders—or requests—to a T. Not just that, those walls he had marked with an X, I had knocked them down myself, because, just like him, I didn't trust those pot-smoking overgrown adolescents who just wanted to make a few bucks without breaking too much of a sweat so they could go on paying for Mike's marijuana.

By the time Chris showed up, all the materials he had asked me for were in the mill, and not just those, but others that I thought were necessary. I had also taken care of the basic necessities for him so he could stay there and sleep without dying of hunger or cold. Everything he needed for a comfortable rustic life.

Every time he came and saw how much further it had come along than he had expected, he pretended to be irate. *Bresnam, leave something for me . . . Bresnam, you've taken your name too seriously . . . Bresnam, looks like you're trying to get rid of me as soon as possible . . . Bresnam, seems like I'm bothering you. If you want, I'll stay away, no problem . . . Bresnam, it's my mill; find your own and leave mine in peace . . .* Always in a carefree tone.

I don't know how I managed it, but those three or four days a month

Chris spent at the mill, I managed to free myself from any domestic or professional chores and got my father and Jeffrey to understand, without giving too many explanations, that I wouldn't be around. Just for emergencies.

And what happened when he stayed? Nothing, everything, lots. The important matters were easy. We worked. We listened to music on portable speakers. We took turns. He was more into heavy metal; I was more into pop divas: Madonna, Adele, Amy Winehouse, Alicia Keys, Lady Gaga, Katy Perry, Avril Lavigne, Rihanna, and especially Taylor Swift. A somewhat explosive mix.

We became friends. Close friends. We had that type of friendship that usually forms between the survivors of a catastrophe, an almost immediate, unique, iron bond. But in this case the origin had been something good, a common objective. That's where I started to go wrong. A common objective? No, it was his objective. But I got so wrapped up in it that it seemed like I was the one who had sketched out the plan. I even told my father and Jeffrey to stop going around there so they wouldn't see it until it was done and I could surprise them.

We laughed. We criticized each other's obsessions, which were many. We danced, him to my corny songs and me to his hardcore ones. We drank beer, ate cans of Campbell's black bean soup with hot peppers—his favorite. We held on to each other to keep from falling—literally and figuratively. We didn't judge each other. We didn't have to put up with each other because he was barely ever there. There were no conflicts. We didn't try and please each other because he was happy with you and I was happy with Jeffrey. It wasn't work; it was like being on the playground in elementary school. It was innocent. Innocent? A slow-motion touch of the hands when I passed him a tool. A glance when the sun was almost down. A smile I didn't know I had. A touch that only existed in our wishes. A tickle that had been forgotten. A drunkenness without alcohol. A sleepless night looking at the stars, lit up every ten seconds by the lighthouse.

A summer, spring, autumn and winter camp. A camp you never want to end.

"It's cold," I said, not cold. "Are the heaters on?"

"You don't have to stay, Bresnam."

"I'm the battalion chief, LeCaptain."

Sleeping, embracing without touching. Waking up in a way I never dared to wish for.

———

But this wasn't from one day to the next; this was from one month to the next, that's why it seemed so natural, so right. Because there was nothing more than that. There was nothing sexually explicit, nothing inappropriate that could be picked apart in front of a court of amorous accounts.

And in the meantime, during those long periods of time that passed between each meeting, he went on with his life, I went on with mine, and his letters kept coming, more and more frequent, always with the excuse of seeing if I could do this or that for the mill, but with the part devoted to the typical complaints pushed slowly aside, as though unwanted, to make way for feeling:

Come on, pick up the pace, Bresnam. I want to finish the mill in time for my retirement.

You know what I like best about writing you, Bresnam? You can't answer me.

I want to be there, Bresnam, but not to see you, just because it's getting nice out.

Don't eat my cans of Campbell's black beans and hot peppers, Bresnam. I'm watching you! At least wait for me and we can share.

You know, I've always been a big individualist; I don't like working with a team. But with you it's different, Bresnam. I like having you at my side.

I miss you a little bit, Bresnam. Just a little, OK?

How I want the fall to come, Bresnam. Save one of those pretty sunsets so we can see it together.

Hey, this is important, Bresnam: I'm reminding you that the confidentiality clause you signed also includes you not telling that I cried when we read the end of the second book of the *Hunger Games* together.

Good thing I met you, Bresnam. If I hadn't, none of this would be possible.

You know what, Bresnam? I've stopped having Campbell's black beans with hot peppers, but not because I don't like them. It's the opposite; they're still my favorite. But now I associate them with the mill. I only want to eat them there with you.

You miss me a little, Bresnam? Look, now I regret you can't answer me.

The mill isn't a mill anymore. The mill is a mill and you. (I like the mill more and more.)

I miss you, Bresnam. I even miss Taylor Swift!

Then it was a year since we had met. I was particularly excited to get a letter from him that day. I remembered because it was Panda's birthday. But I didn't think it would occur to him.

A year, Bresnam, today it's a year since we met!

Sometimes I ask myself if I want to finish the renovation. Every day I enjoy it more. At first I was stressed because I thought Alice would catch me. Every time I came or went, it was hard for me to pretend. That's why I take the long route going there and coming back. To go I need time to stop feeling bad, and to come back I need to detox from the emanations of the island. Or are they from you, Bresnam? But now that everything's on track and my plan is going right and reaching perfection thanks to you, I can't wait to escape there. That said, I'm still taking the same route. I'm a creature of habit, you know me by now.

See you soon, Bresnam. I won't tell you I miss you anymore because you know that well enough.

Kisses,
C.

PS: Congratulations to Panda from me. Because, I remind you, he's mine, and well, yours a little bit too . . .

He was always more daring with his letters than face to face. As if he only permitted himself that now not-so-innocent flirtation from a distance. When we were together, he never managed to say the things he would write. So much so that sometimes I felt maybe I was making it up. That those *I miss yous*, *I wish I could see yous*, and *kisses* were nothing more than sweet afterthoughts without any romantic connotation. Which I suppose in part I was thankful for, so I didn't feel we were doing anything bad. But if I scratched the surface, longings for more were there. His longings.

I started to believe our lie, and it felt like what he was doing he was doing for me, for us. Could it be happening to him too? Your name and Jeffrey's barely came up in our conversations. We made decisions together about the tiles in the bathroom and the kitchen. The kind of wood for the flooring and the stairway. Decisions that at first Chris would make without blinking and that in time he needed my advice for. He wanted me to like it as much as he did.

The only thing that remained absolutely free of any kind of intervention was the attic in the mill. That was solely for you, Alice. It was left immaculate and diaphanous, for you to do what you wanted with it. To make it yours.

———

I could even stop here, Alice, forgetting a few paragraphs from the letters. But we still have a year of history left.

The first and only *couple's crisis* we went through was when he found out you were pregnant again. He disappeared. He didn't show up on his appointed day, and I was really worried: I thought something might have happened to him because the letters also stopped for a few weeks. Even though I was absolutely forbidden to call him, I couldn't help calling his business phone from a hidden number. When he answered, I was relieved but furious. I hung up without saying anything. Had he forgotten about the mill? Had he lost interest? Had he forgotten about me?

Bresnam!

Excuse my absence. I've been up to my neck in work, something unexpected came up and I had to cancel my trip to the island. I'm really sorry I didn't let you know.

And plus, I'm going to be a father again!! Tada! Alice is five weeks pregnant. We're really happy, to tell the truth.

Obviously we still don't have any idea about the baby's sex. So let's not paint the walls in the third bedroom till we know, OK?

I'm getting organized to see when I can go there next. I'll let you know.

Take care,
C.

Take care? I cried for half an hour after reading that letter. It was reality slapping me in the face, and it took a long time for me to react. I felt betrayed, cheated and stupid. But it wasn't Chris's fault: I was the one who had betrayed and cheated myself. What was I playing at? Collecting his letters like an idiot, answering them all without sending my responses, keeping them in the same drawer, filed together in chronological order, because who knew if one day that wouldn't be a beautiful love story for us to tell our grandchildren.

Chris's next two visits to the island were horrible, interminable. I had an awful time, faking, smiling, pretending nothing had happened. I could have just stayed away, but no, I wanted to show him that I was super-happy about his good news and that nothing had changed. And though he tried to fake it as well, he too was acting strangely. We had gone too far without going anywhere. He had realized it, I had realized it, and we were dying from the shame, at least I was.

Why had I done something like that to Jeffrey? I asked myself. But there was something that almost irritated me more: Why hadn't Jeffrey done anything about it? If it had been the reverse, I would have confronted him and probably left him. I had neglected the relationship; I was less caring, a little cagey and absent. I had been that way for months. It was obvious something was up with me. Was I still in love with Jeffrey? Or worse: Had I fallen in love with a married man with a kid and another one on the way?

———

I could even stop now, Alice, leaving out a few details. But we still have six more months.

———

I saw it clearly on Chris's next visit. I decided to distance myself, to come over only to make sure everything was going all right. I had a terrible time. I was in withdrawal. My whole body was quivering. Not even by pulling my hair could I resist the force that was dragging me toward him. I was suffering. I was in love. I decided I couldn't go on like that. At least not with Jeffrey. He didn't deserve it. As soon as Chris left, I confronted Jeffrey.

"I don't know if I'm in love with you."

"I don't know if you are either."

"I need to figure it out."

"If you need to figure it out, then you're not."

"Why didn't you do anything?"

"Would it have mattered?"

We cried together and broke it off.

That night I only went home to get the box with Chris's and my letters. I went out the back without my father seeing me. I didn't want to break down in front of him and probably confess everything. I went to the mill to be alone. To burn the letters, to eat black beans with hot peppers and to drink beer. I was going to mourn, twice.

Then the thing Chris and I knew would happen sooner or later happened: he spotted John when he was going to catch the last ferry to Hyannis and turned back instead, losing his shot at getting off the island that night.

When he entered the mill, I was huddled up on the mattress, with the quilt over my shoulders, eating the beans cold straight out of the can. I had drunk two cans of beer. The first thing he said was, "I knew you'd been eating my beans behind my back."

I thought he had come for me, as if he had intuited my breakup with Jeffrey and now saw no more obstacles to our relationship becoming a reality. But it wasn't so.

"Remember when I told you that if I ran into John, I had a plan?" I nodded. "Well, I lied. I didn't. I saw him at the ferry station when it was about to set off, and I scurried away like a rat. I missed the ferry."

"That's how you kept him from seeing you?"

Chris nodded.

"Aren't you going to ask me what I'm doing here?" I asked him.

"This is your house."

"No, it's not my house; it's yours and your wife's and your daughter's and your future child's."

I wanted it not to sound resentful, but I don't think I managed it. In any case he didn't seem to get it, because he had turned all his attention to the bundle of letters, his and mine, lying on top of the mattress. I still hadn't decided whether to burn them.

"What's this?" he asked while reaching for them.

I stopped him.

"Don't even think about touching them," I threatened, grabbing hold of them.

"Have you been writing me?"

I said nothing.

"Did you answer my letters?"

"Some," I admitted. Actually, it had been all of them. "Just with stupid stuff."

"I'd love to read them."

"Once I burn them, they're yours to keep."

"Barb . . ."

"I'm not Bresnam anymore?"

"Barb, let me read them," he said very softly. "I'd love to read them."

"Why?"

"Because you wrote them to me."

"I didn't write them to you. I wrote them for me." I was sulking like a little girl. "You shouldn't be here."

"Neither should you."

"You shouldn't be in my life."

He didn't respond.

"I broke up with Jeffrey."

"Do you want us to talk about that before or after I read the letters?" he asked with a soft, firm voice.

I went back over them all mentally, as if I were capable of scanning their contents in two seconds and detecting any offensive impropriety or excessive expression of love. I wasn't, even less so in that moment, but I was sure there was a little of everything.

"There's no need to talk about this after. And don't read them out loud, please."

I gave them to him, I had no strength left. I wanted him to hold me. Allowing him to read the letters was the best way, maybe the only way, to get that to happen.

Of course you can call me Bresnam. In fact, I would like you to call me Bresnam. Can I call you LeCaptain?

You pick up the pace, LeCaptain. I'll remind you that, unlike you men, women can do more than one thing at a time.

Maybe you like writing me because I can't write you back. But I like writing you because I know you won't read me. Way more freedom to insult you, come what may.

I also wish you were here, LeCaptain, but not to see you. Just to . . . Yeah, I want to see you.

I'll eat your cans of Campbell's black beans and hot peppers if I feel like it. You leave me here adrift for weeks, that's the least I can do. And another reason, a very small reason, I eat them is because they remind me of you. Oops, I know, I'm going over the line . . .

It's funny, even though I know you're not going to read me, there are lots of things I don't dare write to you.

What are you doing to me?! You've got me in a daze! How gross! Idiot, imbecile, showoff!

I'm not going to answer any of your letters because I'm mad at you.

In truth, I'm mad at myself because I like you a lot. I think about you a lot. By the way, remember that Cavaliers T-shirt soaking in sweat that you took off and never found again? Guess who's got it.

I'll save all the sunsets in the world for you. I'll save them all for you in my eyes.

Confidentiality agreement?! I didn't sign anything! Ha-ha. But easy, I'm not going to tell anyone, because I wouldn't be capable of describing what I felt when we were reading the last part of *Catching Fire* together, curled up under the same blanket. I really am catching fire . . .

Why don't you say all those pretty things you write to my face?! Of course I do the same thing. What a pair of cowards . . .

You know what, LeCaptain? I also stopped eating Campbell's black beans with hot peppers because when I eat them, they remind me so much of you that I get sad and nostalgic. Come soon, hurry. I don't even have the energy to insult you anymore.

Sometimes I regret that you can't read me.

I like you a lot, LeCaptain. I think I'm falling in love with you.

Don't write kisses. Give me them.

O LeCaptain, my LeCaptain . . .

I think a lot of the first time you wrote kisses. I still remember the smell of the letter. I need you to kiss me. I need to kiss you.

Hello, LeCaptain:

What a delight to get your letter! And to know you remembered that a year had passed since we met and that you even mailed the letter beforehand so it would arrive today. I have to admit I was nervous, wanting you to remember, because since I got up, I've had it on my mind. After reading your letter I made Panda an apple pie with a carrot instead of a candle and sang her happy birthday from you.

    It's the same with me as with you, even though I don't have a long trip back and forth because I live here, I still need to air out before returning to real life. Normally I go ride Nessy for a few hours until neither she nor I can take it anymore and I've scattered my feelings for you all over the island. I can't bring them into my house, and I don't want to. I don't think I've ever been this corny in my life. It's your fault!

    Did you ever think that what's happening to us might be because we've never kissed? Maybe we should do it to get it out of our heads once and for all. This is a little bit of a torture, isn't it? For you too?

Bresnam

PS: I don't want the renovation to end either. In your absence, I've wrecked things on purpose. I admit it. I'll probably keep doing it. Sue me.

I feel terrible for Jeffrey. Under normal circumstances, I would have already left him. It's not fair to him. But the thing is, in reality, we haven't done anything. All this is nothing more than a fantasy! Though even the fact that I'm fantasizing can't be a good sign.

You showed up in my life at a bad time, LeCaptain. Go, vanish . . .

No, don't ever go. Stay with me. I'm already yours.

I don't really know at what point he finished reading the letters, because the laughter at the beginning gave way to an eloquent silence as he came closer to the most intimate parts. And I had stopped watching him some time before. It was getting late, and I had drunk too many beers. I was curled up in the fetal position on the mattress with my back to him.

First I heard the sound of his hand gathering together the bundle of letters and setting them aside carefully. Then he undressed. He took off his boots, his jeans and his turtleneck sweater, the one I liked because it looked so good on him. He slid under the quilt. I could feel his body heat and his cold feet. I could feel him smelling my hair. I was half-conscious, and I didn't dare move, like someone waiting for prey and not wanting to scare it off. He embraced me from behind. Isn't that what I'd wanted, for him to embrace me? I didn't want anything else. *Don't do anything more*, I thought. And he didn't. His measured breathing inhabited me and freed me from all my tension until I was deeply asleep curled up in his arms.

When I got up, he wasn't there. He had left me a letter.

Hello, Bresnam:

I like you a lot. I have never liked anyone as much as you, except for Alice. Even more, I suspect that the idea for doing all this didn't come to me from listening to the story of Napoleon LeCaptain or even seeing the mill at dusk. I think I got the idea when I saw you.

I couldn't sleep all night thinking about all you wrote me. And while I remembered and I had you in my arms, lots of things occurred to me to write you, all of them pretty, but we have to stop. At least I do.

Nothing is going to happen between us. Nothing else, because clearly lots of things have happened. I swear to you, I would love it, every day I fantasize about it happening. I'd love to know what your kisses are like, smell your hair without pretending not to, but that would turn me into the kind of man I've always hated. I can't do this to my wife, because I love her, I really love her, and I love all we've made together, and I also can't do it to you, but above all I can't do it to me.

I knew there would be obstacles on the road, but this has caught me by surprise. Now I have to turn this into a lie as well. The lie about the lie. I have to convince myself I don't feel anything for you. And that lie is going to be much harder for me than the other one, which I've been preparing myself for since I was twelve. And now I don't know if any of the lies will have a happy ending.

So, now, Bresnam? What do we do? I don't know very well how to proceed, and that's unusual for me . . . I need my battalion chief's help. Help me so at least one of the lies will turn out right!

LeCaptain

I thought he would have left. I almost would have preferred that. But no, he was sitting outside, looking at the sun as it timidly peeped over the calm sea. He had the letters in his hand, his and mine. I sat down beside him. He looked at me a moment and smiled at me. It was the first time I saw him meek and insecure. I smiled back at him, but he wasn't looking at me anymore. I felt good, really good in fact. It had calmed me a great deal to know that our feelings were mutual, that I hadn't invented all those things that had happened without happening. That was enough for me; I didn't need more. We had lived through a brief story of impossible love. It had to end. I took the baton he seemed to have passed off to me. I had come to the conclusion that we had called each other Bresnam and LeCaptain all that time because it distanced us from ourselves, from Chris and Barbara, and from them, Jeffrey and you. Created a barrier against our lives, turning us into actors, so we could act, feel and live things we wouldn't allow ourselves otherwise.

"We're going to burn the letters," I said to him. "Together. And afterward, we're going to finish what we started. We need to take a step back to reach the end. We have to call each other Chris and Barb again. We have to finish the mill."

We burned the letters together. It was a moment of catharsis, of erasing, of purifying ourselves, of unloading and going back to being at peace with ourselves and with life. When we finished, he told me with his eyes watering from the fire and the smoke—at least partially, "I loved you calling me LeCaptain . . . And I knew you had kept my T-shirt."

———

I could even stop now, Alice, leaving out a good number of details. But we still have a little more to go.

———

For the rest of the winter and the beginning of the spring, we continued working very hard. We set aside less room for contemplation and relaxation, but the heaviness of those last visits had dissipated. Breaking it off with Jeffrey had relieved some of the grief I felt when I was next to Chris. I even came to think that maybe my fixation and feelings of love for him had been a mere tool to help me leave my relationship behind. I realized that the best thing possible had happened. I was thankful it hadn't come to fruition, that it hadn't gone any further. That was what I hoped for from Chris. Because Chris was a guy who was worth it. I didn't want to feel I could fall in love with a man capable of cheating on his pregnant wife. I don't know if that ending was the prettiest one, but it was the best one. For all of us.

We went back to having fun, to enjoying that adventure. Like friends. It was nice to feel we were capable of putting things back in their place. We even sometimes joked about what had happened to us as if it had taken place years ago, when we were children or adolescents.

The problem was, much as I had believed the lie that everything was back in order, I was still hooked on Chris. But my fantasies had been reduced to a minimum. I barely thought about those things and they didn't worry me, because I felt good and the spring always brought positive energy to the island. I had gotten back my practical side. The renovation was going ahead and coming close to the end. One of the most intense phases of my life had just ended. It hurt, of course, but there was no resentment, no yearning. Finishing the mill would end everything the right way, and Chris and I could both go on with our lives.

———

That's why it caught me so much by surprise when I received a new letter from Chris. His last letter. He had left it on the doorknob at the entrance to the mill. It didn't have a stamp. I suppose he had written it then and there. It was our last day. We had finally finished the renovation, the only thing left was the attic, the best room in the mill, with its enormous circular window and spectacular panoramic views of Nantucket Sound. Your painting studio. Chris hadn't touched it. It was still completely empty for you to arrange how you liked.

We had agreed to do a thorough cleaning and then toast for having brought the adventure to a close. That's why I'd brought a bottle of champagne and an ice bucket, to celebrate with him. But he wasn't there. Not him and not his Donatello backpack. Instead, there was just a letter.

Dear Bresnam:

I'm writing you numb and weak, with my vision blurred. Dizzy and with the worst headache of my life. I haven't slept in two days. I can't concentrate and I'm scared, which is something that has rarely happened to me in my life.

I haven't managed to believe the lie about the lie. I think I've gotten you to believe it, and even Alice. Both lies. But I haven't been able to deceive myself. I've been with you in an unresolved fantasy that has gotten bigger and bigger. And I can tell it's about to explode inside my head. That's why I'm going.

I'm going to stop coming, dear Bresnam. We've pretended to get over this together, like two reasonable adults who know how to put things where they belong and live together in harmony. But what's certain is that every day, I still want to kiss your dimples and smell your hair without faking, among other things. So there's no point in continuing.

I can't take failure, and right now I feel like I'm failing. With everyone at the same time. And someone has to come out of this a winner, right? What happened, Bresnam? What happened to me? What happened to us? This was supposed to be my life's dream, the one I've been saving up for since I was twelve, right? It was supposed to be. And we had just enough money to finish the mill. I say it in plural because you supervised it almost better than I did. The Donatello backpack is empty. It can't be just by chance that I went to Dan's True Value to buy a lock for the door of Alice's studio, so she and she alone could have access to her world. But I can't stop asking myself if that passion I missed, that I needed, that I found in the mill and with you, had to do with something lacking in my relationship, with a lack of excitement. If my great gesture of love had to do with an absence of love. I thought before maybe I was clipping Alice's wings and wanted to give her new ones so she could fly, and now I'm asking myself whether I'm the one with his wings clipped, if deep down all this isn't for me, so I can fly. Because I'm the one who's scared of flying. Not her. I refused to believe it. Because this was a dream for us, for the family, but especially for Alice. And yet, however much I want to convince myself of the contrary, I can't manage it. I want to erase it from my mind and I can't, and it's something that I have to figure out, to clear up.

I always thought this wouldn't last, that the novelty of it would lose its grip on me. But more than two years have passed. It stopped being a novelty a long time ago, and I'm just as trapped, or more so. I need time. I'm going back to reality, I'm going to leave this lie behind. I want to be with you, but I love my wife. She is my reality, she and my daughters. It's not an act of sacrifice and generosity; it's an act of selfishness. I'm doing what I think is best for me. I want to be a good husband, a good father, a good person. For me. And for that to happen, I have to go back home, which is something I haven't truly done these past few months. It's time for me to be back with my wife and bring a precious little girl into the world.

But I swear to you I will come back with my problems solved and my questions cleared up. Clean. It may be weeks or months, but I'll come back. I just don't know with whom or for whom. I'm not asking you to wait for me. Don't do it, Bresnam. Even if that's on my list of fantasies. It survived the burning of the letters because it was in my head, and now it's burning inside me. I need for my head to stop burning.

And I know we agreed we'd stop calling each other Bresnam and LeCaptain. But for me, you will always be my Bresnam. And I will be your LeCaptain. Always yours.

ILYSM, Bresnam.

And you too, Barb.

PS: You've managed to do something no one has done before: make me follow Taylor Swift on Instagram. (I needed to finish by trying to get a smile out of you.)

He got one. Surprisingly, he got one. And then I realized that I too hadn't believed the lie about the lie. I don't mean his lie about the lie. I mean my lie about the lie. I was still in love with him. And I would wait for him until he returned. No matter how long he took.

———

I could even stop now, Alice, leaving aside several more details. And this time, there wouldn't be anything left to say. As you already know, Chris died a few hours later.

Barbara

JUNE 13, 2015–JUNE 9, 2016

"BARBARA, YOUR FILLING'S going to have to wait, but you're going to be a big help. Can you assist us in pulling a wild colt into the world?"

At first I didn't recognize you. Then I saw Olivia, with her freckles and rosy cheeks, straggling in with Chief Margaret. I had seen dozens of photos of you. Chris had shown them to me. Now you were on the island, giving birth to your second child in the dentist's office. I was so shocked, I got dizzy. Not at first, because I thought I was the one with the most experience bringing babies into the world and that they needed me. You needed me. Chris needed me. I held out until your baby peeked her head out. And I thought, *She's not a breech birth, and she doesn't have the umbilical cord wrapped around her neck; everything's OK.* Then I let myself go and it hit me.

What did you expect, that a colt would come out of my womb? I heard you in an echo, already off in the distance.

More than a month had passed since Chris had left the island. I had taken his silence as him undergoing the necessary process of re-connecting with reality. I knew I wouldn't get any letters or visits, and that was fine. I wasn't yearning for them. I had entered into an auto-programmed state of hibernation, like the crew of a spaceship crossing the silent darkness that separates Earth from a faraway, unknown planet. That meeting brought me straight back, without the necessary decompression. Where was Chris? What were you all doing there without Chris? I didn't understand anything. I thought he would show up any moment. Maybe he had gone to the mill to wrap his present and give you all a surprise, and things had just happened in a rush. But no, he wouldn't have come back without telling me. What he wanted to resolve wasn't going to be resolved at least until what had just happened had happened: the birth of your daughter. And plus, while they moved you to the ambulance boat, I heard you calling your mother to tell her what had happened and say they'd be taking you to Cape Cod Hospital, that you were fine and that the girl seemed to be in perfect health. Not a single mention of Chris.

When I was back on the farm, I hit *67 and called his business phone. It rang five times and went to voicemail. That scared me even more. Chris had told me he never had his voicemail activated. I hung up without leaving a message. What was happening?

I caught the ferry to see if his truck was still parked at the Hyannis terminal. It was.

I called Mark to ask him for another appointment for the filling. And in passing I asked him a few questions about you. *How crazy was what happened with that girl, right? What was she doing on the island? And her husband? How terrible, missing out on your daughter's birth. He wasn't with them?* He told me it had all been so fast that there wasn't much time to talk about practically anything.

I tried to convince myself that everything was OK, and by OK, I mean that he was alive, that the birth had happened when he was off on one of his business trips and that you had talked to him before. The thought didn't get me far because it didn't make any sense that you were on the island without him. None at all. I called his business phone a few more times, always with the same result: it went to voicemail. Something was wrong.

It was two days before I dared to type into Google: *Chris Williams + WTT + Providence.* The third result sent me to the webpage of the *Providence Journal* obituary section, where I found his entry. A photo of him smiling with the following text below it:

WILLIAMS, CHRIS M., 35, died on May 13, 2015. Beloved husband of Alice and father of Olivia Williams; son of Christopher Sr. and Betty Williams; brother of Tricia; and grandson of Arthur and Lisa Williams and of Alfred and Josephine Reis, deceased. Chris graduated cum laude from the University of Virginia with a degree in business administration and was the owner of WTT. He was an intelligent, effervescent, sincere, strong and hardworking man who lived life as an endless series of adventures. Chris was a committed father and husband. He always supported the people he loved and made the world shine with his presence. Chris will be loved and missed by all those who knew him. We will never forget you. RIP.

Chris had died. And I had lost my will to live.

———

It was hard for me to gather the necessary energy to go to the Swan Point Cemetery. The thought of seeing you there made me panic, but I had to do it. I needed to be near him. I wanted to say goodbye to him. I didn't manage to.

I didn't ride Nessy again after the day I found out about his death. Horseback riding for me is like breathing, an automatic, involuntary function. It gives me life. My father got worried. Jeffrey got worried. I was incapable of telling them anything. They didn't understand what was happening to me. *Honey, tell me what's up. Maybe I can help you*, my father said. But I was catatonic. I didn't react and I started to shut up inside me everything that I could. At night I would go to the mill, lie down on the mattress and hug the quilt even though it was the middle of summer. It didn't smell like Chris anymore, but I imagined it still did, and I would cry all night regretting that I hadn't pushed things further, that I hadn't tried to snatch him out of your hands, even if you were pregnant.

I rewrote the letters we had sent each other, his and mine. It was easy to burn them at the time because I knew them by heart. I had read them dozens of times. I was sure I had forgotten some details and omitted information, but the important thing, the basic thing, our story, remained intact. And when I finished recollecting them and rounded off the collection of missives—with the days when they were sent included—I started writing more letters. New ones. I went on with our story, Letters that I would slip through the slot in the door of the mill. I didn't dare go back inside.

———

I felt guilty. Very guilty. In my mind I couldn't stop analyzing all the variations that would have prevented him from leaving. I didn't know the details of his death, just that he had died the same day he left the island. That two days before he couldn't stop complaining—even though he wasn't a whiner at all—about how he felt dizzy, his vision was blurred, and he had a bad headache. Symptoms that seemed psychosomatic, the prelude to reaching a complicated decision like leaving his dream half-finished.

I thought about going to see you; I needed to talk, to share my mourning, but I barely had any strength. I didn't dare leave the farm. As if there weren't any oxygen past the fences marking the borders of the property. The last time I had left not just the island, but even the farm, was when I went to the cemetery. My father brought a psychiatrist, a very prestigious one from Boston, friend of a friend of a friend, who was on vacation in Nantucket. He diagnosed me with depression and agoraphobia.

Right when all this was unraveling, Jeffrey was happy and was getting over our breakup. He had his emotional life back; he was going out with a girl from Martha's Vineyard, from a very good, proper family. Even so, he was as worried as my father or more so, and he came to see me every day, though many times I wouldn't even leave my bedroom. Then one day he confronted me.

"This is because of that guy, the one who came here, right?"

I didn't answer.

"You don't have to tell me what happened. I don't need to know. Because what I do know is you're in love with him. Sometimes I would fly over the island, not because I wanted to spy on you, but because I didn't have any other option, and I would pass close to the mill and see you from up there, working, fixing the roof, painting boards, taking a dip to cool off or drinking a beer, and I could tell. From up there, I could see what you were denying down here. But from up there, I didn't care. Because up there, you see everything with a different perspective. You realize how small and insignificant we are. And that's what we're going to do right now, go up in the seaplane."

He dragged me gently to the hydroplane. From then on, he took me out every day for an hour. First along the coast, by Cape Cod, in circles, always without losing sight of the island, and little by little, it started to go away, almost without me realizing it, naturally. It seemed as if I were tracing a new map of my life. The tide of blame and affliction that had wiped away everything slowly started to recede, making way for a deep and heavy grief. The grief I didn't mind; it felt like a friend I enjoyed passing the time with. It wasn't aggressive. I let the grief get into bed and sleep with me. I gradually got my appetite back and resumed my activities on the farm. I started to open my doors, or at least stop closing them.

———

Then you showed up, Alice. You moved to the island. And what seemed like it might be a new setback to my delicate state had the opposite effect. I liked it. It intrigued me so much that it awakened me. Why had you decided to come live here? Had Chris talked to you about the island? No, it didn't make sense. Because in that case you would have come to claim what was yours. The mill, the land and the pony. And why did you lie about the date and the circumstances of Chris's death? You told Miriam your husband had died two months before the date in an airplane accident. What were you hiding? Why didn't you ask about Chris? I couldn't find an explanation for all that.

Maybe you had discovered part of Chris's lie, or part of the truth, depending on how you looked at it. In any case you'd had to have been following some clue he had given you to make it this far. You'd found a crack in Chris's master plan, a crack you could slide into. But it was obvious that clue hadn't led you to me, because you didn't approach the farm or the mill, and because I crossed paths with you several times— sometimes because I made it happen with my heart pounding violently beforehand—without getting any kind of reaction or response. But maybe you weren't lost, just looking for Chris.

I never sought you out, never started a conversation with you, out of pure wariness, because I always had this gnawing question of how much you knew; did you know who I was? I didn't want to seem false or hypocritical pretending to be nice with you when you might know my history with Chris. So I gave you your space, your time, so things would happen naturally, getting myself ready for the moment that sooner or later would have to come. Because if not, what was the point of you coming to live here?

Alice, you helped me break out of my cage. It was a very slow process. At first, I was afraid of you, I thought you were stalking me, watching, following, spying. That at any moment you would corner me, and I wasn't ready for that. But when I started to realize you didn't associate me with Chris, I relaxed, and little by little, I became closer to you. I was so curious that sometimes I followed you—I had the feeling sometimes that I was spying on you. I even went to Karen's birthday just to be with you.

Then my father came in and stole the show. In his life's slow unraveling, his path to forgetting, his longing to reunite with my mother, he started to frequent your house, the house my mother lived in when she was a girl. I even came to think my father knew everything. And when I say everything, I mean everything: that he was faking his episodes of Alzheimer's to provoke an encounter between us. But no, unfortunately, what was going on with my father was involuntary and irreversible.

Alice, you helped me get over Chris's death, because meeting you and your daughters brought me closer to him. I lived anchored to an unresolved fantasy of our future together that his death had shattered, and the shards were still inside me, cutting and wounding me. Little by little, the three of you pulled out all those slivers of glass that had grown into my body, and that opened a path to the certainty that Chris had done what he had to do and that I wasn't his soul mate. You were, Alice. I wanted to hate you, and I ended up being on your side. On both your sides, on the side of your family. It happened the day Snow White gave birth to Sunset. That day I took a photo of you, a true family photo. That photo made me feel I finally had Chris back. I had re-encountered him through you all. You had helped me to say goodbye to him and carry on with my life. And after all you had done for my father, it was my turn to help you. So you could say goodbye, too, reconcile with him and get on with your life.

When I left the photo on Chris's tombstone, I thought about putting a rock on it so the wind wouldn't carry it away. To be sure you'd see it, but I didn't, because that photo wasn't for you. You already had yours. That's why I took two. That one was for Chris. His dream, our adventure, had reached its end. It had worked. And now, from the grave, he was the one who had to make the final gesture. Hand over your gift to you, the key that would open the mill, your retreat, your painting studio. It wasn't up to me to do it. It was up to Chris whether that photo would still be there when you all arrived—because I knew you would go—a few hours later. I couldn't force it; I could only give it a little nudge.

That's why when I saw you come to the farm today, many days later than I'd imagined—I suppose because of your own inner struggle—I knew by your expression what you were here for. And you knew by mine that I knew. And that I was here for whatever you needed from me.

PART FIVE

ALICE IN WONDERLAND

"So long as I get *somewhere*," Alice added as an explanation.

"Oh, you're sure to do that," said the Cat, "if you only walk long enough."

She generally gave herself very good advice, (though she very seldom followed it).

It's no use going back to yesterday, because I was a different person then.

"Who in the world am I?" Ah, *that's* the great puzzle!

"Would you tell me, please, which way I ought to go from here?"

"That depends a good deal on where you want to get to," said the Cat.

"I don't much care where—" said Alice.

"Then it doesn't matter which way you go," said the Cat.

—Lewis Carroll, *Alice's Adventures in Wonderland* (1865)

WHEN I RETURNED home, it was as if I had been absent for years. After traveling through Chris's life, I felt so changed, I was afraid my daughters wouldn't recognize me.

I kept going over it in my head for three days straight. But not because I was looking for inconsistencies or omissions. It was clear Barbara had spent a long time waiting and getting ready for that moment. But to me it seemed like a different story—sometimes Chris's story, sometimes Barbara's, sometimes both of theirs. I wasn't really in that story.

Barbara had asked me if I wanted to go inside the mill, but I wasn't ready yet. If it was a gift from Chris to everyone, I should "unwrap" it with Olivia and Ruby. Besides, I felt like it was a special place for the two of them, for Chris and Barbara. Secret. Forbidden. The only way to break that perception was to go in there holding my daughters' hands.

And so, June 13, Ruby's first birthday, I took them. It had been exactly thirteen months since Chris's death.

"Honey, I have something to tell you," I said to Olivia. "And I'm going to tell you because I know you're a big girl."

"Of course, Mommy. I'm a very big girl."

"Oli . . . Would you be able to take care of two ponies instead of just one?"

Olivia was so overwhelmed with emotion, she didn't know how to answer.

"Panda is yours too. For you and your sister. Panda and Sunset belong to both of you, for you to take care of. Always."

Olivia started crying.

"Why am I crying, Mommy? I'm happy . . ."

"Because you're really excited. Sometimes you cry from joy."

"But is that good?"

"Of course, my love, it's really good."

We went with the ponies to the mill. Olivia on Panda and Ruby on Sunset, held up by Barbara. On the way I cried, imagining Chris experiencing that moment with his three girls. Four in this case, I thought, looking at Barbara. She was his girl too. And against all odds, I smiled without stopping my tears. I felt reconciled, I didn't know if with Chris or with Barbara, but I didn't care, I felt good. Olivia saw my tears.

"Are you crying from joy too, Mommy?"

"Now I am, Oli."

"Is it your first time too?"

"No, I've cried from joy once or twice before. When you were born, for example."

"Oh sure," she said. Then she pointed at something: "Look, the pretty mill."

"You know it?"

"Of course, we've come here lots of times when we're riding ponies. I told you before."

It was true. Once she told me that on the farm there was a mill and that Barbara had explained to her what it was used for before. I had seen it too on several occasions, from the ferry, Mark's boat or Kissing Tree Mountain. And I always had the same reaction as my daughter: *Look, the pretty mill.*

I didn't tell her it was ours, that her father had left it for us. Too many emotions for one day. And I didn't know if I wanted her to start asking questions. It wasn't a day for questions.

"Wow, it's all new!" Olivia exclaimed as she entered the mill and walked up the spiral staircase, counting the steps, of course. Though at that moment, those numbers seemed to me like a blessing. Olivia blessing every corner of the mill with her innocence and light.

Then we reached the attic. The door. And I saw the lock. Instinctively, my hand grasped the chain around my neck where the Master Key hung. Finally. I know it's impossible, but I think I felt it vibrate. A current of energy. An imaginary magnetic field. The law of attraction between two objects. Two people. As if the only thing that had brought me there had been that key hanging around my neck.

Barbara took charge of the situation immediately. "Oops, there's nowhere else to go from up here; let's go downstairs, Oli." She took Ruby in her arms and grabbed Olivia's hand and took them downstairs to show them where they would sleep every time they came to the mill.

"So we can stay and sleep here?" Olivia asked, ecstatic.

"Of course, anytime you want."

"And Panda and Sunset too?"

"Of course, Panda and Sunset too. But outside, waiting for you to come out, to take you wherever you want.

"And Pony can stay outside too?"

"No, Pony can't stay outside."

I mixed up the keys. I first stuck in the one for the attic in the house instead of the Master Key. They were the same size, but one of them had a big glob of red paint on it, round enough that you could tell it apart by touch. I laughed. That was a very tender moment for me. A moment of absolute climax broken by a slight slipup. Or maybe it wasn't a slipup. Maybe what I understood was that both keys opened the same thing: the same lock, bought at the same place, guarding the same thing, with the same purpose. My island. My world. The big difference was that the door the Master Key opened didn't lead to confinement; it led to a window. My window on the island. On the world. A place of personal realization to do whatever I wanted. A place in singular. A place where I could be myself, just me.

I looked at my feet as I entered—because I knew Chris would have made me go in with my eyes closed—and I sat on the floor in the middle of the room. White oak floorboards. My favorite. I stroked them. A tear fell onto the wood. I traced it with my hand. It took me a while to look up and contemplate the panoramic view from the enormous window. The beach, the dunes, the choppy sea. I realized just then that the beach before my eyes was the one from my recurring nightmares. My unconscious hadn't wanted to torment me; it had simply given me a clue I didn't know how to read.

Then I saw something: a dollar. It was in the center of the window, stuck to the glass with Scotch tape. I got up and went over. On it, in Chris's handwriting, were the words:

Let's start saving for our next dream.
I love you, C.

I cried again, and though all my emotions were still as turbulent as the sea and my thoughts as disordered as the sand on the beach, I understood that I, too, had been preparing myself for that moment for a long time, because I was surprised at my ability to put everything in its place. I was happy that thirteen months had passed. I needed thirteen months to face the secret/lie/mystery of Chris. I didn't try to understand it at all or judge it or classify it or figure out if it was good or bad. I limited myself to assimilating it and accepting its history as true. I felt relieved. A weight had been lifted off me. The weight of guilt, of wondering what I'd done wrong. I didn't want to get lost in analyzing it or trying to discover if all I'd been told was true. Among other things because there were lots of parts I didn't like, that hurt me. It was a tale with a marvelous beginning and a tragic end, with dark and bittersweet parts, and if I didn't watch out, I could get lost in its twists and turns and spend another year suffering.

––––––––

Laughter, the sound of games and a phrase of Barbara's brought that line of thinking to an end. I didn't know how much time had passed.

"Come on, Olivia, let's take a photo of Pony on the pony."

"No, not that, not that! Not Shesnotapony!" Olivia screamed.

"Yes, come on, you'll see how fun it is," Barbara insisted.

She's in trouble now, I said to myself. I stood up and looked out the window in time to see Barbara scoop Pony up in her arms.

"Come on, Pony, up you go," she said, putting the little creature on top of Panda.

That wasn't what tugged at my heart. It was Olivia's scandalized cry blending with uncontrollable cackling. It was that she managed to tolerate Pony coming over to her, touching her and even sitting on her most prized possession. The gift from her father's last trip: Panda.

Then she rode around the mill, toward me, as if she knew that I was peeking out—that indestructible connection—and said to me, "Look, Mommy, Shesnotapony on the pony."

She began to shriek and laugh again.

And I stopped crying and laughed along with her.

DURING THE FOLLOWING weeks, I thought seriously about leaving. Abandoning the island. I could finally go back now. Dismantle everything. But I didn't. Where would I go back to? I had a house, a mill, two girls, two ponies, a dog and a guppy in frail health. I had lots of questions to resolve. I had resolved one, the ancestor, the mother of all questions, but I felt I still wasn't done. *Help me continue*, Julia had asked me. Those words didn't stop resounding in my mind. I also wanted that, to continue. I needed it.

I had an inevitable sensation of emptiness. No, weightlessness. Because it was a good feeling, like when you do a top-to-bottom cleaning and throw out the useless things you've been piling up. Because the majority of the space in my head had been taken up by dirty, heavy things. Noise. I was glad for that feeling of lightness. The diaphanous space Chris had given me. But also, I was afraid of getting lost, of not having an objective. My motivations had changed, transforming, growing, setting down roots that were still furtively clutching me. I had found something that suited me. Something I liked. It wasn't just a way out; it was a path toward life. My life. Miraculously, I had stopped judging myself, at least for the moment.

––––––

I met with Miriam so she could show me places for rent. We had spent a few weeks without seeing each other, letting a prudent amount of time pass so everything would settle in a natural way. To avoid talking about spy clocks or my intentions. To clear up our friendship and resume it without black spots. But no matter how much we pretended everything was OK between us, nothing was like before; there wasn't the same feeling of connection. And there was only one way to make it better. Just like she had made a grand gesture toward me—rebuilding the clock and putting it back up in the kitchen—I had to do the same for her. And there was only one that was good enough: telling her the truth. Not what I had been doing on the island, but what had brought me there. To tell her about Chris, about Barbara, about the mill.

Weeks later, when I finally got the lease at a really good price for a shop right in front of Le Café on Grand Avenue, I decided to tell her. But while we uncorked a bottle of champagne and toasted to celebrate, Miriam jumped the gun and told me she considered the deal she'd just given me—not taking her commission—a going-away present, because she was leaving, abandoning the island, going away to live in Pasadena, California. She needed to start from scratch, as far as possible from her terrible ex. Then she smiled at me and told me she could see I had found whatever it was I was looking for on the island and that she was really glad, but that she hadn't found whatever it was she was looking for. We hugged a long time and promised each other we'd never lose contact.

I didn't tell her what I was supposedly going to tell her.

———

After I threw Frank out of my house so rudely, he hadn't shown back up. And it had been some time since the fishbowl in Family Pet Land had burned out. I was worried and I felt bad.

I kept looking at his Victrola portable record player, the one he had left at the house, the one he always brought over. It was precious, to tell the truth. A vintage jewel. Too bad it didn't work. I thought I might be able to use it somehow.

———

"Hi, Frank," I said, entering Family Pet Land with Ruby and Pony. Olivia was on the farm with Barbara just then, riding Panda.

"Hello, Alice, Ruby and Pony. How can I help you?" he answered a little curtly. I could see he was still hurt.

"We're not here to buy anything. We're here to give you a present."

"Me, why? It's not my birthday, far as I know. But there are times lately when I don't even know what year I'm living in."

"No, it's not your birthday, not as far as I know either. But it doesn't have to be for you to get a present, right? Because the other day Barb told me Rose used to live in our house when she was a girl. Is that right?"

"You live at Forty-eight Shelter Road?" he asked me, as if he'd never been there before. I nodded. He immediately relaxed. "Well then, yeah, what a nice coincidence."

"The thing is, see, I was going through the attic, where I keep my junk, and it's a wreck because I barely ever go in there. I found something. And I said, hey, this isn't mine. So I thought, we should see if it belonged to Rose."

"What did you find?"

I showed him the record player case. He recognized it immediately.

"The Victrola! My Lord, what memories this thing brings back."

"I plugged it in at home to see if it worked, but no luck."

"It ended up breaking from so much usage. We cranked it up so her parents wouldn't hear us while we were kissing and canoodling," he said, excited. I'd managed to rescue that naughty, lovesick little boy. I missed him.

"Well, with your and Rose's permission, I took the liberty of making a few modifications to it. You have a plug?"

I went behind the counter, where Frank had pointed, and plugged in the record player. I put it on the table and opened the lid.

I had replaced the old turntable with a translucent hard plastic one with a rose—painted by me—right in the middle. Yeah, it was a little corny, but I couldn't think of anything better.

"Now when you turn it on, you won't be able to listen to your favorite songs, but you'll at least be able to remember Rose's light."

I turned it on and the rose lit up, filling the room with a warm light.

"And here, where you used to change the RPM, now it changes the shade of light it emits."

Frank was visibly touched.

"Thank you, dear. You're a great daughter," he said. And this time, it didn't bother me.

"Oh, and when you want to come by the house to remember old times, you don't have to knock on the door or bring the record player. It's best if it stays here."

———

Then Jennifer met someone. *That was fast*, I thought. But it turned out it was an old friend of Stephen's who had phoned Jennifer to offer his condolences when he found out about the death. After that courtesy they exchanged a few emails and calls—sometimes via Skype. He went on vacation to Nantucket. And since it was so close, they met to have a coffee. They connected. They started to see each other once a week. He'd go get her on his boat, and they would sail around with Berta, because Jennifer didn't like the gossip on the island. It irritated me because even though this Chad Miller was attentive, well-mannered, rather attractive—if less so than Stephen—there was something about the way he acted, his prissy correctness, that grated on me. Everything about him seemed to be a little forced. I couldn't trust that man. I really cared for Jennifer. She'd had a very tough time and it had taken her a long time to put her life back together and I'd have been happy for her to fall in love again, obviously. I just wanted to be sure that it was with the right guy, not just the first one who showed up around the corner in Nantucket.

And so I decided to track him and put a snitch on his boat. I wasn't going to let my friend be with the wrong man. Not on my watch.

———

Then Mark came back from his boat trip down the East Coast to spend a few weeks with Oliver, shut down his practice and get his things before moving permanently to New York.

Julia was very sad. She wasn't taking antidepressants because of the pregnancy and had given up on her novel. She confessed to me that she still hadn't told Mark she was pregnant, because she didn't want it to affect his decision and force him to stay out of a sense of obligation. To complete the picture, it turned out Olivia was very upset because lately Oliver didn't want to see her or play with her. I asked her why, and in a sea of tears and a chaos of arguments, she said things like: *Because he says I don't have a father . . . And maybe he's going to end up without a father and it's my fault . . . Because I told him things about not having a father . . . And now those things are going to happen to him . . . And he doesn't want us to be friends anymore. Do I scare fathers, Mommy . . . ?*

That relationship, that family, was a complete wreck. I felt that it had been slightly my fault. First for my intervention; then for my absence. Everything seemed so far away to me. As if it was something I'd done in another life. Till then, all my interventions had had positive results for some people—Miriam, Frank, Jennifer, for example—but with Julia and Mark, it had failed. I still remembered that image of them during the Labor Day picnic, seated under a parasol, their backs to each other. An incredibly graphic portrait of the lack of communication and crisis in a couple. I intervened, I got in the middle, and for a while, I managed to make everything better for each of us separately and for the three of us as a group. And now we were back where we started. No, it was worse. Much worse. Julia, pregnant and depressed. Mark leaving the island with not a clue as to his wife's pregnancy. Oliver in the middle of all that, suffering. And me? And me, what? *You count, too, Alice. How do you feel about this situation?*

I had been searching for the perfect equilibrium between Mark and Julia, a way to position myself to not lose either of them. And when I realized that couldn't be, I stepped aside. But it seemed a little unfair, as if I had been playing, using them, and then getting rid of them without caring about the consequences. My abandonment had caused hardships, and so I felt obliged to do something. For months I hadn't done anything because I didn't know which path to take. And there was just one reason for that: I hadn't decided how I wanted this story to end—or to continue.

My mind veered toward the most immediate thing, the biggest. Chris. Chris and Barbara. That story. That experience had to have taught me something; open your eyes. That was where I needed to find my answer. Every trip that's really worth it leaves its traces.

Then I realized that I hadn't finished the journey. I had followed the path that led to the mill, but I hadn't reached the end. Not till I read the letters.

Barbara had them set aside in order in a small box, and she was not surprised when I went to visit her at the farm and asked her for them. On the contrary, she knew it would end up happening. "You have copies? Just in case I destroy them," I said, trying to make the moment seem less heavy.

"No, I don't have copies. Take them home. Read them and do whatever you have to do with them."

———

Without a doubt, it was the most intense moment I had lived through since Ruby was born. And I say *lived through* because it was tied to life, not to death—as was becoming the custom up to then. And because it was also like giving birth. It was pulling out something that had been gestating inside me for more than thirteen months. Because I saw him. I saw Chris. In front of me. The real Chris. The one I loved madly. The one who had disappeared. He wasn't the distorted figure full of question marks that I had lived with since his death. I saw him more intensely than when I looked over his photos and videos. It was as if he was in another dimension. I could touch him, caress him, hug him, kiss him and even slap him, scream at him, curse him, for leaving us. I couldn't stop crying. And I wanted to hate him, I really tried. I wanted to get out all the rage and aversion I felt when I read some parts. I thought it was necessary to get rid of all the rancor and rejection to be able to go on with my life. But I couldn't hate him—maybe because it was something I'd already done. Just as I couldn't destroy those letters. Painful as it was to admit it, it was probably the best treasure I had found. But that treasure wasn't mine.

———

The day after I read the letters, I went to see Mark at *The Office*. I had to let myself be carried off by that river of energy and emotions.

I thought I was going to say goodbye to Mark, untie the moorings. It wasn't easy for me, because I still wanted him, emotionally and sexually. But I was going to reestablish our equilibrium because that was what I had decided to do. *Mark, what we had wasn't a love story; it was a survival story*, I considered telling him. But of course, love stories, the good, true ones, never start out as such.

On the way to the sailboat, contradictory phrases kept ringing in my head. *Where I'm going, I can't take you, Mark, and even less where I'm coming from, but where I am. I need you. We're not compatible. It's not a question of compatibility, it's a question of desire, of wanting, of what you need. Are you going to finish or keep going? Think in the now.*

Seeing him checking out the rigging, all those phrases melted together and the knot of doubts and fears about Mark came undone.

At some point, when I had asked Mark why he hadn't told me about

Julia's affair, he said something that was the closest thing to a declaration of love: *When you like someone a lot, you try to hide your defects at all costs.*

So while he still had his back turned to me and hadn't yet noticed my presence, I decided to paraphrase him:

"I've also hidden some of my defects, mistakes, errors, weak points, shit, call it what you want. Almost all of it."

Mark didn't turn around until I'd finished. His eyes connected with mine without the need for more words. He must have understood all that as my way of replying to his declaration of love, because under the thick beard he'd let grow, a smile crossed his face. And I felt the closest thing to butterflies in my stomach that I could allow myself just then.

"Shall we take a ride?" he proposed.

I nodded.

Once we were far from the island, we made love. I knew it would happen. I had thought everything over and made my decision. Because everything went in one direction: farewell.

And he sensed it.

"I have the feeling you're saying goodbye to me. That we're saying goodbye. Are we?"

Then I realized you had to say goodbye to some things to keep moving forward.

"Yes, we're saying goodbye . . . but to be able to continue."

And when I was sure he'd understood the positive side of my words, I added something fundamental for that continuation to be possible:

"I can't be your Samantha. And you can't be my Paul."

"I know . . ." he said without a glimmer of frustration. "I'm happy with you being my Alice. And me your Mark. I don't mean today or even tomorrow. Because I know you can't right now. And I can't either, to tell the truth. But I'd like to think that someday it will be possible for us to sail together, not just in the boat. You think it could be possible?"

I answered him with a look. A look that was neither planned nor practiced. A look I framed with the breeze from the sea. For him.

I believed I had come up with a lovely goodbye, and it turned out I had arranged an emotional future. Far from frightening me or putting me on the defensive, it comforted me, and I let myself go. It made me feel a drunkenness that had little to do with the glass of wine I was having on the prow with Mark, naked, covered only with a blanket, the same blanket. I rested my head on his shoulder, grabbed his arm and said, "I think it's time to go back home."

———

Four days later, I went to the beach to spend the day with my girls, and I was able to see Mark and Julia in the distance, walking along the seashore in silence with Oliver in the middle, holding—or clutching—his parents' hands, forming a circuit between them. They had just told him the good news: he was going to have a sister, and there were going to be two houses on the island, Mom's house and Dad's house. All the good stuff in two houses. Twice. At some point, I don't know if before, during or after they crossed in front of me, Julia, with a barely noticeable but growing belly, turned to me and smiled at me in a way as minimal as it was significant. That was the day Mark was supposed to have left the island for good.

———

Toward the end of summer, I changed my route when I went running every morning so that I always ended up at the mill. I hadn't gone back inside since the day I went with my children. It still intimidated me. And every time I got there, while I drank water and recovered before turning back, I wondered whether to turn the mill into my new base. Until one day, I cast the idea aside because that wasn't Chris's purpose. He wouldn't have liked it. It was going to serve the end it was conceived for. A place for personal realization.

I met with Barbara to formalize the transfer of the mill, and she told me one of the conditions she had given Chris when she sold it to him was that he couldn't change the name, and he had agreed, but now she did want to change it and call it Chris Mill.

"You like it?" she asked me.

Chris Mill. The X on the map, the treasure I had looked so long for.

"I like it," I answered.

I wanted it to stop being Chris's island. To give his name to such a concrete thing in such a concrete place freed the rest of the island for me to take possession. To make it mine.

I rescued the Diego Sánchez Sanz picture, which was still exiled against a wall in the garage, and took it to the attic in the mill. I didn't mind looking at myself there. After I hung it, I took the lock off the door.

Then I swam nude in the sea. There was no one there. I took the Master Key off the necklace and threw it far away, the farthest I could, to the depths of Nantucket Sound. I didn't need it anymore.

———

"Hey, Oli, one question. Now that we've been living on the island for over a year, do you still like it?"

"Of course."

"More or less than the last time I asked you?"

"More, because now I have Sunset and Panda."

"I'm glad. But you know, we've still got a deal. And if you ever decide you want us to go back to Providence, you tell me and we'll go. Deal?"

"Deal. But one thing, Mom."

"Shoot."

"Could you show me God's game?"

"What do you mean, God's game?"

"Yeah, because you play with God."

"What do you mean?"

"Because you bring Flint back to life all the time. Every time he dies, you bring him back. He's dead in the water, I touch him with my finger and he doesn't move, and when I get back from school, he's alive again. You bring him back."

I look at Olivia as if I didn't know what she was talking about. She laughs.

"I caught you, Mommy! Every time you do something good or bad, I know."

I want to hug her, kiss her and tell her how smart, as well as obsessive and compulsive, she is. But I decide to teach her a little lesson.

"Oli, we live on an island. We're surrounded by thousands of fish. Why do you want to have a fish in a fishbowl?"

She's the one who teaches me a lesson:

"Because we're like Flint. We live in a fishbowl. We're fishes and the island is our fishbowl."

THE BEACH IS deserted. The grain ears dance to the tune of the southwesterly wind. It's a calm, balmy day at the end of September. A flock of robins flies in a beautiful choreography of abstract shapes. Chris looks calmly out at the sea. He's barefoot, with khaki pants rolled up a few times. He's at the edge of the shore, the sea at his feet. Olivia, Ruby, Pony and I are walking along the beach and about to pass behind him. He turns. He looks at me, at us. I don't need to look at him because I've already found him. Chris knows it, and he smiles. We pass by. He doesn't follow us; he lets us go on, away, because he knows he won't lose us anymore and that if we get lost, we always have a meeting point, up at the mill.

Acknowledgments

To my father and my brother, Ignacio, for always going ahead of me in literary and cinematic matters and forcing me to follow their path. Which I almost never manage to do. I love you both.

To Ana Hernández and her little eyes, which were the first ones that peeked into the novel.

To Sara Muñoz, who read three different versions with equal passion and attention (here's hoping I didn't displease her).

To Oskar Santos, my most faithful friend/reader, curmudgeon and critic.

To Curro Novallas, among other things for taking care of Brigi during my trips to the United States to gather material.

To David Serrano, among other things for accompanying me on several of those trips and for being the first to encourage me to turn this story into a novel.

To Elías León Siminiani, among other things for always showing me other paths, even if I never take them.

To Quim Gutiérrez, among other things for always being by my side to snatch me up if I falter.

To Andrés Torbado, for being my friend first and then my agent. Take care of me, please.

To other crucial names on my island: Antonio, Raúl, Jaf and Joserra.

To Ainhoa Ramírez, Sandra Collantes, Cristina Sutherland and Lola Castejón for helping me file down the rough spots and polish the novel.

To Belén Rueda, Lluvia Rojo and Gail Siegal, for taking me under their wing in New York when I was looking for inspiration.

To my nieces Olivia and Ruby, for lending me their names, their smiles and their expressiveness for my characters.

To Héctor Colomé, for being my example in life. This novel is about a woman who grabs onto a secret and an island to get over the loss of her husband. Like Alice, I grabbed onto the novel like a lifeline; I took refuge in it; Olivia and the island to bear the long and dark illness that took him away. We miss you very much, Héctor.

To my mother, yes, again. Because she is my mother and because she'll be crying right now after reading the previous paragraph. Don't worry, Mamá, everything will be fine, you'll see.